Much Ado About Lewrie

Also by Dewey Lambdin

Much Ado About Lewrie

An Alan Lewrie Naval Adventure

Dewey Lambdin

ST. MARTIN'S PRESS
NEW YORK

MUCH ADO ABOUT LEWRIE. Copyright 2019 by Dewey Lambdin. All rights reserved. Printed in the United States of America. For information, address St. Martin's Press, 175 Fifth Avenue, New York, N.Y. 10010.

www.stmartins.com

Maps by Cameron MacLeod Jones

The Library of Congress Cataloging-in-Publication Data is available upon request.

ISBN 978-1-250-10366-6 (hardcover)
ISBN 978-1-250-10367-3 (ebook)

Our books may be purchased in bulk for promotional, educational, or business use. Please contact your local bookseller or the Macmillan Corporate and Premium Sales Department at 1-800-221-7945, extension 5442, or by email at MacmillanSpecialMarkets@macmillan.com.

First Edition: May 2019

10 9 8 7 6 5 4 3 2 1

To George and Olga Webster, my long-ago agents who took a chance on an Un-published writer back in 1988, liked what they read, and offered representation . . . which caused me to get "over-served"

Full-Rigged Ship: Starboard (right) side view

1. Mizen Topgallant
2. Mizen Topsail
3. Spanker
4. Main Royal
5. Main Topgallant
6. Mizen T'gallant Staysail
7. Main Topsail
8. Main Course
9. Main T'gallant Staysail
10. Middle Staysail

11. Main Topmast Staysail
12. Fore Royal
13. Fore Topgallant
14. Fore Topsail
15. Fore Course
16. Fore Topmast Staysail
17. Inner Jib
18. Outer Flying Jib
19. Spritsail

A. Taffrail & Lanterns
B. Stern & Quarter-galleries
C. Poop Deck/Great Cabins Under
D. Rudder & Transom Post
E. Quarterdeck
F. Mizen Chains & Stays
G. Main Chains & Stays
H. Boarding Battens/Entry Port
I. Cargo Loading Skids
J. Shrouds & Ratlines
K. Fore Chains & Stays

L. Waist
M. Gripe & Cutwater
N. Figurehead & Beakhead Rails
O. Bow Sprit
P. Jib Boom
Q. Foc's'le & Anchor Cat-heads
R. Cro'jack Yard (no sail fitted)
S. Top Platforms
T. Cross-Trees
U. Spanker Gaff

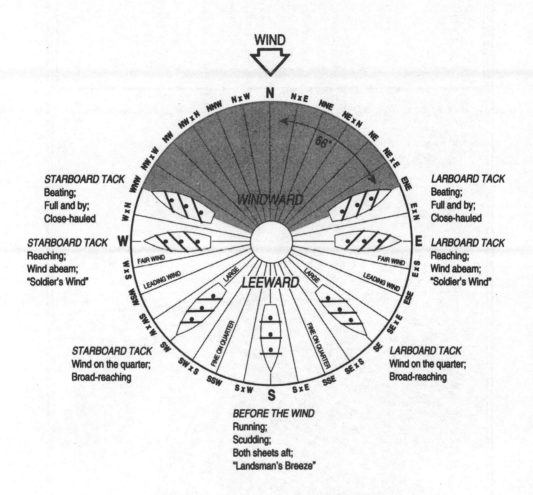

POINTS OF SAIL AND 32-POINT WIND-ROSE

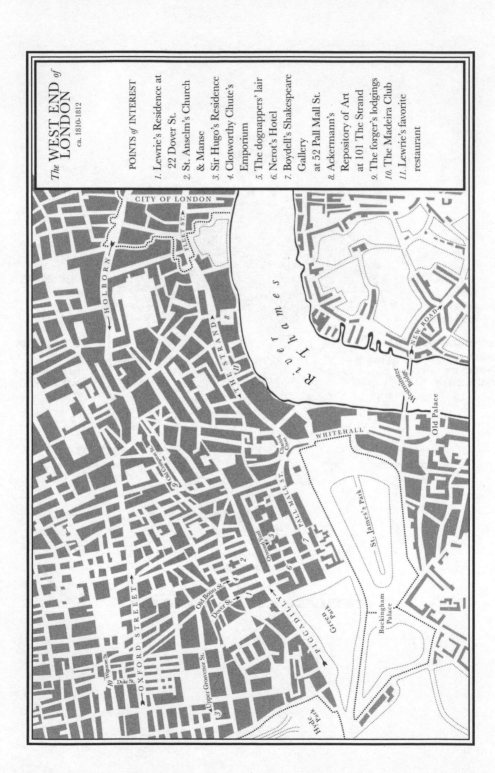

The WEST END of LONDON
ca. 1810–1812

POINTS of INTEREST

1. Lewrie's Residence at 22 Dover St.
2. St. Anselm's Church & Manse
3. Sir Hugo's Residence
4. Clotworthy Chute's Emporium
5. The dognappers' lair
6. Nerot's Hotel
7. Boydell's Shakespeare Gallery at 52 Pall Mall St.
8. Ackermann's Repository of Art at 101 The Strand
9. The forger's lodgings
10. The Madeira Club
11. Lewrie's favorite restaurant

CITY OF LONDON

HOLBORN

FLEET ST.

THE STRAND

River Thames

WHITEHALL

Westminster Bridge

Old Palace

St. James's Park

Charing Cross

Orange Yard

OXFORD STREET

Wigmore St.

Dale St.

Upper Grosvenor St.

Old Bond St.

Dover St.

PICCADILLY

PALL MALL ST.

Green Park

Buckingham Palace

NEW ROAD

Hyde Park

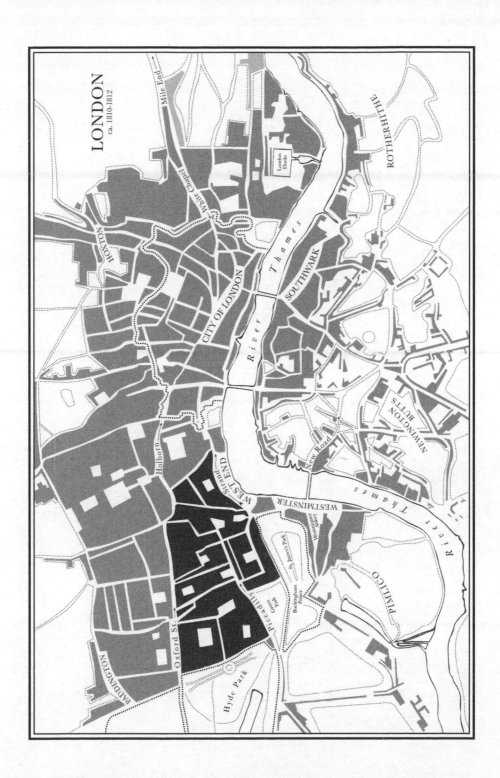

BOOK ONE

On me the tempest falls. It does not
make me tremble. O holy Mother Earth,
O Air and Sun, behold me. I am wronged.

AESCHYLUS, *PROMETHEUS
BOUND*, 1089

CHAPTER ONE

I s'pose they call this a black study, Captain Sir Alan Lewrie thought as he slowly paced the length of HMS *Vigilance*'s poop deck; *Or is it a* bleak *study?* he wondered.

His hands were clasped in the small of his back, and he found the toes of his freshly-blackened boots of more interest than the sights of the anchorage in which his 64-gun ship, and the transports of his wee squadron lay. He clewed to a single deck plank, sanded to pale white, one foot after another 'til he fetched up at the flag lockers and the taffrails and looked down over the stern, the windows at the rear of his great-cabins, and his ornately railed gallery. At present it was awash in bed linens and some of his linen shirts airing in the sun after a wash in fresh water brought from shore.

Lewrie slumped on the taffrails most lubberly and lifted his gaze at last to the middle distance, up to the Nor'east. Somewhere out there a traitor rested on the seabed, anchored by chains round his ankles, bobbing perhaps, with arms upraised, for the fish to nibble on. Lewrie thought that too quick a death. Had he gotten hold of that arch-criminal, that mercenary back-stabber who'd cost the lives of some of his sailors and Marines, whose betrayal had decimated the troops of the 94th Regiment of Foot, *Don* Julio Caesare's death would not have been so quick. One hundred lashes of the cat o' nine tails, with salt and lemon juice smeared on his ravaged back; keel-hauling along *Vigilance*'s bottom and the razor-sharp barnacles that she had acquired since her last dockyard refit.

His end? Lewrie's hands tightened on the taffrails, wishing that he could have strangled the bastard, not once but several times 'til the light left his eyes at last.

But no, Lewrie had been denied that pleasure. *Don* Julio had been a greedy tyrant, a bully to his own subordinates, who had doled out the least of the profits of their criminal enterprises that he would grudgingly spare, and it was his greed—and perhaps his dealings with the French—that had pushed Caesare's *capos* to do away with him, at last.

"Boat ahoy!" a Midshipman of the Watch cried.

"Pusser's boat . . . returnin'!" the bow man of the 29-foot barge shouted back. "'E'll need a workin' party!"

Lewrie stepped to the larboard bulwarks to look out and down at the approaching boat, noting the heaps of sacks and the bushel baskets piled deep along the centerline of the barge. Mr. Blundell sat aft by the barge's Cox'n, looking quite pleased with his shopping trip to the markets of Milazzo, up the peninsula.

Once anchored and back from their latest, disastrous raid on the Calabrian coast, after the dead they had managed to recover had been buried alongside the Army's small cemetery ashore, and the men who had been wounded had been seen to at the large tent hospital at the 94th Regiment's camp, Lewrie had at last declared a Make And Mend Day, today, and it was a very reluctant batch of sailors who answered the summons to fetch the Purser's goods aboard.

Lewrie paced forward to the larboard ladderway of the poop, looming above the quarterdeck, waist, and sail-tending gangways, which spurred a few more hands to rise from their amusements and go to the larboard entry-port under his stern gaze.

"Lemons and oranges, lads!" Mr. Blundell hallooed to encourage them, "Figs and dates for your duffs! Fresh bread and butter, onions and scallions, hard sausages and fresh cheeses!" Blundell tried to sound "matey," but it was a waste of time on his part, for a "Nip-Cheese," a Purser, was never loved in the Royal Navy, nor rarely trusted, either. Even in the officers' mess, he *sold* needful things and desirable items to his fellow wardroom members and his prices were always suspect.

"Not a morsel of it to be issued free," someone on the quarterdeck below sourly commented, "th' money-grubbin' bashtit."

"Aye, mate," a compatriot bemoaned, "Wot's 'e payin' fer fresh fruit, five pence a peck? 'E'll flog it t'us fer a penny apiece!"

Not much had amused Lewrie since their return, but their comments did bring a wee grin to his lips. He leaned his hands on the larboard bulwarks by the top of the quarterdeck ladderway, lifting his eyes to the Army camp, and his grin disappeared.

There were uniformed soldiers astir ashore, soldiers on parade without arms, performing the jerky slow-step on their way to the cemetery, led by a two-wheeled cart. Even at that distance, Lewrie could recognise Leftenant-Colonel Tarrant and Major Gittings standing near freshly-dug graves with their feathered bicorne hats at their sides. Tarrant's large, shaggy hound sat at his master's feet, quiet for a rare once. Two more badly wounded men had passed over, to be added to that grim plot of earth with its flimsy wooden planks that stood in lieu of permanent headstones.

Lewrie shut his eyes, dreading a summons from his own Ship's Surgeon, Mr. Woodbury, to conduct yet another funeral for one of his own sailors who did not survive his wounds.

"Please God, no, not another," he whispered, for he had read the rites at sea for those whom they had been forced to leave behind, at the entry-port for those who had expired on-passage, and for the men who had died in that *ad hoc* Army hospital since.

Lewrie pursed his lips and looked out to sea once again, look anywhere but at yet another funeral. A wee zephyr of a breeze arose for a minute or so, barely rippling the harbour waters and stirring his coat tails, and it had a touch of coolness to it; as it should since it was late Autumn in the Mediterranean, in the year of 1810, though Sicily still looked lush and green. Of a sudden, Lewrie was thirsty, and with a need to go to his quarter gallery and "pump his bilges," though what he had to do below once after was another onerous duty to be borne. He had not yet finished his report to Admiralty about their latest fight; had not yet found a way to make it sound any less than the monumental cock-up it had been, treachery and betrayal for French gold no matter.

Captain Sir Alan Lewrie, Baronet, was not used to failure and defeat. He had always managed to pull his chestnuts from the fire, and turn the tables on his country's foes, one way or another, and wring out a victory for King and Country. Lewrie heaved a heavy sigh, squared his shoulders, and slowly descended the ladderway to the quarterdeck and the door to his great-cabins, where those grumpy sailors stiffened and doffed their flat, tarred hats, and his Marine sentry stamped his boots and presented his musket in salute.

"Good eats tonight, lads," Lewrie said as he entered the door, "even if it costs a penny or two."

"Er . . . aye aye, sir," one of them dared reply.

A good long pee, then a tousle with Chalky first, Lewrie determined to himself; *the cat's always in need o' diversion. And so am I.*

He played with his cat 'til Chalky wanted lap more than he wanted to chase a wine cork on a ribbon; he dug his latest mail from home from a desk drawer and re-read his wife's missives, his eyes raised in longing to the portrait of Jessica that French *émigré* artist, Madame Berenice Pellatan, had done of her.

Finally, there was nothing for it but to gather his notes about the battle, and start a fresh draft. Once back in port, Lewrie had spoken with Lt. Greenleaf and Marine Captain Whitehead, who had been in command of his ship's landing force, and Lieutenants Fletcher and Rutland, who had commanded the landing boats and their armed crews from the troop transports, as well as getting Colonel Tarrant's and Major Gittings's observations concerning the battle that had broken out just East of Monasterace.

In the beginning, the landing looked to be a raid on a promising target. The coastal fishing village of Monasterace had not been reported to have a garrison beyond a small company of artificers from the French Commissariat to repair any supply waggons making the long detour cross bad mountain roads from Naples to the towns that French soldiers actually occupied, most especially their main base at Reggio di Calabria. Destroying that stock of wood, iron forges, leather for reins and harnesses, and the vast stockpile of grain and hay for the horses, mules, and oxen would worsen the trouble of supply for the French. And, if they could land predawn, they had hoped to catch several waggon convoys encamped at Monasterace for the night, setting them all on fire, and slaughtering the draught animals, as they had in previous raids. It had sounded a rosy proposal; too rosy, for it was based on *Don* Julio Caesare's lies and assurances.

Back-handed compliment, Lewrie thought with a sniff; *we must be a real thorn in the Frogs' side if they bribed him with ten thousand gold coins.*

Colonel Tarrant had estimated that a French brigade of at least two regiments of infantry, a battery or two of artillery, perhaps twelve pieces in all, and what had appeared to be a full squadron of cavalry had been hidden in the village's houses, and behind the low ridge back of town by about a mile. Once all his troops were ashore, they had rushed out to form for battle, and the artillery and cavalry had appeared in front of the ridge.

Lewrie, stuck aboard *Vigilance*, had loosed his experienced gunners on the village, first, from a quarter-mile offshore, breaking up their initial formations, turning some of his guns upon the Frenchmen attacking his sailors and Marines just West of town, and with aimed fire, with crude sights notched into the muzzles and cascabels of his 18- and 24-pounders, had protected his vastly out-numbered men with a hail of hard iron shot. He had turned his guns onto the right flank of the French troops marching to engage Tarrant and the 94th, decimating them before they got to close range. After that, he could do nothing but pace and fret, unable to see anything in that vast cloud of musket smoke.

Greenleaf and Whitehead had gotten their sailors and Marines off their beach and back aboard, fetching off their wounded, but had to leave their dead where they lay.

He did not learn it 'til later, could not see it happening at the time, but Lieutenants Fletcher and Rutland, fearing that the 94th would break and swarm the transports' barges, and their lightly armed oarsmen, and creating a mass slaughter, had determined to split their two hundred and forty sailors into two units, and had gone inland several hundred yards to form on either flank of the infantry, adding their musket fire to whittle down the French. Lt. Rutland, unable to see what to shoot at, had even led his party out to his left, then straight out at right angles to the French, forcing enemy soldiers to turn about, bunch up, and creep back towards the centre of their lines, which had panicked the French behind them.

Then, perhaps in desperation, but at the perfect moment, Colonel Tarrant had ordered a bayonet charge over the waist-high stone walls behind which his regiment had formed, and the panic had become general, with French soldiers breaking and running, tossing aside weapons and any item of gear that might slow them down, out of that accursed smoke cloud and into plain view of Lewrie's guns once more, and despite the lack of explosive shot, it had been the French that had been properly decimated. They had retreated all the way to the long, low, ridge, out of range of *Vigilance*'s guns, and their cavalry had never tried to engage, for fear of those guns, even after the bayonet charge had ended with panting soldiers scattered Hell-to-breakfast, more intent on looting discarded French packs for money, strong spirits, and souvenirs.

The enemy remained Quiescent for the better part of two hours as the 94th gathered its Wounded and Weapons, re-formed and in Observation, out of range. Our troops' Re-embarkation and Departure from the beaches went Un-Interrupted, and no enemy scouting parties dared come down to the shore 'til after all ships had hoisted anchors and had made Sail.
I Submit, My Lords, that though we were Betrayed, HMS Vigilance, its officers and men, and the men of the 94th Regt. of Foot gave a good Account of themselves in the face of greater Numbers and what should have been overwhelming Force. Had the Enemy Genl. commanding handled his troops better the Outcome might have been much Different.
I would like to particularly commend . . .

Here, Lewrie paused and tapped the wooden end of his steel-nib pen against his teeth in thought. Fletcher and Rutland for joining the fight to such good results, of course he must mention them. From his own ship, Captain Whitehead of the Marines and the Second Officer Mr. Greenleaf, and his much younger brother-in-law, Midshipman Charles Chenery. Lt. Dickson, though . . . he'd been ashore, and had had the inspiration to take a boat crew and row one of the landing barges offshore, then further up the coast and land her deep on the sands to form a breastwork to protect Whitehead's and Greenleaf's left flank.

The only problem was that Lewrie *utterly despised* Lieutenant John Dickson, who had been a perfect trial since he had arrived in command of their fourth transport, *Coromandel*. His ship was the largest, so he assumed that he should be in command over *all* four transports, instead of Lt. Fletcher who had held that post since the squadron had been formed at Portsmouth. By the time *Coromandel* had sailed into harbour, Dickson's haughty sneers at how low and stupid he regarded his crew had dis-affected them all, and he highly resented any officer who came aboard to train his sailors in how to bear, land, and retrieve soldiers, even Lewrie himself! He carped and complained, had tried to toady, and had ended causing a wee dumb-show mutiny that had let slip one of *Coromandel*'s landing barges in-tow during the night, along with two oars missing from another!

Lewrie had written Rear-Admiral Sir Thomas Charlton, to which his squadron answered, asking if he had the right to remove Dickson from command and replace him with an officer from *Vigilance*'s wardroom. Charlton wrote back allowing it, for the Good of The Service, even if Lewrie did not fly a Commodore's broad pendant. Thankfully, Lt. Rutland, the Second Officer, had volunteered, hoping to make a name for himself (he was married with two children and lived mostly on his Navy pay) that would advance him into command of a warship.

Of course, Lewrie had had to take Dickson aboard as the junior-most officer, for even Lieutenant Grace, risen from Ordinary Seaman during the Nore Mutiny of 1797 to a commission, out-ranked the man, and a most wary eye he had kept on Dickson since, but still couldn't figure the fellow out. Aboard *Vigilance*, Dickson was competent but guarded, not making much effort to make any friends, and keeping his arrogant dismissal of the hands under wraps.

"No, Dickson," Lewrie decided at last, dipping his pen into the inkbottle, "I'll pretend you weren't even there. Take that, ye top-lofty bastard. Think my sailors are the scum of the earth, do you? Take that!"

He went on to cite other Midshipmen who had stood out, then a list of petty officers and a sailor or Marine or two who had risen to the occasion. Then, sadly, a list of those who had fallen, and those who had expired in hospital since.

Lewrie leaned back after closing the inkbottle and wiping his pen clean, looking up at the deck beams overhead and rolling his neck to ease the stiffness.

"Something else t' drink, sir?" Deavers, his cabin-steward, asked as he finished folding and stowing away the last of the laundry.

"Aye, Deavers, I'd admire a pint of ale, if there's any left," Lewrie replied, standing up and looking round his cabins, noting that his bed-cot was re-made with fresh linens, his spare sheets stowed, and the stern gallery now clear of drying cloth.

"I b'lieve there is, sir," Deavers said, going to the ten-gallon anker stood upright next to the wine cabinet. "Right, you lads. Get on your way. Time for skylarkin'," and the two young cabin-servants, Tom Dasher and Robert Turnbow, dashed out to the quarterdeck, whooping with glee to have some free hours before supper to play with the other ship's boys.

"Deavers, do you ask the Marine sentry to pass word for Sub-Lieutenant Severance," Lewrie said as Deavers sat a foaming pint of ale on his desk in the day cabin. "Time for him to scribble the fair copy of my report. Once he's here, he'll be needin' a pint, too."

"Aye, sir," Deavers replied.

Lewrie thought of going over to the starboard side settee and plopping himself on its soft cushions, boots up on the old brass Hindoo tray table, but . . . those cushions reminded him of Jessica, who had had them made for him before he sailed.

He sat back down behind his desk, drew out some stationery from a drawer, re-opened the inkbottle, and began to write . . .

My Dearest Girl, My Wife,
By the time you receive this letter, a report from this quarter to Admiralty will have shewn up in the papers, and I would not wish you to be Upset. Firstly, let me say again how much I miss you and long to be with you. Secondly, I am Well and Un-harmed. We did have a Scrape with the French, though, a most Desperate Scrape, from which We, and I, your Brother Charlie, and the 94th Regt. escaped with a fair amount of Credit, even if I do say so myself. Charlie is well, though he was grazed by a musket ball along the side of his head, and is bursting with Pride over his shaved pate and his Turban of a bandage. We were sold out to the French, you see. . . .

CHAPTER TWO

"*H*mm, I tend to agree with your assessment, Sir Alan," Colonel Tarrant told him after Lewrie had summarised the highlights of his report to Admiralty. "If only, mind, to make me feel better about my losses. Up, boy! Fetch, Dante!"

Lewrie had come ashore to post his latest mail with a mounted courier to Messina, and a visit to the hospital pavillion to see to his wounded men. Lt. Col. Tarrant had been there, doing the same, and they ended up strolling the edge of the parade ground, with Tarrant's boisterous dog tagging at their heels, bounding and whining for play. Off he went in a dash to fetch the stick that Tarrant had hurled.

"Dante visited the hospital?" Lewrie asked. "I'd have thought your surgeons would object."

"Oh, he's welcome with my soldiers," Tarrant said with a wee laugh, "They like him, and Dante adores everybody, and all the attention they give him. He's come a long way from an abused, half-fed farm dog. Perhaps too far. Try as I might to convince him that his pallet by my bed is his place, I wake almost every morning to a wet tongue on my face, and five stone of aromatic dog sprawled atop me."

"And that's why I keep cats," Lewrie sniggered. "Though, in my last ship, Bisquit slept in my cabins, and preferred the Turkey carpets. When he wasn't wandering the lower decks, looking for a handout. It's best I left him in London with my wife and her dog, for live gunnery exercise, and battle, had him terrified down on the orlop, in a perfect shiver."

"Caruthers," Col. Tarrant said of a sudden, coming to a halt as his dog pranced back with the stick in his mouth. "Damn that man. I'd wager he's either envious, or crowing with glee to see us come a cropper."

Brigadier-General Caruthers commanded an infantry brigade of three regiments closer to Messina, an ambitious fellow hell-bent on doing something more glorious than drilling and practicing for an invasion from mainland Italy that would most-like never come.

Earlier in the year, Rear-Admiral Charlton had used his ships and Lewrie's experimental squadron to ravage the Southern Calabrian coast, from the "toe" of Italy to the start of the "heel," and there had been enough troop transports gathered to land Brigadier Caruthers's brigade as well. It had not gone well for Caruthers, since the ships that carried his soldiers were civilian hired transports with only a few small rowboats, so that only two of his regiments had gotten to shore. His part of the expedition had taken so long that the French had had time to march one of their brigades— foot, horse, and artillery—to drive him off, and it had been the trained, skillful gunners aboard *Vigilance,* and some captured French howitzers taken from a pre-invasion supply depot, that had saved his bacon. The man had gotten his battle, and his victory, after all, along with praiseful accounts of it in the London papers, and Caruthers had been mad for more of the same since, pressing Horse Guards and Admiralty for Navy-manned transports and landing barges so he could emulate what Lewrie and Tarrant were doing, on a much larger scale, of course.

Frankly, Brigadier Caruthers would have preferred to take over the whole enterprise, absorb Tarrant's 94th Foot into his brigade, so he could stage a full-scale invasion into Italy, and rage up and down the countryside with a proper Army of several divisions, like Wellesley, or Wellington, or whatever they were calling him these days, was doing in Portugal and Spain.

"I'm sure we'll hear from him," Lewrie said with a sour look, "Perhaps a lecture on how we should have been equipped with flying artillery batteries, limbers, caissons, and horse teams, and tell us exactly how to do it."

"*If* the bloody French are deaf, dumb, and blind," Tarrant spat, "and *if* they allow us a whole day to get all that ashore. He will need tents, of course . . . can't have a proper camp without tents . . . and cookpots, ration waggons with even *more* horses. And, Caruthers and his officers simply *have* to fetch along the mess silver, and a string of hundred guinea horses to ride."

"He did look particularly grand astride a captured horse," Lewrie added with a laught. "Had one shot out from underneath him, and he made sure t'stick *that* in in his report!"

"Better a horse than one of your damned barges, I suppose," Tarrant chuckled, cocking his head towards Lewrie. "Yays, I imagine that we'll be getting an 'I told you so' from the man, as soon as he can gallop out to visit us. And only God knows what he's been saying to the General Commanding at the *castello* to have a hand in the next raid. Take over the whole operation? Swap my regiment for one of his? God save the Ninety-Fourth if he manages that."

"Surely, you have a rebuttal argument in mind, sir," Lewrie said. "He'd have to pare his plans back sharply if he wishes to emulate our way of doing things. Even if he *did* manage to get some Navy-manned transports, with the proper sort of landing barges, his troops would have to be trained, first. Time, money, sailors to man the ships and barges? Gettin' my few was like pullin' teeth, and I've been told I'd only see another the *other* side of Hell!"

"My dear Lewrie," Tarrant said, trying to ignore the dog, who was now trying to put his paws on his chest, "does it come to that, I trust you will support me to the hilt before *he* takes charge."

"Count on me, sir," Lewrie vowed. "We've come to work too well together to let some interloper make a muck of things."

Dammit, he had come to like Tarrant! Unlike the bulk of Army officers he had met, Col. Tarrant was one of those rareties, an officer who took his chosen profession seriously, studied examples from the past, and was clever enough to emulate the successes and eschew the failures, and husband his soldiers and their welfare as if they were kinfolk. Well, perhaps the men of the 94th *were,* in a way, for the regiment had been raised at Peterborough and the near environs, all neighbours and fellow workers before they'd taken the King's Shilling, as were the officers, and Tarrant.

They worked well together, Lewrie and Tarrant, and over the months Lewrie felt that a true friendship had been formed.

Of course, he'd back him in keeping his regiment out of the hands of glory-seeking butchers like Caruthers!

"Here, Dante," Lewrie coaxed the dog, patting the chest of his second-best uniform coat, "Want some 'wubbies'? Want me t'throw yer stick?"

"Mind, now," Tarrant cautioned, "if I receive orders from the General-Commanding, there's little either of us can say."

"We'll cross that bridge when we come to it," Lewrie assured him, taking the stick from his hands. Dante stood on his hind legs, pawed at Lewrie's coat, seized the stick and got down on all fours to growl and toss his head as if killing a rabbit, then dropped it at Lewrie's feet, looking anxious, his tail thrashing.

"Ready, ready, set? Go, boy!" Lewrie said, hurling the stick a good twenty yards, and the dog bounded after it to almost catch it in mid-air, give it another thrashing, then lower his front end, daring them to chase after him if they wanted his prize back. Tarrant made a short mock dash as if to chase him, and Dante wheeled about and ran a wide circle round them.

Damme, I miss Bisquit, Lewrie thought, amused, with all of his cares temporarily forgotten; *Cats just don't do "fetch"!*

In the officers' wardroom, Lewrie's particular bug-a-bear was writing another of his long letters. Fourth Officer John Dickson was penning his own sour assessment of the battle at Monasterace, guarding it from the idle curiosity of his fellow officers with his left forearm. He had written one letter to his father, another to one of his principal patrons, a senior Admiral, and this one would be going to yet another patron, kin on his mother's side of the family who held a position on the Board of Admiralty.

Dickson was proud of his own small part of *Vigilance*'s landing party, and made his movement of one of the barges further up the beach to form a breakfront to refuse the left flank. "Refuse" was not a nautical term, exactly, but that was how Lt. Greenleaf, the big, noisy lout, had termed it, and Dickson thought to repeat it in his letter, to show how knowledgeable he was. He was also proud to mention the three Frenchmen he had slain, two with his pistols at close range, and the last with his sword, bloodied in desperate combat. He had not seen the action on the other side of the seaside town when the French marched against the 94th Foot, but he had heard what other officers had said of it, when he had encountered them ashore once the squadron had returned to their anchorage. What Lieutenants Rutland and Fletcher had done with their sailors and shore parties out on the French flanks had sounded grand, but that would not do for his purposes.

Placing the sailors of the beach guard on the firing line could have re-sulted in their Destruction, leaving the 94th stranded and forced back to the boats with not a single clue as to how to save themselves, in great Dis-order. The enemy laid a trap which could have put paid to the whole Endeavour. The Betrayal only goes to show why it is impossible to de-pend on Foreigners to gather Intelligence, since there is no Faith in them, a fact that should have been Obvious to Capt. Lewrie and their hapless Foreign Office agent, Mr. Quill.

He thought to describe Quill in the worst light, how gawky and book-ish a spectre he was, too trusting and ineffective, instead of the intrepid sort of spy needed in such a post.

"Scribble, scribble, scribble, hey Dickson?" Lt. Greenleaf teased as he pulled a clean shirt over his head after a scrub-down with a sponge and some shore water. "I swear, I never knew a fellow more fond of ink! You write more than the Captain's clerk, Mister Severance, haw haw!"

"Aye, admit it, Dickson," Lt. Grace, the Third Officer, said, looking up from a novel he was reading at the other end of the mess table that sat down the centreline of the wardroom's deal-and-canvas "dog box" sleep-ing compartments, "You're desperately sweet on *some* young miss back home."

"As I said before, I send one long letter to my father, and he separates out the parts addressed to mother, brothers and sisters, and cousins," Dick-son easily lied, though he did shift his arm to guard it more closely, wary of their curiosity which could expose his intent. Frankly, he felt irked with their presence, but there was no other place where he could write barring his small bed box, and hiding himself there, behind a louvred and insub-stantial door, would raise even more suspicion. The finished pages were face-down on the mess table, secured under his right elbow. "At least I now have something to write *about,* as I'm sure you have as well. Let my family know that we've had a battle, and that I'm well."

He would have said something disparaging about Monasterace but bit his words off, sure that his messmates thought much better of it than he did.

"Ah, there I was, surrounded by Frogs with levelled bayonets, my bark-ers empty, my sword broken," Greenleaf hooted in mirth, "and me an inch away from being a pin cushion? Why, they killed me, of course. But then . . . !"

"Slew seven with one blow!" Lt. Farley, the First Officer added, laughing out loud. "Seven, no . . .'twas ten!"

"And the cowardly French ran like hounds," Greenleaf roared.

"We all gave creditable accounts of ourselves," Dickson said in a drawl. "Could have been much worse."

Farley, who had been aboard *Vigilance* and had not taken part in the landings, frowned as if Dickson had slighted him, which did not signify to Dickson; he didn't really care a fig for any of them, and was just waiting for the day when his kin and his patrons plucked him out of this shambles and found a berth for him in a fine frigate, where he really belonged, where his natural superiority of breeding and experience would let him shine.

"What are you reading, Grace?" Greenleaf asked as he sat down at the mess table and began to shuffle a greasy old pack of cards.

"An old Smollett . . . *Peregrine Pickle*," Grace told him. "The Surgeon, Mister Woodbury loaned it to me."

Greenleaf's response was a gruff, inarticulate grunt. He laid out a row of cards to begin a hand of solitaire.

Their fun was over, and Dickson could get back to criticising Captain Lewrie, Quill, the Italians, and the whole experiment that was sure to fall apart the next un-looked-for blow.

CHAPTER THREE

Nothing else for it, then, Lewrie thought; *We did our best to put a polish on it.*

His report, what Col. Tarrant wrote to Horse Guards, and what the officers off the transports had said in their reports might put a good light on their actions, or nothing would deflect blame from official quarters. And, what Lewrie's detractors would make of it was what Lewrie feared most.

He'd learned from several sources, his long-time compatriot James Peel with Foreign Office's Secret Branch, chief among them, that there were officers in the Royal Navy with whom Lewrie had served in the past, that were definitely *not* his admirers. Even a man he'd held as a good friend from his Midshipman days, Keith Ashburn, thought him . . . "insouciant," a slacker who did not take the stern duty of being an officer, a Post-Captain in the Royal Navy, seriously, counting on luck to get by, and sure to foul up and get a lot of good men killed, someday.

Others were jealous of that luck, of his prior successes when it came to prize-money, in being in the right place at the right time to be in combat, and to be mentioned in Despatches. His son Hugh's Captain Chalmers of the *Undaunted* frigate, thought Lewrie a Corinthian, a rake-hell, a reckless fellow who openly kept a mistress at Gibraltar and Lisbon, and certainly not a Respectable Person, and not much of a Proper Christian, either. Fellow

Mids, fellow Lieutenants whom he had outshone, grumbling under their breaths and waiting for a chance to get their own back.

And all of them had powerful, well-placed patrons and kinfolk who could blight anyone's career, even a Nelson or Pellew, if they supported their protégés, or their sons, cousins, or favourites!

What did Lewrie have for patrons? Junior Admirals who had been Captains when he knew them, Captains more senior to him who flew a broad pendant as a Commodore, an old friend in Lord's whom he'd known at Harrow, a supportive older man in the Commons, some few gentlemen in middle-rank public service offices; all the old Admirals that he could have counted on were long-retired and no longer influential, or they were no longer alive. So, who could speak up for him, now?

It must here be noted that Alan Lewrie had never been a fellow big on introspection. He'd been a thoughtless, idle rake-hell and a Buck-of-The-First-Head with no clue to the next morrow before he had joined the Royal Navy—well, in point of fact *dragooned* into life at sea by his own father, Sir Hugo St. George Willoughby who'd needed Alan far overseas and a year out of touch so he could use Alan's inheritance from his late mother's side of the family to pay off his creditors before they called in his debts and slung Sir Hugo into prison.

Alan Lewrie was a fellow who would *never* be thought of as "too clever by half"; that was a trait of the Scots, who tended to be much better educated than English gentlemen, and both cleverness and well-educated were shunned by fellows like Lewrie like the Black Plague!

Besides, he had learned early-on to doubt the use of cleverness. Every time he had imagined that he had the upper hand, a clear view into things, Dame Fortune had always come down from Mount Olympus and kicked him in the arse, just to let him know that he was *not* a "sly-boots" and would never be.

It did not help Lewrie's fretting to recall how callow and ignorant he had been when reporting to his first ship, HMS *Ariadne*, in 1780. That could make him wince to this day! There were twelve-year-olds in the Midshipman's cockpit on the orlop who'd known *bags* more than he did. Lewrie had learned his knots, the rigging, sails, a passable smattering of navigation, had survived his many trips aloft despite his shivers of dread of becoming a bloody, burst bag on the deck if he lost a handhold, or a skitter of the footropes.

For Christ's sake, he, like most of the hands brought aboard by the

Impress Service, the tavern "rondys" for volunteers, or by hook or by crook, he could not swim a single stroke!

No, real introspection might be asking too much of Alan Lewrie, but he did know himself and his nature, after a fashion, and he did not, could not, take himself too seriously, for at least he knew his faults, his lacks as a Proper Commission Sea Officer, and as a man, but he could deal with them, and sometimes laugh at himself, even if he sometimes felt himself to be the hugest fraud.

Lately, junior officers who served with him, who had been Mids aboard some of his early commands, surprised him by expressing trust in his knackiness, and in how *able* he was when it came to engaging the enemy, in how he went about commanding a warship.

More fools, they, he scoffed to himself, wondering what they would say or think of him if they really knew him; *Still, give a dog a good name, and he can go far. Until he mucks things up for everyone to see!*

It was almost enough of a conundrum to make him gnaw on his finger-nails, sulk and mope, pace 'til his feet hurt, or . . .

Go fetch his long-abandoned penny whistle from one of his sea chests, and try to tootle a few simple tunes to get back in practice. A loss by foul betrayal or not, there was little that he could do about it, now, and either he would be exonerated or not; brought low and shamed as a failure, or not, relieved or recalled, or left in command and told to carry on.

It didn't bear thinking about—so he didn't.

The tune of *"Pleasant & Delightful"* wafted upwards through the opened windows of the great-cabin's coachtop on the poop deck, out past the quarterdeck door, and faintly muffled down through deck beams to the officers' wardroom below; stumbling and with some awkward notes due to bad fingering. The Marine sentry at the Captain's door began to whistle under his breath with a faint grin on his face.

Liam Desmond, Lewrie's "Black Irish" Cox'n, drawing a drink of water from the scuttlebutt in the waist, winced a bit, for he was a very musical fellow on his *uillean* lap-pipes. "Been a while since he's played, A little rusty, he is."

"A little, ye say?" the Stroke-Oar from Lewrie's boat frowned. John Kitch was in no way musical himself, only able to keep time with spoons on his thigh. "Th' Cap'um orta find another hobby, Liam."

"No, really, John," Desmond objected. "Afore he got this ship, and th' squadron, he had more time, and he was much better."

"Well, if that disaster puts paid t'all our raidin', he'll have all th' practice time he wants," Kitch pointed out.

Above them on the quarterdeck, pressed against the cross-deck hammock stanchions, Midshipman Dunn espied something flying on the signals tower ashore, went to the binnacle cabinet rack to fetch out a day-glass, and read it. He lowered the telescope, tugged down his short coat hem and his sleeves, and went to the Marine sentry.

"I have to tell the Captain that there's a signal ashore," he said with sudden fifteen-year-old importance.

"Midshipman Dunn t'see the Captain, SAH!" the sentry bawled, stamping his boots and slamming his musket butt on the deck.

The music stopped of a sudden with a final, surprised *tweet*.

"Enter!" came a shout from within.

Dunn tucked his short-brimmed hat under his arm and stepped in, spotting Captain Lewrie seated on the starboard side settee.

"What is it, Mister Dunn?" Lewrie asked.

"Flag hoist ashore, sir," Dunn crisply reported. "It says 'Q here,' and 'Conference, Query.'"

"Ah," was all Lewrie said in reply, leaning forward to place his penny-whistle on the low, round brass table. "Very well, Mister Dunn. Do you hoist a signal to say that I will come ashore, then pass word for my boat crew to muster."

"Very good, sir," Dunn answered, performed a sketchy bow from the waist, more a jerk movement, then turned about and departed, and could be heard yelling for the boat crew.

"Now we'll see what Mister Quill has to say for himself," Lewrie muttered as he rose from the settee and fetched his waistcoat, coat, and cocked hat.

At least he won't be amused, Lewrie told himself after he left the barge at the make-shift landing pier at the beach; *And I won't have t'suffer Quill's donkey-bray*.

Mr. Quill was Foreign Office's Secret Branch representative on Sicily, the unlikeliest spy that anyone could imagine, which might be his salvation from enemy agents. He had been recruited from the libraries at Cambridge, and he looked the part. Tall, lanky as a scare-crow, with a cadaverously lean face, dark hair clubbed back in a short queue, pale skin as if he only stirred out after midnight, and dressed in black from head to toes in a churchman's "dominee ditto," replete with black cotton stock-ings over spindly thin shanks. He resided in the dockyard area of Messina in miserly poor lodgings, where Lewrie and his cabin steward Deavers had had to sleep over one night, half-awake to the sounds of bawdy, drunken revelry outside, and the scurry of rats and mice within.

And when the poor Mr. Quill found cause to laugh out loud, he *did* bray, along with a snigger, and a sound somewhere betwixt a man drowning and gasping for air, and consumption. Dis-concerting as he was, Quill was the fellow who gathered the information about where the squadron and the troops of the 94th went ashore, right down to beach conditions, slope, and dimensions, and the depths of the water from the surfline to where the transports, and *Vigilance* with her supporting artillery could safely an-chor, through his contacts among the criminals who could sail over and pretend to fish or trade whilst they gathered their intelligence, all for a hefty fee from British purses and money chests.

Lewrie made his way up from the beach on a well-worn path that was muddy when it rained, despite beach sand being spread along it, and was dusty today under a mild Autumn sun. Col. Tarrant's dog, Dante, saw him coming, perked up, and came trotting to greet him with a new toy in his mouth, anticipating play. Mr. Quill and Tarrant sat upon the raised wooden gallery in front of his quarters, most-like with mugs of ale or glasses of fruity white wine in their hands, and, of course, Quill did not deal well with the dog; he sat bunched up with his heels under his chair, elbows close to his sides, dreading a burst of exuberant affection.

"Well, hallo, Mister Quill, Colonel," Lewrie said as he neared. "Mister Quill, how d'ye keep?"

"Only tolerably, Sir Alan," Quill nigh-mournfully replied, lifting his mug of ale in salute. "Everything's a muddle, I fear."

"Sit you down and join us, sir," Col. Tarrant invited. "Carson!" he called to his orderly, "A mug of ale for Sir Alan."

"Right-ho, sir!" Corporal Carson agreed.

Lewrie asked no questions 'til the ale had been fetched, and he had taken a welcome swallow, noting that it was not the local swill, but good British ale with a crisp, refreshing taste.

"So, what's acting in Messina, Mister Quill?" Lewrie asked.

"A slightly promising development as regards our cut-throats and crimi-nals, Sir Alan," Quill said, making a sour face. "A shift in allegiences, as it were. Our new premier *capo di capo*, *Signore* Lucca Massimo, has made it clear to his subordinate *capos* and their henchmen that it is in their best interests to shun future dealings with the French over on the mainland, and show more patriotism that is in Italian interests. I've been assured, again, that *Don* Lucca is *our* man, heart and soul . . . and a flood of English guineas, hah!"

"We're still being played, you mean," Lewrie stated.

"For every shilling, of course, sir!" Quill mirthlessly agreed.

"And, Mister Quill has brought me a rough copy of his report to his superiors in London, Sir Alan," Tarrant stuck in.

"Yes, I explained that it was the late *Don* Julio's greed that sold us out, and that despite the well-laid ambush, we acquitted ourselves well," Mr. Quill related, "as well as could be expected given the odds against us." He shifted forward on his chair to impart his latest intelligence. "I have learned through Mister Silvestri's contacts, and a fine set of informants he has managed to recruit, let me tell you, that there is a certain French general, despatched South to deal with us by Marshal Murat in Naples himself. His predecessor has recently been demoted, and sent to count spare boots for his failure. Along with him, the Colonel in command of their cavalry was demoted for his reluctance to advance within range of your guns, Sir Alan, and support the infantry. I included those tidbits in my report," he added, with a scary-looking grin. "I trust that my observations will go a long way as to your, and Colonel Tarrant's, absolutions, heh heh."

Oh, don't laugh! Lewrie thought; *You'll frighten the dog!*

And, at those times when Mr. Quill thought that he had done something, or said something, clever and "Spy-ish," his ill-featured phyz could take on an aspect that could curdle milk.

"So, what are your thoughts on our new benefactor, sir?" Col. Tarrant asked after a deep sip of ale, and a wee smack of his lips. "He really wasn't here long enough for me to take his measure."

"Uhm, well," Quill mused after a deep draught of his own. "He is much more civilized than the late *Don* Julio."

"He can eat with a knife and a fork," Lewrie quipped.

"And most elegantly, too," Quill rejoined. "*Don* Lucca is . . . ah, dare I say, distinguished. As you saw when he was here to inform us that *Don* Julio had been . . . supplanted, he dresses sobrely, without flash, and bears himself with a certain gravity, as if he comes from a middling family of some local importance, from Sicilian gentry . . . thought certainly one long-involved in the criminal syndicate. He is a most serious fellow."

"He'll have someone's throat cut and not crack a smile, do you mean?" Lewrie japed again.

"My but you're cheery today, Sir Alan," Col. Tarrant chuckled.

"I am certain that *Don* Lucca could prove to be even more dangerous than any of his associates," Quill said, "but, odd as it may sound, once he's pledged his word to aid us, I suspect that he's the sort who would stick to his bargain. Personal honour seems to mean much more to him than *Don* Julio. I believe we can trust him."

"So long as there's a regular supply of British guineas," Col. Tarrant supposed aloud, with one leery brow up.

"Guineas, and weapons," Mr. Quill told them. "His *capos* over on the mainland have heard of what a few small bands can accomplish in the wild woods in the mountains since we supplied my assistant, Mister Silvestri, with a couple of hundred-odd muskets and ammunition, and *Don* Lucca has gotten requests for their henchmen to be armed, as well. Probably for armed robberies, but," he said, shrugging.

"Can you lay hands on another lot?" Lewrie asked. "How soon, and how many? I'll send Lieutenant Farley off in a couple of ship's barges as soon as they arrive."

"No trouble," Quill assured them. "I'll write Gibraltar or Lisbon. Both garrisons are storing goodly stockpiles of muskets taken from the French in Spain and Portugal, beyond what General Wellesley issues to Spanish and Portuguese troops.

"As for their distribution, *Don* Lucca assures me that he has the boats to smuggle them over, on his own," Quill went on, between sips of ale, "so your barges won't have to be risked. After all, his criminals are much better smugglers than we are. I dare say they'd put our smugglers back in England to shame, hah hah!"

"I don't suppose that *Don* Lucca has any specific places in mind that he suggest we raid?" Lewrie asked, wishing that it wasn't rude to ask for a refill of ale before his host offered.

"He's said nothing upon that head, Sir Alan," Quill told him. "He is more than willing to gather information on what *we* determine, that would be *our* bailiwick. Once we choose, he and his syndicate will do all we ask them to to speed our way."

"At least he didn't mention Melito di Porto Salvo," Col. Tarrant said with a brief snort of relief.

The late *Don* Julio had pressed them to strike there, right on the "toe" of the Italian "boot," a place with some old fortifications behind the town, artillery batteries either side of the harbour entrance channel, commanding the useful beaches on which they could land, surely had a sizeable garrison, and was uncomfortably close to the main French base and its garrison in Reggio di Calabria. Lewrie and Tarrant had been utterly convinced that the town was home to one of his competitors, or that he'd been laying plans for the squadron and its troops to be destroyed there, long before.

Tarrant's dog padded over to Lewrie and put his head and shoulders in his lap, sniffing at Lewrie's ale mug. In a twinkling, the dog had his muzzle deep inside and lapping.

"Oh, don't let him do that, Lewrie!" Tarrant snapped, a bit put out. "Down, Dante, bad dog! If he gets into some ale, it makes him as gassy as so many cows!"

"No no," Lewrie said, raising the mug above his head, though the dog tried to scramble after it, making Lewrie shove him away. "Damme!"

"You'll be needing a fresh mug," Tarrant said, "and a refill, I expect. Carson? A fresh mug for Sir Alan, and refills all round!"

Good dog, Dante, Lewrie thought with a grin; *It's rather good ale, even after gettin' shipped so far!*

"Uhm, pardon my asking, sirs," Mr. Quill asked, "but . . . where *are* we to strike, now? Saddle up, again, after being thrown, all that?"

"Lewrie?" Tarrant prompted, as if a plan could spring forth all ready for execution from a tactical or strategic genius.

Lewrie paused for a long moment before confessing "I haven't a single clue."

"Ah, hmm," Tarrant said, clearing his throat. "No . . . ?"

"But for Melito di Porto Salvo, we've attacked almost all of the seaside ports and villages along the coast, sirs," Lewrie said, with a negative shake of his head. He summoned the mental picture of the map in his mind; Bova Marina, Brancaleone just East of Cape Spartivento, Bovalino, Locri and Siderno, Marina di Gioiosa Ionica, Rocello Ionica, Monasterace? They had bombarded Catanzaro Lido but had not landed, for there was a large French garrison there; the same for Crotone.

There was a little place betwixt Monasterace and Catanzaro, the wee fishing village of Soverato, halfway up the instep of the "boot." And, they had made few appearances on the Western coast as yet, not since destroying the ancient Roman bridge right on the coast above a village called Pizzo, which had caused the supply detour and bottleneck over the mountains that kept French garrisons fed and armed.

Soverato? What would be the point, far East of where the supplies crossed the mountains and returned to the long coastal road.

"No, Colonel," Lewrie slowly admitted, "at the moment, there's not a place that springs to mind worth attacking again. Locri and Siderno, where we began in the early Spring, and burned up the French invasion depots? They're on the new supply routes, but we have no idea if they've been garrisoned since, or if anything worthwhile is stored there."

"I could go back to Messina and confer with *Don* Lucca to see what he knows," Mr. Quill offered, looking a bit worried that Lewrie didn't produce a wickedly sharp idea that instant. "And, he can send a boat with a letter to Mister Silvestri, asking for his input."

"That'd be good, thankee, Mister Quill," Lewrie told him with a lift and tilt of his dog-licked ale mug. Corporal Carson came out of Tarrant's quarters with a fresh mug, and a pitcher to top them up.

What the Devil do they expect of me? Lewrie asked himself; *They imagine I'm a Wellesley, a Napoleon, or Horatio Nelson? I ain't* that *clever, never have been!*

CHAPTER FOUR

*I*f Lewrie was well and truly stumped, he could find an host of useful diversions 'til something, anything, sprang to mind that would not be a total catastrophe—he'd had enough of those lately, thank you very much.

HMS *Vigilance*, a two-decker 64, needed a good scouring, fore and aft, from bilge ballast to the mainmast truck. There were frayed and worn rigging to be replaced, pulley blocks to be lubricated, trash to be swept, and decks to be washed, then holystoned to new whiteness. The guns had to be washed, too, blacked with paint, and recoil and run-out tackle and breeching ropes to be seen to, solid iron roundshot had to be filed to a more perfect roundness, then gun drill performed without powder or shot to keep *Vigilance*'s already experienced gun crews back to the rhythm of three rounds every two minutes for the long 18-pounders on the upper deck, and two shots in three minutes of the lower deck 24-pounders.

Boarding nets had to be repaired, then lowered to the waiting barges, and the Marines in their shirtsleeves had to practice going over the side and into those barges, then back to the weather decks as quickly as possible. Musket practice fired at bobbing casks, pistol work, then cutlass, hatchet, and boarding pike drill should they have to repel boarders, or fight for their lives on some beach, as they had at Monasterace. And, of course, drill after drill for all ships to row ashore, take troops of the 94th aboard, dis-embark them back into the barges, and land them ashore at their encampment.

Lewrie's crew even spent a morning hunting rats when the number of vermin became too obvious, and the many cats and terriers aboard could not keep up. Nest after nest were discovered and decimated, and most admitted that it was a delightful thing to do, with a contest pitting larbowline division against starbowline division after the kills were tossed into casks and tallied up.

Now, it must here be admitted that Alan Lewrie was, when not pressed by the needs of the Service, and a ship and crew, could be a most indolent fellow, and when ashore on half-pay, was a slug-abed. Nothing delighted him more, at least when he was a young civilian, than to rise late to toast and cocoa, dress smartly and make the rounds of coffee houses and ordinaries with fellow idlers, attend the theatres or bawdier playhouses, drink and be merry, sup late, and go to bed past midnight to do it all again the next day.

Duty, though, his reputation as a "doer," forced him on deck to oversee minor evolutions and repairs, the daily loading of bread and fresh water, fruit, milk, and livestock, even going so far as to peek into the galley and pester the Ship's Cook, Lennox, and his assistants when they used the ship's massive Brodie stove, which could turn out eighty loaves of fresh-baked bread when they had enough ingredients.

To keep fit, Lewrie paced the length of the ship each morning, and led the younger Midshipmen in spirited practices with cutlasses, small swords, and the use of their ceremonial dirks, working up perspiration. And in the privacy of his great-cabins, he hoisted, then swung small buckets with 9-pounder roundshot in them.

He spent a fair amount of time ashore at the Army encampment, hiking through the fruit and olive groves and beyond, and at the firing butts to hone his aim with his rifled Ferguson breechloading musket, a lighter long-barrelled fusil, his Girandoni air-rifle, and his sets of pistols, shooting 'til his shoulder ached and the palms of his hands tingled and stung.

He *knew* that Colonel Tarrant was right; one must get back on the horse that threw you, soonest. *Vigilance* and the squadron of troop transports *must* sail again, stage another raid somewhere on the Calabrian coast before the spirit and morale of both Navy and Army evaporated like steam from a boiling pot.

For almost the entire year, all five ships had spent long days at anchor following a raid; prompting Lt. Greenleaf to comment that it was an odd sort of war they were fighting. But, informants on the mainland, and criminal Sicilians pretending to fish or trade had to "smoak out" the lay of the land and report back on the nature of the sand beaches, the depths of water close inshore, what was worth striking, and if a garrison was present, and in what numbers before Lewrie and Tarrant could agree on where they would strike next. Everyone in the 94th and everyone aboard *Vigilance* knew how it worked, why they delayed, and treated the waits like lazy, idle Sundays, ready to go at it again, eager to give the French another good bash on the nose.

Now, though. Good mates had died, lay wounded and moaning in pain in the hospital pavillion, in ships' sickbays, some of them yet to expire, and some maimed for life, sure to be discharged back into civilian life without limbs, or eyes, or futures.

They had suffered what *felt* like a defeat, had escaped the trap by the skin of their teeth, and this time the delay seemed to sap the spirit from them, despite their officers' assurances that they would strike again, as soon as a good target was found. Lewrie feared that his people no longer felt as if it was a grand game, and had come to dread the idea of sailing into a similar debacle.

In truth, Alan Lewrie felt a niggling worry that a follow-up raid would turn out as badly as the last one, too. Perhaps that was why he could not sit still.

In the times when he felt that he was making a perfect pest of himself, Lewrie forced himself to go over the charts they had used since the first raids in early Spring, reviewing all the details of land, beaches, depth of water, and how difficult was the terrain back of the beaches for his Marines and Tarrant's soldiers. There were piles of hand-drawn maps and sketches to pore over, rough layouts of coastal towns and villages to study—and frets arising over what a forewarned French general or colonel could do to improve defences, or fortify what had been open ground months before.

French Marshal Murat already had sent a new and more industrious officer to command his forces on the coast, someone determined to not repeat his recently demoted predecessor's mistakes. Would he garrison every fishing village? Form mobile brigades that shuttled from Crotone to Melito di Porto Salvo along the vital coast road along with the supply waggon trains? Could they move fast enough to interfere as soon as they learned that the hated British were attacking a place close by?

Lewrie did not know, Tarrant did not know, and most especially, no intelligence from Calabria made Lewrie shift in his chair with an idea that his skin actually crawled with well-hidden anxiety.

One more muck-up like the last'un, and we're done for, Lewrie thought. He craved news from Calabria or *Don* Lucca's henchman as fiercely as he wished to be re-united with his wife!

His barge came alongside the pier that jutted seaward from the beach, bow and stern lines were tied off, and Lewrie at last rose from his seat on a thwart right-aft by his Cox'n, Liam Desmond, and one of the Midshipmen, who in this case was his much younger brother-in-law, Charles Chenery. Using an oarsman's shoulder for support, he stepped on the gunwale then onto the pier, swinging round a piling for a grip.

"Right, lads," he said, "An hour or so to skylark among the local traders, then back to the ship . . . in good time for your rum issue, hey? Mister Chenery, you and Desmond keep a sharp eye on 'em. No excess drink. I'll be ashore 'til mid-afternoon, and will hoist a signal for you to come fetch me."

"Aye, sir," Chenery said, tapping the brim of his hat in salute.

"*Mostly* sobre, aye sor," Desmond japed. "Me an' Kitch'll see t'that."

"Like a fox in the hen coop?" Lewrie rejoined. "Carry on."

He followed the well-worn path from the beach to Col. Tarrant's quarters, quickly greeted by a loping, bounding Dante. Lewrie knelt and gave the big, shaggy hound some "wubbies," then rose and walked on with the dog trotting at his side.

Col. Tarrant and Major Gittings were seated at the outdoor dining table under the canvas fly, having their breakfast, and rose as Lewrie neared.

"Sorry to be late to your kind invitation, sir," Lewrie said as he pulled out a chair to join them. "A last minute detail aboard, and thank you for having me."

"No problem, Sir Alan, none at all," Col. Tarrant told him as Carson the orderly poured Lewrie a cup of tea. "And how do you take your eggs?"

"Scrambled," Lewrie replied as he tucked a cloth napkin under his chin. To Carson's query as to how many, Lewrie told him three.

"A little surprise under your plate cover, Sir Alan," Tarrant said with a grin.

"A grapefruit?" Lewrie exclaimed as he lifted the tin dome.

"Better yet, sir . . . a shaddock," Tarrant said, proudly.

"Oh, wonderful!" Lewrie said in delight. "I haven't had one since last I was in the West Indies!"

"The locals call them pomelos," Major Gittings said, "God only knows why."

"We call them shaddocks after the name of the merchant captain who brought them to Jamaica, was the way I heard it," Lewrie told them, digging a serrated spoon to lift out a sweet, succulent bite. "Ah! Marvelous! If I'd known they grow them on Sicily, I'd have bought up a half-dozen at a time!"

And, after a few minutes, Corporal Carson brought out a fresh plate with his scrambled eggs, three strips of crispy bacon, thick-sliced toast, and a dollop of tattie hash, and Lewrie made free with the fresh butter and a pot of local berry jam. There was hot breath at his elbow as Dante whined for a bite of something.

"Don't encourage him, sir," Tarrant chuckled, "Dante gets his share, and more. When we've bacon, he gets three rashers."

Done at last, and well sated, Lewrie accepted another cup of tea and leaned back. "I may have to take a stroll round the groves, emulating the French and their notion of *digestif*, before we start whacking away at each other."

"Our sporting sword-work can wait," Tarrant said with a wave of a hand as he leaned over a wee candle that had been burning in the middle of the table, set there so he could light a *cigarro*.

"Has anyone heard anything yet from Mister Quill, or from *Don Lucca*?" Lewrie asked.

"No, not a word so far," Tarrant said with a scowl and a squint as the smoke from his *cigarro* wreathed his face. "If we had, you'd be the first we told. This idleness is driving me to distraction."

"And, it ain't good for our soldiers, either," Gittings added. "We can only drill them ashore, and practice boat work so much. It begins to feel pointless, and tedious."

"I know what you mean, sir," Lewrie agreed with a faint growl. "My ship's people know what real preparation, and make-work are, and after a while, scrubbin', polishin', and drills just make 'em surly."

"Well, I do believe that Sir Alan made a good suggestion. We could all use a long stroll, or hike, to work off our breakfasts. Do bring along your swords, and we'll try our skills against each other somewhere out in the woods."

"Well, there are some places best avoided," Major Gittings said with a humourous bark. "Some groves are reserved for the local doxies and their doings, haw!"

"Yays," Colonel Tarrant drawled, amused, "We can't embarrass our troops in mid-rut."

"Sir, it would take a great effort to embarrass our soldiers," Gittings hooted. "They dance out there in the buff!"

After Tarrant finished his *cigarro,* they rose from the table and began their walk, more a leisurely stroll than anything strenuous, with Tarrant's dog loping off ahead of them to explore or sniff at anything that took his fancy, then romping back like a scout sent ahead to report something new and aromatic.

"About here should do," Tarrant said at last in the shade of an olive grove, with branches only a foot or two above their heads. He stripped off his coat and hat, hung them on a limb, and unsheathed his curve-bladed sword. "Care to try, Sir Alan?"

"Right with you, Colonel," Lewrie heartily agreed, shedding his coat and drawing his hanger.

They were, all three of them, long from their formal training in a sword-master's *salle,* and their styles of combat had been honed in a rowdier school since. Colonel Tarrant could be judged the most elegant, holding his left hand in the small of his back, and balancing as gracefully as a man doing a minuet. Major Gittings, when it was his turn, was shorter and bluffer, and more of a slasher, whilst Lewrie used his straighter hanger to thrust and jab to fend him off, countering slashes with their blades ringing.

"Should have invited a fourth," Tarrant said after a few more minutes, panting a little, "Someone's being ganged up upon."

"I fear we are using you horribly, Sir Alan," Gittings said, his ruddy complexion flushed and beaded with perspiration.

"I get too little exercise aboard ship," Lewrie told him, fully in agreement. "This is no bother, really."

Christ, I'm about t'drop! he told himself, breathing deeply and resisting the urge to dash sweat from his brow; *I may be gettin' too damned old for such vigourous work.*

"Let us find some water," Tarrant suggested, sheathing his sword in the scabbard, and retrieving his hat and coat, though he did not put them back on.

"Or some white wine, what?" Gittings seconded, "For I'm fair parched!"

Back towards the drill field and company hut lines they went, 'til they came across a low civilian tent with a rough table in front, upon which sat an odd assortment of mis-matched glasses and mugs, and opened bottles of wine, mostly of the red and rough variety.

"*Vino blanco?*" Tarrant asked. "*Pinot grigio?*"

A silver six-pence coin paid for three glasses, and Col. Tarrant leaned a hand on the table after a first, welcome sip, making it shake and threaten to collapse. Lewrie had a thought to rest his bottom on it, before that, for he felt in need of a sit-down, but was forced to stand and pace about.

"Well, that was a welcome bit of exertion," Tarrant said as he dug into a breeches pocket for another six pence for a second round.

"Oh, aye!" Lewrie said, all but rolling his eyes. "Welcome."

"Something to do to seem as if we're doing *something*, instead of dithering and waiting," Tarrant sourly mused. "We simply *must* find a way to get back into action."

"Show the French that we're not done, not by a long chalk," Major Gittings gruffly said.

"Make the Frogs eat a large crow pie, hah!" Tarrant chuckled.

"Monasterace," Lewrie said of a sudden.

"Monasterace?" Tarrant asked.

"Go right back and burn it to the ground," Lewrie fantasised aloud, with a sly grin on his face. "Take them on and whip them where they imagine they won? It's tempting, if there was a way. It'd give them a huge black eye."

"Hmm, I wonder," Col. Tarrant mused. "They lost a fair part of the two regiments that ambushed us. Surely, they would have to go to their original bases and recover. Why keep troops needed elsewhere sitting round a poor place like that?"

"Oh, I don't know, sir," Major Gittings cautioned, though it was a tempting proposition, "So many supplies camping there for the night, sufficient water . . . Monasterace just might be the best place for them. Set up hospitals and rest their men?"

"But if they *have* moved on," Lewrie said with more enthusiasm, "the only garrison there would be the fifty or sixty Commissariat men who repair the waggons, and issue the hay and oat rations."

"I've still my notes and plans," Tarrant said. "Care to remain ashore for lunch. So we can look them over? Just in case, what?"

"What are we having?" Lewrie asked with another sly grin.

CHAPTER FIVE

*L*ater that afternoon, back aboard his ship, Lewrie dug out the plans for the failed raid on Monasterace, and spent a few speculative hours reviewing them.

His mention of the place had almost been a jape, off the top of his head, but, after discussing the possibilities of re-visiting the town with Col. Tarrant and Major Gittings, a tenuous hope sprang anew. It was a tempting proposition, a most alluring one, to go right back and strike a blow like a boot to French testicles, and one that would go a long way towards restoring the squadron's lustre, the repute of the 94th, and, admittedly, Lewrie's own credit as a successful warrior.

Of course, a potential raid on Monasterace could not happen in the same fashion as the first one. He had placed *Vigilance* a bit to the West of the town and its piers, and had landed his Marines further West to sweep up the outskirts, going for the waggon trains camped on the inland side of the coast road. Tarrant's regiment had gone ashore East of the town, and was supposed to have swept the Eastern outskirts, with one of its Light Companies probing into the streets and houses on that side to root out any stray Frenchmen. They had been landed there for the good reason that the beaches on that side were gently sloped, and broad enough for all eight of the companies to ground their barges together. Unfortunately, they had gotten no further than a low stone wall enclosing a large pasture.

The late *Don* Julio Caesare's amateur spies had fished off the coast, sounding the depths, had gone ashore to drink and eat in the taverns, and chat up the locals, had done some trade in rare goods unavailable under French occupation, and had done some sketching of how Monasterace was laid out, so Lewrie had a good idea of the place.

There was a long stone quay cross the front of the town, about five or six feet above seawater, backed by three short blocks of houses, taverns, a travellers' inn, and some houses. Two main roads or streets led inland to the usual town square which featured the usual church, more houses (some grander than others), and shops where people bought their bread, meats, pasta, and household goods. There were two more roads that ran inland down the peripheries, where there were more houses, more like farm cottages, with styes, coops, and a few barns for goats, sheep, and a few dairy cattle.

Lewrie didn't imagine that there was much left of the seafront left corner of Monasterace, or those smallholding farms, for when the French had sprung their ambush, a few companies of their soldiers had rushed out from that part of town, and to save his Marines from being over-run, Lewrie had turned *Vigilance*'s guns on it, telling his hands, rather loudly and angrily, to turn the place to brick dust!

Which they had, most efficiently.

Beyond where those streets through Monasterace intersected the main coast supply road, Lewrie could see a larger farmstead with two stone barns, a substantial place that probably belonged to some rich family. The Commissariat troops that the French had assigned there were said to live in the house, after turning out the owners, and were using the barns for their woodworking and iron forging to keep damaged or worn-out supply waggons in decent shape.

To either side in the broad pastures of that farmstead were the encampments for the waggon trains, enclosed on the sketch with a set of dashed-line circles. There was a long, low ridge beyond, almost a mile off from the town proper, and *Don* Julio's scouts had not been allowed to wander that far without arousing suspicion and arrest, but they had seen large tents set up to shelter the immense piles of hay the size of hillocks, and the sack upon sack of oats for the draught animals.

"Burn those and it'd make a glow like Mount Etna," he muttered under his breath, drawing the attention of his cabin servants for a moment.

How long would it take the French to gather enough replacement grains and feed, he wondered? How many convoys would have to be diverted from human and military supplies just to nourish the horses, mules, and oxen? Weeks, Lewrie imagined! And wouldn't *that* put the Frogs' noses out of joint?

And if a successful raid could be pulled off, God only knew how many supply convoys would be encamped for the night, draught animals turned out to graze in pens un-harnessed, the usual troop of cavalry escorts to each un-saddled, the troopers asleep in their bed-rolls, with their knee-boots off, and their mounts bound by their reins to ropes stretched between trees. They had found the same conditions at Bova Marina, had set fire to the waggons, panicked the cavalry horses, routed their riders, and had even faced down a weak charge, infantry counter-charging cavalry, a rare wonder. Hundreds of beasts had been slaughtered, over an hundred and fifty waggons torched, and hay and grain had been turned to a bonfire. All that would have to be replaced, too, at great cost to the French, and the supply convoy schedule set back so far that Marshal Murat in Naples would have to request aid and replacement from the far corners of Napoleon Bonaparte's empire!

Lewrie shut his eyes to picture that in his mind, a small grin tweaking the corners of his mouth. If only, he fervently wished!

Lewrie shook his head, though, and returned to the crude sketches atop his desk, Hmm, though . . .

If the town didn't have a garrison, if that brigade was no longer there, the idea was to block the waggon trains from escaping, and burning and slaughtering everything, so . . . how were they to go about that?

The town don't matter, Lewrie thought; *It's what lies beyond.*

He reached into a desk drawer to fetch out a lead pencil, paused as he held it over the sketch, then doodled a brace of transports West of the town, and another pair to the East, with two broad arrows jutting ashore, across the coast road to the camp sites, and driving into the heart of Monasterace to entrap the convoys' waggons, blocking the escape by holding the road.

His Marines and the armed sailors who would row them ashore, he thought to land directly on the town quays, over one hundred and ten men in all, right through the town and out the other side to attack the farm-stead house and barns where the French artificers slept and kept their forge waggon, woodworking, and harness repair shops.

Now, where could he place HMS *Vigilance* and all her 24-pounders and 18-pounders to the best effect? There were many two-storey homes in

Monasterace's centre, along with the church and its spire, and the substantial home and offices of the town's government. His guns could not shoot through them or over them; the roundshot would land somewhere a mile or two far out in the countryside, shattering the odd tree, perhaps. Besides, if, on the off chance that there was no fresh French garrison placed there, there was no reason to bombard the town, bringing fresh woe and ruin to long-suffering Calabrians, who lived a hard-enough life already.

Mr. Quill's informant network had visited Monasterce, too, and had gathered that the town's inhabitants were praying that the heretical French, who brought no priests with them and rarely entered the local church except to gawk, who swilled in their taverns and the seaside inn, elbowing good Italians out of the way, who took over the one wee brothel as theirs, and made rude approaches to young wives and the un-married daughters, would just go away, die, or burn in the fires of Hades.

Lewrie recalled a report from that visit that stated that the Commissariat troops were regarded as less-evil than most, kept in firm check by their officers, and actually paid full value for what they bought. No, it was the escort cavalry troopers and waggoneers who were the worst, who would swarm the town after dark with all the swagger of a conquering horde of Goths.

God let us kill a bunch of them, then, Lewrie prayed.

Vigilance, though; she'd have to anchor close off one of the landing beaches to support that half of the 94th Regiment with gunfire, leaving the other half un-covered. He needed another warship, though he doubted if that ship's gunners would have the experience and skill to fire roughly aimed shots at any threat that arose.

He *could* write to Rear-Admiral Sir Thomas Charlton and ask for re-enforcement, but, could Charlton spare a frigate or a brig-sloop that could get close ashore in shallow waters? And, could that ship shoot accurately enough?

Lewrie heaved a petulant sigh and gathered up all of his charts and sketches, stuck them in a side drawer of his desk, and leaned back in his chair, running his hands through his hair in frustration.

He had no idea if a return raid could be pulled off, no clue as to whether there was a new French garrison there, and, so far, no information from anyone.

"Bugger it," he muttered, rising from his desk to go to the starboard side settee grouping and plop down on the settee with a whoosh.

Eight Bells chimed in pairs from the forecastle belfry; Four in the afternoon, and the end of the Day Watch, the beginning of the First Dog.

"Sun's below the main yardarm, Deavers?" Lewrie called out.

"Ehm, just about, I reckon, sir," the cabin steward replied.

"Have we any ale left?" Lewrie asked.

"Some Eye-talian beer, sir," Deavers told him with a *moue* of distaste. "Not *too* bad a batch, really."

"Tap me a mug, then," Lewrie told him, putting his booted feet up on the low brass tray-table in front of him. "I'll follow the sage advice of a Greek poet, Aristophines."

"What advice was that, sir?" Deavers asked as he fetched a mug.

"'Quickly, bring me a beaker of wine so that I may wet my mind, and think of something clever,' hah!" Lewrie quipped.

A sponge-down, a close shave, and a decent breakfast started Lewrie's day. There was toast, oatmeal with fresh butter and honey, and a small pot of coffee with sugar and a flask of cream bought off a passing bum-boat from Milazzo, cow-cream, not the milk from the on-board nanny goat. Chalky's bowl was at the foot of the long table, where he broke his fast on oatmeal with butter, a crumbled slice of toast, some wee chunks of cheese, and sliced and quartered sausage. To keep the cat fed, Lewrie always made sure that he went to sea with no less than an hundredweight of sausages, and Italy, and Sicily, were awash in a myriad of sausage varieties. Lewrie even awarded himself a short link sausage with his breakfast, something spicy, garlicky, and tasting heavily of fennel that made him burp a time or two.

"Midshipman Malin t'see the Cap'um, SAH!" the Marine sentry on his door bawled.

"Enter," Lewrie called back as he sugared and creamed a third cup of coffee.

"Sorry, sir, but there's a signal hoisted ashore," the Mid said. "It's Request Presence."

"Oh, very well," Lewrie groused, frowning. "Pass word for my boat crew to muster, and I'll be on deck, directly."

"Aye aye, sir," Malin replied, backing up towards the door.

"Keep the cat amused, do, Deavers," Lewrie said, removing his napkin and taking a last, large sip of his coffee. "Warn Yeovill that I may be ashore past dinner, so he's not to prepare me anything."

"Aye, sir," the cabin steward said.

Here we go, again, Lewrie thought as he shrugged into his coat and snatched his older cocked hat from a peg in an overhead beam; *Pray God it's good news for a change, or intelligence about what the French are doin' over yonder.*

For late Autumn in the Mediterranean, it was a rather cool day, with a low-lying fog that clung to the anchorage waters, the beaches, the Army encampment, and filtered through the fruit and olive graves. Lewrie could see about 100 yards through the mists as he trudged up the path to Col. Tarrant's quarters. As he got nearer, he could see that a two-wheeled farm cart stood by the small grove of trees near Tarrant's quarters, drawn by a single mule that was resting with one hind-hoof cocked, munching from a feed bag. And there was the young imp, Fiorello, who was Mr. Quill's lad-of-all-work, sitting on the edge of the raised wooden gallery, munching on a bunch of grapes.

So Quill's here, Lewrie thought; *Let's see what he's brought us.*

"*Buon giorno, Signore Looie,*" Fiorello called out.

"*Buon giorno,* Fiorello," Lewrie replied. "Don't let the dog eat you," he added as the door opened and Dante came dashing out, to have himself a good shake, before bowling the lad over, raising a squeal of delight.

"Ah, Sir Alan, one hopes we did not interrupt your breakfast," Col. Tarrant said as he welcomed his guest in. "Coffee, sir?"

"Please," Lewrie told him, taking off his hat and sitting down at the dining table. Major Gittings was there to one side, and at the foot of the table sat dour and dark Mr. Quill, with a packet of papers before him.

"Mister Quill, how d'ye keep?" Lewrie asked as Corporal Carson fetched a cup and saucer, and poured him some coffee.

"Main well, sir," Quill said with a rictus of a sociable grin, "And you, sir?"

"Impatient, but tolerable," Lewrie told him.

"We thought it best to wait for you to arrive, Sir Alan, so that Mister Quill would not have to repeat himself," Tarrant said, stirring up a fresh coffee of his own. "So, sir . . . what's acting over on the mainland? You have news of what the French are doing?"

"I do, sirs," Quill told them as he opened his packet. "As we learned earlier, the French General of Brigade who sprang his trap on you, and mucked it up so badly, has been replaced by a General of Division by name of Paul Ducote, a fellow with somewhat of an aggressive reputation. He's one of Murat's favourites, and was promoted in person by Bonaparte himself, after distinguished service at Austerlitz.

"He's gotten re-enforcements down from Northern Italy, mostly allied troops. It is rumoured that he favours Germans and Poles, not Italians, if he can't have Frenchmen."

"What sort of Italians?" Major Gittings asked.

"My aide over there, Silvestri, has gathered that Ducote is to be re-enforced with Genoese and Milanese troops, sir," Quill said.

"All fine for him, but . . . what's he plan to do with them?" Col. Tarrant asked. "Do we have any idea what he'll be doing differently?"

"A waiter at his temporary lodgings in Reggio di Calabria did over-hear a discussion, Colonel," Quill went on. "He is aware that we only have four transports, so he roughly knows that the Ninety-Fourth is not a full, ten company regiment. Yet, he berated one of his officers who suggested creating large garrisons in every coastal village or fishing port. There was some talk of mobile forces, in strength, to roam the coast. Brigades, per-manently on the move?"

"That would close the window on opportunities," Gittings said with a growl.

"He'd need a regular relay of supply convoys to do that, would he not?" Lewrie asked. "Christ, how many re-enforcements is he going t'get?"

"French troops have been seen leaving Reggio di Calabria, Melito di Porto Salvo, Catazaro, and Crotone," Quill told them. "Infantry and cav-alry, Cavalry makes sense, does it not? They could be very mobile, and have been wasted in garrisoning the larger towns. Silvestri says that in the last few days, there have been more of them prowling round the moun-tains, putting pressure on the partisan bands.

"Then, there are the semaphore towers they're building," Quill stuck on almost as an afterthought.

"Oh, bugger!" Col. Tarrant spluttered. "Alerts could spread the whole length of the coast in minutes!"

"And what could they do about it if they *were* alerted?" Lewrie scoffed. "We'd be long gone by the time they could respond. Besides, semaphore towers did the Spanish no good on their Southern coast back three years ago, before they changed sides. I burned my share of them, and eliminated the trained people who operated them. In Spain, there were usually no more than twelve or fifteen people at each tower, and that included cooks, bakers, and servants. They're nigh-defenceless."

"And, if this Ducote means to defend them against us," Major Gittings pointed out, "he'd need a full company of infantry at each one. How far apart, ten miles or so, and still be readable by day or night? Every eighty miles would take an average French regiment! He wouldn't have any infantry left to protect anything else!"

"And we wouldn't have to do anything to them, Colonel," Lewrie added with a chuckle. "A pair of brig-sloops or small frigates could be given that chore, and would relish it. Our smaller ships have been at that sort o' work all along the French and Dutch coast for years! I'll write Charlton, and he can have ships off the coast within a week, smoaking them out and burning 'em down. He's offered any assistance I could ask for. So far, I haven't needed to."

"Well, if that's so . . ." Tarrant said with a shrug, turning to Quill. "Has your man, or his informants, told you anything about our last target, Monasterace?"

"Monasterace, sir?" Quill replied, going owl-eyed in surprise. "He did mention something, I do believe, but it didn't signify with me at the time. A moment, sirs," he said, flipping through a stack of loose papers he had brought along. "Ah." Here it is.

"According to our partisan informants, sirs, Monasterace is back in business. Waggon convoys coming and going, camping for the night, with small cavalry escorts, the same as usual."

"The French brigade we met?" Tarrant pressed.

"They went into camp in the fields below the ridge for a few days, burying their dead, and setting up hospital pavillions," Quill said, with a jerk of his head towards the one that still stood at the 94th's camp, "They commandeered waggons to carry most of their wounded away to better facilities, then marched off towards Catanzaro, leaving the worst wounded behind, with a medical detachment of twenty or thirty surgeons and orderlies. That's still there . . . or it was at least a week ago."

"And they didn't leave even a small garrison behind?" Gittings asked.

"Well, no, Major," Quill told him, perplexed. "Monasterace is the same place it was before. Why? Are you thinking of going back to finish the job?"

"We are, indeed, Mister Quill," Tarrant told him with a stern nod. "If the town is as un-protected as your informants say, going back will finish the job we intended, *and* give this new French general a *real* blow to begin his command."

"Hmm," Mr. Quill said, fingers steepled beneath his nose for a long moment, before his long, lean face broke out a boyish grin, and he began to titter. "I quite like it, hah hah!"

Fortunately for all, and the dog, Quill did not break out into a full donkey bray/gasping man laugh, this time. Lewrie un-crossed the fingers of his right hand in relief.

"We may do it differently, this time, but if we can get ashore quickly, we can scoop everything up," Col. Tarrant said.

"Might you require an additional scout, sir?" Quill asked him, "More information anent the beaches, or something? I could contact Silvestri, or *Don* Lucca's men . . ."

"I think we have enough from the initial studies to make do," Tarrant said, "along with our impressions gathered from what we experienced whilst we were there."

"If we sail within a day or two, things should remain as your people reported, Mister Quill," Major Gittings added.

"The long way, roundabout Sicily, though," Lewrie cautioned.

"Even so, we've run the same risk of surprise each time we have done so, and surprising the French is the main thing," Tarrant said. "I just dislike extending my time aboard a ship, on an un-certain sea, at the mercy of foul weather. Brr!"

"One would never suspect, sir," Lewrie told him. "You bear your misery main-well. Like General Wellington on his way to Portugal . . . the Captain of his ship warned him that they were in for a stormy night, and he was reputed to say that he would not take off his boots if that was the case, hah hah!"

"On the contrary, Sir Alan," Tarrant replied with a shy smile, "I do not remove mine 'til we're safely back *here*!"

"Fog's burning off at last," Major Gittings commented, rising from his chair to stretch, pace to the edge of the raised gallery, and clap his hands in the small of his back, deeply inhaling the moist, rich morning smells. Over his shoulder he asked "Should we stage a last boarding drill before we go, sir? Shake the cobwebs off our men?"

"That might be a good idea, Gittings," Tarrant said, dabbing at his mouth with a napkin. "After we tell them that we're going back into action, at last."

"I would suppose you'll not have room for Brigadier Caruthers's men, yet," Quill tossed off, "Not 'til you get more ships."

"Caruthers's men? Certainly not!" Tarrant said with a sniff. "They're not trained for our sort of work, and I'll be damned if *that* man gets a hand in our line!"

"Then what is he training them for, sir?" Mr. Quill asked, all at sea once more.

"Training them? Training them, sir?" Col. Tarrant erupted with fire in his voice, chin-up as if challenged.

"Well . . . ?" Quill stumbled, "the last time I rode past his camp, just this morning, really, I noted that he had erected a wooden wall, Colonel. About twenty feet high, about fifty feet long?"

Under Tarrant's fierce glower, Quill seemed to be melting into his clothes, wincing as if pummeled.

"There are stairways on one side that lead up to a platform. Once Fiorello and I got close enough," Quill went on, "we could see that there are rope nets hanging down the other side, just like yours, Captain Lewrie, and there were soldiers . . . oh, about two hundred of them, on the platform, and clambering down the nets."

"God damn him!" Tarrant roared, frightening his dog to its feet, barking in alarm. "God rot and damn his eyes and blood! If he's got his hands on boarding nets, I'd wager he's laid hands on some transports! The sneaking, conniving, ambitious . . . usurping bastard!"

"If more transports are coming, sir," Lewrie had to point out, "no one's told me. I haven't gotten anything from Admiral Charlton, Commissioner Middleton, or Admiralty. And, I strongly suspect that if Brigadier Caruthers has been authorised to use one of his regiments as amphibious troops, Horse Guards would have written you of it."

"Nonsense, Lewrie!" Tarrant countered, forgetting his usual "Sir Alan" in his wrath, "that drunkard General Malcomb over at Messina probably told him to go ahead, and that's all the authorisation that that ruthless grasper needs! Transports are coming, you mark my words. London simply hasn't told us, yet!"

"Or, he could just take our transports for his own use," Major Gittings gloomed.

"Oh, for God's . . . damn, damn damn!" Tarrant spluttered.

"This could be very bad," Gittings prophecied.

"Sorry I mentioned it," Mr. Quill all but whispered, completely cowed.

Lewrie could almost feel sorry for the Foreign Office agent. Quill, he thought, was an ill-omened bird, and a most strange one, with a penchant for bringing useful information, sauced with a dollop of bad news, and too socially inept and awkward to keep the two separate.

Well, almost sorry.

CHAPTER SIX

*I*n the grim silence that followed, Quill, like the "spook" that he was, seemed to dissolve into thin air; one moment he was there and the next moment he wasn't, out under the trees next to the cart that he'd ridden from Messina. Major Gittings plumped himself into one of the chairs to scowl, whilst Colonel Tarrant paced with his hands in the small of his back, grumbling under his breath.

"Brandy!" Tarrant commanded of a sudden, halting and looking up. "Hear me, Corporal Carson?"

"Brandy right away, sir!" the orderly barked from the pantry, almost stomping his booted feet, followed by the *thock!* of a cork being pulled, the clink of glasses, and some welcome gurgling noised.

"Well, at least Caruthers doesn't have his own transports, yet," Col. Tarrant said, relaxing a bit after letting out a whooshing breath, "he hasn't gotten his soldiers trained to the work, either, and, God be praised, he hasn't ridden into camp waving orders that let him lay claim to ours. Could be worse."

"If he *does* have orders from God knows who," Gittings grumbled, "it would be nice to not be here when he does."

"Monasterace?" Lewrie suggested. "If your troops are back in fighting form, my ships are more than ready."

"Hmm, Monasterace, yes," Tarrant agreed, sitting down as the brandy arrived. "You have your sketches, Sir Alan?"

"I do, sir," Lewrie said with a grin, "I'd thought we might land either side of the town, with my Marines and armed boat crews to land on the town docks and march straight through."

"Half the regiment to either end of the town, and block the roads to pen all the wagon convoys in their night camps," Gittings posed, leaning over the rough map. "Full dark, long before sunrise, I take it?"

"Worth the risk, I think," Lewrie agreed.

"The Frogs'd never suspect us to be that brazen," Gittings said with a wee chuckle.

"Brazen, indeed," Tarrant commented, leaning in over the map, too. "Simple, direct . . . un-expected. I like it. Let's do it, soon as we can. Now, as to the detailed planning. Let's do it, now. You will dine with us, Sir Alan?"

"Of course, Colonel," Lewrie quickly accepted the offer.

"Passably good brandy," Gittings said, after a tasting sip.

"Portuguese, I believe," Tarrant told them. "You will wish to sail round-about Sicily, again, Sir Alan, for secrecy's sake?"

"Aye, I would, sir," Lewrie told him. "We'd give the game away even did we sail down the Strait of Messina at midnight, with all the ships' lights doused."

"Then I shall stash a bottle of this brandy to comfort me and my dread of the open sea on the journey," Tarrant told them.

It was mid-afternoon when Lewrie summoned his boat to come and fetch him, with a fresh sheaf of notes and orders in a side-pocket of his uniform coat. On the way out to where HMS *Vigilance* lay, Lewrie regarded his command with a fresh and appreciative eye, and, admittedly, with some pride.

The up-thrust of her jib boom and bowsprit looked aggressive, guarded by the crowned and seated gilded lion figurehead with one paw raised to shade its bright blue eyes to scan the horizons. All three masts towered high overhead, stout and solid, sails harbour gasketed to yardarms laid square amid a myriad of halliards, braces, clews and jeers, running stays and standing stays and shrouds in a display of geometric perfection. Her black-painted hull was still fresh enough and shiny enough to mirror sun dapples from the harbour waters like a darting cloud of fireflies, and the deep horizontal gun stripe had been washed free of gunpowder smut, chequered with gun-ports opened for a cooling breeze on the lower deck, and a hint of hard, black iron guns bowsed securely to the port sills.

Her coppering that showed along her waterline, well . . . it was not pristine and new-penny bright any longer, and as his barge came alongside the starboard boarding battens, Lewrie could frown at the sight of green weed waving at him in nigh foot long strands, hinting at the foulness that had accumulated on her quickwork below the waterline, and the many barnacles that lurked there could only be guessed at.

How long was she in commission when I took her over from that Captain Nunnelly? Lewrie asked himself as he prepared to rise and take hold of the main channel and battens and man-ropes; *The poor old girl is in need of a haul-out, and a hull cleanin'. Pray God it ain't too soon. We've still things t'do with her!*

"Toss oars!" his Cox'n, Liam Desmond, ordered as the barge butted against *Vigilance*'s hull. Lewrie stood, put a foot on the gunn'l, steadied himself on an oarsman's shoulder, and laid a hand on one of the man-ropes to stretch a booted foot out for the lowest batten.

Up he went, clambering the battens 'til the "dog's vane" plume of his cocked hat showed above the lip of the entry-port, signalling the side-party to doff hats, present arms, and for the Bosun's silver call to tweetle him a salute. Once safely inboard again, Lewrie doffed his hat in salute to the flag aft and the officer of the deck, after Lewrie's characteristic shove from the bulwark and a hop-skip stamp of his boots on the deck.

"Ah, Mister Farley," Lewrie said to the First Officer, who was sheathing his sword after his salute, "I'd be pleased did you hoist Captain(s) Repair On Board. Two-gun General Alert if you have to. Once the transport commanders are aboard, do join us."

"We're going somewhere, sir?" Lt. Farley asked, perking up.

"Ssh," Lewrie sniggered, laying a finger on his lips, "You didn't hear it from me. Yet."

The quarter moon had set almost two hours before, and false dawn was yet to show itself as one lone chime of the bell at the forecastle belfry rang out, a hushed and timid *Ding!* quickly muffled with a hand laid on the metal. One Bell of the Morning Watch, and half past Four in the morning.

Off the larboard bows, two guarded flashes from hooded lanthorns winked to life, just as quickly shuttered; *Bristol Lass* and *Spaniel* furtively announcing that they had come to anchor off their designated beaches, and were ready to embark their troops. Two more flashes off the starboard bows told *Vigilance* that *Lady Merton* and *Coromandel* were anchored East of Monasterace.

The night round *Vigilance*, out to sea, and up and down the shore was still as black as a boot, but, surprisingly, everyone aboard and on deck could see their objective remarkably well, for the seaport town, showed quay-side lanthorns, and the richer houses, warehouses, taverns, and inns had lanthorns by their doors, and some windows showed light from candles, almost delineating the total span from West to East. And behind the town, there appeared to be a sea of red or amber campfires, smouldering low and only now and then tended, as if an entire park had suffered a brushfire that had burned itself out.

Is this going t'work, please Jesus? Lewrie thought, fretting.

Mr. Quill's information about the lack of French troops could be days out of date since they had sailed from Milazzo four days past. *If* there were no troops beyond the small cavalry escorts. *If* there was no field artillery batteries camped for the night!

"Three flashes from all four transports, sir," Lt. Farley said in a loud whisper. "They're going in."

"Thankee, Mister Farley," Lewrie replied, feeling a lump in his stomach, a distinct sinking feeling that it could *still* all go smash. He looked for the transports, but could not make out their hulls, or the eldritch, ghost-like sails being reduced. He looked aloft for his own, and only imagined that he could discern them. *Vigilance* loafed along, barely making way, under greatly reduced sail, and even the usual rush of the sea down the ship's flanks, and the thrashing of her forefoot and cutwater was dim and distant.

Colonel Tarrant and Major Gittings had decided that *Vigilance*'s Marines and armed boat parties would land on the town's quays later than their own landings, using five men from each of their two-dozen barges as a light flank company to cut the town off as they carried out their assaults down the coast road into the waggon camps, with Lewrie's portion coming ashore when it was a little lighter, to avoid confusion and mistaking each other, resulting in needless casualties. *Vigilance*'s sailors and Marines were to clear the town *after,* in case French soldiers and waggoneers were there, wenching or drinking.

In point of fact, in the full darkness, *Vigilance* would not come to anchor 'til they could see if there were any targets upon which the guns could safely fire!

Lewrie felt himself all over for the twentieth time, groping at his pockets and waistband for his two pairs of pistols, loaded but not yet primed, for the reassuring hilt of his hanger, the pre-made cartridge pouches for his pistols, the priming flask, spare flints in his breeches pockets, and the sailcloth sack and wooden canteen that held all the things he thought necessary.

For this time, he would be going ashore with his men. It could go so badly that he could do nothing else. And, truth to tell, the qualms of doubt and lack of information that he had felt on their previous landings, the feeling that he commanded all but was in charge of absolutely nothing *drove* him to go ashore!

Perhaps it was the faint light from the many guttering campfires ashore, but even with a night-glass, Lewrie could make nothing out on the flanks of Monasterace, where the 94th was now landing; nor could he make out the barges stroking ashore. Even the dim phosphorescence of boat wakes and oar splashes failed him this time, so he could but guess how close they were to their beaches. Lewrie would have to wait for more quick flashes from handheld shuttered lanthorns. He cursed under his breath, feeling as if he could jump out of his skin!

"Captain sir?" came a whisper by his right elbow, and Lewrie did have to stifle an alarmed "eep!"

"Yayss?" he drawled back to cover his small scare.

"The barges are drawn up to either beam, sir, and the Marines are standing by on the sail-tending gangways," Lt. Grace reported with a hissing note to his lowered voice.

"Very well, Mister Grace," Lewrie answered, "Are you ready to go as well?"

"Aye, sir," Grace told him, "even though I'm to only guard the quays, and the barges. Mister Greenleaf loaned me a second pair of pistols, just in case."

"Let us pray you won't need them, Mister Grace," Lewrie said.

"I was hoping that I would, sir," Grace said, with a chuckle, and Lewrie could picture the young fellow's sly grin. Every officer in the Navy, every Midshipman, craved action, glory, and honour, for that was the lifeblood of advancement, and fame.

"Light up in the East, sir," Lt. Farley pointed out in a louder voice. "Three . . . four flashes. Major Gittings's half of the regiment is ashore."

A minute or so later, and there came four flashes from West of Monaste-race to tell them that Colonel Tarrant and his four companies were ashore, and feeling their way inland to the coast road and the sleeping convoy camps. The night, the sky, was still black, though, with not a hint of the greyness of false dawn. HMS *Vigilance* and her landing party would have to idle off shore, and wait.

"Come on, come on, come on!" Lewrie muttered, impatiently.

Lewrie tried pacing the quarterdeck, hands in the small of his back, head down in search of his boots, play-acting a stern and stoic senior Post-Captain of the Royal Navy, and trying not to trip over the odd ring-bolt.

Stoic, mine arse, he chid himself; *I've been play-acting this role half my born days! Oh, I'm such a fraud sometimes!*

"Firing, sir!" Lt. Farley yelped. "By volley, it looks like!"

Lewrie jerked his head up and rushed to the landward bulwarks to see. Yes! There were yellow-amber tongues of flame from the muzzles of mus-kets, smaller bursts from priming pans as flints rasped on the serrated frissons, and fire flashed down touch-holes to ignite the powder charges of Brown Bess muskets, rough lines of them under the command of Ma-jor Gittings on the East. The men on *Vigilance*'s decks strained and cocked their ears, but the crackling sound of burning twigs that musket fire made could not reach them.

A second volley of quick, bright flashes erupted, this time it was closer to the outskirts of the waggon camps on the East, but was still silent. Four companies of the 94th could be fixing bayonets, rushing forward with savage battle cries, spreading death and panic as they went, but that was happening in silence, too.

"Firing on the West, sir," Lt. Farley reported, pointing over the star-board bows as Colonel Tarrant's troops got into musket range.

Lewrie looked aloft, hoping for greyness in the skies, looked East towards a sunrise that was just not coming fast enough, muttered "Mine arse on a *band-box*!" and slammed his fists on the bulwarks. "Come on, sunrise!"

His ship was now West of the town quays and sailing even further West. They might have to wear about in the darkness to stay close to their ob-jective, and that would take long minutes on such a scant wind.

"Fetch-to, Mister Farley, fetch her to!" Lewrie snapped, straining to look down the sail-tending gangways, imagining the chaos as men sprang to tend braces, shoving armed Marines aside in disorder. Damn it, it had to be done!

Lewrie could *feel* Lt. Farley's stupefied look on the back of his neck. "Pass word for Captain Whitehead and his Marines to get on the boarding nets and go over the side, to make room."

"Aye, sir!" Farley said, raising a brass speaking-trumpet to yell "Boat crews and Marines . . . man your boats! Hands to the sheets and braces, tail on, and prepare to fetch-to! Helmsmen, hard up to windward," Farley ordered in a lower voice to the men on the wheel.

"Mister Grace, do you board a barge to larboard, whilst I board one to starboard. Mister Farley, I leave you in command," Lewrie said as he groped for the ladderway down to the ship's waist.

"Very good, sir," Farley said more formally, probably doffing his hat in the dark, if Lewrie knew him at all.

Lewrie swung a leg over the starboard bulwarks along the sail-tending gangway, bumping into sailors, found a secure foothold on the thick boarding nets, belly against the bulwarks, and began a clumsy, slow descent.

"Is there a barge under me?" he called down.

"Best ya shift three foot t'your left, sir," a sailor warned.

"You are almost to the gunn'l Captain sir," Marine Lieutenant Venables cautioned. "Another foot or so to your left, and we'll catch you if you slip."

Lewrie completed his spidery move to his left, lowered himself to another foothold, and felt his bum slapped by the loom of an oar that one of the boat crew held aloft, waiting for a Cox'n's order to lower it into the thole pins.

"Make room with those musket barrels," Venables told his men.

"Aye, don't goose me up my fundament," Lewrie japed, even as he lowered himself one more tier of horizontal ropes, and swung a booted foot, seeking the barge's gunn'l.

"Not quite yet, sir," Venables told him. "Two more down."

This time there was wood under his boot sole, and helpful hands reaching up to steady him as he lowered his left foot to find a solid wood thwart, shoulders to steady himself upon, and a seat far aft by the sailor who would handle the tiller.

"Bit of wot whalermen call a sleigh-ride, sir," the Cox'n said. "With th' ship still under way."

The barge was still bound to the ship with bow and stern lines, and one bank of oarsmen gripping the bottom of the boarding nets, so the barge was bumping and being sucked hard up to the hull by the wake that rushed down her side.

"Do we go now, sir?" Lt. Venables asked, eager to do something.

"No, not 'til it's lighter, as Colonel Tarrant planned," Lewrie had to tell him. He looked shoreward, up and down each side of Monasterace. At water level, the view was not as good as it had been from the quarterdeck, many feet higher up. There were continual musket flashes from both ends of the town, now much closer to the outskirts, and it seemed a bit lighter yonder, as if some waggons had already been set alight. Along the town's quays and in upper-storey windows, lanthorns were now lit, windows were flung open.

"Fetched-to, sir!" Lt. Farley shouted down from above.

"Hell's Bells, Mister Venables," Lewrie decided of a sudden. "We are here, ready to go. The town's wakin' up. Why the Devil not? Hoy, Mister Farley!" Lewrie shouted, cupping his mouth.

"Sir?"

"Order away boats!" Lewrie yelled.

"Aye aye, sir!" Farley replied, "All boats, cast off! Away all boats!" he roared, his voice tinny from the speaking-trumpet.

"Shove off and free lines," the Cox'n ordered. "Out oars, starb'd. Fend off, larb'd. Out oars, there, and give me way!"

"Your men loaded, sir?" Lewrie asked the young Marine officer.

"Loaded, but not primed, sir," Venables told him, his right hand flexing on the hilt of his sword. Lewrie looked at him, actually *seeing* Venables as the first inkling of dark blue greyness lifted the curtain of the night.

Guess I got my timin' right, after all, Lewrie told himself with glee.

"Toss oars," the barge's Cox'n ordered in a low voice as all four barges ghosted forward on the strength of the oarsmen's last strokes. "Boat yer oars, Ready the gaff, bow man, an' we'll tie up larb'd side to."

There was a motley assortment of small rowing boats and fishing boats along Monasterace's quays, bound to bollards, ring-bolts, and pilings by single bow lines. Bow men in all four barges used their gaffs to shove them aside, or hook on and drag their boat forward the last few yards.

"Jus' cut their bow lines t'make room," Lewrie's Cox'n urged.

Lewrie, his armed sailors, and Marines could now hear the commotion that the 94th had created; steady musket fire crackling up and down their ranks, feral shouts, now and then a loud explosion as one of the burning waggon's cargo of gunpowder or premade paper cartridges exploded. They could smell the stench of burning wood and canvas, and the bellows, terrified brays, and neighing from frightened oxen, mules, and draught horses could be heard from the stock pens.

Lewrie half-stood, to see above the level of the stone quays, and found the waterfront streets astir with milling, gabbling, gesticulating Italians, barely dressed in the first clothing that came to hand, dashing about as if Attila and his Huns had come with rape and loot on their minds.

"Lash alongside, there," the Cox'n snapped.

"After you, sir," Lewrie told Lt. Venables.

"Marines! Up on the quay and form ranks!" Venables ordered.

"Marines!" Capt. Whitehead, his senior, was also shouting, "Prime your firelocks! Form, form, form!"

The streets, crowded with panicky Italians but a moment before, emptied as they stampeded up the side streets deeper into town, wailing in terror, women screaming, children yowling and weeping as long as their parents were yelling, taking the arrival of *Vigilance*'s shore party as demons and monsters risen from the sea!

Lewrie stood on the barge's gunn'l, reached out to take hold of a bollard, and swung himself to a sitting position on the quay, turning and rising, dusting off the tail of his coat and the seat of his breeches.

"What's that foul stench?" Capt. Whitehead wondered aloud.

"An host of Italians with the shite scared out of them?" Lewrie japed.

"Garbage, I think, sir," Whitehead said with a shrug and wrinkling his nose. "Should I advance the ranks, sir?"

"Aye," Lewrie agreed. "Search all the houses and such as you come to them, in case there are Frenchmen lurkin'. I'll be along, shortly, soon as I prime my pistols. Mister Grace?" he called over his shoulder.

"Here, sir," Grace piped up.

"Post your men either end of the quay, and at the mouths of the streets leading into town," Lewrie said, his hands busy with pistol pans and a priming powder flask. "Stay out of the taverns, mind."

"As we did before at Bova Marina, sir," Grace replied. "Should I post Desmond and Kitch to that duty, again, sir?" he added, grinning at the memory.

"Oh, God save us," Lewrie said with a mock shiver. "They'll *swear* they'll keep sobre, but return aboard with wine kegs under their arms!"

"They were *sort* of reliable," Grace smirked.

"*I Francesi?*" Marine Lieutenant Venables was shouting to the few townspeople who hadn't scampered off. "*Francesi in città?*" His Marines were making rapid searches of the first buildings, and not being too gentle about it, briskly entering the ground levels, with other men aiming their muskets at upper-storey windows.

"Or old Pat Furfy, sir," Lt. Grace said of a sudden, grinning in remembrance. "Your Cox'n's mate? Lord, the lengths he went for drink."

Liam Desmond and Pat Furfy had fled their village in Ireland for mysterious reasons, steps ahead of British authorities, and had ended up in the hands of the Impress Service at Chatham, and shoved aboard Lewrie's first Post ship, the *Proteus* frigate. Grace, his father and grandfather, had taken the Joining Bounty about the same time after their fishing smack had gone down, leaving them and their families penniless, and it was the Graces, Liam Desmond, and Pat Furfy that had stood by Lewrie during the Nore Mutiny of 1797.

"The Chinese Magnolia," Lewrie laughed out loud. "The plantings 'tween the guns!" For Pat Furfy had sworn that it was that very sort of tree that stood in front of his old mother's rough cottage, and a mob of other drunken revellers had ripped it from the garden of the Governor-General's house at St. Helena, all the blossoms plucked off and waved or worn as cockades. HMS *Proteus* and her whole crew, had been banned liberty on the island as long as she was in commission!

"A damned good sailor and fighter, a good shipmate. I miss him," Grace said.

"Aye, I still miss him, too," Lewrie admitted, "Though he kept me busy, haulin' his chestnuts from the fire. Well, carry on, Mister Grace. I'll follow our Marines, and see what devilment they stir up."

Furfy, God! Lewrie thought; *I still hope it wasn't him who fed the Governor-General's wife's lap-dog to one of the circus lions and choked it to death on its collar!*

"Clearing the town, sir," Captain Whitehead crisply reported as Lewrie caught up with him. "There were a couple of drunken Frogs in a tavern. Commissariat men, they claim. I've put them under guard, so the townspeople don't tear them limb from limb. They're getting their courage back, sir . . . Dutch courage."

They strode the length of one of the main streets, into the wide town square before the church, where knots of civilians were emerging and coalescing into mobs with farm implements and clubs. As Marines trotted through with bayonetted muskets to continue their searches in the houses and shops behind the square, there were even some cheers raised, some redcoat backs patted in passing, and some wakened boys in their nightshirts trotting alongside, or trying to march.

Up ahead, round the Northern outskirts of Monasterace, a volley of shots rang out, sending Marines up against the walls of buildings, some kneeling with their muskets levelled.

"Second rank . . . fire!" someone ordered, prompting another flurry of gunfire. It sounded like Lt. Rutland, appointed to the command of the transport *Coromandel*.

"Rutland! That you?" Lewrie shouted as loud as he could.

"Captain Lewrie, sir? Aye, it's me, with sixty men." Rutland called back. "Mister Fletcher is off to the left, and we've caught a pack of drunken Frenchmen between us. Mostly un-armed and staggering. Don't advance beyond me, or you might walk into a cross-fire. There's a brothel yonder, where they came from. I was about to search it."

"No, you keep the pressure on 'em, Mister Rutland," Lewrie decided, "The Marines and I will search the brothel."

That raised a quick *Hurrah!* from the Marines, for there would be naked women and opened bottles in there, and there might be time for a quick romp and a drink or two.

"Good Lord!" Lewrie gawped as he got beyond the last buildings in town to take in the full view of the French encampments, and what Col. Tarrant's regiment had achieved, so far. There were enough of the waggons set alight to bare the entire seene. There were at least six separate waggon camps present, hundreds upon hundreds of canvas-covered four-wheel conveyances packed wheel-to-wheel. The stock pens for each convoy boiled with stirring, galloping, frightened horses or mules, panicked by the gunfire, the rising smoke smells, and the glare of flames. Somewhere, oxen bellowed, stamped, or pawed the ground in dread. Lewrie could dimly make out lines of tents further inland of the coast road, where cavalry escort troops had slept, and cooked rations. Were those French soldiers dashing back and forth, rushing to the lines where they had tethered their mounts, gathering their boots, saddles, saddle cloths, and arms?

Six convoys, six troops of escorts, that's . . . three hundred and sixty cavalry! Lewrie realised; *If they get mounted and organized . . . Oh, Christ on a crutch!*

There were a couple of shots fired nearby, louder than the rest.

"Upper windows in the brothel! Fire, lads, fire!" Whitehead ordered, pointing with his drawn sword. "Mister Kellett! Take a file of ten and clear the ground floor!"

Muskets banged, and the window sills, shutters, and upper sashes were splintered, glass panes disappearing in shards. Lt. Kellett led his men through the stout door and into the ground floor tavern, raising shrieks of alarm from the whores inside. Several women came dashing out the door, clutching what little they wore about themselves in haste, covering bare breasts or chemises with colourful shawls.

More shots from the windows, answered by a volley, and someone inside gave out a scream as he was hit. Stout low boots thundered on the stairs inside, Marines were yelling. There was another scream of agony, a shot or two, the sound of doors breaking, another flurry of gunfire, and a uniformed Frenchman in a blue tunic appeared in one of the windows, howling as he was bayonetted, and riddled with lead balls from shots fired from outside, too.

"The Frogs're comin' out, lads!" someone yelled, followed by three bodies being heaved out the windows to thud on the stony soil, and all the Marines gave out a great cheer.

"What's next?" Whitehead demanded, eager for more action.

"Let's send a runner to Lieutenant Fletcher and his shore party," Lewrie suggested. "There's that large farmhouse and barns up ahead . . . where they keep their forge waggon and repair facilities. If Rutland can take it under fire from the right, and Fletcher the left, we can attack it from the front."

"Sounds good, sir," Capt. Whitehead agreed with a firm nod of his head. "Mister Venables, pick a runner to go off to the left. I'll brief him on what to say."

"Rutland, I'm coming to you," Lewrie yelled over to the right. "Don't shoot me, right?"

"Right, sir," Lt. Rutland called back, sounding amused for a rare moment, for he had proved to be a terse and dour fellow.

"We're going to take on the big farmhouse and barns ahead of us," Lewrie told him once he'd spotted him and approached him. "You look most piratical, may I say, Rutland?" for Lt. Rutland's battered old cocked hat was askew on his head, he sported a heavy cutlass instead of his slimmer smallsword, hung cross his chest on a baldric, four pistols jammed into coat pockets and his breeches waistband, and on his shoulder he'd slung a Tower musket, with all the accoutrements.

"Came prepared for a fight this time, sir," Rutland explained. "Not like the last neck-or-nothing battle we stumbled into here."

"Enjoying yourself?" Lewrie asked.

"I will own to, ah . . . certain, ehm . . . excitement, sir," Lt. Rutland cautiously expressed himself, not the sort of man to blurt out his personal feelings, or display much joy over anything.

"Fletcher and his men will fire on it from the left, and I and Whitehead will take it on from the front," Lewrie told him. "Do link in close to our right-hand end, close enough for orders to be passed."

"I will advance my party now, if I may, sir, and look for any decent cover," Rutland said with a nod of understanding, and Lewrie let him deploy.

Lewrie turned to eye the farmhouse and barns, now silhouetted by fires that had sprung up behind it, making it look grimly formidable.

Wish I'd brought my Ferguson, Lewrie thought, chiding himself for imagining that it would have made him too clumsy on the boarding nets. He was, like many of his sailors who'd come from mill towns or cottages, unable to swim, and a fall into dark waters from the nets, wide of one of the barges, and he'd have sunk under all the weaponry he was already carrying. There were many upper-storey windows in that farmhouse, now turned amber and glittering with reflected fires, and a breech-loaded rifle would have come in handy at daunting or killing the French.

"Runner's on his way to Mister Fletcher, sir," Whitehead said, whipping the tip of his sword through high grass and bracken round his feet. "My word, I do believe that Tarrant's men have set the stores of hay afire!"

There were very large canvas pavillions back of the stock pens, piled high with bound sheaves of hay, stacked round the tent poles vertically like they would be in the English countryside. And under that canvas that protected the feed from the weather, there would also be mounds of bags filled with oats. Now, smoke and flames were boiling from beneath the canvas, the outer edges of one vast pavillion alight like a burning sail, the fire eating its way to the tops of the tent poles, and little blazing mice-like flames skittering up the support ropes.

The Marine private who had borne the message to Lt. Fletcher's party came panting back, musket held cross his chest, and slammed to a boot-stamping stop by the officers. "Mister Fletcher says he's ready t'give fire when ordered, sir! His sailors're stretched out t'cover the side windows, an' the ones in front, too."

"Ready when you are, sir," Whitehead told Lewrie.

"Very well," Lewrie said, drawing his hanger. "Let's be at it."

"Lieutenants Venables and Kellett," Whitehead roared, "Form your platoons in two ranks! Load and prime! Ready? First ranks, do you give fire!"

Over thirty muskets went off nearly as one, muzzle flames stabbing the dawn, quickly followed by Rutland's and Fletcher's weapons. The farmhouse and barns were an almost impossible hundred yards off, too far for any sort of aimed fire, but lead balls spanged off stone walls, making quick flashes and the zinging sounds of rounds flying off in ricochet.

"Second ranks will advance three paces, first rank stand fast, reload," Whitehead snapped. He waited to give his men time to reload, then ordered "Both ranks, advance ten paces!"

There were muzzle flashes and the sound of gunshots from the farmhouse, and Lewrie distinctly heard a bee-like buzz of a ball go past his head.

"First rank, fire!" Whitehead roared, stepping out in front of his men to join that first rank. "Reload! Second rank, three paces forward . . . aim and fire!"

That was closing the range to about seventy yards, about as far as one could expect smoothbore muskets to be aimed and actually hit. Meanwhile, Fletcher's and Rutland's men on either flank were peppering the building's sides, and firing obliquely at the front. But more of the enemy returned fire. More bees hummed past, and a Marine fell.

"Marines, ten paces forward!" Whitehead yelled, "Fix bayonets!"

"They sound more like pistols," Lewrie commented as he stood by Whitehead's elbow. "The French, sir! Cavalrymen in there? Short-range musketoons, not muskets?"

Whitehead cocked his head to one side to listen more closely, a frown on his face, then pointed his sword at the farmhouse. "Marines! Charge! Get in there and *murder* those bastards! *Charge!*"

Off they galloped to cover the last fifty yards or so to the farmhouse, howling like fiends, muskets poised stiffly in front of them, and the wicked blades and points of their bayonets glittering in the firelight. Lewrie got swept up in the spirit of the charge, running even with the first rank, though behind Whitehead and the two Lieutenants.

There was a stout double door to the front of the farmhouse, and it was locked and barred, but the windows of the ground floor were open, shutters swung back, and Marines spread against the stone walls either side, firing and jabbing to clear a way, then rolling inside over the lower sills. Gunshots erupted inside, men howled and roared, and surprised shouts turned to cries of pain and curses.

"Doors, open the doors!" a Sergeant was roaring, and a moment later, wood bars were lifted from iron brackets and flung aside, and the doors swung open to admit Marines who had been peering upwards with loaded muskets to cover the upper-storey windows.

"Huzzah!" was the cry as they trooped in, Lewrie carried by the haste of the Marines either side of him. He found a large room in the centre of the building, a substantial stairway with a landing leading upwards. There were two large rooms either side of the entry, filled now with Marines, and several Frenchmen on the floor, some dead, and some rolling about to clutch at their wounds and cry out in pain. A quick bayonet thrust took care of those.

"Up, lads! Follow me!" Lt. Kellett yelled, waving his sword and taking the stairs to the landing two at a time, flanked by men with loaded muskets. There was a volley of fire from upstairs, and one of Kellett's Marines fell dead, tumbling back down the stairs, hampering the advance of the rest for a moment.

Lewrie went to the back of the farmhouse, right through the dining room and the kitchens, where fires still burned in the chimney nooks, and the beginnings of breakfast lay scattered about. He tore the rear door open and had to duck back as several French cavalrymen, clumsily retreating in their high boots, took time to turn and shoot at him, and he *really* wished that he'd brought his Ferguson rifled musket.

"They're making for the barns!" he yelled to caution his men, drawing one of his single-barrelled pistols, but the range was too far, and he didn't try to cock it. "They're getting' away!"

There was a volley from the left, and he stuck his head out once more to see Lt. Fletcher and his sixty armed sailors out in the open, taking the barn under fire, and cutting several retreating French down before they could reach one.

Thumps, stamps, boots hammering hard enough to shake dust from the wood rafters and upper floor planks, the clash of swords or steel bayonets, some shots, as if a battle royal was going on up there.

"Ground floor's cleared, sir," Capt. Whitehead panted, wiping blood from the blade of his sword with a scrap of window curtain. "You say they're bound for the barns?"

"Aye," Lewrie told him. "Look out!" he yelped as he spotted movement from a corner of the kitchens. He re-drew that pistol, got his wrist on the dog's jaws and pulled it to full cock as a Frenchman came rushing out with a short *sabre-briquet* in his hands.

Bang! and Lewrie took the man square in the chest, knocking him back to crumple in the dark corner from which he'd sprung.

"Commissariat," Whitehead commented, looking at the dead man's uniform, and the odd fore-and-aft red cloth cap with a long tassel that he'd worn. "Not real trained soldiers. He looked terrified, but I do thank you, Captain sir."

"It's gotten quiet upstairs," Lewrie noted, re-loading his pistol. "Your men must have done for them, at last."

"Not without casualties, I fear," Whitehead said, pulling a face. "Quite a melee, it sounded. In the barns, are they? And open ground 'twixt here and there, and the sun's almost up. It'll be nasty work, winkling the French out of the barns."

Whitehead had gone to a kitchen window for a look-see as he said that, and as he turned to return to Lewrie, a musket ball ricocheted off the lower stone sill, caroming round the kitchen.

"There's someone over there with a proper musket, and he's a good shot," Whitehead said, as if pointing out the danger of attacking cross that open ground.

Lewrie drew his hanger and put his hat on the tip of the blade, then went to the window to raise it into view. A few seconds later, the distant marksman could not resist the bait, and a musket ball came through an upper glass pane. For a quick second or two, Lewrie swung over to peer directly out, then ducked away.

"Oh, I don't know, Whitehead," Lewrie said with a wry smile, "I think they don't have enough gun-ports."

That prompted the Marine officer to press himself against the wall, sidle to the opened back door, and dare a quick look.

"There's the double wooden doors, either end," Lewrie told him, "but no ground floor windows. There are square wooden doors either end of the loft, where there are hoists, and on either side of the long walls, there's one wee window. All easily kept under fire to pin them down. If we rush 'em, and they bar the big double doors, we have them trapped inside with no way out."

"Attack the long side, then, and there's only the one window in the loft to shoot from, yes," Whitehead agreed, perking up. "Fletcher and his men can deal with the Western end of the first barn, Rutland the East, 'til we're up against the wall and ready to rush in one of the ends."

"Anything handy round here t'make torches with?" Lewrie asked, poking round the shelves of the kitchen. "Some olive oil'd be welcome, too. Of *course* there's olive oil! What'd Italy do without it?"

"Burn the doors if they're barred, yes!" Whitehead enthused, joining him in the hunt. Whitehead yelled for his Lieutenants to come join them, and explained what was wanting, and how they would attack the first barn. One of the stout kitchen tables, and the finer dining table in the next room, were stripped of their legs, and cloth curtains, towels, and table-cloths were wrapped round them and soaked in olive oil.

"Runners to Fletcher and Rutland," Lewrie insisted, his excitement growing. "Tell them what t'shoot at, and to cease their fire, just before we have a go at the doors."

It took long minutes for runners to dash over to the parties of armed sailors, brief them, then dash back again. Surprisingly, there was little fire directed at them, for the good reason that there was little room for French soldiers at their windows to shoot, shoulder to shoulder.

"Best we leave the house through the front door, sir," Whitehead suggested, "trot out left 'til we're facing the barn's long wall, and then rush it. Let's light the torches, now, lads. There's a decent fire in the kitchen hearth. And mind those jars of olive oil."

Lewrie re-loaded the single-barrel pistol that he'd fired, and primed the pan as the torches came to life, and then they all went back through the house to gather at the Western corner.

"Venables, take your platoon out, form ranks square to the barn, and leave room on your right for Kellett's lads," Whitehead ordered.

"Right, sir," Lt. Venables snapped, "Let's go, men."

Off Venables's half of the Marines went at the double-quick, to form two ranks. Once in place, Kellett's Marines followed him, and almost in parade ground order. Two musket shots were fired at them from the one loft window, and both missed completely.

"Venables, give that window fire!" Whitehead yelled. "Kellett to advance. Twenty paces forward!"

Venables's Marines raised their muskets to their shoulders, took rough aim, and discharged their pieces most leisurely, fire rippling down the first rank as steady as a metronome, blasting glass panes from the loft window, ringing off the stone wall round it raising wee spurts of rock dust and flakes, and a few shots right through the opening, daunting the French inside. And, when Kellett's men were in place, Whitehead ordered them to open fire, and for Venables's men to advance twenty paces beyond Kellett, and reload.

Meanwhile the armed sailors under Fletcher and Rutland peppered the ends of the barn, shivering the wood doors and loft openings. At an idle pace, Whitehead and Lewrie walked towards the barn between the Marines, swords in their right hands and a loaded pistol in the left.

"Do you think the French are beginning to see that their shelter might be a death-trap, sir?" Whitehead asked, almost strutting, a wide grin on his face.

"Too late for 'em now," Lewrie agreed with a firm nod. "If they try t'dash out, Fletcher and Rutland and their men will cut 'em down, and outside the barn, there's nowhere for them to run!"

Several alternate advances later, all of Whitehead's Marines were against the barn's wall, several of them aiming upwards to cover that small window. If the French inside wanted to shoot at them, they would have to lean far out to expose themselves at very short range.

"Oil and torches here," Capt. Whitehead ordered, leading them to the Eastern end that Rutland's sailors were shooting at. A quick peek round the corner, and Whitehead was back. "One door is closed, the other on the far side is open, and I saw several Frogs in there, round the first stall on the fight, and behind the closed door. Ten men, Sar'n Wager, ready to rush in, smash one of the oil jars against something, and heave in a torch. Mister Kellett, be ready to join in with your men."

"Right, sir," Lt. Kellett agreed.

"Time for Rutland t'cease fire," Lewrie decided, taking off his hat and stepping clear of the barn to wave it in wide arcs, wishing that someone . . . anyone . . . had thought to fetch a signal flag along. But, he saw Lt. Rutland stand, wave his own hat in reply, and musket fire ceased.

"Go!" Whitehead snapped, clapping Sgt. Wager on his shoulder.

Ten men ran round the corner of the barn, bayonetted muskets at the ready, firing past the open door. There were three Frenchmen there, backs against the planks of the stall, using a stone door pillar for a firing post, and they were blasted away with stunned shrieks. Sgt. Wager threw the oil jar inside with a wild swing behind the closed door, heard a welcome shattering against the opposite stall planking, then tossed in the torch. Someone inside began howling and screaming.

"Go!" Whitehead ordered, and Kellett's men rushed round the corner, swung the closed wooden door open, and dashed inside with feral howls. They were checked for a moment as a French soldier tottered out, whirling round in an insane dance as every stitch of clothing from his waist down crackled with flames. Whitehead shot him in the head to put him out of his misery.

"Let's take them!" Whitehead yelled, waving his sword to lead the rest of his men into the barn, and the melee was on.

Lewrie joined the rush, sword ready, but pummeled by the armed men either side of him. The first party of Marines were rushing down the long aisle of the dim barn, bayonetting panicked French soldiers, butt-stroking them in the face, making bloody teeth fly like a sleet. Muskets banged from both sides.

Christ, there must be dozens *of the bastards!* Lewrie thought as he wriggled free of the press of bodies, found a Frenchman in front of him with a cavalry sabre, and shot him in the chest. Another came at him with a bayonetted musket, jabbing, but Lewrie hacked with his hanger into the forestock wood to push it aside, smashed the metal hilt of his sword into the man's mouth, then back-slashed and ripped the side of his neck open, deep enough to sever an artery, and the man fell to his knees, dropping his musket to put his hands to his throat as blood sheeted his brightly laced coat plaquet.

"Fight fair, mine arse!" Lewrie roared.

The French in the barn who still could dashed for the far end, flung the double doors open, and poured out into the open. At least six of them got shot at once by Lt. Fletcher's sailors, and the will to fight left them. Muskets and musketoons were hoisted butt-high, and swords were tossed aside as they knelt to surrender.

"Take their boots and shoes!" Whitehead was yelling as his men prodded the French to their feet to herd them out the far end of the barn. "Rip them off! There's a good fire by the entrance! Burn them all! Gather them up, Sar'n Daykin!"

"An' pat 'em down proper for hidden weapons," Sgt. Daykin roared to his men, a chore taken up enthusiastically, resulting in an excuse to turn out pockets and rucksacks for tobacco, brandy, coins, watches, and souvenirs.

"Went well," Whitehead said, joining Lewrie at the far end of the barn. "I have four men down with light wounds, nothing serious, it seems."

"You speak good French, do you, sir?" Lewrie asked, looking at the second barn that stood at right angles to the one they'd cleared.

"Passably, aye, sir," Whitehead replied. "Why?"

"I want you to shout over to that second barn," Lewrie chuckled, "and warn them that if they don't come out with their hands in the air, and those hands empty, we'll set them on fire, too, and burn 'em all up. No escape possible, just death."

"You ah, *don't* speak French, Captain sir?" Whitehead asked, as if such a skill was the possession of every English gentleman.

"My French, sir, is so poor that they'd just laugh and not take us seriously," Lewrie said with a *moue* and a shrug.

"Hallo!" Whitehead roared, then began to deliver that threat.

Lewrie stood by him, idly waving a burning torch.

CHAPTER SEVEN

*T*he French in the second barn saw sense, and came out with their hands up; Commissariat artificers for the most part, with those tasseled red fore-and-aft caps on their heads.

"You gotta see what's in 'at barn, sir," Sgt. Wager reported to Captain Whitehead. "Biggest blacksmith shop ever I did see."

Whitehead and Lewrie went inside, and both uttered a surprised sound together. There were two portable iron forges mounted in the backs of waggons, which could be stood up on iron legs. There were bag upon bag of coal and charcoal, several anvils of various sizes, hammers and tongs, iron-working tools, pre-made waggon wheel rims by the hundreds, and blank horse and mule shoes by the thousands.

"All this has to go, sir," Whitehead said.

"Well, it won't burn," Lewrie japed, "and I don't see it movin', even if we put the whole Ninety-Fourth to the task."

"Keg after keg of screws, nuts, and bolts, by size, too," Capt. White-head pointed out, running a hand into a keg and letting the handful trickle to the floor. "The other barn, sir, that's full of lumber to repair the carts and waggons. And there's nigh an acre of sheets of leather for reins and harnesses."

"*That'll* burn," Lewrie decided, glad that they could accomplish *some* harm to the French. "This lot, though . . . hmm. The forges and anvils. They can't do much with the rest of the goods in here if we roll the forge waggons and anvils down to the harbour and dump them in the sea. Can you arrange some men t'do that, Whitehead? Have 'em tell Mister Grace that he's t'use his men to row the stuff out far enough."

"They'll find the forges, sir," Whitehead grumped, thinking it pointless. "There's no way to load them in a boat and take them out to deep water. The anvils and such, aye, but . . ." he ended with a shrug.

"Then let's find some gunpowder and blow them open in place," Lewrie extemporised. "God knows there's tons of powder out in those waggon camps. Let's go find some."

They went out through the rear doors of the second barn, then stood in awe for a long moment, nigh stupefied by the sights and the sounds. They had been too busy to take much notice, and the crackle of musketry and fireworks popping of pre-made paper cartridges by the bundle had become a background noise.

They faced a sea of flame, and great, towering, rolling clouds of dark smoke blown by the morning's sea breeze East down the coast, and inland towards the low ridge a mile away. Hay and grain sacks had mostly burned out, the grain still smouldering, and producing lighter grey smoke. The tents were gone, the individual encampments of waggons seethed with fire, and crackled with tiny explosions of cartridges, and larger bursts of powder kegs. They could feel the heat, hear the roar, and were buffeted by the wind as the fires drew air to feed themselves.

"I don't think we'll find kegs of powder left in all that, sir," Whitehead said, licking his dry lips and coughing as tendrils of hot smoke swirled past. "This must be what the Great Fire of London was like."

"Well, let's load the anvils into the forge waggons and roll 'em down to the quays," Lewrie decided. "We'll think of something. We'll set fire to both barns before we go."

"I'll see to it, sir," Whitehead promised, turning to find his Lieutenants and set people to work.

Lewrie paused a moment longer, taking it all in, dis-appointed that he could not contribute more mayhem, but delighted with the destruction that the 94th had wrought. Raiding Monasterace again was the right idea.

All that damned cavalry, though, he worried; *Where the Devil did they get to? If they managed t'ride off and organise themselves, is Tarrant's regiment in trouble? And, with all this bloody smoke, the ship can't see anything t'shoot at!*

Far off, barely noticed above the roar of the fires, he thought he heard a bugle, but couldn't be sure. Seconds later there *might* have been a long rattle of musketry; it might have been yet another waggon full of French cartridge ammunition, detonating, but he couldn't tell. Once more he felt as if he was in overall command, but had no control over anything that happened beyond his sight, and the delight he had felt vanished, replaced by a general dread.

"Don't know what to do with the forges, sir," Lt. Grace told him once the Marines had rolled the waggons to the quays, and the anvils had been dumped into the water. "Without gunpowder? Perhaps we could send to the ship for some?"

"Might take too long," Lewrie gloomed.

"Beggin' yer pardon, sor," his Cox'n, Liam Desmond, spoke up. "The fire boxes can't heat up proper if we took axes to the iron. I expect we can find some axes here in town. Same goes for the flues from the bellows. And they'd need fresh leather for the bellows."

"Desmond, you've hit the nail square on the head!" Lewrie congratulated. "Aye, scrounge up some axes and let's see what some strong arms can do!"

Minutes later, sailors were clanging away with a variety of axes, some blows bouncing off, wickedly sharp blades turning on contact and ricocheting dangerously close to feet and legs. Some blows left dents in the thin wrought iron fire boxes, but some hacked into the metal and had to be jerked free, making slits through which air would flow if the French tried to use them. Some metal-headed mauls bonged off the forges, making even deeper dents that constricted the volume of the fire boxes.

"Sir! Sir!" The much older Midshipman Kinsey off *Coromandel* came rushing from the town square to the waterfront.

"Yes, Mister Kinsey? What is it?" Lewrie asked.

"Mister Rutland sent me to find you, Captain Lewrie sir," Midshipman Kinsey said, a little out of breath. "He and Mister Fletcher are returning to the landing beaches, and getting the barges ready for the Ninety-Fourth to re-embark."

"Very good," Lewrie said, then asked, "What have they heard from Colonel Tarrant? Has he been in action?"

"The last runner from the Ninety-Fourth that reached us said that they were inland of the waggon camps, would try to slaughter all the draught animals, but that they were short of ammunition, sir, and may not have enough for that."

"No mention of French cavalry? A relief column?" Lewrie pressed.

"Nary a word upon that head, sir," Kinsey said, shaking his head.

"Well, if they're back near the horse pens, they must have come back this side of the French camps," Lewrie speculated aloud, hoping that Tarrant was headed for the beaches and the boats, if he thought he could not shoot all the horses, mules, and oxen.

We've been ashore, what . . . three hours or more? he thought; *Time to get in the boats and scamper!*

"Your men having fun, sir?" Kinsey asked.

"Oh, the axes and such?" Lewrie said. "We couldn't find any gun powder t'blow 'em up. Care to try your arm, Mister Kinsey?"

"I should be getting back to the beach down yonder, sir," the older Mid replied, after giving the clanging and banging a look. "I do wish you luck with those, though, sir," he said, doffing his hat in a parting salute, as some of the burlier Marines took over from the sailors, attacking the flues that were made of thinner iron to render them useless. Desmond and Kitch had found some coals and firewood, and were setting the leather bellows on fire. The Italians that had fled the British at their first appearance were now gathered round and celebrating, cheering each axe blow or maul strike. Music was struck up, and some young men began dancing, and large straw-covered demijohns of wine were passed round to fill hastily gathered glasses.

"Aha!" Capt. Whitehead cried, "The Army's here at last!"

A young infantry Ensign came trotting onto the quays from the town, waving and calling Halloo. "I've a message from Colonel Tarrant for Captain Lewrie, sir!"

"Here, lad," Lewrie said, walking to meet him.

"Sir!" the Ensign said with a doff of his shako and a short bow. "The Colonel says to tell you that he is withdrawing to the beaches for evacuation!"

"Thank God," Lewrie said, "It's about time. Has your regiment been in action? What of all the escort cavalry, where did they go?"

"About a third of them ran off without their mounts, sir, and the rest rode off beyond the last waggon camp. They did charge us, but we had the waggons for shelter, and saw them off right smartly. Then, we burned that encampment, and they couldn't ride through it, and with all the smoke, we retired quite easily without any further bother, sir. My Colonel apologises that we expended most of our ammunition and could not deal with the draught animals. We took down the oxens' rails, and stampeded them."

"Casualties?" Lewrie asked with a wince, fearing what the young fellow might report.

"Very few, sir," the Ensign proudly said, his chin up.

"Very, very good, then," Lewrie said, letting out a pent breath. "You'll be wanting to rejoin your company. My best regards to your Colonel, and tell him he and his men have done damned well."

"Yes, sir, and I will," the lad said, saluting and bowing once more, then trotting out to the West.

"Think we've done real damage to these forges, sir," Whitehead commented. "They won't be using these again. All that's left is to set the waggons on fire, and go back to our ship."

"Aye, Captain Whitehead," Lewrie said, relieved. "Light them up, and let's be going. Mister Grace? Man your boats!" he shouted. "We are going home!"

CHAPTER EIGHT

*O*verall, casualties among the troops of the 94th Regiment, and Lewrie's crew had been light, even though the Marine complement had been reduced to 67 total, including the three officers. Those who had perished ashore had been fetched off, this time, and interred at sea, out of sight and, hopefully, out of mind.

And nothing buoys the morale of a military unit, or a ship's crew, more than a victory, along with the idea that they had extracted their revenge for the earlier debacle.

Perhaps that explained the festive air at the 94th encampment, a mood that spread to the sutlers, vendors, and Sicilian visitors to the place. The 94th had musicians organised into a small band, though no one could call them talented, or well equipped; fifers, drummers, a few brass instruments, but they tried. No, it was the local civilians with their violins and stringed instruments playing Sicilian airs that provided the background to the general exuberance.

Even anchored out the furthest from the beach as HMS *Vigilance* was, the music wafted out to reach her, if the wind was right, and the ship's few musicians, official or amateur, felt free to strike up their own tunes, and belt out cheering songs.

Lewrie wished that he could go ashore and partake in the revels, as half his crew had done, but there was his official report to Admiralty to write, and boast about the results, with the proper modesty, of course, whilst still making mention of his personal participation.

He had been ashore, briefly, to attend a conference with Col. Tarrant and Major Gittings shortly after all ships had dropped anchor, to tote up the results, and congratulate themselves. By rough count, Tarrant thought that over 360 waggons full of vital supplies had been burned, over 100 French troops had been killed, two cavalry charges had been fended off, with many horses galloping off riderless, and all the repair facilities and feed stocks destroyed. All the French they had captured had lost their weapons, and their footwear, to the bonfires, and two officers had been brought back to be turned over to the Commanding General's staff in Messina and interrogated before being released on their parole.

At last, after several hours of finger-cramp and ink smudges on his hands, and time to mull over the right word or phrase, he could cite officers and men who had rendered special service, including the sailors and Marines who had scandalised the forges, pleased to mention Desmond and Kitch for how to go about it. He at long last concluded with the required "I am your Most Humble & Obedient Svnt," sat back and tossed his pen into a drawer, letting out a long, weary, but satisfied sigh. His clerk, Sub-Lt. Severance could pretty it all up as he wrote the fair copy, and Lewrie could turn his mind to happier things.

Another letter to his wife, first off. Over the months he had described what Sicily was like, what the coasts of Calabria looked like, wishing that he had but a tithe of her talent for drawing. He teased her with descriptions of the local fruits, wines, and food, of how the locals dressed. The wind brought the sounds of the impromptu festival taking place ashore, for half a minute, and he began to construct an image in his mind that he could describe the carnival atmosphere for Jessica, casting a longing look at her portrait as he did so.

Along with some boasting, too, he thought with a self-deprecating laugh at himself.

"Midshipman Dunn t'see th' Cap'um, SAH!" his Marine sentry on the quarterdeck bellowed.

"Enter," Lewrie idly bade, rolling his head to ease a kink in his shoulders and neck.

"Captain, sir," Midshipman Dunn said once he was in front of the desk, "The Army has hoisted a signal ashore. It's Have Mail!"

"Aha!" Lewrie shouted in glee, slamming a hand on the desk-top. "At last!"

It had been weeks since the last time that anything had arrived from home, and everyone's hope that there would be mail awaiting them once back from Monasterace had so far been dashed.

Dame Lewrie, his darling wife, Jessica, was a prolific writer, and when mail did arrive, Lewrie could usually count on at least ten or twelve letters. Even the inconsequential ones were as precious as golden guineas.

"Care for a run ashore, Mister Dunn?" Lewrie asked, grinning like a schoolboy and rising from his desk.

"Aye, I would indeed, Captain sir!" the lad piped up, ashiver with the prospect of a closer look at the doings ashore.

"Have the Bosun round up a boat crew and go fetch it for us," Lewrie ordered him. "And let word of the mail's arrival be known to the ship's people as you go."

"Aye aye, sir!" Dunn cried, wheeling about and clapping his hat on with only the sketchiest parting salute.

"How's that sound, lads?" Lewrie asked his cabin servants, and they were all for it. Deavers hadn't heard from his widowed mother in Staines for some months, and Dasher, who had no family that he knew of, was almost jig-dancing in anticipation of newspapers and a copy of *The Marine Chronicle* or *The Tatler* that he could puzzle over and make out the words slowly. Hope of hopes, might Dame Lewrie send him one, as she had back in the Spring?

"Come on, come on, come on!" Lewrie muttered under his breath as he stood near the quarterdeck's hammock stanchions, drumming fingers on the canvas cover that protected the many sausage-like rolled up hammocks from rain. Midshipman Dunn was taking his own sweet time to return to the barge with the mail sacks, and the barge crew seemed too eager to stray from the landing jetty for a quick jesting word with a pretty Sicilian girl, or sneak a wee glass of wine, no matter what the senior Able Seaman who served as the boat's Cox'n snarled at them.

Vigilance had hoisted an answer to the shore signallers, then put up Have Mail to the four transports. They all had sent a boat over to *Vigilance* in anticipation, where mail sacks to the various ships would be sorted out.

Lewrie snatched a day-glass from the compass binnacle cabinet and peered hard at the shore to see what the delay was, beginning to fume. As glad an occasion as it would be, he was building up a scathing rant, ready to peel some skin off Dunn's fundament. At last! The mail sacks were in the barge, the oarsmen had slouched back to the boat, and the boat was finally shoving off!

"Put your backs in it!" Lt. Greenleaf shouted at the boat through cupped hands. "Get a bloody way on, you slow-coaches!" That raised a torrent of jeers from the crew that remained aboard, in full agreement with him.

"Coming? So is Christmas!" Lt. Grace yelled, laughing.

Dignity, dignity, Lewrie chid himself; Act *like a Captain, for Christ's sake!* He put the telescope back in its place and clapped his hands in the small of his back, pacing the quarterdeck play-acting the patience he did not feel. Sub-Lt. Severance came out of the cabins, taking a break from copying the report to Admiralty in a copper-plate hand much more legible than Lewrie's, and shaded his eyes to watch.

"It appears the other ships' mail is already sorted into sacks, Mister Severance," Lewrie told him. "Only the one for us has to be sorted out."

"Ready and willing for it, sir," Severance said with a pleasant tone to his voice. "It'll be nice if there's some for me in the lot. I'd begun to believe that my parents and friends lived in Siberia!"

"And . . . at bloody last!" Lewrie muttered as the barge came to the starboard boarding battens. Would he have letters in his hands? No, not yet, for the other ship's boats swarmed Dunn's boat, and he had to toss their sacks to them, first.

"Arr!" Lewrie snarled in mock anger, then spun about and went into his cabins, vowing that he *wouldn't* have Dunn bent over a gun to "kiss the gunner's daughter," not even if it killed him. "Arr!" he growled louder in relative privacy, in his best piratical way.

Long minutes went by before the Marine sentry announced Dunn's request to enter the great cabins.

"Mail, sir!" Dunn proudly reported.

"Arr!" Lewrie growled, putting on a good frown. "Give it me."

"Ehm, aye aye, sir," Midshipman Dunn said, much abashed.

"Mister Severance, let's be about it, then," Lewrie ordered.

The sack, a heavy and bulging one, was hefted to the top of the dining table, the lashings undone, and its contents spread out in a heap that threatened to spill to the deck. Chalky, Lewrie's cat, was there in a twinkling to paw at the pile, skittering letters hither and yon, pouncing on a pile like a hound diving into deep snow.

"You silly little bastard," Lewrie said, snatching the cat from the table and setting him on the floor, where Chalky found the deep recesses of the mail sack equally thrilling. "Any wager you like to make, for sure he'll end up peeing on it," he told everyone. "Whilst I am waiting, I'd admire some cool tea, Deavers."

"Right away, sir," Deavers replied, going to pour a tall glass, though with half an eye on the mail over his shoulder.

Lewrie stood apart, though keeping a sharp eye on the pile that was meant for him; something from Admiralty on top, bound in ribbon with a wax seal, aha. What, then? Another from Admiralty? Hmm.

Finally sorted out, Severance stood at the door to the cabins to pass bundles out to representatives from the wardroom, midshipmen's mess, senior Warrant Officers' mess, for the Marines, and the biggest for the Bosun and his Mate to take to the waist for delivery to the seamen.

"Your mail, sir," Severance at last said, delivering a goodly pile to Lewrie at his desk.

"Thank you, Mister Severance," he replied, "and did you receive what you hoped for?"

"I did, and thank you for asking, sir," Severance said with a pleased grin.

It was quite a feast to sort through; there were letters from his father, Sir Hugo St. George Willoughby, his son Hugh, even one from his eldest son, Sewallis, something from one of his old compatriots at Harrow, Peter Rushton, now Viscount Draywick, and one from the old scamp, Clotworthy Chute. And of course there were letters from Jessica, a whole nine of them. One of them was much thicker than the rest, a sure sign that she had done a watercolour sketch of something that she had done with their house, or its back garden.

"Ooh!" Dasher marvelled, for Jessica had sent him one as well. He squatted far aft by the transom lazarettes to open it and read it.

Official bumf first, dammit, Lewrie thought as he broke the wax seal on the first letter from Admiralty.

To Captain Sir Alan Lewrie, Bt.

 Sir, it has come to the attention of the Board of Admiralty that your ship, HMS Vigilance, 64, has been in Full Commission for over three Years, and with the better part of this last year past, has served in tropic waters.

 You are Required and Directed to make the best of your way to

Portsmouth, there to Pay Off and turn HMS Vigilance over to H.M.
Dockyards for a total Refitting.

"What? What? What the bloody Hell?" Lewrie spluttered. "They can't just up and . . . ! God Damn my eyes! Mine arse on a band-box!"

He read it again, then a third time, but it remained the same brutal and direct order, against which he could not argue, even by long distance letters assuring the Lords Commissioners that his ship was still in usable condition! In hopes that the second missive from Admiralty might say "Just kidding!" or provide some amelioration, he ripped it open savagely, turned it right side up and read . . .

> *To Captain Sir Alan Lewrie, Bt.*
> *Upon receipt of this letter, the Lords Commissioners inform you that the*
> *Ad Hoc Squadron under you current Command is to be Re-enforced by*
> *the addition of five more transports rated as Armed Transports with*
> *Naval crews and Officers. Horse Guards has allotted one Regiment*
> *from the Light Infantry Brigade based at Messina. You are Required*
> *and Directed to turn over your Command to First Class Commodore A.*
> *Grierson, HMS Tethys, 74, who will arrive Shortly, accompanied by*
> *the Frigates Hero and Electra. Once Relieved, you will obey the earlier*
> *Instruction to make the best of your way . . .*

"God Damn it!" Lewrie all but howled. "Relieved! By that . . . that top-lofty sonofabitch? They've given him a First Class broad pendant, and Captain t'run his ship for him? Jee-sus!"

He'd met Captain Grierson in the Bahamas back in 1804, and he'd taken an instant dislike to him, which was pretty much mutual. That fool had sailed his squadron up the Nor'east Passage to Nassau, New Providence, flying no flags as a poor jape that had put the island in a perfect terror-ridden panic that a French invasion force had come to conquer them. There had been fearsome rumours that a real French fleet was bound to the West Indies, after all, and Lewrie had taken his frigate and his weak squadron of brig-sloops out to face them, no matter the overwhelming odds against him, and the weight of metal that Grierson's 64 and his frigates could fire at him.

Grierson had found it a most delicious jape, owl-eyed that anyone would dare take him on, and thinking Lewrie a fool for doing so. It had gotten

worse from there, for Lewrie had had fame and battles to boast upon, Cape
St. Vincent, Camperdown, and Copenhagen fleet battles, that he knew
Horatio Nelson personally. That Lewrie had the leg over an attractive
"grass widow" that Grierson desired. It was no wonder that Grierson hated
him as much as Lewrie hated him.

Now he would have to stay long enough to go through a formal change
of command ceremony, and eat that man's shite, give Grierson command
of the transports *he* had assembled, give him the boarding nets, barges,
and tactics that *he* had created, use the concept that *he* had thought up, and
let that fool try to accomplish anything with it?

*Oh God, Brigadier Caruthers knew all about it before I did, before Tarrant
did,* Lewrie furiously thought; *Perhaps even before Rear Admiral Sir Thomas
Charlton did! Grierson and Caruthers, two peas in the same ambitious pod! Poor
Tarrant, poor Ninety-Fourth, and whichever regiment that Caruthers picks.*

"Something wrong, sir?" Deavers dared ask, whilst the other two lads
sat dumb-struck and mouths agape in wonder.

"Something *quite* wrong, aye," Lewrie blurted, then waved a hand in
the air as if to drive that impulsive statement from their minds. "Something to deal with, is all."

He turned away with those damning letters in his hands, to go out past
the wood door and the screen door that kept Chalky safe from falling overboard, to his rarely used stern gallery.

Who can hate me this *much?* he asked himself; *Who knows how much I
detest Grierson? Whoever they are, they couldn't have picked better if they tried!
God rot that simperin' whoreson! Grierson, in a two-decker seventy-four? He's
not the sort t'close the coast to even* decent *gun range. Two frigates come with
him, hey? That's generous! I'd imagine they're Fifth Rate thirty-eights . . .
nothin' but the best for* him! *Captained by close relations of his? Some of his
toadies?*

Lewrie could see no way that this new combination could work.

Grierson's flagship drew too much water to get in close enough for ad-
equate gunfire support, and even combined with two big frigates, which
might be able to get close offshore, none of those ships would have notched
their guns or trained their crews in aimed fire.

And where'd they dredge up a brace o' fine frigates? he asked himself. What
had Nelson said when searching for the French fleet in '98, before he found
it at Aboukir Bay? *"You will find this lack of frigates graven on my heart."*
There were never enough to go round, especially Fifth Rate 38's; Sir
Thomas Charlton was badly in need of a fresh pair, and just might appro-

priate them and give Grierson a couple of brig-sloops in exchange. The thought of that cheered Lewrie for a brief second. Little else could, or did.

I'll have t'tell Tarrant and Gittings, Lewrie told himself, and went to the larboard corner of his stern gallery, taking hold of one of the ornately carved and white-painted columns so he could lean out to look shoreward, and cock an ear to the sounds of festivities.

Lewrie shook his head, and thought that bad news would best be delivered on the morrow.

He would be going home, his long naval career seemingly at an end, and with so many un-named opponents standing against him it would be un-likely if Admiralty ever offered him command of another ship. At least he would not be "Yellow Squadroned" as a fool or incompetent, but would still be on Navy List, perhaps even slowly climbing the ranks to the top of the Captain's List and make Rear-Admiral, as people senior to him and older died or were forced to step ashore due to their infirmities.

And he would be with Jessica.

He thought to write her, that instant, before realising that any letter to her would probably arrive the same time he anchored at Portsmouth, or later. Admiralty would not receive his report of the first action at Monasterace, much less the more-successful second 'til long after *Vigilance* began to pay off.

"Surprise, surprise, girl," he whispered, picturing her opening the door of their house to find him standing there. "Hope you like it."

BOOK TWO

O shore and sea more sweet to me than life!
What luck to come so soon to lands I love!
GAIUS PETRONIUS, XL AL474

CHAPTER NINE

*G*rey, overcast, and gloomy were the seas and skies far out in the Bay of Biscay, which HMS *Vigilance* had all to herself. Once leaving Gibraltar and sailing past the bustle of merchant traffic and military convoys that sustained Wellington's campaigns in Portugal and Spain, and so far out to the Westward of the coasts of hostile France, there had not been any sail to be seen in days.

Vigilance practically snored along at an average of eight knots, under all plain sail, heeled a bit to starboard by the Westerlies off the open Atlantic. Admiralty's order to summon her home had used the usual phrase, "making the best of your way," not the more-demanding "with all despatch," and Lewrie felt no desire to hasten his passage. Seven or eight knots was perfectly fine with him; why rush with wild abandon to lose his ship, his command, and his pride?

The winds were a bit nippy, so he emerged from his great-cabins in an older undress coat, buttoned over his chest for a rare once, and a dingy white civilian wool scarf round his neck. He took the doffed hat salutes of his watch officers with a grumpy nod of his head, and went down the ladderway to the waist for a quick overview of the gun deck, taking his time to get to the forecastle ladderway up to the bows. *Vigilance*'s sailors and Marines were accustomed to their Captain's strolls, several in succession at least once a day for exercise, fore and aft, then over again. They were also accustomed to Lewrie's usual good mood, his grin and nod to people on deck, on watch or out for fresher air and some skylarking. He would actually speak to some, even go so far as to josh. But not today. Taking a cue from Lewrie's faint frown, they busied themselves at their assigned tasks, turned away to avoid eye contact, and silenced their conversations 'til he was past.

"Poor fellow," someone whispered, who blacked an 18-pounder.

"Poor us," one of his mates in the gun crew added. "'Ere we fin'lly get a good Capum an' a jolly ship, an' Admiralty pulls h'it h'out from under us."

"We'll be scattered like chaff t'the wind in a week," another said with a sigh.

Lewrie made his way up to the bows by the starboard cat-head which hung the second bower anchor, joining Lt. Rutland and the Sailing Master, Mr. Wickersham, and the Bosun, Mr. Gore.

"Ready, sir," Wickersham told him.

"Right, then," Lewrie said with a nod. "Heave away."

"Heave away!" Wickersham shouted to a leadsman in the starboard foremast chains, and the heavy deep sea lead, the "dipsy," was swung as far ahead of the bows as the man could, splashing into the water, and him and his mate paying out the hundred fathom line.

"Well-waxed, was it?" Lt. Rutland asked in a grunt.

"Oh, aye Mister Rutland," Bosun Gore assured him. "I seen to it myself."

Lewrie leaned on the bulwarks to look overside to watch the deep sea line pay out rapidly, then took a few more steps forward where he lifted his gaze to the far Nor'east horizon. He'd consulted charts before leaving his cabins, and knew that yesterday's Noon Sights had marked their progress and position as well to the Nor'west of France, and the peninsula of Ushant. His ship was close to the Channel approaches, even at the "slow-poke" pace he'd determined. Lewrie could imagine that they would be able to make out the landfall of the Lizard by sundown, though *Vigilance* was still far short of that mark.

"Slack line, sir!" the leadsman shouted. "With ten fathom o' line t'go!"

"Haul in, haul in," Lt. Rutland shouted back. Thankfully, the dour fellow knew better than to sound eager to know the results. That would irritate the Captain.

The lead weight only weighed about twelve pounds, and with both hands hauling it came in quickly, finally emerging into the daylight.

"I'll be having it, lads," Mr. Wickersham said, and one sailor clambered up the lower stays from the channel platform as high as the top of the bulwarks to hand it over for inspection.

Wickersham turned it up to eye the waxed indentation in the bottom, using a fingernail to peel off some shell and rub them between his fingers. He got a daub of a peculiar blue-grey mud and silt on his fingers next, rolled it, sniffed at it, and even touched his tongue to it as if sampling a dainty, unfamiliar foreign made dish.

"Well?" Lewrie demanded with a curt snap.

"We are in Soundings, sir," Wickersham announced at last, "near the mouth of the Channel. Do we come about to Nor'east, I fully expect that Noon Sights will place us about Fourty Eight degrees North, and Five degrees West, roughtly Due South of Land's End, still over an hundred miles offshore."

"Very well," Lewrie replied to that news, sounding sorrowful. "Damn," he added.

"Damn indeed, sir," Lt. Rutland agreed.

"Well, thankee, Mister Wickersham, Mister Gore," Lewrie said to the assemblage. "You may return to your duties."

Lewrie and Rutland turned away and went down the ladderway to the waist and upper gun deck together, avoiding the activities on the sail-tending gangways.

"I wish you well on your *rencontre* with your wife and family, Mister Rutland," Lewrie said as they paced shoulder-to-shoulder.

"Thank you, sir," Rutland replied, "though, joyous as it will be, I'll be on half-pay before the month is out, and haunting the Waiting Room for appointment to a new ship."

"Aye, a lot of us will be," Lewrie grimaced. "How goes the inventories, sir?" he asked to change the subject, and avoid too much glooming.

"Quite well, sir," Rutland told him. "The yards at Malta and at Gibraltar were able to replace whatever we lacked or got broken during the commission, so we won't be dunned for anything lacking."

Lewrie had taken his own sweet time to enter port at Valletta and at Gibraltar, delaying the inevitable, to requisition new items that were subject to the usual losses, wear, and shipboard accidents. When *Vigilance* dropped anchor at Portsmouth, H.M. Dockyards would find her as fully equipped as a ship ready to sail to foreign stations after a complete refit.

Admittedly, Lewrie had used the occasions to prepare for what he feared would be a very long time ashore on half-pay. He had shopped at the vintners and chandleries to stock up on Sicilian white wines, kegs of Spanish tempranillos and riojas, the *vihno verdes* brought to Gibraltar from Lisbon, along with rosés, brandies, and ports, with even some sherries for Jessica and her lady friends who called or dined at their house. His wine pantry would be bursting with years' worth of drink.

"Thank you also, sir," Lt. Rutland cautiously went on, "For having me back aboard before we sailed."

"My dear sir, I couldn't do without you," Lewrie replied.

"At the least, sir, *Coromandel* won't have Lieutenant Dickson in command of her, again."

"He was a terror, wasn't he?" Lewrie said with a touch of sour humour. "We did keep a foot on his neck whilst he was part of our wardroom. Pray God he learned from it."

"Oh, I rather doubt it, sir," Rutland dared opine. "A leopard don't change his spots. He was a secretive, pretending fellow. Let's hope Mister Dickson doesn't revert to his old ways, now he's appointed aboard the Commodore's flagship."

The change-over once Commodore Grierson's two-decker Third Rate 74, HMS *Tethys*, and her two Fifth Rate frigate consorts, HMS *Electra* and HMS *Hero* had entered the bay near Milazzo had been about as spiteful and high-handed as Lewrie had expected it to be. In some cases it was much worse.

First had come the signal hoist Captain Repair On Board, with *Vigilance*'s number, summoning Lewrie barely a minute after Grierson's flagship's anchors had bitten into the sea bottom.

The welcoming interview if one could call it that, had set Lewrie's teeth on edge. He had been directed aft to the great-cabins by a senior Midshipman, and had been admitted. Lewrie had been surprised to see that Grierson had assembled all of his Commission Officers and Marine officers in his cabins, all in full best-dress uniforms.

Lewrie had recalled from his meeting with Grierson in the Bahamas in 1804 that the man insisted on all officers of his ship and squadron be properly attired at all times when on deck. Grierson, of course, probably had spares that he hadn't even worn yet, for he came from a wealthy family, but that was a burden on Lieutenants and Mids, whose pay could not support that, unless they had family money, too.

Grierson himself was turned out in a gilt-laced coat, epaulets, and snow-white breeches, silk stockings, shirt, and waistcoat. He introduced his Flag-Captain, who was there to run his ship, taking all the work of sea-faring off Grierson's shoulders, then his officers.

"Gentlemen, I give you Captain Alan Lewrie," Grierson announced.

"Sir Alan, if ye please," Lewrie had corrected him, rather perkily and sunnily. "The Baronetcy came extra."

As soon as Grierson's ships' topmasts had hove into sight from the Nor'west, Lewrie had made careful preparations, bathing and shaving closely. And when he'd scaled *Tethys*'s side, he'd come with a boat crew turned out in Sunday Divisions best, himself dressed in his best, and neatly sponged, gilt-laced coat, breeches, shirt, and waist-coat a pure white match to Grierson's, and with his rarely used 100 Guinea presentation small-sword at his hip, the star and sash of his knighthood, and his medals for the Battle of Cape St. Vincent and the Battle of Camperdown.

"Ah . . . Sir Alan," Grierson had purred after a stunned second.

"The 'Ram-Cat,'" one of Grierson's Lieutenants whispered to another, hand over his mouth, but still loud enough to be heard, which forced Grierson to snap his head round and glare, as if he'd just heard someone shout "Mutiny!"

As Lewrie recalled, Grierson had been a rather tall, lean fellow with a square-jawed, handsome face, a man who considered himself quite the la-dies' delight, a charming, well-to-do "comer" in the Navy, and a topping conversationalist, dancer, and a genius at cards.

Good living had taken Grierson to seed a bit, though, packing on more than a few pounds; one stone or a stone and a half, Lewrie had estimated as he gave him a long, slow once-over, taking note that Grierson's waist-coat was strained, and that his uniform coat sported no medals. Grierson, in the newest London style, wore a turned-up shirt collar, which added bulk to the flesh below his chiselled chin, and he now combed his hair for-ward *à la* Ancient Roman style, and his sideburns had been grown out down to the lobes of his ears, also combed forward. The man stood behind his desk, possibly, Lewrie fancied, to hide how tautly his breeches fit his thighs.

"As of the minute of my arrival . . . Sir Alan," Grierson began with a wee simper and a purse of his lips, "you and your ships come under my command."

"What, before the official change-in-command ceremony?" Lewrie had quipped. "Before I bring you up to snuff as to the condition of my trans-ports, and what we've accomplished with 'em lately?"

"Well, if you *wish* to stand on protocol," Grierson had purred, "there will be plenty of time for that review afterwards, to ah . . . discover the results of the pin-pricks you've made here."

"I note that your ship is equipped with boarding nets for your shore parties and Marines to speed their way, sir," Lewrie changed the subject, "though I must suggest that you implement some changes we've found necessary. It's the tumblehome, sir."

"The tumblehome," Grierson repeated. "What of it?"

"The slab-sided transports do fine, but your nets will lay flat to your ship's sides, and your people can't get a fingernail's grip on their way up or down, sir. We had to work some four-by-fours onto the inner side of the nets, else we'd have drowned the landing party, first try. Debarking from your warships might prove trouble, if you don't know what you're doing."

God, he'd been very happy with that innocent-sounding statement!

"I am certain that I and my officers shall find a way to cope, Sir Alan," Grierson had said, almost glowering. "You will depart this station, soon, I take it?"

"No real rush," Lewrie had shrugged off, "*Vigilance* is to pay off once we reach Portsmouth, anyway. There's bags of time to acquaint you with our doings, assuring your success."

"Oh aye, that," Grierson had said with false sympathy. "Most-like to end up a stores ship, transport, or harbour hulk. There's not much call for sixty-fours any longer. Why, she even may end up *here*," he'd said with amusement, "as an addition to *my* squadron!" And he had spread his arms as if to encourage the toadies and lick-spitters in his wardroom that they should laugh along, as well, which they did.

"One can only hope that she will continue to give a good account of herself, sir," Lewrie pretended to agree, and *not* spit flames.

"In point of fact, Sir Alan," Grierson had gone on, "when looking over the names of the transports coming into harbour a day behind us, I found a remarkable co-incidence. An old Fourth Rate fifty, that you once commanded . . . HMS *Sapphire*, hmm?"

Now *that* had felt like a studied insult, at Grierson's request, or a slur dreamt up by Lewrie's powerful detractors, one more of the Death of A Thousand Cuts he must endure. He had felt as if he'd been sliced halfway to the bone, then doused with salt and lemon juice!

"We did quite a lot with her when I had her, sir," Lewrie told the assembled officers. "Raiding the South coast of Spain when they were French allies in Eighteen Oh Seven and Oh Eight, then raiding the North coast after the French marched in, and Spain changed sides. We took a *lot* of prizes, and *Sapphire* and the other ships of my squadron took on and beat four big French frigates, and sent them to England, where they were all bought in," he could not resist the urge to boast, "and made us all a pretty packet of prize-money, sir. It will be a delight to see *Sapphire* again, still in service to the Fleet. She was never the swiftest ship in the Navy, but she was the stoutest and the bravest."

"Well, the French do not seem to have the nerve to come out and offer combat," Grierson had said, as if to shrug off that boast as an old war story, "but, we shall do what we can to discomfit the French over on the mainland. Ehm . . . you flew a Second Class broad pendant then, Sir Alan?"

"Once in the Bahamas where we met, and then off Spain," Lewrie replied.

"A pity Admiralty did not see fit to let you fly one here," the Commodore simpered, rubbing in the fact that he had been a First Class Commodore with a red pendant, not the inferior one with the one white ball in the centre. He dared smile, in a superior way.

Lewrie had answered that gloating with one of his best "shite-eating" grins, and felt that Grierson's attempt to top him and bring him down was not going his way.

"You'll be going ashore to speak with Leftenant-Colonel Tarrant, I take it, sir?" Lewrie had posed.

"Oh, not right away . . . Sir Alan," Grierson had waved off as if shooing a pesky fly, "Plenty of time for that, whilst they lick their wounds after your latest raid on . . . where was it . . . Monasterace? We heard of it when we put into Valletta for provisions."

"Why, we've just come back from Monasterace, sir," Lewrie said, "Our covert information people over there told us that the French who tried to entrap us had dispersed, and the place was back to normal business. We burned six whole supply waggon convoys, over three hundred, destroyed their repair facilities, grain and feed stocks, drove off the cavalry escort troops, and killed or wounded over an hundred Frenchmen. You heard old news, sir. *And*, did it with very light loss."

He had adored the disgruntled look of Grierson's face as the man came round from behind his desk, one hand out as if to steer Lewrie to the door. Lewrie shrugged and grinned. There had been no offer to a seat, and no gracious glass of wine had been forthcoming, though all the officers in the great-cabins had sported full glasses.

"Speaking of news, sir," Lewrie had said, standing his ground, refusing to take the hint to see what Grierson would do to evict him, "you must make the acquaintance of our covert people, who bring us information on what the French are up to, and where the plum targets are. Sicilian criminals, smugglers, perhaps even cut-throats, run by a mysterious man by name of *Don* Lucca Massimo . . . and our local spymaster, one Mister Quill. They're a quite colourful lot, I assure you. Though . . . I'd not amuse Quill too much. The results are quite ghastly."

"Aha . . . I see," Grierson had said, sounding perplexed and out of his depth, which Lewrie had quite relished. "I am certain that we will, soon, Sir Alan. If there is nothing else, my First Officer, Mister Ridley, can see you back to your boat."

"Adieu, sir," Lewrie had said, making the slightest parting bow.

"Sir Alan," Grierson had frostily replied.

And that had been their *rencontre*.

"Allow me to say, Sir Alan, that it has been an honour to make your acquaintance," Lt. Ridley said as they emerged onto the quarterdeck, as the side-party stood to attention to render departure honours. "To actually meet one of our authentic and rightly famed sea-dogs and true heroes, is quite notable."

"Oh, pish, sir!" Lewrie had scoffed with a laugh. "I ain't Nelson. Just a simple sailor, me. Put it down to good fortune, and stumbling into the right place at the right time."

"Your modesty does you great credit, Sir Alan," Ridley had said, blushing a little and tentatively offering his hand to be shaken before doffing hats in salute.

"Oh, not all the time, Mister Ridley, not all the time!" Lewrie had japed.

The official change-in-command had been held two days later, after the new transports had come into harbour. Once more Lewrie had gone aboard *Tethys* in his best, and had stood at attention as Grierson had read himself in, savouring each phrase of his Admiralty Orders.

"Commodore Grierson, I stand relieved of command of the squadron," Lewrie had had to intone, hat aloft in salute.

"Sir Alan, you *are* relieved," Grierson had replied, stressing the word "are" and doffing his ornately gilt-trimmed bicorne. "*I* assume command," he'd snapped, eyes alight with glee and triumph. Silver Bosuns' calls had trilled as his First Class broad pendant soared up a halliard on the mizen mast.

It was right after that that one of *Tethys*'s Lieutenants had been sent over to the *Coromandel* transport to read himself into command and relieve Lt. Rutland, then had sent orders aboard *Vigilance* to transfer Lt. John Dickson into his ship to replace the favourite who had been given a plum position.

Dickson, free of having to pretend that he'd been reformed, had smirked his way off, a quim-hair shy of mute insubordination as he'd made his goodbyes, waving laconically once he was in the boat, shouting "Adieu, you lot, and thank God my Purgatory is done!"

Lewrie did try to fill Grierson in on their doings, but he got a brusque rebuffing. He had no wish to get to know the officers off the flagship, nor the officers of the two frigates, though he and his wardroom officers and senior Mids did attempt to alert the officers and crews of the newly-arrived transports what they would be doing in the future, and how best to go about it. They got a warmer reception.

As the Purser, Mr. Blundell and his "Jack In The Breadroom" made their last forays into Milazzo for provisions and fresh fruit enough to last 'til the ship reached Valletta on Malta, Lewrie spent most of his remaining time ashore at the 94th Regiment of Foot's encampment, either trying to smooth the waters 'twixt Grierson and Col. Tarrant, or commiserating with Tarrant and Major Gittings over the rapid changes.

The regiment that Brigadier-General Caruthers had secretly begun to train for amphibious work had left its brigade camp and had marched to Milazzo Bay to begin erecting their own quarters, laying out a large area on the East side of the creek and freshwater source on the other side of the rickety wooden bridge. First, tents went up in company lines, then lumber from the towns about had arrived to floor them and raise sidewalls. Some of the soldiers had been put to well-digging for a surer source of water, and Col. Tarrant had thought that a good idea for his 94th, too, now that they had to share the waters of the creek.

The 102nd had been one of the two regiments that Caruthers had gotten ashore back in the Spring to fight the French, and win the Brigadier some fame, so they were at least "blooded" and understood a modicum of what their new role would entail. Col. Tarrant had developed a wary working relationship with their Colonel, even if he was from Cornwall, and could only be understood half the time.

Near the bridge, a rather lavish headquarters and lodgings had gone up to quarter Caruthers and his immediate staff, though thankfully he had not yet made his presence permanent, and only showed up now and then to strut, preen, and rub his hands in glee.

Naturally, he and Grierson took to each other like a house afire.

Finally, there had been no more plausible reason for delaying HMS *Vigilance*'s departure. Lewrie and his wardroom officers and the Marine officers had been invited to the 94th's officers' mess for a supper and drink-sodden party, during which perhaps *too* many toasts and too many "A glass with you, sir!" happened, resulting in a comic return to the ship long after Lights Out at Nine P.M., in which tarry-handed, experienced Commission Sea Officers could barely find the boarding battens and the man-ropes to aid them up to the entry-port, and Lt. Greenleaf and Lt. Rutland, "tarpaulin men" both, had come aboard in a cargo net, bawling out "Misty, Moisty Morning" at the top of their lungs, unable to find a way to seat themselves in Bosun's chairs.

And it was with heavy heads and bleary eyes that the anchors were hauled up the next morning, the hands sent aloft to make sail, and the guns to be manned and loaded with reduced powder charges. For salutes must be fired in departure to honour the senior officer present.

"If I weren't a gunner I wouldn't be here," the Master Gunner, Mr. Carlisle sang out, pacing down the upper gun deck's starboard battery of 18-pounders, "Number One gun fire!"

"Ow, goddamn!" Lewrie hissed, as the first gun erupted.

"I've left my wife, and all that's dear. Number Two gun, fire!"

"Christ shit on a *bisquit*!" Lewrie groaned, hands on his ears. "Mister Farley, keep an accurate count, and tell me when the very last goes off, for God's sake!"

"Far, far too much brandy," Farley moaned. "That's three, sir, God help me."

Lewrie and Rutland returned to the quarterdeck, where Lt. Farley, the ship's First Officer, stood the Forenoon Watch.

"In Soundings, sir?" Farley asked.

"Aye, in Soundings," Lewrie replied, a bit morosely. "Due South of Land's End, the Master believes." He looked aloft, beyond the sails and rigging to survey the grey overcast. "Pray God we see the Sun when Noon comes round, else we'll have t'trust to Dead Reckoning. Sun or no, I wish to come about to Nor'east, perhaps Half North then. England's up there, somewhere. We'll bump into it, eventually."

"Aye, sir," Farley said with a sage nod. "Ehm, about the cleaning and last-minute painting, sir."

"Aye?" Lewrie asked.

"The lower decks are touched up, sir, and all that's left to do is a daily sweep down and swabbing," Lt. Farley reported, "The sickbay is done, and I've a working-party going over the galley, the cookery, steep tubs, and stove and ovens, with brick dust to buff up the brass and such. The only touching up that's still wanting is the transom and stern gallery, and we've enough white paint left for that. The sea is calm enough to put hands over the side in Bosun's chairs, if you think it safe."

Lewrie imagined sailors dangling from the taffrails, level with his stern windows, and shook his head. "It'd be even safer for 'em if we wait 'til we're anchored at Portsmouth, Mister Farley. Time enough for that then. Carry on with the rest."

"Aye aye, sir," Farley said, touching the brim of his hat, and turning away to attend to his list of chores.

Lewrie crossed the quarterdeck to the windward corner just above the larboard ladderway, his appointed place by right and old custom, and laid an arm along the cap-rails of the bulwarks to lean out for a look forward. Lt. Farley was right; the seas were rather calm today, for the North Atlantic, and the outermost reaches of the Channel. The waves were no more than five feet at their crests, rather long set and marching along in an almost orderly fashion, rolling under *Vigilance* to lift her on their scendings. The jib boom and bowsprit slowly rose and fell against the far horizon, the ship barely hobby-horsing as it would on a more boisterous day. Inner, outer, and flying jibs curved out to starboard, stiff with wind, and the after leeches almost seemed to vibrate.

One hundred bloody miles to Land's End, Lewrie thought, shrugging deeper into his coat and fiddling with the scarf round his neck. *As close as a hop, skip, and jump. Couldn't I just come about to the wind, and head to Halifax? What'd Admiralty say t'that? To the Great South Seas and say I was huntin' the* Bounty *mutineers?*

That put a smile on his face for a moment, quickly extinguished.

There was no way that he was going to keep *Vigilance* and he knew it, no last-minute reprieve would be forthcoming, and, as dilatory as he had tried, a few more days and this would all come to an end with the anchors down in Portsmouth, and the ship swarming with inspectors and petti-fogging officials from the Dockyards; pay clerks to award back-pay to the crew, and jobbers coming out in the bum-boats to buy up the chits for ready money, but at reduced value of what they'd get if they went up to London to cash them.

Lewrie leaned out a little further to look straight down over the side to watch the sea cream down the ship's hull. The bluff bows, forefoot and cut-water, in British fashion, shoved a mass of seawater into a foaming mustachio which spread out to either side, before sucking up against the smoother bulk of the ship, and on a fast day the wake would curve up-wards to somewhere almost amidships, baring the quickwork and copper-ing before it swept on aft into another upwardly-curved wave that joined the maelstrom under the transom and spread out like a fine princess's gown train.

In the bare stretch, Lewrie could see weed, foot-long strands or better, and the strip of coppering that the heel of the ship exposed looked to be speckled with razor-sharp barnacles.

Maybe Admiralty's right, he thought with a defeated sigh; *She's more than due for a cleaning*.

Lewrie shoved himself off the bulwarks and turned about to look the quarterdeck over, hands behind his back, balancing with long-acquired skill on the relatively slight angle of the deck.

His cabin-steward, Michael Deavers, came out of the great-cabins, his hands wringing the apron that he wore over his shirt, waistcoat, and slop-trousers, with a frown on his face.

"Ehm, Captain sir," he began. "We have a problem, aft."

"What sort o' problem, Deavers?" Lewrie asked, wondering what would make the usually calm man look fretful.

"It's Chalky, sir," Deavers almost whispered. "We can't find him."

"What the Devil?" Lewrie blurted, bustling past him into the cabins.

There he beheld Tom Dasher, cradling his pet rabbit in his arms, tears running down his cheeks, and his lower lip quivering. The other cabin ser-vant, Turnbow, was opening all the transom settee lazarette storage, rummaging round and cooing "Here, puss puss!"

"We've looked in every cabinet, sir," Deavers told him, "in the side-board, the wine cabinet, in all your trunks and chests. He's one fond of quiet, dark places, he is."

Lewrie went to the starboard quarter gallery which was usually used as extra cabin storage, now crammed right up to the bottom of the window sills with crates, barricoes, and ankers of wine. Lewrie gave the sash windows a jiggle to make sure that they were fully shut, and latched. "Here, Chalky!" he called out. "Here, catling! Come get a sausage!" There was no response.

They all prowled the cabins together, looking in the covers of the hanging bed-cot, in the lower part of the wash-hand stand where towels, soap, and washcloths were kept. They looked under the starboard side settee furniture, in the dining coach, even the drawers of the desk in the day cabin.

"Chalky?" Lewrie cried, louder, turning round and round. Then a thought came to him, and he went to the doors that led to his stern gallery. Long ago, he had had the carpenters of his ships build a door frame without glass of wood panelling, the frame lined with rows of small nails round which twine was tautly stretched, to keep Chalky from off the stern gallery in search of sea birds, bound behind a screen of intermeshed small stuff.

The iron hook-and-ring latch was open, and the door swung free!

Fearing the worst, Lewrie touched the stouter wood-panelled door and that one swung free as well! He dashed out onto the stern gallery in hopes that the cat would be hunkered down in a corner, but the gallery was bared and empty, spattered with salt water here and there, and almost keening as the cool, nippy wind sang past the railings and pillars.

"Who left both doors un-locked?" Lewrie roared.

"Th . . . the Carpenter and Loftis, the Bosun's Mate, were in for a minute or so, sir," Deavers told him. "The First Officer sent them t'see what needed doin' t'touch up the transom paint an' all."

"While you woz up forrud, sir," Turnbow added.

A half-hour ago, Lewrie thought; *a quarter-hour ago?*

Lewrie leaned on the stern gallery's chest-high railings to peer aft, but what was there to see? A small, mostly white-furred cat trying to swim in the wide, white-foaming wake? Chalky might have slipped out when the Carpenter and the Bosun's Mate opened the doors. He was always crying and chittering his jaws at the sight of any sea bird he could see as they swooped round the stern, or perched on the railings. They might not have even noticed the cat, and had closed the doors as they went back inside, leaving him out there to leap up on the railings and over-balance.

A quarter-hour, Lewrie thought; slumping on the railings; *in that short amount of time, Vigilance could have sailed two whole miles!*

"Goddammit!" he muttered.

Had one of the sailors fallen overboard, there would be no question of coming about and putting boats in the water to recover him.

But for a wee cat, dear as he was?

Lewrie felt a wild hope; their four 29-foot barges were still in tow astern. Could Chalky have scrambled up onto one?

"Mister Farley!" Lewrie yelled on his way to the quarterdeck. "Haul the barges up alongside and look for my cat! He's fallen overboard and he might have landed in one! Smartly, now!"

But no. A quick search of the first two barges, closest to the stern transom showed no cat atop their canvas covers, nor inside them.

"You didn't see a white cat come onto the quarterdeck, did you?" Lewrie asked the Marine sentry at his door.

"Nossir," the Marine told him. And the helmsmen and Quartermasters, and the Master's Mate on watch had not seen the cat, either. Yeovill, Lewrie's personal cook, came up from below and strolled aft towards a ladderway to the quarterdeck.

"Yeovill, have you seen Chalky? Did he follow you to the galley?" Lewrie called down.

"Oh, no sir," Yeovill assured him. "He never has, really. Is he not in the cabins?"

"No, he's not," Lewrie said, despairing by then. "He's fallen overboard."

"Oh Lord, I'm so sorry, sir!" Yeovill exclaimed.

"Carry on, Mister Farley," Lewrie said, re-entering his cabins. He unbuttoned his coat and threw himself onto the settee.

"We're sorry, sir," Deavers said in a pained voice. "Chalky was good at slinkin' round and hidin' himself, then comin' out t'pounce on a foot or an ankle. Nappin' in odd places? We never noticed that he wasn't here 'til we began sweepin', and he dearly loved t'bat at the brooms and . . ."

"C . . . couldn't we turn round and look for him, sir?" Dasher asked in a wee, distressed voice, still cradling his doe rabbit.

"Too late, Dasher," Lewrie said, massaging his face with both hands, feeling the moisture at the corners of his eyes. "The ocean's too big, and he's so small. How long can a cat swim? I don't know. We'd go back for a man, but . . ."

"Our fault, sir," Deavers asserted. "For not keepin' our eyes on him."

"No," Lewrie told him. "He was always here, and you had no call to keep watch over him. It's not the Carpenter's fault, either. It's just . . . bad luck, that's all."

"Would you be likin' a drink, sir?" Deavers shyly offered.

"We still have some American corn whisky?" Lewrie asked.

"Just a little, sir," Deavers had to admit. "But there's some of that Portuguese brandy that you liked."

"Aye, fetch me a brimming bumper," Lewrie asked. He lowered his head to rest his chin on his chest in sorrow, trying not to weep, but . . . upon the bright red settee cushions that Jessica had had made for him, there was white strands of fur.

Oh God in Heaven, how much more must I suffer? Lewrie thought, close to wailing out loud; *how much more must I lose?*

CHAPTER TEN

My dearest darling wife,
Any letter I could have sent you from Sicily would have arrived the
same time as me and my Ship, if not still languishing in some mail
bag at Malta or Gibraltar, but . . . I am of this moment at Ports-
mouth, and I am come Home! It will take some time to pay Vigilance
off and turn her over to the Dockyards, but I will soon be in London,
and in the arms of the sweet Lady whom I dearly Love. My Return is
not without some Personal Grievance on my part, but Admiralty
ordered us Home, and replaced me in command of my small Squadron,
the Details of which I shall relate to you once we are Together again,
but, in all Respects, I am Glad of the Results of it, to be with you
again.
*   A little more time, I assure you, dear Jessica, and my Coach will*
clatter up to our door, bearing your brother Charlie as well, and we will
lay on a Celebration.

Your loving Husband, Alan

He folded it upon itself, dribbled some wax to seal it, and put his everyday seal stamp on the wax. That letter joined a substantial pile that he had
already written on-passage, to his father, Sir Hugo, his sons, wherever their

ships were, to old friends he'd served with, and the ones under which he'd
served, whom he could call his patrons. Those letters bore his complaints,
and simmering temper, expressing the unfairness of it all.

"Bloody Hell and brimstone!" he could hear Lt. Greenleaf on the quarterdeck outside, railing at yet another Dockyard clerk. "You've had us lay
out and account for every bloody sand-glass three times already! D'ye
want the egg-timers from the galley, too, hah?"

"It is my duty, sir, to . . ." the clerk spluttered back.

"Aye, yours and the *last* three cod's-heads who've come asking!" Greenleaf fumed. "Are you in the pay of the French?"

Lewrie put all his letters in an empty bisquit bag, then went out onto
the quarterdeck to whistle up an idle Midshipman to bear them all ashore
to the Dockyard's post office, just in time for the finale of Greenleaf's ti-
rade.

"Sir, all I know is that my employer sent me to . . ." the clerk was whing-
ing, trying to edge round Greenleaf and flee, his dignity and authority be
damned.

"You're a know-*nought!*" Greenleaf barked. "Here's the numbers, which
haven't changed since the first of you lot showed up, so there. Take the
account and beggar off!"

"Something the matter, Mister Greenleaf?" Lewrie calmly asked. The
clerk took his interruption as a chance to fly down the starboard ladderway to the waist, and tug his clothes and his feelings back into order.

"We've never seen the like, sir," Lt. Greenleaf fumed, taking off his hat
to run an angry hand through his hair. "Pulley-blocks, rammers, galley
implements . . . the yard clerks say new'uns, perfectly serviceable ones, are
dirty, damaged, or won't believe our accounts one day to the next. It's as
if the senior clerks yonder in the warehouses are determined to find any
fault they can. Bosun Gore is about ready to pull his hair out, 'cause his
account books have ink smudges, they don't think he's truthful, even if
his stores are all there, right to the last length of small sutff and waxed
twine. I've paid off more than one ship, sir, and I've never been subject to
anything like this . . . none of the officers and warrants have."

"God, wait 'til Gun Wharf sees our guns," Lewrie said, thinking of the
aiming notches he'd had cut into the muzzle bells and base rings and what
those worthies might make of them. Might they accuse him of defacing
Crown property, declare the guns useless for further service, and charge
him for their loss? Gun Wharf hadn't said a word when he'd paid off *Sapphire* and landed her artillery, notched in the same way.

"It's as if someone's *paid* them to find fault, sir," Greenleaf spat, shaking his head in disgust.

"Perhaps they are," Lewrie said, enigmatically. "My respects to Mister Farley, and inform him that I am going ashore for a bit. Call out my boat crew, if you will, Mister Greenleaf."

"Aye aye, sir."

Lewrie dropped off his mail at the post office himself, then he betook himself to the red brick building which served as the offices of the Port Admiral. He had found that Admiral Lord Gardner, feared by one and all who had ever suffered one of that worthy's tongue-lashings, was actually a rather easy man to deal with, and he hoped that he was still there. Once inside, he requested an audience from a Post-Captain who served as the Port Admiral's second. Unfortunately, that office was no longer filled by Captain Nicely, who had been the soul of helpfulness, but by another fellow whom Lewrie did not know from Adam. An audience? Simply out of the question this week; Admiral Lord Gardner was much too busy. The best Lewrie could do was to request pen and paper, write the Admiral a letter laying out his grievances anent de-commissioning and the yard's petti-fogging, and bow his way out, considering a toothsome dinner at The Grapes. That establishment had been his refuge when in need of overnight shore lodgings, and they had always set a fine table, but . . . he had a boat crew waiting, with time on their hands, with Stroke Oar John Kitch, and his long-time Cox'n, Liam Desmond in charge of it, two fellows who could turn up a keg of ale in the middle of a desert, and make it Fiddler's Green.

No, he had to go back to *Vigilance* before they just naturally got into trouble.

"You account for so many kegs of powder and so many round shot expended during the course of your commission, sir," a spindly, grey-haired clerk from Gun Wharf quibbled a day later, as the main course yard dipped and swung to hoist out the first of the 18-pounders from the upper gun deck. "Yet, sir. You are now in possession of shot and powder in full sufficiency."

He was a very well-dressed fellow for a clerk, clothed as well as a London banker.

"Whilst operating out of Sicily, we provisioned from Malta when in need, sir," Lewrie told him, "and on our way home, we put into Valletta to re-stock, then again at Gibraltar, so we would have all that we might need should we run into a fight on our way home, d'ye see?"

"Hmm . . . gun tools . . . flexible rammers, wood-handled rammers, powder spoons, and wormers," the clerk muttered, running down a list of things which would go ashore with each gun. "Flintlock strikers?"

"Three broken and replaced, sir," Lewrie replied.

"I . . . see," the clerk said warily, "And one dozen flint spares for each gun, six-pounders to carronades, bagged, I take it?"

"You'll find all the tompions aboard, too, sir," Lewrie pointed out. "Recently re-painted the proper red. And, if you look close, you will find that all train tackle, recoil, and run-out rackle is in new and serviceable condition, as are all the breeching ropes and truck-carriages. The axles freshly greased, as are the carronade slides."

"I must see for myself, sir," the clerk insisted with a wimpy little attempt at a grin. "We must be thorough."

He stepped over to a row of 18-pounders laid out in a line, ready for hoisting overside to the waiting barge. One of his helpers was kneeling, entering serial numbers into a ledger to see if they all matched those issued when *Vigilance* had been taken out of ordinary and re-armed under the unfortunate Captain Nunnelly, whom Lewrie had supplanted.

"Odd, sir," the helper said, fingering the muzzle ring of one of the guns. "They all look as if they've been sawed at."

"Sights, sir," Lewrie said.

"Sights?" the older clerk scoffed. "On naval guns, haw haw!"

"They work," Lewrie assured him. "I had sight notches filed in the guns of my last two ships, and trained my gun-captains to use 'em for closer shooting."

"Never *heard* the like, sir," the older clerk sniggered as if it was the greatest jape. "Why, one could almost say that they have been damaged."

"A skilled artillerist are you, sir?" Lewrie asked. "Or do you just count them? My guns were breaking French regiments ashore at a mile away to support the troops I landed."

The fellow bristled, plucked at his neck-stock, but did not make a reply.

"Lash her up, there, lads," Bosun Gore was shouting at the men binding the gun's barrel ready for hoisting. "You men! Tail on the yardarm lines and be ready to lift away!" Brace men, stand ready to swing it out!"

Would the Gun Wharf official accept them, or would he balk and quibble some more? Lewrie glared at him, and the man seemed to melt. He nodded curtly, and the working party put their backs into it, and off the deck and into the air above the bulwarks the 18-pounder went.

"Good," Lewrie said with a satisfied nod. "Good."

Now, who else *do I have to over-awe?* Lewrie thought.

"Boat ahoy!" a Midshipman called to an approaching cutter.

"Letter for your Captain!" came an answering shout.

"Come alongside!"

Lewrie left the ship's waist and went up to the quarterdeck to see what the letter was about, leaving the clerks standing about, glad to be shot of them for a moment.

A minute later, and an immaculately uniformed young Midshipman scaled the boarding battens, saluted, and handed over a wax-sealed letter, taking a breathless moment to look all round at the activities and the swarms of working parties as if he was in the Navy, but not yet of it.

Lewrie went into his great-cabins, tossed his hat at a wooden peg on an overhead deck beam, and sat at his desk to open and read the letter, noting that it was from Admiral Lord Gardner.

My dear Captain Sir Alan Lewrie,

I have reviewed the letter you left at my offices this two days past, and I quite agree that the egregious Manner in which various Officials of Portsmouth Dockyards have comported themselves anent the De-commissioning of your Ship, HMS Vigilance, seems to have been conducted much more Scrupulously than necessary, reminiscent of the Spanish Inquisition. I have made it Known among those various Officials that I have counted you as admirable Officer since our first Dealings in 1804, and that such Zealous, yea Over-Zealous handling will not be Tolerated. I do pray that you find the Onerous Process of surrendering your Command more Pleasant in Future. Once the Process is done, do inform me, and I will be delighted to dine you in, at a Date and Time to be determined.

"Well, bless my soul, we're saved!" Lewrie shouted to the deckheads, thrusting the letter upwards. He put the letter in his desk, and returned to the quarterdeck with a jaunty step, and, admittedly, a touch of swagger. "How does it go, Mister Farley?" he asked the First Officer, who was just coming up from the waist.

"Well, it's rather odd, sir," Farley confessed, "We were ready to wrangle with the clerks come aboard, but . . . all of a sudden they have turned into baa-lambs."

"A bit of influence from on high, sir," Lewrie boasted. "It matters who you know, sometimes."

"Let's be thankful for that, sir," Farley said with a laugh, "from whatever quarter. We should have all the upper-deck guns off by dusk, I'd imagine, I'm saving the forrud end of the waist for the carriages, then we'll begin with the twenty-four pounders from the lower deck tomorrow after breakfast."

"Very good, sir," Lewrie replied, grinning as he looked aloft at the mastheads which had already had the topmasts struck down to a "gantline." "I believe things will go much easier, the next week or so." He lowered his gaze and spotted John Kitch loitering round the bottom of the larboard ladderway, looking up, his flat-brimmed hat in his hands, turning it round and round.

Lewrie went down the ladderway to the waist.

"Beg pardon, Captain sir," Kitch spoke up, "but, could I have a word with you?"

"Aye, Kitch," Lewrie agreed, savouring his wee victory.

"It's about the draughts, sir," Kitch began. "I'd like to go wherever the Navy sends me, sir."

"Oh. I had hoped that you'd come up to London with the rest of us, and . . . wait 'til I got a new command," Lewrie said, surprised.

"I did that the last time, sir, and . . . well, idle and pleasant as it was . . . I ain't cut out to be in service to any house, not even yours, Captain," Kitch slowly explained. "The Navy's the only Life I knows, sir, and ya can't make a silk purse out of a sow's ear."

"You've talked it over with Desmond?" Lewrie asked.

"He thinks I'm daft, sir," Kitch admitted with a grin, "but I've good prospects, being rated Able Seaman and all, laid by some money from prizes, and my mind's made up, sir. I hope ya forgive me for jumpin' ship, as it were, but . . . there it is."

"Well, I'm going to miss you, Kitch, as will Desmond," Lewrie told him. "But, I quite understand, and wish you well wherever you end up. Who knows, you could strike for a petty officer's berth if you wanted. Quartermaster's Mate, Gunner's Mate?"

"Mast Captain's my best bet, sir," Kitch allowed. "I never got mathematics wrapped proper round my head. That, or Bosun's Mate."

"Ah, too damned many things to count as a Bosun's Mate," Lewrie said with a laugh.

"Long as I got ten fingers, I could cope, sir," Kitch said as he knuckled his brow in a parting salute.

Immediately after Kitch turned to go, Lewrie had only taken a few steps before his long-time Cox'n, Liam Desmond, was there, hat in hand.

"Kitch speak with ya, sor?" Desmond asked.

"Aye, he did," Lewrie replied. "Don't tell me you're next to go."

"Ah, no, sor," Desmond said with a shake of his head. "Like I told ya at th' Nore, sor, I'm yer right-hand man, long as ya need me. But, like Kitch told me, how he ain't keen on bein' a house servant in livery, well . . . once you're settled in London, sor, I might be more use to ya down at Anglesgreen, seein' t'th' livestock an' such. Grew up workin' th' farm back in Ireland, least 'til ya get orders back to sea. I could do ya better there."

"And poppin' into the Old Ploughman for some of their ale?" Lewrie teased.

"That, an' their pot pies, sor, aye," Desmond chuckled. "A fine way t'end a good day's work."

"Well, I'll have Deavers, Dasher, and Turnbow, so I should think I could spare you, Desmond," Lewrie allowed. "It wouldn't have a thing to do with their waitress, Miss Abigail, would it?"

"That'd be pleasant, too, sor," Desmond confessed, blushing.

Two days later and John Kitch was gone, along with over seventy sailors summoned to be transferred to a Third Rate 74 just fitting out after a complete refit in the yards. Her new Captain was not a fellow whom Lewrie knew by reputation, and had evidently had bad luck at his recruiting "rondy," unable to attract enough men to work his ship out of harbour. Lewrie spoke with them before they departed, assuring them that their new Captain would be getting a fine draught of Ordinary, Able, and Landsmen sailors who knew their jobs well.

And, slowly, *Vigilance* lightened and floated a bit higher as the last of the guns, truck carriages, tons of roundshot, and gunpowder were landed ashore, as the large water butts sufficient for six months at sea were broached and drained into the bilges, then pumped out overside, and the butts broken down into hoops and staves. Salt meat casks beyond the immediate needs of the dwindling crew were swayed out, then sent to the warehouses. Barrels of cold tar and pitch, kegs of nails and screws, the Sailmaker's locker and Bosun's stores dis-appeared, so *Vigilance* could show the world even more of her barnacles and weeding, and expose the upper plates of sea-stained copper.

Each day, another draught of man were ordered off, and the pay clerks came aboard to issue them their chits for back-pay, with the Purser and his Jack-In-The-Breadroom carefully itemising deductions due Mr. Blundell's accounts before the final sums were written down.

Lewrie's own cabins began to resemble an empty garret as rugs were rolled up and bound, the settee grouping and the Hindoo brass tray table were wrapped ready for removing, as the wine cabinet and wash-hand stand were emptied and stowed in protective scrap canvas, with particular care for the day-cabin desk and impressive sideboard in the dining coach. Crates, kegs, ankers, and barricoes of spirits and wine were piled high.

"What about the dining table, and chairs, sir?" Deavers asked.

"Mmm, sort o' rough, ain't they?" Lewrie said, giving the set a good looking over. "I don't have a dining room big enough for 'em, and my wife'd shriek in horror if she laid eyes on 'em. I bought it all from old Captain Nunnelly, 'cause *he* said he had no more use for 'em, either, so . . . let's just leave 'em. What'd I pay him, twenty pounds? I can't remember. Small loss."

And, eventually the morning came when Captain Whitehead and his junior officers and Marine complement left the ship, leaving no more than two-dozen crew still aboard, in addition to the Standing Officers who would serve as harbour watch and shipkeepers when *Vigilance* left the dockyards and was laid up In-Ordinary. Even the Midshipmen were paid off, and the only one left aboard was Charles Chenery, Lewrie's brother-in-law, who would wait to coach to London with him and the men of Lewrie's small retinue.

Scows were hired for the next morning to take aboard all of his goods and furnishings, and dray waggons were contracted to deliver it to London. Lewrie at last went ashore to dine with the Port Admiral, Lord Gardner, and *Vigilance* was no longer his own.

The next morning, the last official paperwork was looked over and signed, and the ship became just another de-commissioned hulk in the harbour, worn and tired, streaked with salt stains, and not one stitch of canvas bound to her bare yards. The only thing grand that still adorned her was her gilt-crowned lion figurehead, left to peer with one paw shading its eyes for an open and fair horizon that she might never see again.

"Come on, Charlie, lads," Lewrie beckoned by the dray waggons and large coach, "let's get aboard and set out for London."

"It doesn't seem fair, sir," Charles Chenery griped, looking back at their ship as if drinking in the last drops of her courage and spirit. "We did so many grand things with her."

"Aye, we did," Lewrie agreed, forcing himself not to despair. "And Life itself ain't fair, right, or just. Come on, let's be on our way. We may have to stay overnight at Guildford if we don't get a move on." Or even Liphook."

Lewrie looked to the top of the coach where several chests and sea bags were lashed down to see if all was in order. He spotted the wicker cage that Chalky would have been in, no longer carried inside the coach, but relegated to excess baggage.

Just dammit all to Hell! he thought.

CHAPTER ELEVEN

*T*hey did have to take lodgings overnight just outside Guildford, and an expensive proposition that was, what with coachman, drivers on the drays, and Lewrie and his retinue to feed and bed down, plus their breakfasts the next morning, and a light dinner to tide them over short of London.

But, eventually, after Kingston, their destination lay before them. It was a sunny Autumn day, with high-piled white clouds slowly coasting Eastwards above . . . well, above a faint grey haze of coal smoke that almost obscured the many Parish Church steeples and the soaring domes and towers of the greater cathedrals. City bells could be heard chiming even before they got near Southwark and the expanse of the Thames.

Soon, soon! Lewrie silently urged the time and miles to pass as his return to his home, and reunion with Jessica, drew nearer, making him fidgety and anxious for the first sight of Dover Street, and the first glimpse of his dear wife's face. He had sent along a letter the day before they set out, alerting her to his expected arrival, but the lateness of their starting, and the need to stop at Guildford, put paid to his expectations. He hoped that she would not have been too dis-appointed.

His head was out the lowered sash windows in either coach door, having to share with the other passengers crammed into the interior as landmarks passed by. Westminster Bridge, then up Whitehall past Horse Guards and the Admiralty to Charing Cross, then a short jog down Pall Mall to Wardour Street for another turn onto Piccadilly at last, then . . . a right turn into Dover Street.

"Huzzah! Will ya look at that!" Lewrie cried as he espied his house, its door and the Doric lintel above it adorned with a draping rope of long-stemmed flowers twined together. "We're here!"

He bolted from the coach the moment the coachee drew reins, dashed to the door and raised the well-polished brass pineapple door knocker to pound it for admittance.

"And where the Devil did *that* thing come from?" he muttered.

"Coming!" a muffled voice inside said.

A key clacked tumblers in the lock, and a bolt screaked as it was turned, and the door swung open to reveal his old cabin servant, Pettus, now the house butler.

"My stars, Captain Lewrie, sir!" Pettus gushed, beaming. "Come in, sir, and welcome home at last! Dame Lewrie? Ma'am? It's . . . !"

Lewrie stepped inside, sweeping off his hat to fling at the entry hall sideboard. Charles Chenery joined him, just as Jessica came down the stairs from the drawing room above in a rush, ladylike demeanour be damned, her shoes thudding on the stair treads. She paused for a brief moment at the foot of the stairs, her lovely face breaking into an expression of utmost joy before they rushed each other so he could gather her up in his arms and lift her off her feet to press her whole length against him, face burrowed against her neck, and hers against his.

"Oh, my Lord!" she said, sounding breathless and on the edge of tears, "My love, my dear love, you're back!"

"Jessica, I've longed for this moment," Lewrie swore to her as their lips met in a long soul kiss. And there were tears moistening her cheeks that he tried to kiss away.

"It's been too long, dearest Alan," she said, shuddering.

"I'm home now. Hope I make up for the absence," Lewrie said, on the edge of a silly laugh.

"Good to see you, too, sister," Charles Chenery said, "Oh, ware the hounds!"

Bisquit, and Jessica's Cocker Spaniel, Rembrandt, came thundering upstairs from the kitchen and cellar, barking and baying. Bisquit bounded round Lewrie and his wife, whining pitifully, 'til Lewrie let Jessica go to kneel down and pet/tousle with his old ship's mascot and almost got bowled over as Bisquit pressed against his chest and licked his face, tail whipping madly.

"Welcome home to you, too, Charlie," Jessica said, welcoming her younger brother with a fond embrace, and a peck on the cheek. "My word, but you've shot up like a weed! You are all out elbows and wrists, in need of a new uniform, I dare say!"

Her dog looked a little puzzled about Lewrie's arrival, but he knew Charlie of old, and barked for attention and reunion "wubbies."

"Darling, you remember Deavers, Desmond, Yeovill, Dasher, and Turnbow?" Lewrie said as he got back to his feet.

"Indeed I do," Jessica sweetly said, greeting them all, giving Dasher a tousle of his hair. "There's fresh bedding belowstairs, and cook has planned a feast for all tonight. Father will sup with us, Charlie, along with Madame Berenice, of course. Should we have your luggage brought in, dear?"

"Oh, of course," Lewrie said, turning to his men. "My furnishings can go into the coach house out back. My desk, hmm . . . there's a small room just above the entry hall. That's a good place for it and all my books. Sorry t'put you to work so soon."

"We'll see to it, sor," Desmond told him, tipping Pettus a wink, who doffed his dark coat and traded it for a dark green apron suitable for work.

"You must show me all you've done since I've been gone, love," Lewrie bade, and Jessica was girlishly happy to oblige, almost skipping on light feet as she led him into the front parlour, her art studio.

To Lewrie's lights, she was even more fetching than when they had first met, when he'd first become entranced and besotted. She wore her long, dark hair coiled up into an ornate coif, baring a little of her graceful neck. Her eyes seemed to sparkle, large, expressive, and a peculiar shade of blue darker than the normal hue. She wore a fine white-lace trimmed gown of pale blue with half sleeves, below her elbows, a low, square neckline, and puffed at the points of her shoulders, her neck set off by an ivory cameo on a thin gold chain. Her gown was high waisted, set off with a white sash, and falling straight—Lewrie lastfully took note—over her firm, flat belly and slim hips.

She had re-painted the front parlour a much paler, softer hue of yellow than it had been, and Lewrie had to admit that the vine-like white plaster work she had contracted looked particularly smart.

In the dining room beyond, past the rarely opened door from the front parlour, Jessica proudly showed off some new items she'd bought, a

Wedgwood fruit *compote* and a brace of flower urns in pale blue and decorated with white scrollwork, that now sat on the sideboard. Lewrie's coin silver candelabras and table decorations that he'd brought out of storage were on prominent display, too.

"Those Venetian *bombe* chests look simply wonderful either side of the stairs," Jessica gushed, "I love that splendid red colour, do you not? Oh, and our front door! A brass kick plate on the bottom, and the new door knocker? The old iron one with that grotesque face like a gargoyle was just hideous! It made my skin crawl every time I had to use it. But, the bright brass is *much* nicer, and a pineapple represents hospitality. I *would* have had something nautical installed, if I could have found one. Now, here in the morning room . . ."

At the back of the first storey sat a much smaller dining room for taking breakfast *en famille,* and Jessica had not done all that much to it, but for the walls being covered with some of her framed artwork; landscapes, boats, and city scenes, along with some animals.

"Now, look out the windows and see the back garden!" Jessica insisted with another bout of pride. "The gazebo, the crushed gravel walks, and the flower beds? I've planted nothing *too* demanding of my gardening abilities, mostly flowers and herbs native to England, so I *trust* they will thrive. A proper English garden, if I do say so myself. Want to go see it? We can have tea!"

"I want to see that harpsichord, first," Lewrie said instead.

Up they went to the drawing room, where room had been made for the instrument, and even Lewrie had to admit that it was a handsome piece. Jessica sat down and played a hymn, her long, talented fingers lovingly stroking the keys.

"So *much* nicer on the ears than a piano forte," she beamed, swaying a bit to the metre, then did a little "doodle-doodle" and turned on from the keys on the bench and laughed. Belowstairs, the sound of music of *any* kind set Bisquit to baying in his attempts to sing along, which made Lewrie laugh out loud, too.

"It *is* nice, and I see what ya mean about a softer sound," he agreed. "Aye, tea'd be nice, but I should see about the lads, and what they're doing with my cabin furnishings and stores. I bought up lots of wine on Sicily, Malta, and Gibralatar that needs stowing."

"Oh, delightful!" Jessica exclaimed, springing from the bench to put her arms about him. "And, I've a surprise for you, as well."

"Mmm, and what is that?" Lewrie asked, feeling lusty, again; he had actually managed to remain faithful and celibate all the time he'd been gone, though not without fearful temptations, and that crinkly-dry spray of rosemary still rested in his desk drawer.

"There's a shop in New Bond Street, Martini and Company . . ." she began to explain.

"Aye, I've shopped there before," Lewrie interrupted.

"The owner is on very good terms with America, and gets goods that most Americans would not offer any longer to Englishmen," Jessica went on. "All this talk of how we seize their merchant ships, take men off if we think they're British deserters?"

"Aye, 'Free Trade and Sailors' Rights,'" Lewrie said with a nod. "It's been in all the papers."

"You *do* make this difficult, Alan my dear," Jessica said with a faint cross look. "Martini's managed to import gallons and gallons of American corn whisky. It was a bit dear, but I bought you four stone crocks of it . . . twenty gallons, all told. For your homecoming! For a present."

Lewrie picked her up off her feet once more and twirled her round the drawing room, hooting his surprise and delight. "My God, you're a bloody wonder, my girl! Whoo! What a gift! I *adore* you for it!"

"I spoke with Mister Martini personally," Jessica said, better pleased with her husband than she'd been a moment before. "Did you know that the Rebels made him a prisoner for a time 'til Thomas Jefferson, whom he knew, set him free? And Jefferson became one of their Presidents. I'm told they are still fast friends."

"Martini's is good for all sorts of things," Lewrie told her. "My father and his servants shop there regularly. And so should we!"

"Go see to your things, darling," Jessica fondly said, giving him another long kiss. "After, we'll have our tea, if the weather will co-operate."

"Excuse me, then, dear Jessica," Lewrie said at last, letting her go and stepping back. "What did Romeo say, 'parting is such sweet sorrow' . . . all that?"

"Go! I will be here," Jessica laughed, almost sticking her tongue out at him. "The important thing is, so will you."

There were chests to be fetched up to the bedchamber, civilian clothing hung in the *armoire,* cabin furnishings stored in the groom's lodgings above the stables in the un-used coach house, and an ocean of wine and spirits put away in the pantries in the kitchens. They had to hail a handcarter to shift Charlie Chenery's dunnage to his father's house at St. Anselm's manse, and the dray waggoners to be paid. That took at least two hours, hindered by the curiosity of the house dogs. At last, Lewrie hung up his uniform and changed into a fresh, clean shirt, buff trousers and black coat, with a burgundy waist-coat and a black neck-stock, traded Hessian boots for a comfortable old pair of buckled shoes, and trotted downstairs to the kitchens and out the door to the back garden.

"Sir Alan, sir?" a man in a white apron asked.

"Aye?" Lewrie said, stopping by the door.

"Hazelwood, Sir Alan," the man said, naming himself. "I am cook to the household. And a fine feast Dame Lewrie has demanded of me for your first night home from the sea, sir! I assure you that you will enjoy it."

"Well, I'm sure I will, Hazelwood," Lewrie said, looking the man over closely.

Must be a good cook, Lewrie thought; *he's round and well-fed as a hog.* He found it odd, though, that Hazelwood sported a Frenchified moustachio, and topped off his clothes with a high, puffy white hat with many folds.

"A feast for six, Sir Alan," Hazelwood promised.

"Six?" Lewrie asked.

"Sir Hugo Willoughby, Reverend Chenery, Madame Pellatan, you, and Dame Lewrie, and Midshipman Chenery, sir," Hazelwood almost simpered as he ticked names off his fingers.

"Ah, my father, aye," Lewrie said with a nod; he had hoped that rencontre with the old rogue could have waited 'til a later day. "I believe my wife said something about tea in the garden?"

"The water is aboil at the moment, Sir Alan," Hazelwood said, rising on his tiptoes in an odd fashion. "May I ask, though, Sir Alan, what am I to do with but the one rabbit?" he said, pointing to a cage which held Dasher's pet doe, Harriet. "It won't even make soup."

"Feed it, Hazelwood," Lewrie told him. "That's not for eating, that's Dasher's pet."

At that moment, Lewrie's shipboard cook, Yeovill, and Dasher came in from the coach house with his tools of the trade; pots, pans, iron skillets, mixing bowls, measuring cups, and bottles of various sauces, looking for a place to store them.

"I did not order anything," Hazelwood said, stiffening, tilting up his nose. "What is all this?"

"Hazelwood, allow me to name to you Mister Yeovill, who is my personal cook aboard ship," Lewrie said, "and one of my cabin servants, the aforesaid Tom Dasher. Lads, the cook, Mister Hazelwood."

Their responses were more like grunts, and an "Aha!" from the house cook.

"I'm sure that your Mister Yeovill will enjoy his long rest," Hazelwood simpered, "since these are *my* kitchens."

Oh, this'll be joyful t'deal with, Lewrie cringed to himself.

He went on out the stout rear door, up the stone steps past the water pump, and into the back garden, a smile creasing his face as he spotted Jessica, already seated at the table in the gazebo.

"Done with your duties, dear? Good. Let me show you round," Jessica said, springing from her chair to join him on the lawn and the white pea gravel walk. "Isn't the garden ever so much nicer?"

"It is indeed," Lewrie had to admit. "You've simply done wonders."

The day was just warm enough, and the air in the garden lush with the aromas of blossoms and new-mown grass. Jessica led him round to admire the flower beds, naming them by turn, though the varieties went right past Lewrie's head; he knew colours, and whether they were tall or short, skinny or bushy, and that was his horticultural knowledge, and all he needed to know.

Pettus, now the house's butler, came out with the tea tray and fixings, whilst Jessica's personal maidservant, an adorable blonde woman named Lucy, brought out an array of pastries and wee edibles.

"Shall I pour, sir?" Pettus asked, and at Lewrie's nod, did so. Jessica preferred her tea with lemon slices, as long as lemons were obtainable, whilst Lewrie went for sugar and heavy cream.

"How do you like shore duties, Pettus?" Lewrie asked as he eyed the sweet rolls, jams, and butter.

"Oh, it's quite fine, sir," Pettus vowed, looking away, and at Lucy, "Dry, warm, safe in stormy weather, and . . . filled with infinite possibilities."

"Thank you, Pettus, Lucy," Jessica said, sounding as if she had acquired the manners and authority of a proper housemistress. "I will ring if there's anything else."

"Yes, ma'am," Pettus replied, and Lucy dipped a wee curtsy as they both went back into the house.

"There is a reason for us to have a talk, Alan dear," Jessica said, leaning her head towards him.

"About my father being invited?" Lewrie japed, mouth filled by a sugar and cinnamon stuffed tartlet.

"No, not that," she said with a wee laugh. "It's about Pettus and Lucy."

"What about 'em?" Lewrie asked.

"They have fallen in love, and wish to marry, Alan," Jessica told him. "Normally, that would mean that one, or both of them, would have to leave our employ, but . . . if we allow them, to ah . . . ?"

"Leave? Why?" Lewrie spluttered after a sip of tea.

Long ago, when Pettus became his cabin steward, the lad had just been scooped up by the Press, roaring drunk in the pit of Hell after losing his employment at a Bishop's residence, and separated from his true love, a girl named Nancy. Lewrie shook his head in the negative.

"I was wondering, though, if we . . ." Jessica was saying.

"Damned if they'll have to leave, darling," Lewrie told her and took her by surprise. "Not only can they stay on, we'll throw them a wedding." After another sip of tea, he turned his gaze to the coach house. "There's rooms yonder, for a coachman and a groom, and it'd make a cozy lodging for a married couple, what? Of course, we'd have to find some stray cats, and Bully, t'clean out all the rats and the mice, first, but . . ."

"Oh, my *word*. Alan," Jessica gushed with joy, "you *do* have the soul of a romantic! I was hoping and praying that you could see your way to keeping them on! Oh, let me kiss you! My dear love!"

That he would definitely allow! And, they could kiss and hug in the privacy of their own, walled garden.

"They'll be needin' furnishings, though," Lewrie speculated.

"Clotworthy Chute's emporium?" Jessica suggested.

"Perfect!" Lewrie exulted, sitting back down, but holding her hand in his left as he raised his tea with his right.

"Hoy, Bully, stop 'at!" Dasher yelled as he came running from the back door to the basement, mingled with the barking of the dogs. "Cap'm Lewrie, help! They's after Harriet!"

The rabbit was bounding about the garden in great leaps as the dogs, Bisquit, Bully the wee terrier, and Jessica's usually docile spaniel, Rembrandt, chased after her.

"No, dogs!" Jessica shouted. "Not my flower beds, my herbs!"

"Bisquit!" Lewrie roared in his best quarterdeck voice. He rose to intercept them. Though it was a weird sort of chase, for none of the dogs had ever seen a rabbit outside of a cage, and Bisquit had shown no interest in the rabbits or quail in the forecastle manger; and it was good odds that Harriet had never seen a dog aboard ship, either. She might have been running and hopping to enjoy a wee bit of freedom, and the dogs were

loping, not running after her just out of curiosity. The rabbit dashed between Lewrie's feet, did a bound or two beyond, then got cornered by the
back wall and gate and the stable. Bully gave out a series of sharp barks,
getting into the spirit, which prompted Bisquit to let go with a few.

"Don't let them hurt it!" Jessica entreated, staying on the raised gazebo
platform as if the rabbit was a very large mouse.

Penned into a corner, Harriet did a great bound off the stable wall, right
back at the dogs, leaping over Bully, who turned a back flip in surprise,
and Bisquit collided with him, sending them both sprawling. Jessica's dog
stopped and sat on his haunches, letting out a very confused "Whuff!"

Up the steps of the gazebo, then round the other side of the garden, Harriet flew, brought short at last at the back wall where Dasher caught her
and scooped her up. The confused dogs trotted over to look up at the rabbit while Dasher stroked her, had a sniff or two, then dropped their front
ends as if inciting more play.

"Bad dogs," Dasher chid them, cradling Harriet protectively, "Bad
dogs!"

"Let's get her into her cage," Lewrie suggested, walking over to ruffle
all three dogs' fur. "Maybe Harriet'll end up chasin' *them* like she did
Chalky, hey?" Lewrie plucked a dandelion at the edge of a flower bed and
offered it to the rabbit. "Jessica, want t'meet the rabbit?"

"Oh, she's darling!" Jessica cooed as she stroked Harriet's ears and head.
The rabbit squirmed to free her front paws so she could eat the dandelion. "She keeps in a cage? Perhaps, if the dogs are kept in the house, your
pet can have the run of the garden, now and then. She surely can't eat half
what the squirrels can, Dasher."

"Oh, thankee, ma'am, thankee! She'd like that!" Dasher beamed.

"What's next, dear?" Jessica asked Lewrie. "Parrots? Pigs rooting up
the lawn? I like animals, but a menagerie is not what I envisioned."

"You must admit that it was amusing, for a bit," Lewrie said as he tossed
off a hapless shrug.

Thank God she smiled at that moment and began to titter. "You and
our beasts are amusing." She linked arms with him.

"I'm pleased that you're pleased," Lewrie replied, giving her a hug.

CHAPTER TWELVE

*S*upper would be at seven, and the guests were told to arrive by six, giving everyone a chance to catch up on their doings over the year. Sir Hugo, Lewrie's father, turned up in grey trousers strapped under the insoles of his low boots, with a cream waist-coat and black coat, in the finest Beau Brummel fashion, with his usual close-fitted white wig that, at first glance, resembled an actual head of hair.

Reverend Chenery was black from head to toe but for the white bands at his collar, of course, beaming with joy to have his son home, in one piece, and in good health. Young Charles Chenery had changed into some of his old civilian suitings that, unfortunately, looked as outgrown as his uniforms, and Jessica gently chid him about it. The lad had earned some prizemoney from his time aboard HMS *Sapphire*, so he could remedy that fault in short order, and with no need to draw upon his father's finances, which Lewrie expected were as lean as they were when they'd sailed for Italy. The Reverend's hobbies were just too expensive. *He'd do better betting on horses*, Lewrie thought.

Madame Berenice Pellatan, was, as usual, the fashion plate of the gathering, rigged out in a colourful, nigh gaudy, gown with white shawl, and a high-piled older-fashioned wig sprigged with artificial flowers and butterflies. The French emigré artist who lodged at the manse at St. Anselm's out of charity and taught drawing to the parish children swept in with the grandeur of a *vicomtesse* of the greatest airs. Frankly, she'd always gotten up Lewrie's nose, but, it seemed as if she would play the honoured widowed aunt to the Chenery family 'til the Second Coming.

"*Chevalier* Alan, *enchanté*" she cooed as she offered a hand to be kissed. "Ooh la, how delightful to see you and young *M'sieur* Charles, back from your travails at sea. And Dame Jessica, how happy you look, how *beau* your appearance, to be re-united with your husband! Why, I could almost imagine your are dancing on your tiptoes!"

"Just this afternoon, Madame," Jessica japed, describing the "rabbit hunt" in the garden, to the amusement of all.

"Ah, *le aperitifs*!" Madame Pellatan gushed as wine appeared, accompanied by some pastries.

"The wine is a light, delicate *vihno verde* from Portugal," Lewrie told everyone. "Found it at Gibraltar before we sailed for home."

"Ah, marvellous," Reverend Chenery said after a tentative sip.

"Alan brought home a grand selection of wines," Jessica added, "Spanish, Portuguese, Italian, and Sicilian. Sherries, ports, brandy, that are growing rarer on the London market."

"I could almost be termed a smuggler," Lewrie japed.

"Any Madeira, or Rainwater Port?" Sir Hugo asked.

"Some Madeira, but not Rainwater," Lewrie apologised, "it's as rare as hens' teeth. I think George Washington, a great lover of a Rainwater Port, bought it all up years ago, hah hah."

"Pity," Sir Hugo grumped, "the club hasn't seen a single bottle available in ages."

That led Reverend Chenery and Sir Hugo to talk about the Madeira Club, which Sir Hugo and some others had founded, and how it had been planned as a gentleman's club and lodging for people who would never be invited to join White's, Almack's, Bootles or Brook's.

"Ladies and gentlemen," Pettus announced at last, "supper is now ready to be served." And down from the drawing room they trooped, to the dining room below to seat themselves, sorting themselves out in descending order of status.

There was a first course of green salads, dressed with oil and vinaigrette, with a Sicilian pinot grigiot; there was a passable approximation of a French vichyssoise with potatoes and leeks, with a rosé; and a loud declaration from Madame Pellatan on how close it was to the real item, of course; then came spatchcocked pigeons done in a mild pepper and tarragon sauce, with a cabernet sauvignon, followed by a main course of prime rib of beef, la-dled in *au jus*, with a claret. Removes consisted of peas, stewed carrots, Brussels sprouts, and roast potatoes *au gratin*. With enough wine, the table conversation became lively and amusing, too.

Halfway through the pigeon course, though, Reverend Chenery and Madame Pellatan took notice that Lewrie and Charles Chenery were both tapping their warm, buttered, and fresh-baked rolls on the table top.

"I say, Sir Alan . . . what are you doing?" Chenery asked.

"*Oui,* how perplexing," Madame Pellatan commented, looking about her fellow diners to see if they agreed.

"Oh, that?" Lewrie said with a grin, and took a large bite of his roll. "It's a habit one develops at sea."

"Should we tell them, sir?" Midshipman Chenery asked him with a puckish grin.

"Perhaps it's not fit for proper company, Charlie," Lewrie said with a grin of his own, and polished off the rest of the roll.

"Whyever would one do it, though?" the Reverend pressed.

"You see, father," young Chenery said, beginning to chuckle. "We don't have fresh bread at sea."

"There's room in the big oven apparatus in the galley to bake loaves, but no one ever knows how," Lewrie explained. "Not enough eggs or milk, or yeast . . . we only have ship's bisquit after a few days out of port."

"And a hard tooth-breaker it is, after a few weeks," Chenery added. "We have to soak it in wine or water to make it edible." He raised his hands to help describe a small, rectangular, and unleavened chunk of thick cracker. "It's brought aboard and stowed in cloth bags, hanging every-where there's room. We, ah . . . tap it on the table to scare things out of it."

"Scare what out of it?" Madame Pellatan demanded.

"Weevils, ma'am," Chenery told her. "Weevils and . . . such."

"Ooh, *alors, mort de ma vie!*" she gasped, fanning herself.

"At least it doesn't go mouldy, like fresh bread," Lewrie said, hiding his glee at her reaction.

Sir Hugo sniggered knowingly, for he'd seen more than his share of Army bisquit, and Jessica laughed right out loud, putting her napkin to her lips, joined by Lewrie and young Chenery, leaving the Reverend, his father, and the pale-faced Madame Pellatan to titter, politely.

God, what a lot of make-up! Lewrie thought, looking at her; *It stands out when she's white as a sheet! Well, she* is *French.*

"Cook tells me he's fashioned a tasty dessert for us tonight," Jessica promised as the dinner plates were cleared away. "He said a sweet, white wine goes well with it."

Everyone turned to watch the arrival of the sweet course, expecting a duff or pudding with a brandy sauce, but it turned out to be an apple pie, still warm from the ovens, with thin slices of aged sharp cheddar over it.

"Oh, good ho!" Charlie Chenery cheered as a slice was put before him, leaning over to smell it and make yummy noises. "How I have longed for a decent apple pie. Sicily only had jam turnovers."

"Mmm, cinnamon, brown sugar, and . . . honey?" Rev. Chenery said after a taste. "And do I sense a touch of lemon juice, as well?"

"Whatever you taste, sir, it is magnificent," Sir Hugo raved.

Once the last moist crumb had been pressed between the tines of their forks and eaten, and the last sips of wine had been downed, Madame Pellatan and Jessica shared a look, prompting Jessica to rise from her chair, which drove everyone to their feet.

"Madame Berenice and I will be in the drawing room, gentlemen," she announced. "Join us at your leisure for some music, and cards perhaps?"

"Nothing too complicated, madame," Sir Hugo jested. "We must not tax my son's wits too far, especially after such a fine repast."

"And I don't know if my son is good at cards, either," the Rev. Chenery added with a wee whinny of a laugh. "He was hopeless before he went to sea. Whist is quite beyond him, alas."

They bowed the ladies out, then sat back down at the table, now bare of a tablecloth, and out came the port, along with clumps of red grapes. Politics, doings at Court, some not-too-lewd gossip and how the Army was faring in Portugal and Spain? Lewrie wished that he could undo his breeches buttons after such a grand meal. And yes, all of the men remarked that he'd brought home an excellent sort of port.

"It seems, Sir Alan, that you barely left, yet here you are, back again," Rev. Chenery asked. "Is there a tale in that?"

"A most miserable one, sir," Lewrie growled back, and proceeded to lay his complaints before them on how he and his ship, his command in Mediterranean waters, had been taken from him, and why.

"It was so utterly unfair," Charles Chenery contributed, "just as we were really hurting the French . . . hitting our stride." After that sneer, he tossed back half a glass of port most manly.

"Surely, you've developed patrons, son," Sir Hugo said.

"None as powerful as my detractors' patrons, it seems," Lewrie groaned. "Commodores and Rear-Admirals low on the lists."

"Well, you always could rub people the wrong way," Sir Hugo said with a snigger, making light of it.

"Ah, what a vote of confidence," Lewrie shot back.

"I gathered that the Captain's replacement, Commodore Grierson, and the conversion of our last ship, *Sapphire,* to an un-armed troop transport that came with him, was a studied insult," Charles Chenery told the table with a knowing nod of his head.

"We've despised each other since the Bahamas in Eighteen Oh Four," Lewrie agreed. "Well, at least Dame Lewrie will be happy. Against such unknown foes, I may end up ashore and on half-pay 'til . . . the end of the bloody world!"

"Hmm, perhaps then, Sir Alan, you would have time to participate in a grand expedition that is being organised," Rev. Chenery hinted. "Lots of exploration, adventure, and an opportunity to re-write the history of the discovery of North America."

Oh, Christ on a crutch, he's still on that? Lewrie thought with a stifled groan, and *not* rolling his eyes. He looked down table to young Chenery, who *was* looking at the ceiling and sighing.

"An expedition, sir?" Sir Hugo enquired.

That opened the door to a new topic of conversation, which the Reverend dominated, about rocks erected and carved along the shore in New England that were in Phoenician, and had been translated to state "Phoenician Trading Station," the tales of many pit mines scattered throughout the Ohio Territory and what the Americans called Michigan where massive amounts of copper had been brought up; how the plates of copper were found in the same hourglass shapes on both sides of the Atlantic, bound together the same way. The Phoenicians and Carthaginian people, the sailors of Nineveh and Tyre in later days had made up the merchant and naval feets of Rome, and about the fifteen-year-old Emperor Valentinus the Second had supposedly sent ships West to find him a refuge before his mother and a Gothic general in Roman employ murdered him.

"And, Sir Hugo, we've learned that Roman coins have been found, washed up on beaches in Massachusetts," Rev. Chenery expounded with joy, "bearing the likeness of Valentinus the Second, and dated during his short, unfortunate realm, hah!"

"That Dago, Columbus, bedamned, hah!" Sir Hugo enthused.

No one noticed that Lewrie and his young brother-in-law shook their heads as the same time; they had both heard it all before, and it was beyond them by now to even toss in the occasional "my word," "do tell," or the odd, appreciative grunt.

"Phoenician ships, crews that would fight and die if anyone followed them past the Pillars of Hercules," Rev. Chenery rhapsodised, "Roman ships, some as big as the sort that carried Saint Peter to Rome, hundreds of passengers, even Vikings sailing past Iceland and Greenland to a land they called Vinland, far enough South of our Canadian colonies where wild grapes grow? My brother, who is a Fellow in Antiquities at Oxford, several of his contemporaries, and some enthusiastic patrons are laying plans, making preparations, for such an expedition. They have discovered a world traveller and adventurer whose exploits have resulted in a couple of books, and some contributions that he brought back to the British Museum, a Major Beresford, late of the Thirty Third, to provide the organisation."

"The Thirty Third Foot, hey?" Sir Hugo said. "The 'Havercakes,' a damned good regiment." Will this expedition be jumping off anytime soon, Reverend?"

"We would hope to have all in place by the Spring of Eighteen Twelve, if not earlier," Chenery told him. "Are you enticed?"

"Hmm, marching through Massachusetts, into the Ohio Territory, and up towards the Michigan Territory," Sir Hugo mused aloud, "Brr, not me, personally. I ain't the stout man I used to be. Why, it'd involve *years* of grubbing and digging, sir! In Indian lands, I take it? A large, armed party? And, I expect that the Yankee Doodles'd think us an invasion force, haw! No warm welcome there, either."

"Well, if not personal participation, one could invest in . . ." Rev. Chenery tossed off, but Lewrie had had enough.

"A last toast, gentlemen, and I think it's time to join the ladies," he suggested, instead, topping off his port glass and offering larboardly round the table.

"If you would allow me, Captain sir?" Midshipman Chenery asked. He raised his glass, still seated Navy fashion, and said "It is Monday, so . . . gentlemen, I give you . . . Our Ships At Sea."

"Our Ships At Sea!" they chorused, and tossed their port back to "heel taps."

In the drawing room, they got up a four-handed card game, easy to play and quick, with no wagers, whilst Jessica played her precious harpsichord, and Lewrie had to admit that no matter what the end price had been at Clotworthy Chute's emporium, it had been worth it, and it did have a softer, rounder, more pleasant tone than a piano forte.

Of course, Bisquit and Rembrandt, who had sat by the dining table with longing looks (for that was where the *food* was!) joined them in the drawing room to lay before the hearth to enjoy a warming fire, and Bisquit now and then whined and bayed along with the music, as he was wont to do, with Rembrandt contributing a *whuff* or a whine here and there.

"It doesn't irritate him, father," Jessica explained, "I believe that he tries to sing along."

"It's be a deal worse if I played my penny whistle," Lewrie said from the card table.

"Hah!" Charlie Chenery piped up, "If the Captain tootled a tune, Bisquit'd come running up from belowdecks to sit outside the door, or go to the poop and look down through the skylights in the coach top to bay and sing."

"We should have a duet, then," Jessica suggested, laughing.

"Still packed away at the bottom of one of my sea chests," Lewrie told everyone, "It's best there, believe me."

Before it got too late in the evening, or the London fog became too thick, their guests departed for their own homes, Sir Hugo graciously offering his coach to see the Chenerys and Madame Pellatan to St. Anselm's manse.

Candles were snuffed, fireplaces banked on the first storey and in the drawing room. Door and window locks were seen to against the ever-present foot pads and house breakers, and Lewrie saw Jessica up to their bedchamber with a three-candle bright pewter holder.

Jessica took the small dressing room as Lewrie stripped off his civilian suitings, neck-stock, shirt, and laid everything out atop a chest for morning. In a chest of drawers, he found a cream-coloured nightshirt that fell just below his knees. Looking out the window to the back garden, he noted that the fog was thickening, bringing with it a slight chill. He added a couple of lumps of coal to the fireplace and gave the fire a hopeful poke or two. Wonder of wonders, at the foot of the bed sat a new pair of bear-skin house slippers that came up above the heels, and he slipped those on, too. He thought to get his dressing robe out of the armoire as he listened to Jessica, humming a light, happy tune.

Lewrie sat on the edge of the bed, letting out a pleased "Aah!" and looking forward to the moment when he and Jessica rolled into bed, after all the months apart.

He began to develop a monstrous cock-stand. At last, and celibacy could go to the Devil and shake itself!

Jessica came from the dressing room in silk slippers, a cotton nightshirt, and her favourite embroidered dressing robe, chastely folded over her body, and bound shut with a sash.

"Oh, it is so good to have you home, Alan," she cooed, coming to embrace him and rest her head on his shoulder. "Shall I let you sleep in as late as you like, this morning?"

"That sounds heavenly," Lewrie cooed back, brushing back her hair to nuzzle on her neck and an ear. "More to the point, you smell heavenly, *feel* heavenly."

"There is a flask of brandy on the night stand," she said, stepping back half a pace, "and some water for when you rise."

"Mmmmm," he purred, grinning.

"I will say goodnight to you, then," she said.

"Hmm? What? You'll . . . ?" he stammered.

"Unfortunately, my love," Jessica explained, "your arrival coincides with the arrival of my time 'under the moon,'" she delicately put it, "and we both agreed that neither of us thought such a time as one suitable, or welcome, for intimacy. You have been *so* understanding about my feelings on the matter, for which I thank you, and adore you."

"Under the . . . ? I say!" he spluttered. That enormous erection was much like a marlingspike, forcing his nightshirt to jut out like it was pushed by a tent pole, and he bundled up his dressing robe to cover himself from the waist down. "I'd thought . . . !"

"I *know*, my dear," Jessica said with a winsome pout, "the timing of it distresses me, too, and you know how much I have come to enjoy our pleasing and passionate hours. Believe me when I tell you what a trial it has been for me to sleep alone all this time, without your touch, without . . ."

"Uh huh!" was all that Lewrie could say, mouth agape in shock.

"It will only be but a few days, darling," she told him, "then I will give you a *proper* homecoming. You *do* understand, don't you?"

"Ah, ehm . . . uh, aye, if we must," he stammered.

She embraced him one more time, shared a long, lingering soul kiss that set off fireworks in Lewrie's head, then she stepped back, said goodnight, blew him a last, promising kiss, and went to one of the spare bedchambers.

As she opened the door, Bisquit slipped into the room to sniff and push his muzzle against Lewrie's shins, and Lewrie bent down to ruffle his fur.

"Mine arse on a band-box, dog," he muttered, "Thank your lucky stars you ain't a bitch. I'm so randy th' crack o' *dawn* ain't safe!"

Lewrie sat on the side of the bed, picking up the flask of brandy and giving it a jiggle.

"Full, by God," he muttered, "a whole pint, and I think that I'm goin' t'need it. *Jee-sus*!" He rolled onto the bed, fussed with the feather pillows to prop him up on the headboard, and gave his erection a look. It was still as stiff as a pistol barrel, and a flick of a finger on its head barely moved it. He looked round for a scrap of cloth. It had been quite some time since he'd resorted to self-stimulation, "boxing the Jesuit and getting cockroaches" as his old Midshipmens' berth had called it.

"Well, damme," he said, pulling the cork from the brandy flask to pour him a good measure in a small snifter. He was more than ready for a good, lubricated sulk.

Bisquit padded round on the hearth stones before the fire, but found no comfort. Of a sudden, he bounded atop the bed, found that the mattress and the bed covers were softer, and flattened himself on the quilt. Since Lewrie did not immediately object, Bisquit wormed his way up along his right thigh, took a sniff and a squint at that odd mound under the nightshirt, then worked his way further to lay his head on Lewrie's stomach, letting out a whiny sigh.

"You're my bed partner, hey, Bisquit?" Lewrie whispered to him. "Let's pray ya don't have fleas." He tipped his snifter to the dog, and took a deep sip, wondering where in the kitchen pantries Jessica had stored that American corn whisky.

CHAPTER THIRTEEN

$\mathcal{T}$here didn't seem to be much point in Lewrie calling upon the Admiralty, but there was Charles Chenery to think of, so the two of them went through the motions of dressing in their best uniforms and coaching down to Whitehall for several wasted hours in the infamous Waiting Room. Just once a week, so it didn't look as if either one of them were really begging for active commissions.

The Autumn weather was good enough for strolls round the many shops, bookstores, trips to the tailors to up-date their civilian clothing, and clothe Charlie in better-fitting uniform items. Then, there were horses to hire for rides in Hyde Park. Sir Hugo rode with them now-and-again, as did Jessica, though she was finishing a portrait for an important client, a member of Parliament, reported to be a "comer." Frankly, Lewrie found the man entirely too dashing and far too handsome, and who showed up for his sessions at least three days a week, a little after breakfast. Lewrie hadn't reckoned on Jessica's clients coming to his house on such a regular basis, but, whilst he was away, the first storey front parlour had become more than a workshop studio. When he brought it up, Jessica had laughed it off, assuring him that if anyone ever got fresh, Pettus would be there to set the cad straight, and see him off. She had done three portraits this year, for £25 apiece, and with the sales of her animal and children's paintings, was well on her way to another £100 year, saving on the household budget, hardly ever having to dip into the "pin money" he had settled on her for the upkeep of their house.

"Besides, darling," Jessica had reasoned with a smile, "you are now here, so if anyone thinks to play the cad, *you* can set him straight, along with Desmond and the rest of your men. His sessions will soon end, and if I do manage to engage another commission before Christmas, it will most likely be a woman. All the others have been, so far."

Lewrie also worried what his neighbours would think of a house on Dover Street being turned into a commercial enterprise, engaged in Trade, of a sorts. He thought to raise that topic with her, but had enough sense not to. He just made a point to be home with no shopping or riding scheduled on the days when the young M.P. showed up, all full of himself.

At his father's insistence, they attended the Madeira Club for suppers several times, taking Charlie with them once. The place had been expanding the last time Lewrie had been in London, absorbing the house next door, and adding a billiards and cards room off the old entry foyer and lobby, opposite the original Common Room. There were some new members, an host of unfamiliar faces, but some of the Old Guard still held court, relishing the deference that the newcomers offered them; there was old Mr. Giles, cackling over the recent profits in his leather goods trade, Mr. Showalter, still in the House of Commons from what seemed a safe borough, winning re-election on a regular basis; even former Major Baird showed up once. He was now deep into his father-in-law's iron smelting business, and had to come down to London at least once a month; and still chasing "quim" in Covent Garden out of range of his wife. And, of course, there was still Mr. Pilkington, still lean and gloomy despite the sumptuous meals that the club laid on, who'd rail over the national debt that the wars were costing the country, sure that it would all go smash.

At least the suppers were splendid, and the club's wine cellar could still offer the best selections in town, as fine as any of the prestigious gentlemen's clubs.

"Do we always dine so grandly?" Lewrie had cause to enquire at breakfast. There had been rashers of bacon, kippers, and sausages to choose from on the sideboard, scrambled eggs with hashed potatoes, thick slices of toast and butter and jams.

"Well, not usually, dear," Jessica told him over the rim of her tea cup.

"In winter, oatmeal with treacle, toast, and jam, is the usual fare. Soups and stews for dinner, and chops and vegetables for supper. Why, Alan? Do we over-feed you?" she asked teasingly.

"Any more celebratory meals and I'll need new trousers and breeches," Lewrie said, patting his midriff. "It ain't the costs, it's the *amount*, and the waste. Even the *dogs* can't eat all the leftovers."

"Well, I do imagine that part of it is Hazelwood, showing off his culinary skills, now that he has good reason," Jessica allowed. "Is it not pleasing, after the sparcity of ship-board fare you described?"

"Pleasin', aye, darling," Lewrie told her, "but every day can't be a feast day. I'd settle for *one* meat with breakfast, not three. And when winter comes, oatmeal and treacle sounds just fine."

"I will speak with him, then, darling," Jessica promised. "Yes, the house can go back to its old regimen, with perhaps but the one grand meal for Sundays . . . and when we have guests."

"That sounds fine, then," Lewrie said, stifling a burp. He had in point of fact loaded his plate with bacon, gone back for sausages, and sampled the kippers, too.

"Excuse me, Sir Alan," Pettus said, stepping into the Morning Room, "Ma'am, but we have callers."

"This early?" Lewrie griped.

"Your father, Sir Hugo, and a Midshipman Hugh Lewrie, sir," Pettus announced.

"Good God! Hugh?" Lewrie whooped, tearing off his napkin and rising so quickly that he almost tipped over his chair. "See 'em in, Pettus. See 'em in!"

He stayed in the morning room just long enough to take hold of his wife's chair to ease her to her feet before he dashed out into the hall to greet them in the foyer.

"Hugh, good Lord, where did you spring from?" Lewrie exclaimed as he greeted him, shaking his hand vigorously, and giving him a pat on the shoulder. "I do believe you've grown even taller!"

"Hallo, father," Hugh said in return, clapping Lewrie on the shoulder for a moment, "It's good to see you again, too!"

"Showed up at my door not an hour ago," Sir Hugo said. "And I thought to re-unite you at once."

Hugh had always taken after his late mother, Caroline; lighter hair, and a good head of it. He had grown to be almost two inches taller than Lewrie, and in the last few years since they'd last seen each other in Lisbon, Hugh had filled out at the shoulders, lean in the hips and waist, and had sprouted long, lean legs which made him appear even more impressive.

"You wrote that *Undaunted* paid off," Lewrie said.

"A real pity, that, father," Hugh said with a wee laugh. "She was a fine ship, and fetched us all a shower of prize-money. When you directed the squadron, we did very well upon that head, but, after Admiral Popham took command, and expanded operations, it came in like a winter snow, just piling up and piling up, hah hah!"

"Oh, Hugh," Lewrie said, stepping back a pace to stand by hise wife, "allow me to name to you Dame Jessica Lewrie. Jessica, this is my younger son, Hugh, now a Passed Midshipman between ships."

"Mister Lewrie," Jessica said as she dipped him a cursty, with a graceful incline of her head.

"Dame Lewrie," Hugh replied, with a formal bow.

"How odd to say!" Jessica said with a wee laugh. "*Mister* Lewrie, as if I'm addressing your father as if I'd never met him!"

"Get Sewallis here, and it *could* become confusing, Ma'am," Hugh told her with a chuckle of his own.

"I met him, when his frigate was launched at Chatham," Jessica said brightly, "Sir Hugo and I coached down, and it was ever so delightful an event."

"Indeed it was," Sir Hugo said.

"Coffee, tea, or have you eat yet?" Jessica offered. "I could have our cook prepare a breakfast for you."

"Grandfather laid out some quick food, soon as I surprised him," Hugh said, "but tea would be nice."

"Yes, let's go up to the drawing room and send down for tea," Jessica said. "How wonderful! Now, I have met all three of Alan's offspring. I am told, however, Mister Lewrie, that you may be the pluckier of the boys? The more playful than your brother Sewallis?"

"Well, he always was the book-ish sort, Ma'am," Hugh laughed.

Once seated in the drawing room abovestairs, Hugh commented upon how tasteful he found the furnishings, and had to stroll over to stare at his father's portrait.

"Quite a remarkable resemblance, father," he said. "So life-like!"

"Jessica painted me right here, in the front parlour," Lewrie was proud to say. "In fact, she accepted my request for her hand the day it was hung."

"You don't say!" Hugh exclaimed. "How fortuitous!"

"Heard from Sewallis, have you, Hugh?" Lewrie asked him as the tea things arrived, along with a plate of sweet bisquit and ginger snaps.

"Oh, rarely," Hugh said, accepting a cup and saucer, pouring in some cream and spooning in some sugar. "His frigate is on the North American Station, sailing out of Halifax, from there down to Spanish Florida and back. It didn't sound all that exciting to me. And since the *Leopard* had her fight with the American frigate *Chesapeake*, the Yankee Doodles have banned British warships from entering any of their ports, so, it sounds like a lot of sea time but little more."

"All that 'Free Trade and Sailors' Rights' talk?" Jessica asked.

"You keep up with such things, ma'am?" Hugh asked, surprised by a woman who followed the news.

"Well, of course, Mister Lewrie," she told him. "I am now part of our Navy, in a manner of speaking, and what may affect my husband affects me."

"Now you're a Passed Mid, Hugh," Lewrie enquired, "have you any word on when you gain your Lieutenantcy, and a new ship?"

"Well . . ." Hugh replied round a bite of ginger snap, "that was why I came to London. To see if you could be of any assistance."

Come t'the wrong shop if that's so, Lewrie sourly thought, wondering how to break the news.

"I may not be as much help as you imagine, lad," he had to tell him. "As I told your grandfather, I'm a bit under a cloud, which is why I'm ashore on half-pay at the moment."

"Envy, jealousy, spite and vindictiveness," Sir Hugo gravelled, working his mouth sourly, "and influential patrons who'd have shoved Admiral Nelson aside, so long as their protégés got advanced."

"I cannot pretend to understand all of it," Jessica chimed in, "but Alan has been treated in the vilest manner by people who either lack the skill, or the good fortune, to accomplish anything on their own."

"I . . . see," Hugh said, looking crest-fallen and asea, darting glances at everyone. "Well, ehm . . . I suppose I'll just have to trot up to Admiralty and take my chances in the Waiting Room. Brrr!"

"Surely, Captain Chalmers put in a good word for you," Lewrie said.

"I'm told he did, father," Hugh replied, "as he praised all of his officers and Mids when paying off *Undaunted*. But then he was off to commission a new frigate at Chatham. And, there was Lisbon," he added with a shrug and a grimace.

"What about Lisbon?" Sir Hugo asked.

"Well, some of the older Mids and I took a day's shore liberty, and we got a bit . . . pickled in a series of taverns, met some girls," Hugh tried to shrug off . . . or shrink into his coat . . . "took them to supper, and dancing, and were stumbling about, hanging on each other and laughing fit to bust, when Captain Chalmers came round the corner and glared at us as fierce as Moses did before he broke the *first* set of tablets. The next morning, he had us in his great-cabins and took a strip of flesh from all of us."

"Oh, God," Lewrie snorted in humour. "I can just imagine it . . . disgracing the uniform, the Royal Navy, England itself? Drink, lust, dancing, public inebriation, and fornication?"

"That pretty much covers it, aye," Hugh confessed.

"Captain Chalmers is a doughty fighter, and an excellent sea Captain," Lewrie explained to the rest, "but a holy terror when it comes t'Bible thumpin' . . . pardons, my dear," he added, leaning over towards his wife. "He always thought that I was doomed to Hell 'cause I was never *serious* enough for him."

Gawd, I was about t'blab all my doin's, mistress and all! he almost blanched; *Not bein' serious she'll understand.*

Thank God Jessica found that amusing.

Thankfully, the dogs took that moment to dash into the drawing room in a noisy tail chase, discovered people, and the aromas of the sweet bisquits.

"Here, Bisquit," Lewrie coaxed, "have a ginger snap and don't go jumpin' into anyone's lap."

"So that's the famous Bisquit?" Hugh asked. "Then who's this'un?"

"That's Rembrandt, my dog," Jessica told him. "Alan left Bisquit ashore the last time he sailed away, and they've become fast friends."

They made a fuss over the dogs, and Bisquit swarmed his master, squirming and tail-wagging for pets and more ginger snaps, climbing halfway into Lewrie's lap trying to lick his face.

"Let us show you round, Hugh," Lewrie suggested, and, after the last of the sweet bisquit and a last cup of tea, they all rose to take a tour of the house and the back garden. They ended in the front parlour so Hugh could admire more of Jessica's artistry.

"Her latest commission portrait," Lewrie said, pointing to the framed portrait. "An M.P. from a Kentish borough."

"It's done," Jessica told them. "I've let it dry, and will be picked up today, at last. Do you like the birds, Mister Lewrie?" she said, leading him to some works in progress. One was of a young girl goggling at a linnet sitting on her finger; the other was a parrot of spectacular plumage on a branch with a red berry between his beaks, and one clawed foot reaching for another.

"I had to borrow my maid and our butler, Pettus, to escort me to the exotic bird market near Billingsgate," Jessica said with the faintest of distasteful *moues*. "We could hear the fish-market women and their foul language, even from blocks away. Very educational!" she said with a shy laugh.

"Did you paint it there, ma'am?" Hugh wondered.

"Oh no!" She said with another laugh, "I did the sketching, and noted the colours, then painted it safely here."

"It's done?" Lewrie asked. "And you've no new commission?"

"Free at last," Jessica told him.

"Then, before the season's done, I've an urge to go down to Anglesgreen," Lewrie announced. "Country air, riding, Will Cony's ale, and Mistress Furlough's cooking? Charlotte's staying with the Chiswicks, as usual."

"God, I haven't seen her in *ages*!" Hugh exclaimed. "Aye, let's!"

"Oh, do invite Charlie!" Jessica pled. "He'd adore it!"

"I've a yen for the country, too," Sir Hugo chimed in. "Capital!"

"Charlie?" Hugh asked.

"Jessica's younger brother," Lewrie supplied, "and a Midshipman aboard my two last ships. He's sixteen or so, but he's shaped well. You'd like him, I think, Hugh."

"How *is* Charlotte?" Hugh pressed. "She writes so seldom that I've no idea what she's up to."

"Well, that," Sir Hugo said, making another face. "She's done two London Seasons, and a month at Bath, by now, and is still in search of a suitable husband. Picky thing. And it don't help her temper for her cousin, Diana Chiswick, to be almost engaged."

"You'll see," Lewrie said with a smirk. "We all shall. We'll all pop round the Admiralty to show our faces, then pack and coach down."

"I'll send the Furloughs a letter to prepare them," Sir Hugo promised. "We'll stay what, about a fortnight?"

"Sounds good," Lewrie agreed.

"It will be delightful . . . bliss!" Jessica rhapsodised. "Take the dogs?"

"They'd love it, too, I expect," Lewrie said, smiling widely. "We'll all three leave our address with Admiralty. Nothing will turn up in a fortnight, really. *Dun Roman,* Anglesgreen, Surrey. Sounds grand, Hugh?"

"I agree with Dame Lewrie, father," Hugh Said. "It'll be bliss!"

CHAPTER FOURTEEN

*I*t took two coaches for the trip down to Anglesgreen, Sir Hugo's for himself, Lewrie and Jessica, Hugh, and young Charlie, and a hired coach to carry Deavers, Dasher and Turnbow, and Desmond, who had been long-promised a spell in the country. Yeovill came along out of boredom, since the Lewries' cook, Hazelwood, would not allow Yeovill even to stir a pot in *his* kitchens, and Yeovill wished to get away from the tyrant for a few days.

It was slow going, initially, threading their way through Kingston, then Woking, but eventually the two coaches began to rattle along at a decent trot past the industries and crowds, and into an Autumnal bliss. Sash windows in the doors were lowered, and rural vistas took the place of row-houses and coal smoke. Fields on either side of the road swayed with late season corn crops of barley, rye, wheat, and oats, with farm workers reaping and binding in stooks, and the smell of fresh-cut grain filled the air, rivalling the flowers growing along the sides of the road. Old hedgerows rose here and there, stretching for half a mile or so, then ending to reveal another open field thick with alfalfa or lespedeza being fetched to barns for winter feed for the livestock that would not be chosen for slaughter after the first frosts. For now, cattle, sheep, and pigs grazed and fattened themselves in perfect peace, and likely looking horses gamboled and frisked.

There had been just enough rain in Surrey to staunch the usual dust in the roads, but not enough yet to turn to mud, so they all took turns leaning out the sash windows to inhale the incredibly sweet airs they could never savour in London, even on a rare hot day when no coal needed to be burned to ward off a chill or the dank.

Every couple of hours, they pulled up at a posting house or a village tavern for brief trips to the "necessary," a pint of ale for all passengers, and fresh water for the horses.

"I'll just have a few sips of yours, Alan," Jessica insisted at each stop, "or yours, Charlie. Ale embarasses me." To prove that it did, she had to stifle a ladylike burp after a few sips.

"Refreshing, though," Lewrie teased.

"Immensely," she agreed with a laugh.

"Tomorrow morning," Sir Hugo announced, "I intend a good, long ride up into the woods. Who is with me?"

"I'd be delighted," Hugh spoke up, "then, I suppose I could ride over to Governour's and see Charlotte."

"After dinner, first," Lewrie suggested. "We all can."

"Ehm, we might be a bit short on mounts for that," Sir Hugo speculated as they re-entered their coach. "Might have to take the coach, for those who are short a horse."

"So long as Charlie's a welcome member of the family," Lewrie said, rubbing his chin in thought, "and we don't have a tame mare or gelding for Jessica, shouldn't we see what's on the market?"

"They used to hold horse fairs on the commons," Hugh recalled. "Monday market days, mostly. It was great fun."

"Yes, something gentle, I beg you," Jessica said, pretending to shiver in dread. "You'd really buy me a mount of my own?"

"We most certainly shall," Sir Hugo declared.

"You don't ride often, ma'am?" Hugh asked her, and Jessica explained that she adored horses, but only rode when visiting her sisters or vicar brother's country parishes, and converting from childhood to a proper lady's sidesaddle had taken the joy from the endeavour.

"I'm *sure* to topple off backwards," she confessed with a rueful expression. "Our city parish doesn't require saddle horses. Even my father walks, or hires a hackney, to perform his duties. Charlie is the only one in our family who seems to have developed a seat." She patted him briefly on the knee. "Galloping rented horses down Hyde Park with the other imps, most-like."

"Taking turns, 'cause we didn't have enough coin to hire mounts for all of us," the younger Chenery sniggered.

"Oh, that one poor horse!" Lewrie quipped.

Guildford came and went, then the land became rural once more; at last, the turn approached for them to take the road to Aldershot, Farnham, and Fleet. And on that road, not three miles on, lay the village of Anglesgreen.

The fields and hedgerows they clattered past belonged to their neighbours, the farmhouses, rich or poor, and the laborers' cottages on the great estates, were landmarks from long country visits since 1784, even before Sir Hugo had purchased 320 acres from the late and un-lamented Phineas Chiswick for his estate. It was where Lewrie and his late wife, Caroline, had rented 160 acres and had run up a house, new barns, and stables near her brothers, Governour and Burgess—the same farm and house that uncle Phineas Chiswick had sold out from under Lewrie following Caroline's death, so Burgess and his bride, Theodora Trencher, would have a country seat.

The tannery loomed up, blessedly now out of business, shuttered but still slightly redolent of vile fumes when it rained. No one had done anything with it, and the workyard and spaces between buildings were now spiked with saplings and oddly tinged long grass.

Further along on the right lay the brickworks, which was still a going concern, and a source of employment. It seemed that the owners had branched out into dressed stone, as well. Roundabout sat cottages for workers, neat and pleasant.

A low stone wall ran a quarter-mile past the brickworks framing a field where cattle grazed, just 50 or so acres where the Embleton estate came close to town. And then came Anglesgreen's lone church, the very old stone St. George's, and its vast churchyard filled with gravestones honouring both rich and poor, bound all about by wrought iron fencing. Across the road, on their left, lay a maze of middling cottages, each with its back garden and vegetable and herb plots, with small barns, stables, or coach houses to each.

"Willam's Run," Hugh said with delight to spot the reedy stream that ran down the middle of the village, now stone-bridged in two places. Idle fishermen and half-clad boys cast their lines, or dove and splashed in the cool, slow-flowing water, and took time to wave at the coaches as they passed.

There was a wider road spearing South from the first bridge, off which lanes sprouted, where even more, newer cottages and one or two substantial houses sat. A lane ran the length of the stream, the site of a row of shops that had slowly grown over the years.

Then there was what was now being called the High Street, where even more shops did business; small emporiums, dry goods, tobacconist, a greengrocer for those who lived in the village itself and did not have gardens. And, just before the second bridge, there on their right was the Old Ploughman.

"We're stopping here!" Sir Hugo shouted to his coachman. "Ale for all, hah hah!"

In the beginning, the Old Ploughman was a smoky horror, the year of its first establishment lost in the time of William the Conqueror, a public house with smoke-stained walls and ceilings, odds and ends for tables and chairs. When Lewrie had first dined or drank there, a Mr. Beakman and his daughter ran it. It was, in point of fact, the *only* public house in Anglesgreen where Lewrie was *welcome* to drink or dine. The better sorts, of which Lewrie was definitely not one, favoured the Red Swan Inn, a long walk West down the vast commons, red brick Tudor-turned early Georgian and smug in its wealth where the few who earned or owned enough to vote met to elect themselves, or their elder sons, into Parliament or local offices.

When Mr. Beakman grew too old, Lewrie's old cabin servant and "man," then Cox'n, and Bosun's Mate, Will Cony, had retired from the sea minus a foot, but with a slew of prize-money, and had bought the Old Ploughman, married a former house servant at the Lewries, Maggie, fathered a slew of tow-headed boys. He'd prospered nicely, adding a barn and stables, a brew house for his excellent beers and ales, a few more rooms to let for weary travellers, and a covered side garden with a stone-flagged floor for summer diners and drinkers. A white wood plaque by the door bore a representation of the "Post Boy" flag, marking the Old Ploughman as the local mail drop.

"Oh, look!" Hugh exclaimed, looking towards the commons, "Hops! Waggons of hops! I'd wager Mister Cony's brewing up his winter ale, even as we stand here!"

It felt so good to be back, sitting round a large table near the doors to the side garden, which were open, with a slight breeze that brought the smells of new-cut grass and the flower planters made from half-barrels. Desmond, Deavers, Yeovill, and the younger lads took a table of their own close by.

Clump-clump-clump and there was Will Cony, himself, with his wood foot, neatly dressed in breeches, red waist-coat, white shirt and neck-stock, with a publican's blue apron atop his clothes.

"Will Cony, my good man!" Lewrie greeted him, rising to shake his hand.

"Cap'um Lewrie, my stars!" Cony chortled back. "It's been far too long since ya came home. "And Sir Hugo, Hugh, and Mistress Lew . . . pardons, Dame Lewrie! And damn my eyes, if that's Liam Desmond, Yeovill, and Michael Deavers? Welcome lads. Now, who needs an ale?"

All hands shot up, and two of Cony's strapping sons, grown to manhood, and the dark-haired serving maid, Abigail, rushed to fill piggins and fetch them to the tables, with half-pints for Dasher and Turnbow.

"You're lookin' prosperous, Will," Lewrie said after a sip.

"I'm lookin' fat as a boar hog is how I looks, Cap'um Lewrie," Cony said with a deep laugh. Indeed, he had put on considerable weight, his face had turned round, with a double chin, red cheeks, and his hair . . . it had thinned and receded, exposing a ruddy pate.

"Maggie's fine cookin', and your own beer, haw!" Lewrie said.

"Life's good, sir," Cony admitted, patting his paunch.

A moment later and Maggie Cony came bustling out from the kitchen, wiping her hands on a dish clout, bubbling over with welcome, and looking a round match to her husband. She had to give everyone a hug, though she was more reticent with Sir Hugo, Lewrie, and Jessica. Charlie Chenery was new to her, but she gave him one, anyway.

"I've a lovely batch of wee sausages on the grill," Maggie promised, "and some toast and jam'd go nice with 'em. Anyone peckish?"

"I must admit that I am," Sir Hugo said.

Things're lookin' up for Liam, Lewrie thought as he took note at the next table as Desmond flirted with Abigail, and she swished her hair, laughed, and touched him on the shoulder for a second. *Is he goin' red in the face? Liam Desmond, blushing?*

The ale was nice and hoppy, and very refreshing, the perfect blend of bitter and mild, and the sausages were hot and spicy; the toast was browned to perfection, and the jam was a thick apple butter, rich with cinnamon. They all spent a pleasant hour in the Old Ploughman, before it was time to coach on up to the house and get settled in.

"Horses, sir?" Will Cony said as he saw them to the doors, "this Monday market day. Yeomanry muster day, too. Hah! Harry Embleton showin' off his uniform. Quite a fiddle he's workin', Sir Hugo."

"What sort of fiddle?" Sir Hugo sniffed.

"He'll bring ten or twelve horses down from his pastures," Cony explained, "claim that his Yeoman Cavalry regiment needs remounts an' replacements for ones gone lame, or worse, gets the Army t'pay him for 'em, an' pockets th' cash. An' he won't have the time o' day for anyone lookin' for a saddle horse, hee hee. They'll all go for more than ten guineas. Embletons, Oakeses, Chiswicks . . . all the biggest landowners roundabout does it."

"There are other dealers, certainly," Sir Hugo said, frowning.

"Oh, aye, Sir Hugo," Cony said, "men from Aldershot, Farnham, Milford, or Liphook. You'll find somethin', sure, at decent cost."

"I'm relieved to hear that," Sir Hugo told him. "Dame Lewrie, her brother need mounts, tack, and saddles."

"Yer estate manager, Sir Hugo," Cony suggested, "Rainey? He's a good fellow. Pops in here often, and he's a rare judge o' horses. Might fetch him along."

"Well, I'm sure he is, Mister Cony," Sir Hugo allowed, "but I do consider myself able to spot a good mount." It was harder for Sir Hugo to deal with common people as easily as his son did, so he came across a tad sharp. "Good day, Mister Cony, and thank you for your victuals, your excellent ale, and your welcome."

"Always happy t'please, sir," Cony replied, all but tugging the forelock he no longer had. Lewrie shared a look with Cony on the way out to the coach, shaking hands. "It's just his way, ya know, Will," he told him.

"Oh, I knows, sir," Cony replied, "He comes by often enough when he's down from London, an' his money's good."

The house staff at *Dun Roman* paraded themselves on the pea gravel roundabout drive as the coaches rolled up, Mr. and Mrs. Furlough, the older couple who served as butler and cook, and an host of maids and footmen on staff, as well as a few hired on for the fortnight that the house would be full. Welcomes were made, luggage and chests un-loaded and carried in to the various bedchambers. Lewrie's retinue was led to the servants' quarters, where beds were already made up with fresh-laundered sheets and newly aired blankets.

Sir Hugo had not brought his usual valet down, but there was a fellow who'd served him whilst at his estate for some time to do for him. "Mister Chenery," Mr. Furlough said, "this is Richard Standish, here, will serve as your valet whilst you're here."

"Me?" Charlie gawped, surprised. "I'm to have a man? I've never had one before. Aboard ship . . ."

"If you'll follow me, sir," Standish said, waving an arm down a hall, "I'll show you to your bedchamber, and get you settled in."

"Well? Alright, I suppose," Charlie said with a pleased smile and a puzzled shrug. "Lead on, then."

At Sir Hugo's suggestion to limit the number of people needing seats in the coaches on the way down, Jessica had left her maid, Lucy, in London, too, and was introduced to a sweet-faced slip of a girl who would tend to her needs.

Half an hour later, Lewrie and Jessica strolled out to the back garden, which was mostly a well-rolled and well-trimmed lawn, with a few oaks to lend shade. Beyond lay the truck gardens, thick with tomatoes, celery, lettuce and cabbage, radishes and mild peppers, cauliflower, broccoli and Brussels sprouts. Off to one side were small fields for potatoes, turnips, and peas and beans. Day laborers were already gathering the crops for pickling, to tide the house through a long winter, and green tops were being placed in wheelbarrows to feed to the pigs.

Farming, brr! Lewrie thought, looking forward to the day that he inherited all this with a certain trepidation. When he and Caroline had had their rented farm, she, raised on a North Caroline plantation, had been the one who knew how to run a farm, an estate, the pickling and preserving, crops and livestock, and had once joked—at least he *hoped* that she'd been joking—that Lewrie knew how to raise his hat, and that was about all.

He took Jessica's hand as they strolled further along, down to the barns and stables, stout brick structures, to look over the horses.

"Ooh, Mister Deavers, they keeps rabbits!" they could hear Tom Dasher enthusing as they spotted the pens.

"Nothing better than a jugged hare," Deavers called back.

The young lads, Dasher and Deavers, had never dealt with saddle horses, or cattle, or sheep, or pigs. They had been to the forecastle manger aboard ship, but had never seen so many chickens, turkeys, or dairy cows. There was even a large pigeon coop full of strutting, cooing, fluttering squabs! And in the pastures and paddock beyond, well!

"This'un's Anson," Lewrie said, showing Jessica his favourite mount, who came to the stable door with a whicker and toss of his head in recognition, and Lewrie stroked his neck and face, his ears and forelock. "Hmm, his teeth," Lewrie noted. "Gettin' on in years, ain't you, old fellow. He's pushing twenty. I might have to put him out to pasture, and let him enjoy his last years."

"To stud?" Jessica asked, joining him in petting the horse. "I don't know much about that, but . . ."

"Anson's a gelding," Lewrie told her, "and he was only fifteen guineas in his prime, so . . . he'll graze, trot round, socialise with the other horses, and have a good, long rest."

"You'd look for a new one at the market Monday?" she asked.

"Maybe not this year," Lewrie decided. "We'll see, dear."

"Oh, I've come to love it here," Jessica cooed, leaning against him. "If no one minds, I brought my sketching materials. Your father's estate is such an inspiration to me. And the air is so fresh!"

"Well, except for the horse dung at the moment," Lewrie japed. "Let's walk down to the pastures."

Later in the day, as supper was being prepared, Lewrie, Jessica, Hugh, and Charlie Chenery sat on the long and wide front gallery, with lanthorns lit as the dusk crept over the Surrey countryside. Sherry had been served, and they sipped as they regarded the vista. Sir Hugo made his wicker chair creak as he poured himself a refill.

There was a faint wind, just strong enough to sway the hanging planters. The last flocks of birds swooped and swirled in an intricate evening dance above the trees downslope before settling to their nests. Tiny lights as small as fireflies shone from houses, shops, and a few street illuminations from Anglesgreen, from tenant cottages and great houses as darkness crept over the land. Sir Hugo rose and strode out onto the front lawn to peer into the West, and grunted satisfaction that the sunset had been one tinged with red and amber, a sure sign of good weather for the morrow.

"I must say, Sir Hugo, that your estate is a most pleasant Eden," Charles Chenery said.

"Amen to that," Hugh agreed, "Some of the happiest days of my childhood were spent here, in Anglesgreen, the countryside."

"You and Sewallis," Sir Hugo harrumphed, "if it wasn't a pack of setters, it was your wanting otters or fox kits for pets!"

"Or when father sent Charlotte a doll from South America, and a pair of big, hairy tarantulas were in the packaging!" Hugh hooted.

"She didn't mind the spiders *that* much," Lewrie reminisced, "but she wrote me and asked for a monkey!"

"See her tomorrow," Sir Hugo said, "Governour sent a note round that they'd be home . . . with some company," he hinted with a warning nod.

"Company?" Lewrie asked.

"Looking forward to seeing her, again," Hugh said, "her and the Chiswick boys."

"Company?" Lewrie asked again.

"It seems that Governour's daughter, Diana, is affianced at last," Sir Hugo told him, "He'll be there whoever he is. And the young gentleman has brought a friend of his along. Charlotte was introduced to them when she and Diana extended their husband-hunting to Bath, last summer."

"Charlotte may be engaged, as well?" Lewrie asked with a frown.

"It's as may be," Sir Hugo told him.

Oh Christ! Lewrie thought; *Am I shot of her at last? Huzzah!*

Far off, Lewrie could hear cow bells and belled rams leading the way to their feed, their barns. Almost like church bells, he fancied?

CHAPTER FIFTEEN

After breakfast, they rode or coached over to the Chiswick lands, Sir Hugo astride his blooded hunter, fractious from not being ridden often enough, Lewrie on Anson, and Hugh, Jessica, and Charlie going by coach. Down the long, gentle slope and the fine gravelled drive to near the wooden bridge cross Willam's Run, to a fork in the road short of the bridge, and then taking the turning onto another gravelled drive which followed the stream for half a mile before climbing up another low, rolling hill to Chiswick Hall.

The house and grounds had been much improved and made more stately since childless uncle Phineas Chiswick had died, and Governour, who had eaten the old man's bile for ages, had inherited thousands of acres and that mean old miser's wealth. The house staff, much larger than Sir Hugo's, turned out to bow and curtsy to their visitors, the horses were led off for water and oats, the coach un-harnessed, and Sir Hugo led the way inside.

"Aha, Sir Hugo, welcome!" Governour Chiswick boomed, standing by his wife, Millicent. "And Sir Alan and Hugh, aha, both home from the sea, at last! Dame Jessica, and who's this lad?"

"My brother Charles, Mister Chiswick," Jessica told him after a graceful curtsy, "a Midshipman aboard my husband's last two ships."

"Mister Chiswick, Mistress Chiswick," Charlie said, bowing nicely. "Delighted to make your acquaintance."

"The younger folk are in the morning room," Governour said with an expansive wave to show them to a first storey drawing room. "Come join them. Momentous news, hah hah!"

"Something about an engagement?" Lewrie asked on their way in.

"And a fine young fellow, haw haw!" Governour replied.

Governour Chiswick had once been panther-lean, a soldier and a hard man, serving as a Captain in a North Carolina volunteer regiment during the American Revolution, but, after evacuating to England when the war was lost, civilian living had had its way with him.

Governour, wealthy at last, was garbed as fine as a lord, but he had fattened up like a boar hog 'til he resembled the caricature character "John Bull" in the papers and one-sheet cartoons. Now, he was currently elected Magistrate, and was reputed to be a harsh fellow to the people brought before his swift sort of justice. Lewrie had once thought well of him, but over the years, after Caroline had been shot dead over in France during the Peace of Amiens, Governour had turned against him, imagining that his dear sister would still be alive were it not for Lewrie and his adulterous ways when overseas, for Lewrie's whim to go see Paris, when it had all been Caroline's wishes.

"Hugh!" Lewrie's termagant daughter Charlotte cooed to her brother. Much cooler, then. "Father . . . dear."

The Chiswick boys were there, young men now who had nothing on their minds but sport and horse racing, and did *something* round the estate to earn their keep. The daughter, Diana, a girl who Lewrie had always believed to be as silly, simple, and giddy as so many sheep, was standing with a young Captain in the uniform of a Light Cavalry regiment, complete with the new and stylish fur-trimmed pelisse draped over one shoulder, with both gilt-laced sleeves hanging free.

Diana could not help gushing "Sir Alan, allow me to name to you my affiance, Captain Roger Wilmoth of the Fifth Dragoons. Roger, this is Captain Sir Alan Lewrie, Baronet. He's Navy."

It was gauche and out of turn, but everyone let it slide. Full introductions were made all round in the proper way.

And who was the cavalry officer standing near Charlotte? Lewrie was named to him at last, as Captain Alexander Courtney. He was very good-looking, blond, with ringlets at the back of his neck, slim and fit, and his uniform was immaculate, and looked to be costly. Lewrie noted that Charlotte had a possessive hand on the sleeve of his coat.

Can we only hope? Lewrie thought.

"Delighted to make your acquaintance, Captain Courtney," Lewrie said by way of a beginning. "Have you and Captain Wilmoth come a long way?"

"From Aldershot, Sir Alan," Courtney told him, "our regiment has its home station there, just up the road, really. At present, we're the cadre squadron, instead of being in Spain with the rest."

Smooth-soundin' sort, Lewrie thought; *Too bright and chirpy, perhaps? I guess he'll do.*

"I will ring for fresh tea and sweets," Millicent offered, "Sit, please do."

Lewrie thought that Millicent had had a hard life being married to a fellow as blusteringly sure of himself as Governour Chiswick. She was most fashionably gowned and styled, a match to her husband, good enough for a formal ball, but she looked so old and tired for a woman in her mid-fourties.

"Home early, ain't you?" Governour asked Lewrie, and he had to give them all a sketch of his doings off Italy, and how his ship had been recalled to be de-commissioned and re-fitted before he expected.

"No matter the reasons, I am delighted to have him home!" Jessica declared. "And my brother, Charlie, into the bargain, of course."

"And to have Hugh back after his ship paid off," Lewrie added, giving Jessica's hand a pat. "Now if only Sewallis wasn't prowling the other side of the Atlantic, it'd be a grand reunion."

"Both sons in the Navy, Sir Alan?" Captain Courtney said with a faint sniff of surprise.

"Both more than willing," Sir Hugo interjected with a laugh. "I fear Sewallis is headstrong. Ran off and found a Captain and a ship that would have him as a Midshipman whilst we were kitting Hugh out to go aboard a ship of his own, haw haw."

He left out the forgeries that had allowed that!

"Wanted revenge against the French," Lewrie added.

Uh oh, here it comes again! Lewrie thought with dread, sensing Governour's scowl, and Charlotte's quick, indrawn breath and the fret lines that appeared on her forehead. The old recriminations were going to surface about her mother's murder!

"And when do you and your fiancé expect to be wed, Miss Chiswick?"

Jessica unexpectedly asked. She'd been wed long enough to hear all about it from both sides when dealing with the Chiswicks, and Sir Hugo, in the times when Charlotte had husband-hunted in the London Seasons.

"Well, I'm hoping that the nuptials may happen before Christmas, Dame Lewrie," Diana gushed, beaming at her intended.

"How splendid!" Jessica congratulated her. "In point of fact, we will be having a wedding in our household about the same time."

"Master Charles?" Hugh hooted. "Bit young, that."

"No, our butler, Mister Pettus, and my maid, Lucy," Jessica explained, laughing.

"You'll dismiss 'em, of course," Governour harumphed. "Ya can't have married folk in service."

"Mister and Mistress Furlough do quite well in my service at *Dun Roman*," Sir Hugo pointed out.

"Yes, but they're older, and won't have children running about, corrupting the heirs with common mischief," Governour insisted.

"We're converting rooms above the stable and coach house to be their lodgings," Lewrie told him. "Pettus served me well aboard several of my ships, and Jessica would hate to lose Lucy."

"Never heard the like!" Governour grumped.

"Perhaps it's too modern, uncle," Hugh sniggered.

"I've come to know them both, and I don't see why not," Charlotte stated, looking everyone in the face; a *far* too-sweet smile at Jessica and a *very* brief one for Lewrie. Jessica returned a smile in-kind, and Lewrie knew that Charlotte had *something* up her sleeve, for she was never so pleasant as when scheming to have her way. Lewrie's only question was . . . *what?*

"One doesn't raise purebred dogs in the streets with the town curs," Governour grumbled, jerking his waist-coat down below his waist band.

"And is that why none of us are invited to the great houses of the land, sir?" Jessica enquired, still smiling, but with one brow up, a sure sign to Lewrie that she was irked. "A purebred to one set may be thought curs to another."

Governour stiffened so quickly that his substantial jowls jiggled, and he let out a spluttering noise.

"Speaking of purebreds," Millicent interrupted, trying to smooth things over, "we ought to tour the stables. Our boys have acquired a brace of thoroughbred hunters."

"Hundred guineas each," one of the Chiswick boys crowed. "We'll be sailing over the hedges like larks, come fox hunting season."

"Your old horse is there, too, Hugh," Millicent said.

"Mine?" Hugh said, frowning. "Why's he here?"

"Charlotte needed something to ride, Hugh," Governour explained, "and with you gone to sea most of the last eight years, well. Needed saddling and being ridden, else he'd have gone fractious."

"I'd like him back," Hugh said, "for at least the next fortnight."

"I dearly wish we could stay longer in the country," Jessica said, "for I've come to adore it so."

"A fortnight's about as long as we can allow," Lewrie told the gathering, "Hugh, Charlie, and I must be back in London, pesterin' the Admiralty for employment."

"But if you take him back, brother," Charlotte complained, in a sulk, complete with pouty lower lip, "I'll have nothing to ride! Oh, it is so unfair! I've *always* had hand-me-downs."

"On the contrary, Charlotte," Lewrie pointed out, "when you were little, I bought you a pony, when you were older I got you a horse-pony, and then you were living with Governour and Millicent, and I was told you were provided for in that regard, whilst I was away at sea."

"But for the next fortnight . . ." Charlotte pressed.

"You'll have my horse back after that," Hugh told her, sounding a bit vexed with his sister's ways, "and in the meantime, you can go about in a coach. Aye, you'd look especially impressive in Governour's landau, with the top down."

"Isn't there to be horses for sale on the village commons, come Monday?" Captain Courtney said to her as they sat together on a settee. "You might find one to your liking, Miss Charlotte."

Awfully damned free with my *money, are you?* Lewrie fumed to himself as Charlotte cast him a hopeful smile, batting her lashes and widening her eyes.

"We *were* planning on purchasing some new mounts for Dame Lewrie and her brother," Sir Hugo allowed.

"We *could* look for a likely mare or well-behaved gelding," Lewrie said, surrendering when it appeared that he couldn't get out of it.

"Oh, father dear, that would be *wondrous!*" Charlotte exclaimed.

Father dear? Lewrie thought; *I doubt she's put those two words t'gether, the last fifteen years entire! Mine arse on a band-box, it appears I'm buyin' a whole herd o' horses! And I wonder how much peace and quiet* that'll *buy from her?*

CHAPTER SIXTEEN

Diana Chiswick and her fiancé, Captain Wilmoth, and Charlotte and Captain Courtney coached to Anglesgreen's commons on Monday, as they had to St. George's church on Sunday, in the landau with the top down, this time with their mounts' reins tied to the back. In anticipation of her victory over her father, Charlotte wore her best riding habit and boots, with a quirt in her gloved hands.

Sir Hugo, Lewrie, and Hugh rode, while Jessica and her brother were coached in a light surrey.

The Chiswick sons would have come, too, to trot and lope about to show off their hundred guinea hunters, but Governour had chores for them to perform round his vast acres.

The vast rectangular commons no longer looked quite so vast, with livestock pens erected and filled with sheep, pigs, calves, and dairy cattle, and poultry cages. Young roosters for sale to enliven someone's flocks sensed each other and crowed continually in challenge. All along the inland side of the main road there were mules, plough horses, and saddle horses for sale. The Red Swan Inn and the Old Ploughman Tavern had set up open-sided tents to sell beer and ale, and the tea and the town pastry shops had booths for their goods, as well. Farmers and their wives, with children in very loose tow made their rounds, hmming and hemming over likely beasts to shelter through the winter for Spring breeding, and over to one corner by the nearest bridge to the High Street, musicians played, and some couples danced as if it was one of the yearly town fairs.

Captains Wilmoth and Courtney handed the young ladies down, then went behind the landau to take hold of the reins of their horses, and to share a word or two discreetly.

"D'ye think Miss Charlotte will end up with a mount worth fifty guineas at the least, Alexander?" Wilmoth muttered, grinning.

"We'll see how much pelf he has, one way or another," Courtney sniggered.

"Knighted *and* made Baronet for success and bravery, was what we heard last night," Wilmoth told him. "*And* very successful when it came to prize-money. A real name in the Navy."

"Well, *do* tell, haw haw!" Courtney muttered in glee. "That makes Miss Charlotte even *more* desirable."

Lewrie's party found a place behind the Old Ploughman to tie up their saddle horses and stow the light two-horse coach, the "daisy kicker" lads who worked there quick to supply oats and water.

Jessica, too, had come to town in riding habit, her black boot toes showing beneath the hem of her skirt.

"Wearin' breeches under that?" Lewrie teased.

"Of course," Jessica tittered. "I'll not risk myself trying to ride sidesaddle on a strange horse, after all."

"And the whole parish'll be sure that my wife is as scandalous as I am," Lewrie laughed, giving her a brief hug, no matter who saw it. "Aha. Here comes Sir Harry Embleton and his wife. I wonder how many horses he's killed *this* month?"

"What?" Jessica asked, appalled.

"Been mad as a hatter, goes neck-or-nothing all his life," Lewrie told her, leaning his head close to hers. "Racin', steeplechasin', and fox huntin', and there'll be a burst heart or broken legs, and he never thinks a thing of it. The Embletons are *very* wealthy."

Sir Harry Embleton, Bt., came down the long row of horses for sale, astride a glossy black charger of at least sixteen hands, dressed out in shiny reins and saddle, with gilt-trimmed royal blue saddle pad. Sir Harry was equally resplendent in an expensive uniform of his Cololonelcy of his Yeoman Cavalry unit, with a gilt-laced and plumed bicorne hat that was so curved it almost touched his back and came down to below his nose in front. He rode with the reins in his right hand, and his left, holding a quirt, pressed against his gilt and silver trimmed sword belt, one arm akimbo. Needless to say, he surveyed all beneath him—and that included almost everyone present—with cold disdain.

His wife—Lewrie had only met her twice and couldn't recall her name—was tricked out in a matching Army red riding habit, with some gilt trim here and there, and gilt buttons. Her mount was a grey, exquisitely groomed, and was a match to her husband in obvious wealth, though she seemed as weary and worn as Millicent had; a faded beauty with high-piled and styled blonde hair.

Hard on women, Lewrie thought; *to be married to proud, hard men.*

"Sir Harry," Lewrie spoke up, doffing his civilian hat as they rode close by them, and Jessica dropped a graceful, quick curtsy.

"Ah?" Harry Embleton said, taking dubious notice. "Lewrie," he said, touching his hat with his quirt, then riding on. Dame Embleton at least gave them a wan smile, and a nod of her head.

"What's the matter with his chin?" Jessica whispered, once they were out of earshot. "It appears he hasn't any. Or any manners, either."

"Too rich t'need 'em, dearest," Lewrie told her, stifling a good laugh. "His father, Sir Romney, was a most-handsome man, but I've always thought the best part of Harry dribbled down the coachman's leg. There is a tale that the attending doctor pulled him from the womb by his chin. You get a good look at him sideways on, you could swear he resembles an otter, hah hah!" Despised me for ages, he has."

"Whyever would he, Alan?" Jessia asked, linking arms with him to stroll the horse lines.

"Well, at one time, when I was really young and foolish," Lewrie explained, "back in Eighty-Seven, and I'd just come back from the Far East, I rode down to spend some time with the Chiswicks, and Caroline and I spent a lot of time together. Back then, Harry Embleton had his eye on her, too, but . . . she chose me, and Harry bein' Harry, didn't much care for it. There was a hunt party, and somehow my old cat, William Pitt, who'd been stayin' with the Chiswicks whilst I was away, got treed by the pack of hounds.

"I was under the low-ish bough, tryin' t'coax him t'jump down in my lap, and Harry shouldered my horse out of the way, lashin' at the limb and the cat, cursin' a blue streak. I got Pitt to jump down at last, and Caroline rode up with fire in her eyes, called him a cruel brute . . . he said something unflatterin', and she lashed *him* with her reins, right in the face and made his nose spout claret.

"And that's why I'll drink and sup at the Old Ploughman the rest of my life, and not the Red Swan, darling," Lewrie concluded with a laugh. "Sir Romney was gracious enough to invite us to social doings at Embleton Hall a time or two, but Harry and I haven't shared two or three civil words all this time. Holds a grudge well, he does."

"The painting of your late wife hung in our bedchamber here," Jessica mused, turning somber for a moment."

"Done by an exiled artist in the Bahamas, a 'remittance man,'" Lewrie breezed off. "Not really all that *good*, or accurate."

"Ehm, close enough, I'd imagine," Jessica said, "She was lovely, and even average talent limned her so. There was something striking about her eyes, and the hint of a smile. She must have been a spirited woman, someone quite formidable."

"Aye, she was," Lewrie agreed, in sad remembrance, "but . . . so are you, Jessica. More fetching, much sweeter, and dearer to me. I thank the Lord your brother wished to go to sea, and I met you. I dare say you're makin' an honest man o' me, my love."

That was rewarded with a full-throated laugh, a hug, and a stolen kiss.

"Speaking of Charlie," Jessica said, nodding down the line of horse dealers. "I think he's found himself a horse. It is so kind of you and your father to buy him one."

Sir Hugo, Hugh, and Charles Chenery were inspecting a bay gelding, looking at teeth, hooves, and pasterns, feeling over his legs and neck.

"He could do you quite well, Charles," Hugh was saying as Lewrie and Jessica joined them.

"How old, sir?" Sir Hugo asked the owner.

"He's a three-year-old, yer honour," the dealer explained, "he's a good goer, stout and sound. Won't win any races with him, nor force him t'jump hedges an' fences, but he'll bear ya fer hours on end. He's tractable, well broken, Onliest problem, an' I'll tell ya true, is that he tends t'balk when put to steep places, goin' up or down."

"Care to try him, Mister Chenery?" Sir Hugo offered.

"Aye, Sir Hugo, I would. With your permission, sir?" he said to the owner, who handed over the reins and offered cupped hands for his left foot. Charlie got astride, clucked his tongue and kneed his boot toes and off he went at the walk, then a trot, up the road towards the Red Swan Inn, assaying an easy lope.

Charlie was back in five minutes, patting the bay's neck as he returned to the small paddock, the horse arching his neck and lifting his hooves as if as pleased with his rider as the rider was with him.

Twenty five pounds was quoted, Sir Hugo countering with twenty, and, after some haggling, the bay gelding was bought for £23/10, and their new horse was led away to join their others behind the tavern.

They had to step back against the rope lines as a troop of Harry Embleton's Yeoman Cavalry came trotting by by-fours. Captains Wilmoth and Courtney, with Diana and Charlotte, were close to joining them, on the opposite side of the High Street, calming their cavalry horses as the troop passed them.

"So, Sir Alan, Sir Hugo, what do the pickings look like?" Captain Courtney cheerfully asked.

"Found a good mount for Mister Chenery, at a good price," Sir Hugo told him. "Have to lead it home, since all my spare tack and saddles are up at my place."

Charlotte began to skip along the rope lines, stroking and eyeing likely horses, all of them, Lewrie noted, at least fifteen hands high, and conformed like hunters. How much *would* she cost him?

"Oh, hallo, and how are you?" Jessica cooed at a small-ish horse that was pacing round the next paddock. "Come here, sweet thing. I've some treats for you."

"See something likely, dear?" Lewrie asked her.

"That dapple grey, Alan," Jessica said, busy extending a floret of cauliflower over the rope line to entice the horse, which perked up its ears, raised its head and cocked it to one side for a second.

"That cobby, shaggy thing?" Hugh snorted in derision. "Fourteen hands at the most, maybe thirteen."

"Reminds me of the hired prad you ride in Hyde Park," Lewrie said.

"Come here, darling," Jessica coaxed, adding a length of carrot to further entice the horse. That did it. The grey shouldered through its paddock mates in a trot and took the carrot from her flat palm, munching away as Jessica reached out to give her some tentative pats. A snort and toss of its head, and Jessica reached into her jute bag for a quartered apple, which went down well, too. More carrot, more cauliflower, another bit of apple, and, nectar of Heaven, a lump of sugar! There came a whicker of thanks and appreciation.

"Looks stout," Sir Hugo commented, peering the horse over.

"There's a likely mare yonder," Hugh said, pointing up the line. "Let's see her," and they strolled beyond to the next paddock, but were stopped by a loud whinny from the grey, which pressed itself against the ropes dividing its pen from the next up the line, head-tossing and pawing the ground.

"I think I've made a friend," Jessica laughed, going back to give the dapple grey strokes on its nose, face, and neck, and playing with its mane.

"If we *must*," Charlotte could be heard whispering exasperation.

"Father, could you and Hugh go with Charlotte and find her one that you think suits?" Lewrie bade. "Not *too* dear, if ya don't mind."

He turned back to find the dapple grey rubbing its cheek against Jessica as she hugged it and cooed to it, whickering back softly.

"Well, hallo, sir . . . ma'am," the owner said, coming up and doffing an old leather tricorne hat. "Ya like Bobs, do ya? He's a fine little horse, a three-year-old gelding, an' as gentle as a baa-lamb. Fourteen hands as ya kin see. His dam was an ambler, which is why he looks a tad shaggy. His sire was a hunter. Bit of an accident, that."

"You're from Liphook, sir?" Lewrie asked, grinning. "You're the man I rented an ambler from, four years ago, while I was healing up."

"Oh, yessir, that I am! Thomas Jeffcock, an' glad t'make yer acquaintance."

Lewrie introduced himself and Jessica, and shook hands with Mr. Jeffcock. "My wife is in need of a gentle saddle horse when we come down to the country. A baa-lamb, you say?"

"Sweet as honey, sir," Jeffcock boasted, "Bobs has took after people once he was weaned. Loves the attention, pettin', groomin', an' his treats. Loves pears in the Autumn. My daughter and t'other kids've ridden him often. Mixed breed as he is, there's not much of a market for him, so we had him gelded. He's a bit of an imp, Bobs is, and loves t'play pranks. Like t'try him, ma'am?"

"Oh, I would!" Jessica exclaimed quickly. "Have you a saddle?"

"Well, not a lady's saddle, ma'am, not here with me," Jeffcock apologised. "I could ask round . . ."

"A man's saddle will do just as well," Jessica told him, rubbing the top of the horse's nose and pressing her cheek against his.

"Well . . . if ya want," Jeffcock said with a puzzled shrug. "Be back in a tick."

"You're not going to scandalise the whole village?" Lewrie asked.

"Yes!" she laughed, beaming impishly, "I think I shall!"

A saddle and bridle was produced, cinched, then tightened once more after a knee against Bobs's belly. "He thinks it's funny to puff up an' let the saddle slip," Jeffcock explained. He half-knelt, offering cupped hands for Jessica's left foot, and she swung up onto the saddle, looking left and right to slip her boot toes into the iron stirrups. "A good part o' bein' half ambler is that he got his dam's endurance. He's right happy at trot, lope, an' canter, but gallopin' for long don't suit him, ma'am."

"I'll keep that in mind, thank you, Mister Jeffcock," Jessica said with a sunny smile, flicking the reins against Bobs's neck. The gelding swung his head about to look her in the eyes, sniffed at her left boot toe, then nodded his head and set off at a walk up the lines.

"She'll never put him to a gallop," Lewrie told the owner. "In Hyde Park, she rents a grey mare much like this'un."

"An' do she ride astride in Lon'on, too, sir?" Jeffcock asked.

"Unfortunately, yes, when she can get away with it!" Lewrie told him with a laugh. "Ehm . . . not much demand for a half-breed ya say, Mister Jeffcock?"

"Bobs is more a pet, sir, spoiled an' fed year round," Jeffcock said with a speculative look. "Kids'll be sorry t'see him go, but . . . I need the stable space for more likely horses that'll fetch more. I'm thinkin' . . . thirty five pound, sir."

"We'll see how she likes him," Lewrie replied.

Sure enough, up the High Street and in the more open ground by the Red Swan, people were pointing, guffawing, smiling and tittering at the sight of a woman astride a less than impressive horse. That made no difference to Jessica, who was intent on her seat, and keeping her head up and her back straight, and her heels down. It didn't seem to affect Bobs, either, who was now at a gentle lope, head up and nodding. He wheeled round just shy of the stableyard of the Red Swan and got reined back to a canter on the way back.

Charlotte, Diana, and the Cavalry officers were sniggering as Jessica went past them, and Lewrie saw Charlotte sneering openly at the sight. Hugh hadn't seen Jessica ride yet so he stood with his mouth agape; Sir Hugo and Charlie Chenery had, and merely shrugged.

Bobs was well-gaited and obedient to light touches on the reins. He came to a walk, then a halt just by his paddock, and Jessica swung off and hopped down, beaming from ear to ear. "Oh, he's perfect!" she cried, standing by Bobs's head with the reins in her hands.

"You're sure, love?" Lewrie asked, grinning himself. "Mister Jeffcock,

I've been called a fool who always pays full price, but in this instance, thirty five pounds will suit. Shake on it?"

"Yessir, let's do," Jeffcock agreed.

"Now, we'll have to find something suitable for my daughter," Lewrie decided aloud. "You have a horse, dearest." In preparation for purchasing horses, Lewrie had gone to Coutts' Bank and withdrawn £300, all in the new-fangled paper notes, unfortunately, that weren't always welcome in the country, but Mr. Jeffcock was happy to fold the notes and stick them in a pocket of his corduroy waist-coat. And Bobs got another bit of carrot before he and Jessica joined the others.

"That was what you were looking for, Dame Jessica?" Charlotte simpered. "An odd choice of horse, I must say."

"*Exactly* the sort of horse I sought, my dear," Jessica rejoined with a too-sweet smile, listing Bobs's good qualities. "And, have you found Miss Charlotte a proper mount?"

"We have been discussing that fellow there, Dame Lewrie," Capt. Courtney said, pointing to a tall roan. "Fifteen hands, well-formed, and perhaps has a touch of the Arabee in him."

"He's beautiful!" Charlotte enthused.

"He's a stallion, girl," Sir Hugo said dismissively. "Too much spirit for a young lady to handle."

"Looks more a steeplechaser to me," Hugh opined.

"Seventy guineas, though," Sir Hugo added. "From the Embleton stables."

"Fit for the hunt, not a saddle horse," Lewrie stuck in.

"I could hunt, steeplechase," Charlotte said with one of her patented pouts.

"Haw haw haw!" Hugh roared, startling the nearest horses, "You have *never* ridden to hounds, sister, and when dared to gallop cross-country and Devil take the hindmost, you always begged off! You said it wasn't lady-like!"

"Something gentler, Charlotte," Lewrie suggested, "perhaps a mare. Gallopin' on a sidesaddle's too risky."

"Definitely," Jessica said with a deprecating laugh. "I confess freely that I am not a skilled horsewoman."

"Is *that* why you *straddle* a horse . . . ma'am?" Charlotte asked, making it sound close to a sneer.

"Of *course* it is . . . my dear," Jessica replied in kind.

So much for peace, quiet, and "dear father," Lewrie thought with a sneer of his own; *and she ain't even got her horse yet! Should've made her sign a contract, or something.*

"Let's look in the next paddock," Lewrie suggested, but up rode Sir Harry Embleton, Bt., on his tall black charger, still looking imperious, with his left hand on his sword belt.

"Sir Hugo, down from London, hey? Miss Charlotte, Hugh, back at home, what?" he intoned, looking down his nose. He ignored Lewrie and Jessica, turning his attention to the Army officers. "Miss Diana, my congratulations on your engagement. Now, who would these two fine fellows be?"

He was introduced, and leaned back in his saddle, stretching out his elegantly booted legs in the stirrups. "Down from Aldershot, are you? Social visit? We're about to run my battalion through its paces. I trust you'll find my troopers able, hey?"

"But, if you've come to recruit," Sir Harry added, "I warn you now. I'll not have it. I will not give up a single man after training them, equipping them, mounting them, and arming them, hear me?"

"Sir Harry, Colonel sir," Captain Wilmoth spluttered, stunned by such a welcome, "We are not here to recruit. Courtney and I were invited to ride over to post our first banns this Sunday past."

"We'll see about that," Sir Harry warned them. "Lewrie."

"Sir Harry?" Lewrie had to reply.

"Saw that shambles your wife was riding," Sir Harry sneered. "And rather commonly, too. You here to buy horses?"

"For Charlotte, now," Lewrie told him.

"Always happy to oblige my good neighbours, and long-time friends, the Chiswicks," Sir Harry announced, with no change in his angry tone, "I've many fine mounts yonder. Take your pick, Miss Charlotte. For you, Lewrie, and Sir Hugo of course, one hundred guineas will obtain any horse you wish."

"Except for the ones you're goin' t'flog off on Horse Guards for remounts, Harry?" Lewrie said with a sly smile. "How much does the Army pay you apiece?"

Harry Embleton's face went red and flushed, and he rose in his stirrups, astounded to be "fronted" like that. His left hand with the leather quirt rose as if to strike Lewrie, but, considering his past experience with horse whips and reins, he lowered it just as quickly.

"Goddamn your blood, Alan Lewrie!" Harry hissed, then sawed the reins to force his charger to back a foot or two and turn about.

The ladies were scandalised by such a foul curse, the men sucked in their breaths at such a crude effrontery . . . and Lewrie let out a laugh, a long and loud one. "We'll not be buyin' anything from *his* stock," Lewrie told the party. "Let's go look elsewhere. And then, I think it's time for some of Will Cony's excellent ale."

They found Charlotte a suitable horse, a dark brown mare with a set of white feet, white blaze on her nose, and light brown mane and tail. She *seemed* pleased enough, but the mare wasn't a hundred guinea mount, but only fourty five pounds. There would be pouts and a rant later, Lewrie was mortal-certain.

CHAPTER SEVENTEEN

*F*or the most part, the rest of the fortnight in the country went delightfully. Breakfasts simple and tasty, rides cross Sir Hugo's acres, and up the gentle slopes into the woods for the vistas and the cooler air and breezes. Visiting calls upon those families in Anglesgreen friendly to Sir Hugo, and the Lewries, and receiving company for several hours. Fine suppers, music and singing afterwards, and even some impromptu dancing in the drawing room.

Lewrie was happy to see Jessica revel in their brief taste of country life, on her morning or late afternoon rides on Bobs, going so far as to get out brushes and currycombs to groom her horse, instructed by Sir Hugo's head groom. When inspired by something that caught her eye, she simply had to sketch it, fussing and peering over her work 'til satisfied with the composition and the likeness, humming sweetly with a half-smile ever on her lips.

Visitors called upon them, too; Charlotte and Capt. Courtney, seemingly a couple, and Diana and her intended. They were invited to dine twice, and were led round the estate on a mid-day ride. Captain Courtney was surprised by the style of *Dun Roman*, not the two-storey brick pile usually found round Anglesgreen, but a one-level, expansive *bungalow* in the fashion of houses Sir Hugo had gotten acquainted with when serving in the East India Company Army. All found the wide and deep galleries front and back quite novel. And of course, the furnishings and decor were luxurious, if a tad exotic, with collections of Hindoo *tulwars*, daggers, and spears that covered the walls here and there, and the tiger skin rug, head, fangs, and all in one room.

"Why's Captain Courtney hangin' round Anglesgreen so long? Does he not have duties at Aldershot?" Lewrie grumbled one mild and sunny mid-morning as they returned their mounts to the stables after a ride down to the village so Jessica could do some shopping to see just what was available in the stores.

"He *may* be developing a fondness for Charlotte, Alan," Jessica speculated, leading Bobs to his stall and giving him a hug and kiss.

"Accompanying his fellow officer?" Hugh said, shrugging his own puzzlement.

"Shopping," Sir Hugo cackled. "He looks at everything as if he's shopping, and valuing what things are worth."

"I'd have thought that Captain Wilmoth didn't need his best man, if that's what Captain Courtney is, escorting him all hours of the day and night," Charlie Chenery said with a snigger. "Come to think of it, can they *both* stay away from their regiment for all *three* banns to be read at Saint George's? What about the banns at *his* home parish, and introducing Miss Chiswick to *his* family, and the rest of her kin?"

"Enjoy your fodder and oats, sweet Bobs," Jessica said to her horse as he was un-saddled and led into his stall.

"It is most peculiar, yes," Sir Hugo agreed. "Once back in London, I've a mind to call upon some of my old friends at Horse Guards and ask about our Captain Courtney."

"You don't imagine he's a fortune-hunter, do you, Sir Hugo?" Jessica asked as she pulled off her riding gloves. "Weighing up what Charlotte might be worth?"

"He very well might be," Sir Hugo told her. "I've seen the sort in my days in the Army," he said with a prim sniff.

God help us if you haven't, Lewrie thought, recalling Sir Hugo's false marriage to his own mother, his abandonment of her when he discovered they weren't really wed, and skipping off with her jewels, along with the man's long career of wooing, even marrying, rich widows more lonely than wary! It wasn't just stolen loot from the Far East that had bought Sir Hugo his house, his estate and acres, and all of his luxury!

"And Charlotte may be gettin' desperate," Lewrie said. "Mean to say, she wasted two whole Seasons huntin' a husband in London, goin' after someone with a title, and most-like dismissin' a myriad of suitable young men 'cause they weren't lofty enough for her ambitions."

"Good Lord," Hugh exclaimed, "is that the way she's been going about it? What does she expect, the Prince of Wales?"

"Unfortunately yes, Mister Lewrie," Jessica said with a *move* and a toss of her head. "With Alan away, it fell to me and your grandfather to squire her round, when I couldn't talk my way out of it, and your sister went about things with her nose in the air, curt and dismissive to most young men, and all but throwing herself at anyone with a title due them, or great wealth."

"And Governour heartily encouraged her," Sir Hugo added. "He asked me, as a Knight of the Garter, to get her presented at Court! Trick her out in a tiara? I *found* them a perfectly good buttock-broker, for God's sake! Charlotte, I was assured, was introduced to an host of men of good families, and good prospects."

"I'm sorry to say that, once home from arranged social doings, she sneered at them all," Jessica confided to them.

"And, what if this Captain Courtney does ask for her hand," Hugh asked, "what will we do?"

"If he turns out to be a mountebank, a fortune-hunter, I'll tell her 'no,'" Lewrie declared.

"Aye, father, make your enquiries, as soon as we get home. If she really wants him, she'll have to coach off to Scotland, and God help her. She'll still get her 'dot' of two hundred pounds a year, but it's more than likely that it'll go for her husband's mess bills and fancy uniforms."

"Good," Jessica stated with a firm nod, "She never listened to me, or heeded my advice. I'm the interloper who supplanted her mother, after all, near her age. She *has* been a trial, your sister, Mister Lewrie. I'd have thought that having Captain Courtney here, getting a new horse, seeing you, again, after such a long time, would mellow her, but . . . well, you've seen how dismissive she is of me."

"We all know, dear," Lewrie said, taking her hands in his. "And I must say you've borne it like a martyr, and *tried* to befriend her."

"Hear hear!" Sir Hugo boomed.

"Come to think upon it," Hugh japed, "I'm even *closer* to your age, ma'am, haven't known you a dog watch, but *I* like you!"

"Oh, Mister Lewrie . . . Hugh . . . thank you for that!" Jessica said with a whoosh of relief, and a beaming smile. She gave him a tentative hug and a dry peck on his cheek.

"Well, now we're kin," Hugh suggested, "it *does* sound rather awkward to call me Mister Lewrie. I would prefer Hugh. I must allow that I would feel uncomfortable calling you 'mother,' might I be given the right to address you by your given name?"

"Oh, of course!" Jessica replied.

"The Lord pity us all, about Charlotte," Sir Hugo said with a deep sigh as they started to walk up to the house. "Ehm, do any of you feel peckish? Mistress Furlough told me that one of my cottagers got some fine fish from the stream."

"Fish sounds fine!" Lewrie exclaimed.

Other joys of the countryside were the rides that Lewrie and his wife took alone, with a blanket, a wicker basket filled with bread and sandwich makings, a mustard pot, and a bottle of wine, just ambling along 'til they found an open spot with a vista downhill to the fields and the village, or a shady spot up in the woodlot or forest atop the back acres, where they could talk, laugh, and kiss, or even nap and drowse, 'til Anson and Bobs got tired of cropping grass and nickered to be up and doing.

When Jessica got inspired to sketch, she sometimes took Charlie along, leaving Lewrie to try his hand at fishing (at which he was not very successful, or skilled), shooting at targets with firearms borrowed from his father's vast collection, or enjoying a book in the drawing room. Charlie got tired of being shanghaied into escort duties, and usually spent his time round the stables, hanging out and yarning with Deavers, Desmond, Yeovill, and the younger lads.

Desmond seemed to spend quite a lot of his time down in the village, at the Old Ploughman, making excuses to be in the company of Miss Abigail. Yeovill found use of his idle spare idyll in the kitchens, where he and Mrs. Furlough jawed about foreign dishes that did not require "foreign kickshaw" sauces that could go bad so quickly. And she allowed him to prepare a meal, now and then.

And, when the hours grew late, and everyone retired for the night, Lewrie and his wife could toss back the bed covers and make love by the light of a single candle, then snuggle up like spoons, cooing, whispering, and chuckling to each other 'til sleep claimed them, making up for all the lonely nights spent apart and lonely when he was overseas.

⚓

Fortunately, after those first *rencontres* with the Chiswicks, and the Embletons, they only had to see them at St. George's of a Sunday, Sir Harry giving the entire Lewrie party the "cut sublime" as if they were back in London, and they ran into the Chiswicks when all were in the village to shop, up to the moment when Governour took Millicent to the Red Swan Inn for their libations, and the people with Lewrie to the Old Ploughman.

Of course, at the end of their enjoyable fortnight, all of the families shared a last supper, where everyone was on their best behaviour, best manners, and all wearing genteel Public Faces as if they were the best of friends, of kin. And this time, without the presence of Captains Wilmoth and Courtney.

And that next morning, very early, they said their goodbyes to the Furloughs and the house staff, loaded up their chests and luggage, and set off for London. Though not without a tearful goodbye down by the stables, where Jessica found it so hard to part from Bobs, giving him her last pets and strokes, and an apple, a pear, some carrots, and a last lump of sugar. He neighed several minutes after she walked away.

BOOK THREE

I think Crab my dog to be the sourest-natured dog
that lives. My mother weeping, my father wailing; my
sister crying; our maid howling; our cat wringing her
hands, and all our house in a great perplexity-yet did not
this cruel-hearted cur shed one tear. He is a stone, a very
pebble stone and has no more pity in him than a dog.
WILLIAM SHAKESPEARE, *THE TWO GENTLEMEN OF
VERONA*, ACT II, SCENE III

CHAPTER EIGHTEEN

"Going to Admiralty today?" Jessica asked him as they sat down to breakfast their first morning back in London.

"Aye, me, Charlie, and Hugh," Lewrie told her after a tasty first sip of creamed and sugared tea. "Put in an appearance, let 'em know to send any correspondence here, and remind 'em we're still alive and available. And what are you up to today, dear?"

"I'll sort through my sketches and decide which I'll begin work on first."

"Something about Bobs?" he teased.

"Oh, of course!" Jessica sunnily admitted. "Oh, Rembrandt!"

Her dog was at her end of the morning room table, whining for something to eat. Lewrie could look down to his right and see Bisquit, whom he'd already given a bit of buttered toast, licking his chops and shuffling his front paws in hope of more.

"We really shouldn't spoil them with table scraps," Jessica said, even though she slipped Rembrandt a piece of bacon.

"They're *supposed* t'be spoiled," Lewrie said with a grin.

"But, when we have guests . . ." Jessica said with a quick frown. "Oh, well. I suppose we could shut them up belowstairs in the kitchen."

"Where the leftovers are, hey?" Lewrie sniggered.

"Alan," Jessica said, turning sobre. "Do you really imagine that you'll be called back to sea? Call me perverse, but . . . the influence against you seems so powerful that, if you do not get a new ship or a new active commission, it would please me to have you here with me for a long, peaceful time."

"I'd love that, too, darling," Lewrie truthfully said, "but, as long as we're at war I'd feel I was shirking my duty. I have to *try* to be employed, even if it kills my soul to be apart from you.

"Now, when France is beaten, and Bonaparte gets hung, and peace comes at last," Lewrie went on more hopefully, "I'll be more than glad t'stow my uniforms away, deep in a chest, and never set foot on a ship the rest of my life."

"Pray God peace comes soon," Jessica said.

"Amen t'that," Lewrie agreed. "Good omelette this morning. All cheesy and onion-y."

After breakfast, Lewrie went up to their bedchamber to sponge off and shave, then don his best-dress uniform, upon which Deavers had affixed his Knight of The Bath star. He grabbed up his hat and trotted down to the ground storey to take up his showy presentation sword, popping into Jessica's front parlour studio, where she was sorting through her many sketches. He gave her a hug round the waist and a peck on her cheek.

Sure enough, there were several sketches of her horse, Bobs, a colourful hen with her yellow chicks crowding round her, a dairy cow and her calf rubbing cheeks, a village scene with the Old Ploughman in the centre, and a sketch of Hugh standing by his horse's head.

"I may do this one first," Jessica said, spreading out the drawing of Hugh. "I'll re-do it from the waist up, not full length . . . if I can convince him to sit for me, that is."

"And take him away from his entertainments, haw?" Lewrie said with a guffaw. "If he isn't appointed to a new ship, he may have all the time you need . . . and my father'd be pleased t'have it."

"Off you go?" Jessica asked, turning to hug him.

"Off I go," Lewrie replied, giving her a lingering kiss. "And off *we* go. I'll have t'collect Charlie and Hugh, first. Have a good day, my love."

Charles Chenery was easy to round up; he was just coming up the street when Lewrie stepped outside. Some of the prize-money that the lad had garnered under Lewrie's command had gone for a newer, better fitting uniform, and the showy new dirk at his side.

"Hah!" Lewrie greeted him, "Turned out as fine as Sunday Divisions. I'll wager you even washed behind your ears! Let's whistle up a hackney and go pick up Hugh."

Minutes later, Passed Midshipman Hugh Lewrie tumbled into the hired coach, turned out as immaculately as an illustration of what a Navy Mid should look like. Though he did look a bit under the weather.

"Did you go caterwauling last night, son?" Lewrie asked him.

"I played backgammon with grandfather," Hugh sheepishly said, "late into the night, and matching him brandy for brandy."

"Oh, that'll put you in a coma," Lewrie laughed. "The man has a limitless ability to put away spirits. If you nod off, the Waiting Room's the perfect place for it. Coachee? Admiralty if ya please!"

The various roads that led to Westminster were teeming with an host of waggons and coach traffic, making their journey longer than Lewrie had estimated. Somewhere along the way, as their hackney was brought to a full stop, Charlie jerked his head towards Hugh to direct Lewrie's attention. Sure enough, Hugh had slumped down on the bench seat with his head lolling over so far it appeared that he had broken his neck, with his mouth half open, dead asleep!

"Never, Charlie, *never* drink with my father," Lewrie cautioned. "I'm surprised Hugh managed t'dress himself and get the buttons done up in the right holes!"

"Should we wake him, sir?" Charlie asked.

"Lord no, not 'til we get there," Lewrie told him. "Just take off his hat so it don't get crushed."

At last the coach clattered up to the curtain wall adorned with the stone porpoises, and rocked to a stop. Charlie got out first to lower the iron steps, followed by Lewrie, who paid the coachman, and at last, Lewrie stuck his head into the coach to shout "Wakey-wakey, show a leg, lash up and stow!" at the top of his voice.

Hugh came awake with a start, mouth agape, eyes un-focussed, and sliding off the padded bench seat to the coach's floor in a tangle of arms and legs. "What?!" he croaked. "What?"

"We're here, lad," Lewrie said, grinning with delight. "Put a shine on."

Hugh managed to scramble out of the coach and lurch to his feet outside. Charlie handed him his hat, grinning impishly.

They walked cross the courtyard, stopping for a mug of tea for Hugh to brighten him up before confronting the tiler, another of the Greenwich Pensioners who delighted to taunt Captains and Admirals who wished entry.

"Mornin' to ya, sirs," the burly old retiree said, doffing his hat, "an' good luck t'ya all, for it's a rare mob in there, t'day, not a seat t'be had, an' if ya don't have an appointment, God help ya."

He swung the massy door open for them and they strode in, putting on confident faces and determined smiles, which became hard to keep as they beheld the crowd already inside the Waiting Room. Officers and Mids stood arsehole-to-elbow, and every seat was taken, as the tiler had told them. People tried to pace about with an eye peeled for the fortunate fellow whose name was called to be summoned abovestairs, and ready to spring, hurdle, or trample their fellow officers to lay claim to it.

Hell, there's a Rear-Admiral in here! Lewrie thought; *Even the high-ranked are havin' t'beg!*

Clerks threaded their ways up and down the stairs, and in the hallway outside the Waiting Room, at their best pace, some with sea charts fetched from the basements, others with thick sheaves of official papers from one office to the next. Those who didn't have a burden were continually stopped by officers wishing for their names to be noted down as present and seeking an interview.

"Have we declared war on somebody new?" Charlie asked, gazing about in awe. "It looks extremely busy."

"Aye, I've never seen it so crowded," Lewrie said, shrugging, and trying to snag a familiar-looking clerk to the First Secretary of the Admiralty, Mr. Croker. Lewrie had long before labelled the principal pair of clerks as "the happy-making one" and the "bugger off one," the first who did the summoning, and the second who delivered the regrets. He managed to get their names scribbled down and their presence recorded at last.

"I wonder if there's anyone I know in here," Hugh speculated.

"In all my years, I never have run into anyone I know," Lewrie admitted. "Backgammon, was it, Hugh? Did he trounce you?"

"Not at first," Hugh confessed, "but the drunker I got . . ."

"Any wagers on it?" Lewrie asked. "No? There's a blessing. My father showed you rare mercy. The last time I played against him, I lost eleven shillings, and he cackled his glee like a Demon!"

"Well, as I sloped off to bed at last, I *did* hear him wheezing with mirth," Hugh related with a faint groan.

"By the by," Lewrie told him, "Jessica did a sketch of you and your horse, and she wishes to make a portrait of it. She asked me if you'd not mind sitting for her a few times, so she can paint you for your grandfather."

"Oh, well," Hugh said, mulling that over, "I suppose I could. If I don't gain a new berth soon, I'll have all the spare time in the world." He yawned widely, then yawned again, as if his jaw was being un-hinged. Lewrie screwed up his face in imagined pain.

They paced, looking down at the toes of their fresh-blacked boots, and hands in the small of their backs. Hugh and Charlie, with less dignity to preserve, now and then leaned against a wall to chat, out of the way of the press of bodies. Lewrie nodded and smiled at officers he did not know, exchanging pleasantries. He stood, arching his aching lower back, curling his toes in his new boots. Beached Lieutenants chatted him up now and then, wondering if he would be in need of officers aboard the new ship they imagined he was there to get, and he had to dis-appoint them by saying that he was between commands. After a while, he found it harder to say, not without a satisfying snarl. He strove *not* to pull out his pocket watch to see how long they had been waiting.

Finally, hunger drove him to hunt up that clerk, inform him that he and his fellows would be going out to dine, and gathered up Hugh and Charlie to exit the building, cross the courtyard, and repair to an ordinary close by. He treated, since Midshipmen earned very low pay to begin with, and when un-employed did not receive half-pay. A plate of sliced beef, boiled potatoes, rye bread, and mushy peas, with an ale each seemed to restore Hugh, who called for a piece of currant duff with treacle.

"Ehm, how much longer should we stay, sir?" Charlie asked once they left the ordinary and walked back to Admiralty.

"It's half past one now," Lewrie replied, "so, let's give it 'til three, and we'll call it a day. After that, let's come here only once a week. There's too much desperation and misery in there t'suit me."

"And bring along a whacking thick book," Charlie japed.

Once back to their slow, idle pacing about, it was Lewrie's turn to feel the need to yawn, and wish for a chair where he could take a needful nap. He did sneak a peek at his watch, finding that an hour had passed, and there remained but a half-hour 'til his intended departure. He closed his eyes, nodding and lowering his chin to his chest.

"Is Captain Sir Alan Lewrie here?" a clerk called out, waking Lewrie with a start.

"Here!" he called back.

"Sir, the Second Secretary, Mister John Barrow, wishes to speak with you," the clerk imparted. "If you will follow me?"

"I s'ppose I could find the time," Lewrie japed. "Lead on."

He had not dealt with Barrow before, didn't know the man from Adam, and actually had to be shown to the proper office. He entered as Barrow rose from behind his desk and offered him a seat.

"I have read your accounts of your latest doings in the Mediterranean with great interest, Sir Alan," Barrow began, hands steepled atop a pile of documents. "I gather that Rear-Admiral Sir Thomas Charlton and you conceived the idea of amphibious landings, and that you, with the aid of Captain Middleton, brought the concept to fruition. A novel idea, that, and a mostly successful one."

"Unfortunately, Mister Barrow, 'novel' and 'experimental' ideas are usually orphans," Lewrie replied. "But, thankee for finding it successful."

"The First Secretary and I found it odd, though, Sir Alan, that your ship, ah . . . the *Vigilance*, was recalled, and another officer was appointed to replace you, just as you were hitting your stride, as it were," Barrow said with a frown.

"I was appointed to *Vigilance* with two years of useful service left in her before she *did* need a refit," Lewrie admitted. "And, by the time we sailed home, she *was* weeded and slow. I think she could still have served for at least a year's extension. It's not as if we had to chase after French frigates. She matched the speed of the transports, which was all that was needed."

"We found your idea of notching sights on your guns novel, as well, Sir Alan," Barrow went on, shuffling some papers. "Much like the reports Captain Phillip Broke sent us when he did the same. You cited the increased accuracy of your gunners as a factor in supporting what troops you put ashore, as well."

"Did it when I had *Sapphire*, too, sir," Lewrie pointed out. "We got quite good at shooting off the North coast of Spain."

Mr. Barrow made a great deal of that earlier commission, recounting the many prizes taken, the many French supply carriers sunk or run aground, and, most especially, Lewrie's small squadron's complete victory over four French frigates sent to eliminate them.

"We also note, Sir Alan, that you have sent Mister Croker several letters of recommendation for your former officers and petty officers," Barrow said, setting aside the report on the frigate battle, trading it for a thinner folder, which he opened. "We have made appointments for these gentlemen to new ships, but, for some reason, these men still sit idle ashore without employment. We are wondering why assignments from the First Secretary are delayed or set aside, and who might have done so.

"Do you, sir, have any suspicions as to why this would happen?" Barrow asked with one brow raised in significant puzzlement.

"I was called home and lost my command, sir," Lewrie began to fume, "I was replaced by an officer I've detested since Eighteen Oh Four, and it was mutual. He, and others, have much more powerful patrons than *I'll* ever gather. Ruin *my* career? Fine, but to ruin good men because they served under me is despicable! Aye, I've suspicions of who requested it, though I'm not sure of their names, and wouldn't slur anyone without proof. But, I sincerely hope that you and Mister Croker, within your power and high office, can do for those officers, patronage and influence bedamned!"

"And something for yourself, Sir Alan?" Barrow slyly asked.

"That goes without sayin', sir," Lewrie replied with a shrug, "and my career speaks for itself. Aye, I *would* love an active commission . . . though I doubt it'd please my wife," he added with a sheepish grin. "I won't plead for *me*, Mister Barrow, I'll plead for *them*!" he said, jabbing a hand at the folder. "This gross injustice based on envy, spite, and jealousy must be undone!"

"Tell me of those officers you so highly recommend, sir," Barrow asked, opening the folder. "This Lieutenant Farley."

And, one by one, Lewrie laid out his reasons why his officers should be allowed to contribute their talents to the Navy; Farley, he could have a command of his own, by now; Rutland was clever and courageous; Greenleaf went through life like a bulldog; and Grace, who'd come from Ordinary Seaman in 1797, from the Nore fisheries, had turned into a most efficient and able man.

"There was someone you removed from command of one of the transports, Mister John Dickson. What of him?" Barrow asked.

"The very worst top-lofty, arrogant sort, sir," Lewrie related. "He was given a decent crew, decent officer and a Mid, and he ruined them in short order with curses, slurs, and floggings. He has no regard for his men, no respect, and no loyalty. I replaced him with Mister Rutland and brought him aboard *Vigilance*, where he sulked and sang small 'til Commodore

Grierson arrived and took him aboard his ship as Fifth Officer. They may be cater-cousins for all I know," Lewrie said, describing the mini-mutiny that "lost" a barge and some oars aboard the *Coromandel* transport, and Dickson's sneering departure, shouting that his Purgatory was at an end.

"Commodore Grierson, yayss," Barrow drawled, tapping his chin.

"He came in a two-decker seventy-four, Mister Barrow," Lewrie pointed out, "which draws too much water to get close inshore as I did, and his guns are not notched, so I don't know how much help he could be if the troops run into another trap ashore. I've written Lieutenant Fletcher, who *was* senior officer over all transports, and Lieutenant-Colonel Tarrant of the Ninety-Fourth Foot, to find out how they are faring under a new commander, but, I've not heard back, so far. I am concerned that something will go wrong, sir, sooner or later, harming people I've come to admire, and like."

"Is there anyone else you have in mind to recommend, Sir Alan?" Barrow asked with a cryptic smile. "Any protégés?"

"Well, while I'm at it, Mister Barrow," Lewrie said with a grin, "there is my youngest son, Hugh, a Passed Midshipman who just came off the *Undaunted* frigate, Captain Chalmers, who also reccomended him highly, who's looking for a promotion, or a berth as a senior Mid, and my brother-in-law, Midshipman Charles Chenery. I brought them along with me today, just in case."

Barrow made no comment, merely scribbled their names down. At last, he set the folder aside, steepled his fingers again, and said "Mister Corker and I suspect that Lord Mulgrave, the former First Lord, still has a hand in things, most un-officially. The new First Lord, Charles Yorke, will be apprised of these doings, and surely will correct the matter. Thank you for speaking with me, Sir Alan. It has been an honour, and a pleasure, to meet you."

Lewrie got to his feet, got led to the door, and they shook hands one last time.

Well, that's something, at least, Lewrie thought on his way down to the ground storey; *Maybe justice* will *be done.*

Hugh and Charlie peered up at him with hopeful-fearful rictuses of smiles on their faces, brows up in silent question. Lewrie gave them a tight-lipped grin as he got off the stairs.

"Gawd, the looks on your faces!" he teased. "I was given a chance t'put in a good word for each of you. You mayn't be employed, *yet*, but the Second Secretary sounded receptive. Now, let's go home, for we've been here far too long. We'll all of us call on my father at his home for a bit before Charlie and I return home."

"And if he offers us brandy, sir?" Charlie asked, much relieved to hear that there was a chance for a new ship.

"We'll stick to *tea*," Lewrie directed, "and if he's in a good mood, he'll *have* t'offer scones and jam!"

CHAPTER NINETEEN

$\mathcal{A}$fter breakfast the next morning, Lewrie thought to write some letters to old naval friends, and his son Sewallis, who was not the most prolific letter writer; he hadn't gotten one from him for months.

He also thought to use the table in the morning room, but Jessica reminded him that he had a perfectly serviceable study over the entry hall, where they had installed his desk, chart table, and all of his nautical books and maps. Why not use that?

"Good idea," he agreed, and requested Deavers to brew up some of his cool tea, with lemon, sugar, and an admixture of ginger beer.

"And what are you up to?" he asked his wife, noting that she had donned a bonnet and her parasol.

"I thought that Lucy and I would walk the dogs in Green Park," Jessica said, "Their time in the country with us has made the back garden too small for their ambitions, I fear. And bad on my flower beds. Too many squirrels to chase, too many holes dug."

"You might take Dasher and Turnbow along, Jess," he said.

"I can't hear you," she teased. "I don't answer to Jess."

"Dearest, darling Jessica, love of my life," Lewrie said, taking her hands in his, "have a good time, and keep a firm hand on Bisquit's leash."

"Enjoy your letter writing, Alan, my love. Ta!" Jessica said as she pecked him on the cheek and almost danced down the stairs to gather up the dogs, calling for Dasher and Turnbow.

He went to his study, opened the one window facing the street, and sat down at his desk, drawing out fresh paper, and his steel-nib pen, just as Deavers came in with a pitcher and glass.

"Ah, thankee, Deavers," Lewrie said with a brief smile.

"That Hazelwood, sir," Deavers carped, setting the tray down on a side table, "Soon as I got out the tea leaves, he's fussing over me, telling me how to brew it proper, and when I put in the lemon juice and the sugar in the pitcher, not on side plates, he said I was doing it all wrong. Wouldn't hear that it's the way you prefer it, and when I poured in the ginger beer, I thought he was going to have a fit!"

"Damn the man," Lewrie spat. "A damned good cook, but a pain in the arse. Does he still ban Yeovill from the kitchens?"

"Most of the time, sir," Deavers explained, "but for when a pot needs scrubbing, a platter needs fetching, or something menial. This goes on much longer, and we might lose Yeovill. He's been talking of hiring on at one of the gentlemen's clubs, or a restaurant."

"God, I'd hate t'lose him, and his talent with food," Lewrie exclaimed. "He's a wizard, he is. I may have t'have a stern word with Hazelwood. If they can't get along, I'll sack him and put Yeovill in his place." Are you lads gettin' enough at your meals? Same food as the dinin' room gets?"

"Oh, yessir," Deavers assured him, "more than enough, though it may not be as fancy. Hazelwood's a penny-pincher."

"Well, you ever have a complaint, I'll deal with Hazelwood," Lewrie vowed.

He poured himself a glass of his cool tea and took a deep sip, relishing, for it was just as good as it had been aboard ship, then dipped his pen in the inkwell and started a letter to Benjamin Rodgers, who now had command of a Third Rate, and a small squadron, in the Eastern Mediterranean. He vowed that he would not sound *too* sorry for himself.

On the other side of Piccadilly Street, the dogs were having a grand time in Green Park. Crossing Piccadilly, with its myriad of carts, waggons, coaches, and saddle horses, and the throngs of people on foot, had quite dazzled Bisquit and Rembrandt. The sights, and the new *aromas* had them straining at their leashes in curiosity and exuberance. And, there were squirrels, many more than the dogs could chase in the back garden,

impudent squirrels who clung upside down on the boles of trees just beyond a leap's range, chittering amusement and defiance, or openly hopping
cross the grass. There were birds everywhere, people pushing prams,
people walking strange dogs, too, and oh, it was a wonder to the dogs. So
many trees and bushes that they had yet to pee on, so many entrancing
odours! Of course they strained at their leashes!

"Don't pull so, Bisquit," Jessica entreated, slipping her hand through
the loop at the end of the leather leash. "We're here for a walk, not a
run. And I don't know what that mess is, but you're *not* going to roll
in it!"

"Your dog is more used to the park, ma'am," Jessica's maidservant,
Lucy, said, "you've walked him almost daily here. Rembrandt is a sweetie,
yes he *is*!" Lucy praised him, and at the mention of his name, he looked
up at her. "Cross the park, or just round the northern bounds, do you think,
ma'am?"

"Oh, just along the Piccadilly side," Jessica decided. Bisquit stopped
straining at his leash and squatted of a sudden to drop a few "presents" on
the grass. "Feel better, Bisquit?" she asked once he was back on his feet.
"Good dog."

Dasher and Turnbow trailed along behind the women and the dogs, not
quite totally bored with their escort duties, taking in the sight of the various classes of people in Green Park, snickering and whispering comments
about the overly well-dressed and the showy, or about the poor who were
taking an idle morning off, assuming that they were employed at all. They
marvelled at an Irish family, fair-haired all, dressed in their shoddy best
with broken-down shoes, with five children in tow, fitted out with a patch
quilt and wicker basket, looking for a shady place to dine *al fresco*, strutting like lords.

"A basket full o' ale or beer, I'd wager," Turnbow sniggered, "an' nought
more than bread an' cheese, hee hee."

"Who needs th' cheese?" Dasher japed.

Two burly men in cast-off rags and old, grimy tricorne hats, who had
been strolling along the sidewalk, abruptly turned into the park and trotted ahead of their party.

"What?" Turnbow gawped.

"Gi' oos th' dogs!" one of them snarled, taking hold of Bisquit's leash
and his collar.

"Stop! How dare you!" Jessica yelled. "Let go of him!"

The other burly man snatched up Rembrandt, dragging Lucy along with him for a step or two before he pulled out a knife and shoved it at her, making her let go of the leash.

"Help, thieves!" Lucy screamed. "Thieves! Brutes! Help!"

Jessica joined her, yelling for assistance. "You dirty criminals," she cried, poking her open parasol forward as if to use the brass ferrule as a weapon. The man swung a paw at the parasol, brushing it to one side, then back-handed Jessica on the side of her head, knocking her to her knees, her senses reeling. Bisquit and Rembrandt squirmed, barked, and tried to bite the attackets.

"I said, gi' oos th' bloody dogs, bitch! Leggo!" the assailant roared. He scooped Bisquit up, pulled hard on the leash and Jessica was drawn flat on her stomach, dragged by her wrist, crying out, this time in pain. Her fingers on the leash let go, but her hand was still trapped in the loop. The other assailant, the one with the knife, cut the leash just behind Bisquit's collar, and they both turned and ran to the street.

For a numb second or so, Dasher and Turnbow had stood still in surprise, then broke into a run together, shouting "Thief, thief!" or "Dognappers!" or "Ladies gettin' hurt!," pummeling at the men, on their ribs and backs. Their efforts were futile, both being hit and brushed aside. The threat of the knife forced Turnbow to quit.

"See t'th' ladies, Robert!" Dasher yelled, running after them as they reached Piccadilly and scrambled up and into the back of a two-wheeled cart, throwing the dogs in before them. A third thief at the reins whipped up and the cart rattled off at reckless speed, no matter the traffic, or pedestrians, weaving its way up Piccadilly towards Haymarket. Dasher ran full-out, chasing the cart, but ship-board life and its constraints on running caught up with him. Dasher had to stop, finally, bent over with his hands on his knees, heaving for wind, and tears running down his face. He had lost sight of the thieves and the cart, hadn't seen where in all the traffic it might've turned into a side street. He hadn't been able to save the dogs, or defend the Captain's lady wife or her maid, people he truly liked!

He had let the Captain down! All he could do was trudge back to the park, mopping his face with the sleeve of his coat.

"Brutes, animals!" Lucy continued yelling, gathering a crowd of gentlemen, far too late to aid her or her mistress.

"Are you hurt, madam?" a nattily dressed solicitor asked as he offered to help Jessica to her feet.

"My wrist, oh!" she managed to say. "They stole our dogs! They *struck* us! Lucy, are you alright?"

"Yes, ma'am. I'm *sorry*. One of them had a knife, and I was so frightened, I let go!" Lucy wailed, shaking with aftershock. "I let your dog go, and I wish I'd been braver, but . . . I'm so sorry!"

Jessica rolled to a sitting position, clutching her wrist to her chest.

"Let us help you to your feet, ma'am," another gentleman said.

Jessica tried, but her head was spinning, and she felt faint, so she waved off the assistance. "My head is reeling. Let me rest a bit longer."

She reached up to touch the side of her head that the thief had struck and it felt hot and sore. Her fingers came away, reddened with smears of blood. "Oh, my God," she said with a groan.

"Turnbow," Lucy ordered. "Go fetch the Captain, fast as you can."

"Right!" Turnbow agreed, leaping to his feet from kneeling near Jessica. "I'm off!"

Dasher came trudging back from his fruitless chase, broke into a trot to reach his mistress, wriggled through the people who had been drawn to the scene, and dropped to his knees in front of her, gawping to see her bleeding and cradling her wrist.

"Aw, Miz Lewrie, I'm so sorry," he blubbed, "I couldn't fight 'em, an' I tried t'chase after 'em, but they got away, an' I don't know where they went with the dogs."

"Don't cry, Dasher," Jessica tried to say to comfort him. "You and Turnbow were brave fellows, trying to fight two huge men. Brutes! Stealing our dogs, in broad daylight! How horrid! Why? Why?"

Dasher knew why, but he kept mum about a part of his life that he wasn't that proud of.

Lewrie was just applying a daub of sealing wax on a letter to his former First Officer, Geoffrey Westcott, now a Commander with a brig-sloop ravaging the French coast, when he heard someone banging on the front door below him, and through his opened window, the voice he recognised as Robert Turnbow.

"Help! Open the door! Tell Cap'um Lewrie 'is wife's been hurt in the park!" Turnbow howled.

Lewrie whirled to his feet to stick his head out the window, to look down on Turnbow at the door a storey below. "Hurt? How?" Lewrie shouted down.

"Two big, ugly men attacked yer Missuz an' Lucy, sir!" Turnbow replied, looking up and shouting his news. "Stole the dogs, hit yer Missuz on th' side of 'er head an' knocked 'er down! One of 'em had a knife! 'E almost cut Lucy with it!"

"I'm coming!" Lewrie roared, fearful, and enraged at the same time. Down the stairs he dashed, just as Pettus opened the locked door to let Turnbow in. "Deavers, Desmond, Yeovill! I need all of you! You too, Pettus."

Lewrie looked about for a weapon, and his eyes fell on his old hanger, standing in the porcelain umbrella stand. He snatched it up.

"What happened?" Pettus demanded to know, slack-jawed.

"My wife and Lucy were attacked in the park!" Lewrie snapped in impatience, his anger growing. "Lead on, lad," he ordered to Turnbow. "Pettus, fetch all the lads and follow on. Go, lad!"

Down Dover Street Lewrie and Turnbow trotted, Turnbow, out of breath from his run to the house, stammered out details of what had happened, between breaths. Piccadilly Street was still full of cart, waggon, and coach traffic, and they had to weave, skitter ahead of, or dart behind it all in a sea of snorting, neighing draught horses, and shouting waggoners or coachmen, and people cried out in alarm to see a man out with a sheathed sword in his hand.

"There, sir," Turnbow managed to croak, pointing to the knot of bystanders about twenty yards beyond the verge of the park.

"Jessica!" Lewrie shouted. "Jessica!" as they got closer.

"Alan?" he heard her cry out.

"Let me through!" Lewrie demanded as he shoved some bystanders aside, dropping to his knees to slide to her, drop the hanger, and take her in his arms.

"Oh, Alan," Jessica whimpered, throwing one arm round his neck. "They took our dogs, they . . . *attacked* us! I *tried* to keep Bisquit, but . . . !"

"There, there, love," Lewrie tried to comfort into her hair. "Did they hurt you?"

"One of them hit me. My hand was caught in the leash," Jessica said, raising her right arm a bit to show him.

Lewrie saw the dabbles of blood on her temple, where something on the assailant's hand, a ring of some kind perhaps, had opened a small gash, surrounded by a developing bruise. He gently touched at it, and found a knot.

"Oh, my love, my dear!" Lewrie cooed. "We'll get you home, and send for a doctor. Who's that friend of yours, her husband, Doctor . . . ?"

"Stansfield," Jessica said, slowly nodding, though it hurt.

"Lucy!" Pettus cried out as he and the rest of the household got to the scene, rushing to embrace her and press her close.

"Who dares hurt th' Captain's lady?" Liam Desmond demanded, his fists clenched tight. "Any o' th' bastards still around? Ah, yer pardons, Dame Lewrie."

"They're long gone," the helpful solicitor said. "This young lad chased after them, but they got away."

"In a two-wheel cart, sir," Dasher piped up. "Big brutes, they woz. I run as far as Arlington Street, but they woz just too fast, an' I'm sorry I let ya down, Captain."

"They stole the *dogs*?" Lewrie gawped, at a loss as to why anyone would go to such lengths, offer violence, for a pair of dogs.

"Can ya walk, ma'am?" Deavers asked. "Need help gettin' up?"

"I feel a bit faint, and weak, Deavers," Jessica told him.

"Here, lads," Yeovill said, "She can't walk, we'll carry Dame Lewrie home. Play like loblolly boys and make a chair."

Desmond and Deavers, the strongest of all, went to each side to put their arms behind her back, to help her stand for a second, then put their free arms linked together under her bottom. Lewrie went to her side and took hold of her left hand.

She squeezed back, and managed to summon up a brave smile.

"The rest of you lads, find a way t'get us cross Piccadilly, through all that traffic," Lewrie ordered.

"We tried to fight 'em, sir," Turnbow told him, tagging along at Lewrie's side. "Just weren't big or strong enough."

"Not your fault, Turnbow, you tried, and that's what is important," Lewrie told him, "And Dasher? You tried t'fight 'em, too, and then gave chase. That was brave of both of you."

Behind them as they left the park, the bystanders chatted among themselves, and Lewrie faintly heard "That was Captain Alan Lewrie? The naval hero? My stars, him to the life?"

"What's London comin' to, I ask you?" another spoke up. "Crime and assaults in the parks, on a famous man's helpless wife? Tcha!" and "Wot's th' bloody Bow Street Runners doin', then, drinkin' beer an' havin' a pie when things like this're goin' on? *Police* I ask ya!"

They stopped traffic long enough to get across Piccadilly and up Dover Street, and finally into the house, where they lay Jessica on a cushioned settee in the front parlour, her head and shoulders propped up on fetched bed pillows.

When Jessica said she still felt faint, smelling salts were sent for. One maid suggested willow bark tea as a good remedy for aches and pains; who had any? The maid knew a shop, and bustled off to buy some. Was her wrist sprained, or broken? Ice, in quantity, might help, but who had a stock of ice this late in the Autumn? The little maid-of-all-work was given some money and sent off to hunt some up. Deavers was despatched to the Stansfield house for the physician.

If Lewrie imagined that his wife would get any ease, that hope was dashed at once. The physician's wife was a childhood friend, and she lived close by, and attended St. Anselm's Church. She came with her husband, after sending a servant to the Mertons', and the banker's wife arrived a bit later. She, in turn, had sent word to the manse at St. Anselm's, and Reverend Chenery, a hand-wringing, shivery wreck, Jessica's brother Charlie, and Madame Berenice Pellatan were banging on the door not ten minutes later. Next came Mrs. Eaton, a barrister's wife, Mrs. Pryor, another girlhood friend wed to a steam engine manufacturer, and Miss Kensington not long after, after dismissing her elementary classes at St. Anselm's.

If Missuz Heiliger shows up too, I hope she brings a keg o' beer, Lewrie thought as the gathering crowd of sympathisers shoved him out of standing room. Then, damned if round, blonde Betsy Heiliger entered the house almost as soon as he thought it—without beer or ale that her husband's family brewed.

"Perhaps we would all be more comfortable in the drawing room abovestairs," Lewrie suggested. "I'll send for tea."

"That would be best, Sir Alan," Dr. Stansfield said, "thank you," as he bent to his patient. "Hmm. Hah. Hmm. Aha?" he mused whilst examining her. "I fear that the gash on your temple, Dame Lewrie, must be stitched to close the wound. And, I fear that once healed, it will leave you with a faint scar."

"A match to my husband's?" Jessica gamely asked.

"Oh my dear, how brave of you!" Mrs. Merton gushed, and that set off another bout of syrupy condolences and praise from her friends, a fine pack of "chick-a-biddies" in full cackle.

As Lewrie began to herd them up the stairs, Agnes, one of the maids, blew in the front door, waving a tiny paper spill aloft. "Found the willow bark, sir!" she bawled triumphantly, "an' I'll have it hot an' ready in two shakes of a wee lamb's tail, an' th' first'un already be shook!"

"Regular tea for all in the drawing room, too, Agnes," Lewrie reminded her. "Set Hazelwood to that, and you do the other tea, that willow bark, yourself."

"Willow bark tea?" Dr. Stansfield said with a sniff, and a bit of amusement. "A folk treatment for headaches and fevers. Still, I've seen it prove efficacious in *some* instances. Now, my dear, if you can manage to flex your fingers?"

"Ow!" Jessica cried after the effort.

"Hmm, ahh, hmmm," Dr. Stansfield speculated some more.

There came another banging on the front door, not the knocker, but a fist. Pettus and Lucy were in the entry hall, Lucy with her hands to her mouth in concern. Pettus unlocked the door and swung it open, and in came a ragamuffin shop boy with a square-ish bundle on his shoulder, wrapped in burlap or jute, and the little maid-of-all-work, beaming like a cherub.

"Somebody's wantin' a block of ice here?" the lad asked. "Damned near the last of our winter stock. Iff'n ya got a cool larder?"

"Show him to the kitchens," Lewrie directed. "How much?"

"Summer rates, sir," the lad said on his way down the stairs, "Ten shillings."

"Oh, your poor hand, Jessica," Madame Pellatan wailed as she made her way upstairs, the last of the herd. "*Mon Dieu,* if you can no longer paint, or draw?" Jessica let out a mournful wail, at that.

"Enough o' that," Lewrie snapped, wishing that he could boot the old French baggage and her melodrama right up the arse. "I'll leave you to Doctor Stansfield's care, my love," he said as he trudged up to join the others, oath as he was to join them at that moment.

"'Ere, where's me master's money for th' ice?" the lad who had fetched it called out at the top of the kitchen stairs.

"Some peace and quiet, please!" Dr. Stansfield demanded, rather loudly. "Give Dame Lewrie some quiet, in which to rest!"

"Thought she already paid you," Lewrie snapped. "I gave her some money."

"You did, and I did, sir!" the little maid swore. "I give him twelve shillin's!" I still got five o' wot you gimme!"

"Yarr, ya did not!" the shop boy countered. "Ya said yer master would pay when we got here!"

"Did not!"

"Did too!"

"Quiet!" the Doctor roared.

"Oh my Lord!" Jessica exclaimed, partly in pain and partly in utter exasperation. "I need a brandy!"

"Turn out your pockets, boy," Lewrie demanded.

"Don't have none of it on me, yer honour sir," the boy objected, "me master already . . . uh."

"So my maid already paid for the ice?" Lewrie asked, grabbing the scamp by the front of his shirt to give him a shake. "Twelve shillings, and then you demand another ten when you get here? There's boys transported for life for less!"

"Right! Just like I told ya, sir!" the maidservant piped up in triumph, showing Lewrie the five shillings she had left.

"Damn your blood, boy! Get ya gone, and damn the two shillings your master charged. I hope he chokes on it."

"Daughter!" the Reverend Chenery called out as he crept down the stairs from the drawing room. "Is your wrist quite *broken*? I heard you cry out! We are all, this instant, praying for your recovery. A word to the Lord, dearest Jessica? I remember your dear mother's passing."

"Nobody's *dyin'*, for Christ's sake!" Lewrie roared in his best quarter-deck bellow.

"Quiet!" the Doctor entreated, even louder.

"Brandy?" Jessica re-iterated. "Anybody? Ow, ow, ow!"

"And one for me, too," Lewrie demanded, "before I *strangle* somebody!"

The shop boy was shoved out the door, with the little maid sticking her tongue out at him. Reverend Chenery slinked off up the stairs to fret in the drawing room, and Deavers turned up with a brandy bottle and two glasses.

"Hmm, aha!" Dr. Stansfield said at last, sitting back up in his chair. "Your wrist is not broken, Dame Lewrie, merely a bad sprain. I do believe you may regain full motion in a fortnight. Did someone say something about ice?"

"I believe it was mentioned," Lewrie dryly said, "yayss."

"Take a sip, my dear," Stansfield said to Jessica as the brandy glass arrived, "then I shall use a bit of it on your wrist, where the leather of the leash abraded your flesh. Scratches, mostly, and naught torn open." He opened his bag and removed a clean, white handkerchief to dampen and press on her hand and wrist. "A bit on your temple, too, I know, it stings. There, there."

What the Devil's he doin'? Lewrie wondered as he got his glass of brandy, and took a restorative sip, taking a chair nearby.

Dr. Stansfield drew out what looked like a "housewife," a sewing kit with needles and thread, all of which he dampened with the brandy. "Turn your head to me, my dear. You will feel some pinches, but you must bear it. Do you know that King George the Third once had to be operated upon for the stones. He read a book before the surgeons were ready, drank off a brandy, and then underwent the procedure without a single groan?"

"Ow!" Jessica cried out as he made his first stitch.

"There, there, I'll dose you with some laudanum, after. There, there," Stansfield cooed, taking a second.

"Ow, my Lord!" Jessica whimpered, breaking Lewrie's heart. "That is *not* a pinch! Ow!"

Two more stitches—sutures, he called them—were taken before Stansfield snipped the thread with a small pair of scissors, and he was done. "Drink all that up, now, my dear, and I shall wrap your wrist. Brave lady! And could someone fetch several small pieces of that ice, wrapped in a clean tea towel? That will reduce the swelling, which is sure to reveal itself." He stowed away his needle and thread.

"Alcohol, sir?" Lewrie asked, frowning.

"Most apply hot, clean water, preferably boiled," Dr. Stansfield told him, with a faint smile, "to cleanse a wound. I've heard that a sailor will use salt water, but I've found that deep scratches and wounds that break the skin seem to stay fresher, without suppuration, with the application of highly fermented spirits. God only knows why it is, but it seems to avail. Did you know that Galen, the classical healer, used honey, even on deep sword cuts? Imagine! It was once widely used by the surgeons of the Roman legions. Successfully, too."

"More brandy, my good man," Stansfield said to Deavers, who was still standing by with the bottle. Stansfield got a refill, tossed it back for himself, then allowed Jessica another glass. "I will leave you a bottle of laudanum, but you will need something to allay the bitter taste."

"I've some tea in my study," Lewrie recalled, "with lemon, sugar, and ginger beer."

"I'll go get it, sir," Deavers volunteered.

"Only a minim at any given time," Stansfield cautioned, "And the willow bark tea once the pain has abated to a tolerable level."

"Of course," Lewrie agreed, going to sit by Jessica's side.

"Am I marred for life, Alan?" she asked, reaching across her body to take his right hand in her left.

"Tosh, love, it ain't even piratical, and not a patch on mine," he comforted her, only having to lie a little, showing her a gap of less than two inches 'twixt his left hand's forefinger and thumb. "My darling, *nothing* could steal your beauty."

"If you're fibbing to make me feel better, I suppose I could wear my hair in bangs from now on," she said, squeezing his hand and shifting a little on the settee to a more comfortable position.

"We should consider getting you up to bed," Lewrie suggested.

"No, just let me rest here for a while," Jessica demurred, putting on her first smile since the attack. "After the laudanum, I will most likely nod off. We can do that later."

Deavers returned with the pitcher of cool tea and Lewrie's glass from his study. Stansfield had a sniff at it, poured a glass, and added a small, measured amount of the laudanum. Jessica drank it down, thirstily, then gave out a sigh, wrinkling her face up.

"I can taste the laudanum, even through the tea," she said with a sigh. "Brew more of it, do, with more ginger beer poured in."

"I'll get the company herded out, so you can rest," Lewrie told her, rising and patting her hand one more time.

"I'll join you, Sir Alan," Stansfield offered. "They'll listen to a physician's orders, if they won't heed yours, hah hah. My wife can convince the rest that she's no longer in danger."

"Your fee, sir?" Lewrie asked as they went up the stairs.

"After all the good dinners I've eat here, Sir Alan?" Stansfield said, chuckling, "and all the grand conversations? No fee."

Well, there's something *good come of it,* Lewrie thought.

CHAPTER TWENTY

*H*ow they got word of it, God knows, but even Lewrie's father and son Hugh showed up as Lewrie and the Doctor got the women herded out so that Jessica could rest. They exchanged a few comforting words with her, vowed to find the culprits, somehow, and let her drift off to a restful, pain-free sleep on the settee in her studio. Lewrie led them all up to the drawing room, calling for a fresh bottle of brandy.

"Wish I'd been there, 'stead of the lads," Charlie gruffly said, with his fists clenched. "Lord, is *any* place in London safe any more?"

"My neighbour's servants caught a boy trying to snake his way in through the drains," Sir Hugo said with a sniff, "so he could let the house breaker gang in on the quiet. They didn't reckon on a pair of hungry foot-men making themselves some midnight dampers."

"Did they call the police?" Hugh asked.

"Not much point in it," Sir Hugo told him. "The gang must have seen candles lit and scampered. Oh, they turned the boy over, but he kept mum."

"Why try to steal dogs, though," Lewrie wondered. "What use can they have for them?"

Dasher, who had come to collect the tea things, popped his mouth open several times as if summoning up the courage to speak. Finally, he set the tray down on a side table, and went "Ahem. Sir?"

"Aye, Dasher?" Lewrie said, turning to look at him.

"They woz dog buffers, sir," Dasher related, fingers busy on the seams of his trouser legs. "Part o' th' cantin' academy. Criminals, false beggars, house breakers, safe crackers, pick pockets . . . they's all got their specialties wot they call 'lays,' an' put on airs that they're smarter than regular people. Got their own slang language.

"Dog buffers aren't well thought of, even by the beggars, sir," he went on. "They're a mean bunch."

"What do they do with the dogs they steal, then, Dasher?" Hugh asked him.

"Ransom, mostly, sir," Dasher said, turning to face him. "A day or two from now, a wee boy or girl will be at th' door, maybe leavin' a note. Th' owners haveta place a notice in th' paper th' buffers say to, offerin' a reward t'get their dog back."

"How much?" Lewrie asked.

"Depends on wot th' carriers, th' ones who do the scoutin' an' casin', figure wot th' swell can afford, sir," Dasher said. "In their lingo, you an' all gentlemen're swells. Maybe . . . ten pound apiece?"

Lewrie shared a look with his father. "That's dear, but Jessica is that fond of her silly spaniel. And Bisquit has been close to me for years. We'll get them back?"

"Yessir, iff'n ya pays," Dasher assured him. "Ya don't, they's gone forever."

"What happens if we don't pay?" Hugh asked.

"Well, uhm . . ." Dasher said, scuffing the toe of one of his buckled shoes on the carpet, looking down for a moment. "They gotta make *somethin'* outta their snatch, sirs. They's dog fighters wot need dogs for their fightin' dogs t'practice on. They can sell 'em for a few shillin's, It's good odds the buffers'll have a slew o' dogs to ransom, an' they need feedin', so they kill th' ones wot won't earn 'em any money, sell the skins, an' feed th' meat to th' rest. Even eat dog meat themselves, sir. Dog meat ain't bad, sir."

"Good God!" Hugh and Charlie both exclaimed. They had both been raised with dogs in the house, Jessica's Rembrandt, or Hugh bowled over by his brother, Sewallis's, pack of setters.

"Dog ain't bad, indeed," Sir Hugo commented, and everyone had to gawp at him, appalled. "What? None of you have ever been on short commons in the field? Alan, Hugh, Mister Chenery, haven't you ever eat your shipboard rats, your 'millers'? Haw!"

"Well, I suppose a man can never get enough meat, *but* . . ." Lewrie said, "Aye, we've all eat 'millers,' but I draw the line at dogs . . . and cats!"

"Don't know why th' buffers stole th' dogs right out in th' open like they did, sir," Dasher told Lewrie. "Most times, they'll get over a wall or a fence t'snatch 'em when nobody's lookin'. Attackin' women like that's not natural."

"I *will* ransom our dogs," Lewrie vowed, after tossing back his remaining brandy, "but, dammit, I want t'track 'em down, chase 'em to their lair, and *murder* the bastards for what they did to Jessica!"

"Right with you, father," Hugh seconded.

"Count me in, too," Charlie swore.

"Desmond an' th' lads'd be that eager t'help, sir," Dasher said with a gulp.

"And this talk about killin', skinnin', and eatin' dogs," Lewrie cautioned, "We'll not mention any of that round Jessica. She's upset enough."

"Passed, *nem con*," Sir Hugo agreed.

"How to find them, though, sir," Charlie Chenery speculated. "We have no idea where their lair *is*. Dasher? Any clue on where they went?"

"Like I said, sir," Dasher explained, looking sheepish, "I run almost t'Arlington Street, an' their cart was still lashin' on, as fast as Jehu, up Piccadilly, 'til they passed so many coaches an' such that I lost sight of 'em in all th' traffic. I couldn't say where they made a turnin'."

"Doesn't make much sense," Sir Hugo scoffed, looking querulous. as he reached out for a refill, "Shaftesbury, Haymarket, Saint James's Park, Charing Cross Road, or Pall Mall . . . those thieves were running through *good* neighbourhoods. Where would low-born filthy criminals find a hidey-hole in there?"

"They woz both of 'em right nasty beau-traps, sirs," Dasher told them. "Cast-off finery from th' rag pickers' barrows, but dirty an' greasy-grimy. Had a fortnight's worth o' beards, an' th' leader, he said, ehm . . .'gie oos th' dogs,' makin' dog sound like 'doges.'"

"Wapping?" Hugh said, puzzling. "Cheapside? East of Bow Bells? Somewhere that a pair like them fit right in?"

"And it would have to be where no one objects to all that barking all day and all night long," Charlie contributed. "A warehouse by the docks, an abandoned stable . . ."

"A tumbledown house in a stew," Sir Hugo said with a sage nod. "Where, I would imagine, our thieves pay a very low rent, by the month, not the night. They simply *can't* move over a dozen dogs from place to place on short notice. Dasher, you saw only the one two-wheeled cart?"

"Aye, sir," Dasher agreed. "A third man drivin', an' a sorry shambles it woz. Their horse musta been a good'un, though, t'gallop as fast as it did."

"A stable might be just the thing," Lewrie exclaimed, perking up. "A place to feed and keep the horse, where they could keep that cart out of sight 'til they need it, again."

"If it's *their* cart," Charles Chenery commented, "and not one they rented or borrowed for the job."

"Well, there is that," Lewrie said with a sigh. "Damn!" He drummed his free hand's fingers in deep thought. "Aha!" he said at last.

"What?" Sir Hugo asked, glaring at him as if angry.

"We could scour all London, and cross the river in Southwark, too, but . . . like Dasher told us, *they* have to come to *us*!" Lewrie said with a sly grin growing on his face. "Some child waif will come to the house, tell us which newspaper we are to place the advertisement, and how much ransom they're demanding.

"He, or she, will *have* t'go back where the thieves keep all the dogs t'tell 'em that her job's done," Lewrie explained. "They might even pay her a shilling or two, and feed her, or him. Give the child a place t'doss down, as much a part of the gang as any of 'em. Once she, or he, set off on the return journey, we *follow* the child, break in with swords and pistols ready, rescue our dogs, and bloody some heads!"

"I *like* it!" Hugh cheered loudly.

"Ehm . . . wouldn't we stand out like a horde of bare-chested Turk warriors, though?" Charlie countered, looking dubious. "A band of men, with swords and pistols, trailing along, slinking from one shop door to the next? I'm not sure I even know *how* to slink! The waif turns round just once, sees a pack of armed men trailing behind, and she's off in another direction, and we'd *never* find the lair."

"The messenger runs as fast as he can, and perhaps doesn't dare go back to the hidey-hole 'til next morning's breakfast," Sir Hugo gloomily predicted. "Good idea, son, *but* . . ." he added, throwing up his hands in frustration. "Best just pay the ransom and be done."

"Damn!" Lewrie spat, his quick scheme seemingly blocked at both ends. "Damn! If only . . . ! Damn!"

Charles is right, he glumly fretted; *If the messenger doesn't tumble to us, the police constables just might arrest us for going about London armed! And, I don't know how t'slink or lurk, either. But, I know some people who* can!

He stood of a sudden and patted himself down to check for his coin purse and wallet.

"Going somewhere?" Sir Hugo asked him.

"To the Foreign Office," Lewrie told him. "There's someone I must see."

"The Foreign Office?" his father said, completely puzzled.

Reverend Chenery took that moment to clomp up the stairs and enter the drawing room, looking the company over, and getting a look in his eyes as he spotted the brandy bottle.

Damn, is he still here? Lewrie thought; I thought we'd run him off!

"How is Jessica?" Lewrie had to ask, though.

"She is sleeping, thank the Lord," Reverend Chenery told him as he went to the side table and the brandy, looking about for a fresh glass. "Though the laudanum dulls her pain, she still moans now and then, and mumbles in her sleep. It is most pitiful to witness. Ehm, could someone fetch a glass?"

"I'll go, sir," Dasher offered, and trotted off to the kitchens.

"I should look in on her before I go," Lewrie vowed, following Dasher out to the stairs.

"Go?" Jessica's father all but spluttered. "Where does he have to go in my dear daughter's hour of need?"

"The Foreign Office, he said," Sir Hugo informed him.

"The *Foreign* Office? Whatever for?" Reverend Chenery gawped.

"I think I know," Sir Hugo said with a sly smile, which on him looked positively grisly. But he would not elaborate.

"Jessica, I have to go out for a bit," Lewrie whispered as he sat on a chair by the settee where she slept. "I'll try to get back as quick as I can. Am I not here when you wake, and you're up for it, you should let people help you to our bed chamber, and have some more laudanum, or willow bark tea . . ."

She opened her eyes and let out a faint moan, or whimper, as he sat there. "Oh, Alan. I'm having the most horrible dream."

"That's the laudanum," he said, nodding, brushing back her hair and kissing her forehead.

"Our poor dogs," she whispered, "poor little Rembrandt, who would never hurt a soul . . . terrified, crying out, penned up in the dark somewhere strange . . . alien! . . . so frightened, and in the hands of evil, brutal men! I could *see* it!"

"They're bein' held for ransom, darling," Lewrie softly cooed to her,

"I will pay it, gladly, and we'll soon have 'em back, safe and sound. Don't you worry your head about that. Trust me. If you believe you're strong enough, let's get you up to bed. Some soup or a bite to eat, perhaps? Get into your bedclothes, and sleep some more."

"I . . . I think I could," she gamely said, trying to sit up one-handed, awkwardly turning, with his support, to a sitting position.

Lewrie left her for a moment to go upstairs and summon aid to help her up to the bedchamber, got her settled in, then gently kissed her one last time. Lucy and one of the chambermaids shooed the men out of the bed-chamber to help her undress and prepare for bed, dashing off for more cool tea and the vial of laudanum, a fresh, hot cup of willow bark tea, and plumping up all the pillows.

Satisfied that they had done all that they could for her, Lewrie went down to the entry hall, took up his walking stick and a natty civilian hat, and went out into Dover Street to hail a hackney.

From earlier calls, Lewrie knew which floor, and which office, he had to call upon. He entered the outer office and waiting room, and spoke to a fresh-faced young clerk.

"Is Mister Peel in today?" he began.

"Why, yes he is, ehm . . . sir," the clerk told him with a wary smile. "Ehm, are you sure you're in the right place, though? This is ah, a certain part of the Foreign Office that . . ."

"Tell Mister Peel that Captain Sir Alan Lewrie, Baronet, has need to speak with him, at once," Lewrie announced, glad to throw a bit of his rank and minor title about; it always proved useful when needed. "On an urgent matter, tell him."

"Ah, ehm . . ." the young clerk said uncertainly.

"At once, if ya don't mind," Lewrie prompted.

"Yes, Sir Alan," the clerk surrendered, going to an ornate door to the inner sanctum, and squeezing through it, as if swinging it wide open would allow the highest state secrets to fly out. The clerk was back in a bare min-ute, almost bowing and scraping as he bade Lewrie enter.

"Alan!" the senior spy greeted him with both arms out.

"Jemmy!" Lewrie responded in kind.

He had been introduced to Peel . . . "'tis James, James Peel" . . . long years before in the West Indies during the time that France was trying to hold on to St. Domingue, now Haiti, or for Great Britain to seize it, back in the days when that master spy, back-stabber, throat-cutter, and arch schemer Zachariah Twigg, was still skittering like a spider over his schemes, pulling on the webs to play "The Great Game" like a master harpist.

"Something urgent, hey?" Peel asked as he led Lewrie to his inner lair, offered him a chair, and rang for a pot of tea.

"My wife and her maid were attacked in Green Park this morning," Lewrie began, "Jessica was struck on the head, and got her wrist and hand hurt, hanging on to a dog leash. The attackers, dog buffers, took our pets and galloped off in a cart. I *could* pay their ransom and have done, but I want some blood, James. I and my people don't have the skill t'track the messenger back to where they're holed up, but, I recall that Mister Twigg once had a battalion of people who could . . . what he called his 'Baker Street Irregulars,' when he lived on that street. Could I borrow some?"

"Dogs," Peel said, his mouth agape for a moment. "Your *dogs*?"

"I know it's a lot to ask, *and* on short notice," Lewrie said.

"Too bloody right it is, Alan," Peel said, shaking his head in astonishment. "Look here, you *know* what use we make of them, and *yes,* they're still in operation, in even greater numbers than Twigg's days, with a lot more on their plate than before.

There are foreign embassies to be watched, letters to be intercepted, read, copied, or re-written by our best forgers," Peel explained with both hands spread wide on his desk, "Some of our allies spy for the French, ye know, our so-called best friends. Ships from foreign ports land passengers, businessmen, and sailors in the thousands each week, and which of them are here to sneak about and report to the French? Housemaids, mistresses, footmen and page boys, idlers and watchers who keep track of all those people already have their hands full."

"I know, but . . ." Lewrie tried to insist.

"Then there are the *Englishmen* we suspect of traitorous doings, and the servants we've tried to place in their homes and businesses," Peel continued, "who report on what they hear, or read in passing. Besides, Alan, as I told you the last time we spoke, round the time you were getting married, the Irregulars, and what goes on in London, aren't my department. I'm at this bloody desk, reading reports, and rumours, from our agents overseas. Some days it's juicy and meaty, but most days it's as dry as dust. I couldn't prevail on the other department to spare some people, not on short notice."

"A few of your children-watchers," Lewrie pressed, leaning his hands on the front of Peel's desk. "The thieves'll send someone round t'tell me how much it'll cost, and which paper to publish my 'reward.' Just loiter about my street, follow the messenger, most-like a child, and report back. Two or three, at the most."

"Hmm . . ." Peel sourly mused.

"They struck my wife, they would've sliced her maid with a knife if she hadn't let go the leash," Lewrie grimly pointed out. "In broad daylight. In Green Park!"

"Sounds more like a job for our police," Peel said.

"What good are our bloody police?" Lewrie scoffed. "A Frenchified notion! After I and my men get through with the thieves, I suppose we could turn 'em *over* to the police, and let 'em make what case they can against 'em. I just *can't* let the bastards get away with it!"

"Two or three, do you say?" Peel said, head canted to one side.

"Young, innocent-lookin', street waifs, like the messenger will be," Lewrie wished aloud. "Idlers, workmen, beau-nasty, 'fly' cullies. Whatever you can spare."

"You live in Dover Street?" Peel said, sounding as if he would relent.

"Number Twenty-Two," Lewrie told him with a growing smile.

"I'll see what I can do," Peel promised. "Good God! Dogs!"

CHAPTER TWENTY-ONE

*L*ewrie got back to the house in late afternoon, and immediately went up to their bedchamber to see to Jessica, where her maid, Lucy, and Agnes the chambermaid were tending to her.

"How are you feeling?" he asked, sitting on the edge of the bed and taking her good hand in his.

"My wrist isn't hurting quite as badly as it did, earlier," she told him, leaning over to give him a kiss. "I don't know whether it's the laudanum or the willow bark tea that's responsible for that."

"The tea's safer, ma'am," Agnes insisted. "That laudanum can turn good people inta fiends, it can. As bad as cheap gin."

"Both taste horrid, no matter what sweetenings one adds to it," Jessica said, making a face.

"Have you eat anything, dear?" Lewrie asked.

Jessica briefly raised her right hand. "I can barely manage a cup of tea in my left hand, Alan, much less cut things with a knife and fork. I had a bit of soup, in a mug, and some buttered bread . . . with Lucy's help. Soups and broths may be my main meals 'til I heal up.

"I vaguely recall you telling me something about ransom?" she said, frowning. "The laudanum addled my wits, and I'm not sure that I didn't dream it."

"Aye, the dogs were taken for ransom," Lewrie told her. "According to Dasher, who grew up rough in the streets, dog buffers make their living by ransoming the pets they steal. Tomorrow, morning or mid-day, a messenger will come round, leave a note or something, that tells us to place a reward . . . like they were *lost,* for God's sake, in a certain paper, and offer the price the messenger tells us. Don't worry, love. We'll get our dogs back, no matter what they ask."

"Leaving them free to steal them, again, and demand even more money?" Jessica gasped.

"Well, uh . . ." Lewrie said, stumped. He hadn't thought of that! "No, they won't, love. The next time we walk the dogs, *I'll* go with you, or Desmond and Deavers. You and Lucy'll have bodyguards. Bigger bodyguards than Dasher and Turnbow."

"In London," Jessica sighed, shaking her head sadly, "an English city, which *should* be safe. Or have I gone through life with blinders on?"

"You've led a charmed life, so far, darling," Lewrie admitted.

"I suppose," she said with a sigh. "Ehm . . . Alan, I find myself in need of a trip to the ah, necessary. You would not mind absenting yourself for a few minutes?"

"Need help?" Lewrie asked.

"Feminine help is preferred," Jessica said with a quirky smile as she tried to fling back the sheet and coverlet.

"Ah! Oh!" Lewrie gawped, getting to his feet. "I'll ah, go to the drawing room. See if we've a newspaper."

"That would be best, my love," Jessica said as Lucy and Agnes swarmed to tug down her nightgown, turn her cross-wise of the bed and help her to her feet and into a bed gown. "And, after another dose of laudanum . . . a wee one, Agnes . . . I think I will try to fall off to sleep for a while."

"See you at supper, then?" Lewrie assumed. "We'll have our mugs of soup together."

"Go!" Jessica ordered.

Instead of the drawing room, though, Lewrie went to his study to take inventory of his weapons. His everyday short, slightly curved hanger sword was in the entry hall, as was his 50 guinea presentation sword from the East India Company, given after he'd saved several Indianmen off Cape Town years before. There was his old Midshipman's dirk, laid aside for ages after making Lieutenant. His father hadn't spent a lot on it, on any of his initial kit, back in 1780 when he'd been shoved aboard a ship, so he'd be a thousand miles and six months away when Sir Hugo purloined an inheritance from Granny Lewrie, off in Whedon Cross in Devonshire. One of his retinue could use it when they raided the dog buffers' lair. Fusil musket, Girandoni air rifle, or the Ferguson rifled breechloader? No, they would draw too much attention from passersby, as would the over-under fowling gun. But, he had two pairs of pistols, some fine double-barrelled Mantons, and a brace of single-barrelled made by Henry Nock. He'd carry one of the Mantons, and parcel the rest out to his men.

And, there was the hanger sword that he'd been given in the West Indies, the one he'd worn at Toulon in 1794 when his bomb ship had been blown out from under him, and he'd had to hand it over to Napoleon Bonaparte after crawling onto a beach, refusing to give his parole, refusing to leave his surviving crew. He'd gotten it back in Paris in 1802 during the Peace of Amiens, from Bonaparte's hands at a *levée* in the Tuileries Palace. Just before discovering that he and Caroline were to be ambushed and murdered. Just before Caroline had been shot in the back and died at another beach near Calais as they made their escape.

No, he'd not risk that one to anyone else's hand. Swords were out. Both Hugh and Charles Chenery had dirks, and he knew that his young brother-in-law had spent some of his prize-money on a personal pistol; Hugh probably had one, himself, and he was a good shot from all their practicing in the country.

He spent some time cleaning and oiling his pistols, securing new flints in the dog's jaws of their firelocks, assuring himself that a good spark would ignite the powder in the pan when the time came.

"Oh, sir," Agnes said, peeking into the study, "thought you were in th' drawin' room. The Missuz is drowzin' off, an' said she'd sleep for a while. An' don't you worry, sir, I'll keep a sharp eye peeled on that nasty laudanum, t'see she don't take too much of it."

"Ah, thankee Agnes," Lewrie said with a firm nod. "Aye, I've seen men aboard ship . . . Surgeon's Mates mostly . . . who have access to it, and end up dependent. It's worse than a sot and his gin."

"Missuz Jessica asked me t'ask you if ya would be wantin' some tea an' a scone, sir," Agnes went on.

"That was thoughtful of her, worryin' about me in her condition," Lewrie said. "Aye, I am a bit peckish."

"Pot o' tea an' scones'll be ready in th' drawin' room, quick as the shake of a wee lamb's tail," Agnes perkily replied, dropping him a quick curtsy and departing.

His study window was still open, and he heard the pineapple door knocker clapping, then a mumble of Pettus's voice as he opened the door to speak with some caller. A moment later, and Pettus was at the study door.

"Excuse me, sir, but there's a grubby lad in the entry hall who *claims* he's a knife grinder," Pettus said, sounding dubious. "Not to worry, I've posted Turnbow and Dasher to keep an eye on him. He says he wishes to speak with you directly, sir."

"Aha!" Lewrie cried. "It may be the message from the thieves! Aye, I'll come."

Dignity of a homeowning gentleman bedamned, Lewrie went down the stairs to the ground floor and entry hall in a clatter.

"Yes?" he intoned warily when he got there. If this person was part of the dog buffer gang, he wished to strangle him on the spot, soon as the information about the ransom was passed.

The caller was a younger version of a "beau-nasty," dressed in a dark green broadcloth coat that was missing buttons, a buff waist-coat atop a grimy linen shirt with a scarf round his neck, and grey breeches but no stockings, and a cracked pair of buckle shoes. He snatched off a low-crowned, narrow brimmed brown hat that had seen too many rains, and nodded his head in greeting.

"G'day to ya, sir," the lad, who could not have been much older than thirteen or so, cheerily said, "an' blessin's t'this house. My name is Haddock. Someone said you're in need o' some help from th' Irregulars?"

"James Peel sent you?" Lewrie exclaimed, stunned.

"That he did, sir," Haddock said, beaming. "Well, Mister Peel spoke with my director, an' *he*, sent me. Us."

"Us?" Lewrie had to ask.

"First thing in th' mornin', sir," Haddock went on cheekily, "round first sparrer fart time, I'll be settin' up by yer servant's entrance, belowstairs, sharpenin' all yer knives, an' there's to be two girls in th' street, sellin' posies, an' t'other beggin' t'keep watch. When th' messenger comes t'yer door, we're t'trail him, an' tell ya where t'find yer criminals."

"My word!" Pettus exclaimed, not sure of what he was seeing or hearing. "Children?"

Lewrie took a second to glance at Pettus, and saw Dasher and Turnbow standing wide-eyed and mouths agape as if they had run into a ghost in the pantry.

"Best at it, sir," Haddock told Pettus. "Nobody suspects kids, even spies lookin' over their shoulders, an' wary of ev'rything."

"You've followed *spies?*" Dasher exclaimed, his eyes alight with sudden excitement.

"A time'r two, yeah," Haddock proudly revealed. "Don't ya be worryin', sir, we know what we're doin', an' me an' the girls can get so close t'our quarry we could snatch silk handkerchiefs, pick their pockets, or read their palms an' tell their fortunes. First thing o' th' mornin', mind, an' now I'll be goin'."

With that, he lifted his hat to doff, performed a sketchy bow, and spun about to open the door for himself and trot out in the street where he had left a small hand-cart with the tools of his supposed trade.

"Th' tea's ready t'serve, sir," Agnes said as she came up the stairs from the kitchens with a tray.

"Before supper, Pettus," Lewrie ordered. "Let's get all the lads together in the kitchen t'get ready for whatever happens tomorrow. Dasher? Turnbow? You'll need to carry notes to the manse at Saint Anselm's to Mister Chenery, and my father's place to alert my son, Hugh, as to what they'll need to do."

"Aye, sir," the lads chorused,

"We gonna be goin' along, sir?" Turnbow asked, looking eager.

"Not this time, Turnbow," Lewrie told him. "There might be one Hell of a scrape when we corner those rats, and get our dogs back."

With that said, Lewrie went back upstairs to the drawing room to sit on the settee, pour himself a cup of tea and stir in the cream and sugar, then split a scone in half to butter it and smear it with some strawberry jam.

I hope those children are as good as they claim, Lewrie thought as he chewed, and sluiced the bite of scone down with some tea; *Come t'think on it, I hope this plan works. There's many a slip, 'twixt the crouch and the leap. Ha! As many times as my perfect plans've turned t'shite, I ought t'know!*

"But I don't *need* someone to sharpen my knives!" Hazelwood, the testy cook, complained as loudly as he dared when Haddock turned up just after sunrise. "I sharpen my own knives! And I certainly would not trust them to a dirty hobbledehoy, a Gypsy! That boy *looks* like a Gypsy thief! He'll run off with my knives, after I've spent good money on them, and sell them for a *tenth* of what they're worth!"

"Do stop your gob, Mister Hazelwood," Lewrie testily snarled at him. "There's things afoot that *require* Haddock t'be seen sharpenin' knives in the street. We've guests for breakfast, so concern yourself with that."

"But, Sir Alan, sir!" Hazelwood tried to argue. "*What* things are afoot?"

"Gettin' the dogs back is all I'll say of it," Lewrie growled. "You worry about breakfast," he insisted as he went back up the stairs to the entry hall, just in time for his son to arrive. Hugh came in with an overcoat atop a civilian suit, with his dirk at his side and a pistol in the overcoat pocket.

"Brr," Hugh said, headed for the fireplace in the front parlour which was lit. "It's getting on for frost, father. Damned early in the morning, too."

"We'll lay in more coal and wood," Lewrie said. "With luck, our dogs'll have warm hearths t'sleep in front of, once they're back."

"In front of which to sleep," Hugh cheekily corrected him.

"Pedant," Lewrie shot back, grinning.

"Captain Chalmers was a stickler," Hugh shrugged off.

The door knocker thumped, and Lewrie went to open the door, himself. Charles Chenery had arrived.

"Morning, Charlie," Lewrie greeted him.

"Good morning, sir," Chenery replied.

"What the Devil's that?" Lewrie asked as Charles shrugged off his overcoat.

"I brought my dirk, a small pocket pistol, and a criquet bat," he said. "Well, it's hard wood, and somebody *might* find it a useful club."

"Right," Lewrie drawled, dubious. "Come on in and warm yourself. "Our cook's got coffee or tea coming. Anyone in the street?"

"Oh, there's some slip of a girl flogging posies," Charles said, "God only knows who she plans to sell them to this early, a coach or two, and there's some boy at your basement door whetting knives."

"As it should be, then," Lewrie cryptically decided. "There's no telling when the messenger shows up, but there's a good breakfast coming. Even if Hazelwood's in a snit. Why don't you two go into the dining room, out of sight, just in case."

"There's coffee ready did you say?" Hugh perked up after a good yawn. "That's for me. Come on, Charles. Bring your bat," he added with a snigger.

Lewrie went belowstairs once again to check on his men, all of whom were gathered round the servants' dining table, sipping coffee or tea, a rare treat for sailors aboard ship, As best they could, they'd dressed in civilian garb with their coats and hats laid by, but with weapons jammed into their waistbands, and their personal clasp knives in sheaths at their sides, to the consternation of the female servants and the younger lads. Seeing Yeovill armed seemed to put Hazelwood into a nervous, hand shaking clumsi-ness, and Yeovill was making the most of it, grinning evilly at Hazelwood now and then, and honing his knife on a stone from the back garden.

He returned to the dining room above, just in time for the food to ar-rive and be displayed on the sideboard; tatty hash, bacon, wee sausages, and at least a dozen eggs all scrambled in a serving bowl.

"If nothing comes of this morning, at least we'll eat well, hah hah," Charles Chenery chortled as he loaded his plate.

It was about an hour later that Lewrie went up to greet his wife and see how she was faring. The knot on her temple still throbbed, the sutures Dr. Stansfield had taken seemed to be drawing tauter, or so she said, and though her wrist didn't seem so painful, it was hard to move, was still swol-len, and required more of that ice to be bound round it.

"I may be getting better at feeding myself," Jessica jested, in better sprits, "I can pinch off bites of muffins, *clumsily* stir tea with my left hand, and manage to not make *too* much of a mess." She was propped up against the headboard with four thick feather pillows behind her, with a tray cross her lap, and a large napkin covering her breast and lap. "And do you see, Alan? A large serving spoon is the perfect thing for my eggs and potato hash. For the bacon, however," she demonstrated, picking up a rasher and taking a bite, "fingers are the very thing. Did I hear Hugh and my brother downstairs?"

"I invited them over to breakfast," Lewrie told her, hoping she didn't ask *why*. "Boys' day. Some cards, some backgammon," he lied. "I don't suppose you're up for a game?"

"Oh, after some light ablutions, I will drink some more willow bark tea, ghastly as it is . . . perhaps with some honey in it . . . and nap and read. Enjoy your games, dear."

"Enjoy your rest, my love," Lewrie said, blowing her a kiss.

He was halfway down the stairs to the ground floor when someone rapped on the door. Pettus, who was just coming up from the kitchen, froze in mid-stride and shared a look with him before going to unlock the door.

"Yes? What is your business?" he asked the wee urchin waif on the stoop, a raggedly dressed girl of about nine or ten, wrapped in a huge shawl that looked as if it would double for a horse blanket.

"Got a letter fer th' master o' th' 'ouse," she piped, glaring and darting her gaze into the entry hall as if gawking at the finery, then cutty-eyed to left and right as if fearing something out in the street. "Well, take h'it!" she insisted, then whirled about and got out into the street to make her escape.

"What's it say, Pettus?" Lewrie asked once the door was shut.

"Hard to tell, sir," Pettus said, frowning as he unfolded it and tried to puzzle it out. "Here, sir."

Genulmun
Yew want the dogs bak, put word note in the Xaminer paper. Watt kine dogs and watt yew col em. Ten pound eech, koin no paper, or yew never see em agin. Be reddi to pay first wen gerll cum bak.

"Word note," Lewrie tried to de-code. "I suppose he means reward notice. The *Examiner?* Not a Tory, is he? Though I doubt the fellow knows how to read *any* paper."

"Criminal gutter scum, sir," Pettus said with a sniff. "What are we to expect of people in such a low trade."

Lewrie went to front parlour windows, knelt on the cushions on the deep sill, and looked out. He couldn't see the urchin who had delivered the note, but, sure enough, a little girl with a tray of posies was making her way down to Piccadilly Street, and another wee beggar girl was rising and wrapping her blanket round herself, headed in the same direction. Below, in the basement servant and delivery entrance, Haddock was wrapping his whets and tools in a leather bundle. He looked up and tipped his hat, winking, before he set off, too.

Lewrie had told Jessica that it would be an idle day of cards and backgammon, and that was the way that he and the others passed the time, after all, waiting to hear back from the Irregulars. Finally, after what seemed an eternity, there was a rapping of the door knocker. Everyone froze, dice cups and hands of cards held still in mid-air for a second, ears cocked to hear what Pettus was saying belowstairs.

"It's that Haddock fellow, sir!" Pettus shouted up the stairs. "He's back!"

Everyone in the drawing room bolted to the entry hall, weapons stuffed into pockets, and Desmond, Deavers, and Yeovill came up from the kitchens, armed as well.

"Lo, sir," Haddock cheerfully said, doffing his hat to one and all, "We found 'em, an' they didn't go all that far away. They're in Ormond Yard, off Duke o' York Street, in an old barrel-maker's shop. Noisy as anything, with all th' barkin'. Ya can almost find it by the smells, ya can."

"Good Christ," Lewrie exclaimed. "I remember that place, when my father owned a house in Saint James's Square! Let's get our overcoats on, hide away our weapons, and get going. Pettus, could you go flag down a couple of hackneys for us?"

"Yes, sir," Pettus replied, though pausing for a second before doing so. "I still wish I could join you, sir. I'd give anything to face the brute who hurt Dame Lewrie, and my Lucy."

"We'll settle with him, no worry, Pettus," Lewrie vowed. "You will come along to show us the way, Haddock?"

"Yessir," the lad heartily agreed.

Out in the street, they found that the late morning had gone grey, with a low overcast and an unseasonable chill to the air, making their overcoats welcome. Pettus had managed to flag down a pair of hackneys, old and slightly shabby two-horse coaches that had seen better days when owned by private families. And what was this, the coachees wondered; three obvious gentlemen clambering into the first one, accompanied by a gutter urchin? A pack of men who could only be sailors getting into the second, and all going the same place?

"We oughta be gettin' out shy o' th' yard, sir," Haddock instructed, leaning far out the open sash window in the right-hand door as the hackney made its turn into Duke of York St. "Their hidey-hole is at th' far end."

"Pull up here, coachee," Lewrie called out, thumping his fist on the roof of the coach. "Let's go."

They spilled out of the coach, paid the fare, and waited for the sailors to join them.

"Ain't got th' fare, sor," Liam Desmond told Lewrie.

"Ah, shite," Lewrie spat, trotting back to the second coach to hand the coachee some coins before he could rejoin the others and take a peek from the corner of the entrance to the yard. Since all of them were curious, *everyone* had to lean out to scout the yard at the same time, forcing Lewrie to hiss covertly and wave them back, so only he and the boy, Haddock, could lean round the corner.

Ormond Yard had seen better days in Lewrie's boyhood, and gone down since. There were still a few houses that appeared to be occupied, a couple with broken windows that obviously weren't, a tailor's shop, a hatter's,

what looked to be a salvaged brick and stone scrap-yard, a stable and storage lot with a few broken down hackney coaches, and a pile of waggon
wheels, and a row of smaller shops with hanging signs advertising a penny-
ordinary, a dram shop, a tobacconist, and a poulterer's where wood cages
held live chickens, chicks, pigeons, and turkeys. As a commercial yard, it
looked to be a failure going slowly downhill. There were a few workmen,
stable boys, and poor folk about, and even the dram shop and the ordinary seemed abandoned.

"There's big double doors, sir, where they keep their cart," Haddock
said in a whisper. "I took a peek through gaps in the boards. The stable's
most-like where they rent a horse when needed. Listen t'all that yappin'
an' barkin'. It's a wonder the few folk who still live here haven't complained
t'th' police already. All day an' all night, I reckon. They must have dozens o' dogs in there!"

Lewrie gave it a long look, weighing his options. To just march down
the middle of the street like a threatening mob might alert the dog buffers to their presence and give them time to arm themselves. Could they
saunter down to the building at the far end, as if they were shopping?

"Everyone, have a look for yourselves," Lewrie ordered, "taking turns.
It's the old wood building at the far end. Used to be a shop where barrels
were made. The one with the big double doors."

That took some time before each man was satisfied. When Desmond
leaned round the corner, then stood out a foot or so from the wall he leaned
upon, Lewrie spotted something long pushing out his mid-thigh overcoat.

"What's that under your coat, Desmond?" Lewrie asked, "You bring
along your *uillean* pipes?"

"Mister Chenery's criquet bat, sor," Desmond said with a wicked grin.
"He says it makes a fine cudgel."

"Right, then," Lewrie said. "Here's how we'll do it. Pair off into twos,
then we'll stroll down either side of the yard like we're shoppers, or merely
curious, 'til we get to the end. If it looks as if the double doors are barred,
we'll try the single door, off to the right of them. Barge in, take 'em by
surprise, and keep quiet 'til we do. They get warnin', they might fight
t'keep their dogs. Right?"

Everyone nodded their agreement.

"Hugh, you go with me," he ordered his son, and, after a deep breath,
Lewrie stepped out into the street and began to stroll up the yard with his
hands in his overcoat pockets. He and Hugh stayed to the right side of
Ormond Yard, past the houses, the ordinary, and the dram shop. Hugh

un-buttoned his overcoat and checked that his dirk was in the right place, and Lewrie followed suit, putting his left hand back in a pocket, where he had secreted one of his Manton pistols.

"This is amazing, really," Hugh commented, peering about. "This close to Saint James's Square, and the Palace, one'd think that some developers would have bought the whole yard out and run up some fashionable new row or terrace houses."

"By the looks of the place, that may be comin' soon," Lewrie said in agreement. He began to take deeper breaths out of nerves and impending violence.

The man who hit Jessica, Lewrie fantasised; *I hope he's here. If he is, I mean t'hurt him. He had something on his hand. A big ring? If only I can spot him 'mongst the others.*

He looked back to see Charlie Chenery and Yeovill sauntering on the other side of the street, and Desmond and Deavers were behind him, clucking at the birds at the poulterer's, as innocent as anything.

He and Hugh reached the end of the street near the single door entrance whilst Chenery and Yeovill idled on the other side for a few seconds before walking past the double doors, to take a peek through the weathered gaps in the boards, and to see if there was a lock or a bar behind it. Chenery looked at Lewrie and shook his head "no."

No? What the Devil does that *mean?* Lewrie puzzled; *No lock or bar on the doors? No entrance?* He waved Charlie closer.

"No what?" he hissed.

"No way in there, sir," Chenery said. "The doors are barred. I could see a big baulk of timber mid-way up."

"Right, we'll bash our way in here, then," Lewrie decided as he drew his old dirk. "Good shoulders, here, lads."

Desmond pulled out the criquet bat, Deavers produced his clasp knife, and they put their shoulders to the door, making it move a bit.

"Kinda flimsy," Deavers said. "And a one, and a two, and a *go!*"

The door was indeed flimsy, for it slammed inwards quickly, the old hinges breaking free from the jamb at the top, sending the two men sprawling to their knees, and jamming up the others, outside.

"Wot th' fook?" a man inside bellowed in surprise. "Gie at 'em, lads!"

The urchin girl who served as their messenger let out a scream, leaping from the straw-filled pallet she was using as a bed on the dirt floor, and began to run around, looking for an escape. The dogs in their wood box cages began to bay and howl maniacally.

A big man came rushing the fallen door with a large knife in his hand, but Desmond had scrambled to his feet, swung the criquet bat, and hit him square in the face. His eyes crossed, his nose, already broken long before, spouted a gush of gore, and he spat out a pair of yellow teeth as he staggered backwards, windmilling his arms to keep his balance before tripping over his own feet and falling to the dirt like a very large sack of grain, unconscious, in a cloud of dust.

"Oh, yes!" Desmond hooted with glee and rushed forward, cocking the bat over his shoulder.

"At 'em, lads!" Lewrie roared. "Away boarders! Yahh!" he yelled as he ran in with his dirk jutting forward, and his Manton pulled from his pocket in his left hand.

A ratty fellow snatched up an iron poker from the large cooking hearth that barely warmed the large shop and tried to swing his way to the door, but Deavers pulled one of Lewrie's single-shot pistols and shot him in the leg, making him howl, hop about, and stumble even as he continued swinging his poker.

Him! Lewrie told himself, spotting the biggest villain at the rear of the shop who was loping forward with a clumsy-looking pistol in one hand, and a large butcher knife in the other; *He has a ring!*

There was a glint of yellow gold on his left hand, and Lewrie leaped eagerly to engage him. The man raised his pistol, but Lewrie cocked the right-hand firelock of his own on the back of his right wrist, raised his, and fired, just as the burly brute fired his. A lead ball droned past Lewrie's head, but his own had connected, hitting the dog buffer at the point of his right shoulder.

I can shoot better than that! Lewrie chid himself as the brute clapped his left hand to his wound.

"Steal *my* dogs, will ye?" Lewrie roared, "Strike my *wife*, will ye? I'll kill ye for it!"

The man took his hand away from his wound and took a wild swing with the butcher knife, which Lewrie blocked with the blade of his dirk, countering with a jab at his chest, and blocking the next slash with the barrels of his pistol, back-slashing and ripping a gash into the villain's face, making him howl and stagger backwards 'til he fetched up against a large table. One of the table legs gave way and he sprawled on his back and buttocks. Lewrie cocked the left-hand barrel of his pistol and aimed it at his chest.

"You get up, you die," Lewrie warned him, his finger on the trigger, and wishing that the man would try. But no, he'd had quite enough. His left fist opened and the butcher knife dropped to the dirt floor, so he could clap that hand to his face where his blood ran freely, soaking his filthy shirt and coat collars.

"Rembrandt? Bisquit? Here, dogs! Where are you?" Charlie was calling out, trotting down the rows of cages and bending down to look inside them. "Woohoo! I found them, Captain Lewrie! They're here!"

"Ow! Quit tryin' t'bite me, ya hellcat!" Deavers cried as he held the urchin girl's arms behind her. "Somebody, get some rope."

She squirmed, she tried to kick backwards, she writhed and let out a long, feral scream worthy of a panther, as Yeovill found a bit of rope atop an old keg and came to bind her arms above her elbows. She wept, she screeched, then launched into a string of curses not heard this side of Billingsgate Fish Market, before switching over to loud shrieks of "Murder, they's murderers 'ere! 'Elp! They killin' me!"

"Got the others bound?" Lewrie asked as Hugh and Desmond came to lash up Lewrie's foe. Once bound, Lewrie carefully un-cocked his pistol, and shoved it back into his overcoat pocket.

"What's acting here?" someone bellowed from the broken door in an authoritative voice. "You men, show your hands."

Lewrie turned to see three police constables coming into the building, truncheons out and slapping them on their palms.

"Gentlemen," Lewrie began, "Allow me to name myself. Captain Sir Alan Lewrie, Baronet, Royal Navy. These three men are dog buffers who attacked my wife, Dame Lewrie, and her maid in Green Park yesterday, and stole our dogs. We found where they kept them and came to get them back. As you can see, and hear, they've a great many dogs they've stolen, as well. Allow me to name my compatriots . . ." he said with a smile on his face, pointing to Hugh, Charlie, who now had Bisquit and Rembrandt on a leash, or a length of rope, and his sailors.

"Dog buffers, hey?" the leader of the constables said, walking round. "Yes, there's proof of th' puddin'."

"They're all yours, trussed up and ready to go," Lewrie said.

"Got nought t'do wif h'it,' the girl protested. "I jus' like th' dogs, an' come play wif 'em now an' then, yer honour sir!"

"She's the one who delivers their ransom demands," Lewrie said.

"Then it looks like you'll be comin' with us, too, girl," the senior constable said with a grin. "'Yer honour sir,' my eye! Sounds like you've been before a magistrate before. Shots were fired, were there, Captain Lewrie?"

"That one took a shot at me, and I fired back," Lewrie told him. "One of my men fired one shot to put down that'un there whilst he was tryin' t'crack his head with a fire poker. Oh, Bisquit, yes puppy!" he cried, dropping to one knee as his old shipmate broke free from Charlie's grip on the rope and swarmed Lewrie, tail wagging like mad, paws on his shoulders and licking his face, whining welcome. "We'll be gettin' you home, yes we *will*!

"I'll be needin' to write out a report, the attack in the park and all, Captain Lewrie," the constable said, reaching inside his coat for a stub of pencil and some loose paper. "Or, better yet, you could come with me to the station house and write it all up proper."

"I can do that, if my men can get our dogs back to my house," Lewrie allowed. "Hugh, Charlie, can you see them home?"

"Aye, sir," Charlie promised. "Won't my sister be pleased!"

"Uhm, father," Hugh said, arms akimbo as he surveyed the place.

"Yes?" Lewrie said, smiling back, full of triumph for a successful raid.

"What are we going to do with all these other dogs, then?" his son enquired with a thoughtful frown on his face.

"Well, ah . . ." Lewrie replied, looking all round himself. "Hmm. My boy, that's a damned good question!"

BOOK FOUR

Away, you scullion! You rampallion! You fustilarion!
I'll tickle your catastrophe!
WILLIAM SHAKESPEARE, *THE MERRY WIVES
OF WINDSOR*, ACT II 67

CHAPTER TWENTY-TWO

*T*here was no quick return to his house to bask in Jessica's joy and gratitude, no heroic welcome. No, there was the report to the police, laying charges against the dog buffers, and with a promise to show up in court and testify against them. And once that was done, Lewrie had to coach back to the lair in Ormond Yard to see the men of his retinue whom he'd left to guard and tend to the other dogs.

"I made a list, sir," Deavers told him. "The thieves wrote down the names and addresses of all the people they stole dogs from. It's hard to read their scribbling. I guess, in the morning, we could make the rounds and return them."

"Hmm, it'd be easier if they came here t'claim 'em," Lewrie said, "if they want 'em bad enough. I could place an advertisement in some newspapers. *The Times*, the *Gazette*, the Tory *Morning Post*, and even the liberal *Examiner*. Christ, I don't even know where their offices are!"

"Then there's the matter of food, sir," Deavers pointed out.

"Do dogs like raw chicken, or cooked, I wonder," Lewrie pondered. "There's a poulterer right down the yard. He has some plucked, hangin' up and ready to go." Lewrie dug into his coin purse, found that he'd spent a slew on hackney fares, and dug out his new-fangled wallet. "Here's a five pound note. See how much that'll buy."

"On my way, sir," Deavers said with a grin.

"Any *other* problems?" Lewrie asked, spreading his arms wide.

"There ain't much coal in here to heat with, sor," Liam Desmond told him, standing by the hearth and rubbing his hands. "It's sure to be a cool night, sor."

"T'keep the dogs comfortable, *and* the guards," Lewrie agreed. "No coal tonight, perhaps, but the old barrel-makers left a pile of staves and lids, and that low wall o' old barrels and kegs can be broken down and burned."

"Guards, sir?" Yeovill asked.

"There's no way to lock this place up secure enough to prevent other dog buffers comin' in and stealin' the dogs all over again," Lewrie said with a sigh. That meant that he would have to send home for blankets, lots of them, and spare . . . spare everything needful to carry himself and his men overnight. There was no way he would coach home to a good supper, hot tea and muffins, and a warm bed.

"Make a list, Yeovill, of what you'd need t'cook us up a warm supper tonight, and bread, cheese, and beer for morning," he ticked off on his fingers, adding mugs, plates, and eating utensils. "Enough for four," he concluded. "It looks as if I'll be sleepin' rough tonight. When we list everything, trot home and fetch it, and tell my wife that I've still got things to do here."

"Aye, sir," Yeovill said, looking round for pencil and paper.

"The place needs muckin' out, sor," Desmond suggested. "Th' boxes are full o' dog filth an' they may need bathin', to boot. Maybe when th' mornin' comes, we could send for Dasher an' Turnbow t'help out."

"Oh God, brooms, mops, water, too," Lewrie bemoaned. This was turning into an enterprise as daunting as putting a ship into commission!

"That stable, sor," Desmond pointed out. "They got all we need, and I'd bet their stableboys an' daisy kickers'd be willin' t'help if they got a shillin' or two for it."

"There's an ordinary right down the yard, sir," Yeovill said, jerking his head in that direction as he scribbled his list. "Might be good enough for breakfast."

"A penny ordinary, most-like, would poison us by noon," Lewrie scoffed. "God only knows what they serve and call food."

"There's a dram shop, too," Desmond said with a taut, innocent grin. "They're sure to have beer or ale."

"We'll trust to what Yeovill fetches us back from home," Lewrie quickly replied, knowing his Cox'n's penchant for drink, and he'd seen that angelic grin on his phyz countless times before. "Are there any lanthorns or candles in here? We can't stand guard in the dark. Do look, Desmond."

There was one old, battered lanthorn with cracked glass panes, and a stub of a tallow candle inside it, several more tallow candles wrapped in newspaper, but too few candle holders. Yeovill wrote down bee's wax candles to his list, along with empty bottles for holders.

"I got eight boiling hens at the poulterer's, sir," Deavers reported as he bustled back in with a sack over his shoulder, "and a dozen candled eggs for tomorrow. Inspected them myself, so we won't boil up un-hatched chicks. Came to two pounds eight, and here's your change, sir."

"Ah, thankee, Deavers," Lewrie said, pocketing one pound notes and coins. "Can anyone else think of anything necessary?"

"Feather beds, sor?" Desmond quipped. "Beef steaks an' potatoes?"

"There's more than enough chickens for the dogs and us," Yeovill announced after poking them and having a sniff to see how fresh they were. "I'll bring my spices and sauces, and if someone could go down to that greengrocer's and find some potatoes, carrots, peas, and such, I can throw a decent stew together. Here's my list, sir. Add what you think best."

Lewrie looked it over and saw that Yeovill, as usual, was thorough, right down to blankets, candles, and his cooking utensils.

"Looks good, Yeovill," Lewrie told him. "You toddle off home and I'll whistle up a hackney and try t'find all the newspaper offices before dark, so they'll have the advertisements ready to print in the morning. Maybe the constables at the police station know."

"I'm off, then, sir," Yeovill, said, accepting some coins from Lewrie for the fare there and back. "Back in a tick."

Fortunately for Lewrie, the police did know where the offices of the various papers were, since they submitted all the crimes and alarums to them each evening for the next-day editions. A bargain was struck 'twixt Lewrie and the chief constable, alleging that the police had co-operated in the raid that apprehended the thievish gang. Lewrie and the chief constable wrote it together, including the list of people whose dogs had been stolen, and a sketchy description of breed or colour, that their pets could be returned to them if they called in Ormond Yard, at no cost, thanks to the bold action taken by Captain Sir Alan Lewrie, Bt., RN to retrieve his own dogs, with the able assistance of Midshipman Hugh Lewrie, Midshipman Charles Chenery, and several men of Captain Lewrie's household. It took time to write out, correct, and agree on the finer points, then got sent off in the hands of constables going off-duty for the night to the various newspaper editors.

It was nearly five in the afternoon by the time Lewrie returned to Ormond Yard and paid off his coachman, just in time for a fine and misty rain to begin to fall, making his triple-caped overcoat more than welcome.

As he strode past the poulterer's and the stables, now full of tired coach horses neighing for their fodder, the barrel-manufactury seemed almost homey. Smoke was rising from both the hearth and the forge fireplace where barrel hoops had been pounded out from raw iron strips. What windows there were, and the broken single door entry, showed the winking and flickers of an host of candles, and was there a whiff of chickens stewing in there?

What in Hell's this crowd about? he wondered as he got closer, for there were men, women, and children gathered round the door, trying to peer inside, though the women held scented handkerchiefs and wee posies to their noses to counteract the stink, curious despite it.

And, of course, there was the loquacious Liam Desmond telling them all about the raid and what had led to it, his Irish brogue even thicker then normal as he jollied them along.

"Nah nah, ma'am, we're standin' watch over th' dogs, 'cause the real owners ain't come t'claim 'em yet, arrah," Desmond told a lady, "th' dog buffers took no care of 'em, sure, an' we want t'let 'em rest quiet, for a change. Note how they're not barkin' so loud as they did before we busted in? Oh, Jaysus, Mary, an' Joseph, but the rogues put up quite a fight afore we overcame 'em."

"Desmond," Lewrie said, touching the brim of his hat.

"Cap'um Lewrie, sor! Th' very fella who led us!" Desmond said, sweeping his hat off in salute. "*Sir* Alan Lewrie, Baronet, one o' th' fightin'est Cap'ums in the Royal Navy, th' victor of an hundred battles, nigh as famed as Lord Nelson, God rest his soul, arrah!"

There came a chorus of Ooohs and Ahhs from the bystanders.

"People, good evening," Lewrie had to say, doffing his hat again, and plastering a modest grin on his phyz. "Excuse me."

"Th' thieves attacked his good wife and her maid in Green Park yesterday, pulled knives, clubbed Dame Lewrie on th' head when she wouldn't let go th' leash, an' dragged her by her wrist afore they tore th' Capum's dog away. What else could a bold man do, after that, I ask ye all? Still laid up in bed, she is . . ."

Oh, do stop yer gob, Desmond, Lewrie thought, gritting his teeth as he entered the building to peel off his hat and overcoat; *Damme, it's almost warm in here! Still stinks t'high heaven, but the dogs're mostly quiet.*

Empty brandy and wine bottles stood everywhere, sporting tallow or wax candles, throwing an amber glow all round the dog cages and the fire-places. The straw-filled pallet the urchin girl had slept on had disappeared, most-like burned for fuel, along with its lice and fleas. The broken table had been propped back in place atop some old barrels, and smaller kegs sat round it in lieu of chairs. Beds on the dirt floor were marked by blankets, two to a place.

"Ah, Captain Lewrie, sir," Yeovill perkily greeted him, busy at the fire-place, where he'd hung a large copper cauldron, stirring the contents with a large spoon. "I gave Pettus your message to Missuz Lewrie, and she said to tell you that she's thrilled beyond measure to have Rembrandt back. Pettus says her dog's atop her bed, in her lap, and not likely to move, ever. She said it was brave of you, and most responsible to stand guard over the dogs 'til their owners claim them, though she'd love to have you home, and ah . . . hug and kiss you."

Yeovill actually seemed to blush; maybe it was the firelight.

"Hazelwood went raving daft, of course," Yeovill went on, "with all the victuals I fetched off, an apple pie he'd baked, and all of my cooking goods. And his knives, sir," Yeovill sniggered this time at his nemesis's rage. "That lad Haddock may be a canny tracker, but he knows nothing of sharpening knives, and half of Hazelwood's blades are blunted or scarred up with file marks. He swears he hasn't one decent knife left to cut an apple in two, or pare off a slice of cheese!"

"Oh, bugger him," Lewrie said, looking for a keg to sit on. "I see Desmond is in fine form."

"Loves an audience for his yarns, sir," Deavers said, chuckling. "And this'un's gettin' grander with each telling. Care for an ale, sir?"

"Yes, I certainly do!" Lewrie agreed, realising how dry his stay at the police station had been.

"The dogs have been fed, sir," Deavers told him as he tapped an ale in a tall china mug. "That's why they're so quiet, now. Poor wee things. Boiled chicken meat, no bones to choke on. They were really starving. There may be enough left over for their breakfasts, too."

"Good, very good, Deavers," Lewrie said, nodding his thanks as he stuck his nose into the mug and took a deep draught of ale with a smack of his lips and a long, drawn out "Aahh!"

By God, I think you could plunk Yeovill down in the middle of the Egyptian desert, and he'd produce a feast! Lewrie thought as the spicy aromas of the stew, or whatever it was, wafted over him. He took a peek at the hearth and spotted slabs of cheese and loaves of bread.

And when it came time to eat, gathered round the propped up wood table, they had mugs, china plates, bowls, knives, spoons and forks, and the meal consisted of a creamy pea soup, that bread and cheese in liberal slices, a savoury chicken stew loaded with vegetables, and the apple pie for afters.

Yeovill had even taken the time to scrounge up some leaf tobacco for those who had pipes. The pots and pans, plates and utensils were taken to the stables where there was a water pump, to be sluiced out.

An attempt was made to brace the broken door back in place, for show, mostly, and the first watch was set, Lewrie volunteering for the first watch, and letting the others doss down on their blankets. He waited three hours before shaking Desmond awake, then retired himself, after giving his pocket watch to Desmond. The misty rain still fell, swirling like a halo round the few lanthorns in Ormond Yard as he lay down on the lower blanket, spread the other atop him, and added his overcoat atop that, and with his weapons near to hand.

Sleep was hard to come by, though, for Yeovill, he discovered, snored like a steam engine, and the thirteen remaining dogs in their cages whimpered and whined in longing for their masters and familiar places. One young Pomeranian even approached a mournful howl.

I'd get it out and let it sleep with me, Lewrie considered; *but for the probable fleas, and the shite it's lain in. And has anyone bathed and groomed Bisquit and Rembrandt?*

CHAPTER TWENTY-THREE

*W*hen at last the sun rose through a river fog, the fires were in full bloom, again, breakfast was sizzling in Yeovill's skillets, beds were shaken out and folded into a large pile, and buckets of water for the dogs, and human ablutions, were fetched from the stables. There was ale from one of the shops in the yard to slosh down scrambled eggs, sliced potatoes, and toast with butter and jam.

Leftover chicken meat was fed to the dogs, then, one at a time, they were leashed and let out of their cages, then led outside into the yard, where they did their business. As each cage was left empty, buckets of water and mops swabbed them out of the worst filth. Once free, though, the dogs were loath to return to their pens before they were walked up to Duke of York St. at a brisk pace and back.

Lewrie strolled up to the shops, looking for the morning papers, but all he could find was a single copy of the *Morning Post*. Evidently, keeping up with things, and reading itself, were not all that important to the denizens of Ormond Yard, and he couldn't even buy it; it was held at the ordinary for anyone to pick up, like a coffee house.

News pages were always on the inside, with a four page sheet of advertisements on the outside, and there it was, his notice, smack dab in the middle of the first page, large and bordered.

"Oh, good God!" Lewrie muttered as he read it. Someone at the paper had embellished the notice, making their raid sound only a bit less adventurous and dangerous than the Battle of Talavera . . . or one of Liam Desmond's last recitations of the tale to last night's visitors. "Th' owners gonna come an' get their dogs, then?" the publican asked as he swabbed a table top with a tea towel.

"That's the plan," Lewrie told him as he folded the paper back in order.

"Good, 'cause me an' th' missus sleep upstairs, an' th' barkin' was drivin' us both daft," the man snarled. "But, will th' swells who come spend any money round here, I ask ye? Pshaw!"

Lewrie went back to the barrel-maker's, noting that the double doors had been thrown open and the two-wheeled cart had been pushed out of the way. "Airin' th' place out, sir," Desmond told him as he entered. "Don't smell half so bad as before, sure."

"There's still a hellish stink," Lewrie noted, wrinkling his nose.

"Oh, that'd be the 'jakes' t'other side o' th' yard, sir," Liam Desmond informed him, jerking his head in that direction to indicate a row of five sagging doors at the front of a large shed, separating it into compartments no bigger than a "Parish Charlies'" watchman's booth. "I think th' whole yard uses 'em."

"Ugh," Lewrie said, grimacing. "I'd rather do my business right out in the open, on the cobblestones. And with only the one newspaper at the ordinary, it don't bear thinkin' about."

"Ah, someone's comin', sir," Desmond pointed out.

Sure enough, a well-dressed gentleman was stepping down from a hackney in front of the stables, assisting his equally well-dressed wife, and two children, who held to his hand once alit, but tugging in impatience. The gentleman asked one of the stablemen who pointed to the end of the yard, and the adults turned and walked in Lewrie's direction, careful of their footing on some loose cobblestones that could squirt muddy water after last night's fine rain. The children broke away and ran, despite their parents' warnings.

"Please, sir!" the boy almost pleaded, "Is this where the dog buffers kept? Is our dog here?"

"Pudding?" the girl yelled, "Are you here, Pudding?"

To her amazement and delight, one of the dogs inside gave out a quizzical *Whoof?*

"This is the place, young man," Lewrie told the lad. "Go in and claim your dog."

They needed no more encouragement, dashing through the doors and squealing in joy to spot their pet.

Deavers fetched a leash and let the dog out of its cage, handing the leash to the children, which was quickly wound round their legs as their dog, a black-and-white Border Collie leaped, wriggled, and bounded in equal rapture.

"He's here, he's here, he's safe, papa!" the girl shrieked and laughed as her face was licked. She knelt to embrace him.

"One down, a dozen t'go!" Lewrie yelled to his men, feeling an equal delight.

"Good day, sir," the gentleman said as he doffed his hat. "So this is the place, sir? Samuel Putnam," he said extanding his hand. "And you are?"

"Captain Alan Lewrie," Lewrie answered.

"The fellow who raided this stew, sir?" Putnam said, "My eternal thanks to you for doing so. Out children were heartbroken 'til we saw the advertisement. The felons are under arrest? Good, very good, and damn their blood. Ehm, is there a fee?"

"No charge, Mister Putnam," Lewrie assured him. "I rescued both my dogs yesterday, and didn't know quite what to do with the others 'til the police spoke with me. Keep a sharp eye on your dog, though, Mister Putnam. This gang isn't the only batch of dog-nappers. I am delighted that you have him back."

Putnam shooed his children out towards the waiting hackney, not without getting an exuberant greeting from the dog, then got everyone back in and it whipped away.

"Now, that's a good feeling, it is, sir," Yeovill said.

"Damned if it ain't, Yeovill," Lewrie told him. "Those children are happy, the dog's happy . . . and *we're* happy."

Over the course of the morning, seven more parties showed up to retrieve their pets, usually with children in tow who were cock-a-whoop with joy to see their beloved dogs and take them home, again.

Round noon, two hackneys rolled into Ormond Yard at the same time and at least six people got down, and approached the barrel-maker's, a party that had no children with them. For a moment, Lewrie imagined that all the remaining dogs were to be claimed at once, but as they got closer, he changed his assumption. He had been sitting on a keg, dangling his booted feet, but sprang off and went to greet them.

"Have you come for your dogs, sirs, ladies?" he asked, doffing his hat.

"We have not lost our dogs, my good man," a portly fellow said, shifting his walking stick to his other hand to doff his own hat, revealing a sprawling shock of white hair, "We've come to call upon the hero who broke up that scurrilous mob of dog-nappers, Captain Sir Alan Lewrie, Baronet."

"You found me, sir," Lewrie said with a grin. That got a mixed reception, some Oohs and Aahs, an Aha! or two, along with a few pruny faces as they observed his dress. The day had cleared to a sunny and warm-ish one, so Lewrie had doffed his overcoat, coat, waist-coat, and neck-stock, and was in his shirtsleeves, and those rolled to the elbow.

"Then, allow me to express our admiration," the portly fellow said, "We are members of The National Society To Eliminate Cruelty In All Forms Towards Animals." He rocked on his feet and puffed out his substantial chest, performing a sweeping bow.

You'll never make an acronym o' that mouthful, Lewrie thought.

"Delighted t'make your acquaintance, sirs, ladies," Lewrie said instead. The portly fellow, one Mr. Singleton, named his compatriots, though most of their names flew right past Lewrie's ken, sure that he would meet them only once. "A noble goal, I'm sure."

"Indeed it is, Sir Alan," Mr. Singleton said with a fierce look coming over his phyz, "One sees brute cruelty everywhere, daily, in the streets of London. Working beasts starved and beaten to perform far beyond their strength, horses horribly whipped, dogs, cats, and all manner of lesser creatures abused, kicked, and tormented for people's amusement. It is shameful, sir, shameful beyond belief!"

There was a chorus of Amens from the rest of his committee.

"So, when we read of such a noble deed to rescue animals from fear, starvation, and a horrible fate should their owners refuse to ransom them, or do not have the means to do so, we all were quite literally overjoyed, and determined to come honour the man who did such a selfless thing."

"Well, they had my dog, and my wife's dog," Lewrie pointed out, "and they attacked my wife and her maid. Dame Lewrie is still in bed from her injuries. It was partly vengeance, in truth."

"Our condolences to your good wife, sir," Singleton intoned as if he was at a funeral, laying his hat on his heart. "Your act was heroic, nonetheless, and we wish to honour you."

"Come meet my men, who fought with me," Lewrie bade, sweeping an arm inside the building. "I hope we've done enough to rid the place of its odours. There's the cages where they penned the dogs. Allow me to name to you Liam Desmond, my long-time Cox'n, Michael Deavers, my cabin steward when I'm at sea, and my personal cook, John Yeovill."

His men did not pull their forelocks like servants or farm laborers; they doffed their hats briefly, nodded and smiled, then went back to what they were doing. Once more, Lewrie's introduction of common sailors to the committee got a mixed-bag reception.

"We've still got five dogs left, as you can see," Lewrie said, giving them a brief tour, "Counting mine, they had fifteen in all. At ten pounds ransom each, the dog buffers expected a fine profit. God only knows how many they'd stolen overall. Or how many they killed, skinned for their pelts, and ate."

He took secret delight to see them cringe, put handkerchiefs to their faces, or the ladies pulling out their fans to whisk fresh air, vigourously beating the aether.

"Is . . . is that blood?" one of the other gentleman asked with a pale face.

"Probably is," Lewrie told him. "It was a hard, but short fight. We had to shoot a couple of them when they pulled out pistols."

The committee broke into pairs to stroll round the large room, gawking at weapons, the cages, the penned up dogs, the cooking arrangements, and the piles of staves.

"There's still a lot to do to muck this place out," Lewrie went on. "Would any of you care to lend a hand?"

None of them barked an indignant "Certainly not!" but the look of being asked to do something menial was there.

Thought so, Lewrie told himself; *They're talkers, not do-ers.*

"We would . . . all here present . . . and our other members, would wish to honour you, Sir Alan, with a benefit dinner," Mr. Singleton proposed of a sudden, "We hold our monthly meetings at Nerot's Hotel, quite near Saint James's Palace . . ."

"I know the place," Lewrie told them, "A dinner, you say?"

"In a few weeks, and, should Dame Lewrie be up to it, perhaps you both could attend?" Singleton said with a simpering noise.

"That would depend on her physician's advice, sir," Lewrie said with a frown. "But, should she be recovered by then, I believe she'd be delighted, as would I."

Oh, simply capital!" Singleton exclaimed. "Our other members are, I am certain, eager to meet you, as would such members of the public who would also attend, and contribute to the cause."

"We live at Twenty-Two Dover Street," Lewrie told him. "Write me with the pertinent details."

"Thank you, Sir Alan, thank you for your courage, for your brave deed, for your great care for animals!" Singleton cried, shaking his hand, sounding as if he was in some rapture. "We will detain your good works no longer, and bid you a fond, admiring good day!"

With that, they all bowed or curtsied their way out, got back in their carriages . . . personal carriages, not hackneys . . . and rattled off.

"Faith, sir, and what th' Devil was that about?" Desmond asked, amused.

"A flock o' silly geese, Desmond," Lewrie said, chuckling and shaking his head. "Do-gooders out to right the world like those Abolitionists who want to do away with slavery. What'd they call themselves? The National Society To Eliminate Cruelty . . . to something or other. They probably have a 'down' on fox hunting, too. Too hard on the fox!"

"Too hard on th' cottagers, more like, sir," Desmond sneered. "Gallopin' over poor people's farm plots an' tramplin' their pigs an' chickens. Anglo-Irish back home is mad for it. When me an' Furfy was littl'uns, whenever we heard someone blowin' his 'tara tara,' we hid in th' house, or they'da trampled *us*!"

"Sounds more like steeple-chasin' to me," Lewrie said. "That's what does the damage."

"Well, they're both daft, sir," Desmond decided.

"Amen," Lewrie agreed; he knew his limits as a horseman, though he'd done both when he was younger.

"Excuse me, excuse me?" a fine lady, escorted by her maid and a footman called out as she tentatively approached the building after alighting from a private coach with a coat-of-arms painted on the door. "Is this where the stolen dogs are kept? I am looking for my little dog, a Pomeranian. He answers to Precious."

"It is, madame," Lewrie said, "and there *is* a white and tan Pomeranian inside. Do come in!"

Finally, after a hasty dinner of bread, cheese, and some apples from the greengrocer, and more ale, the last dog was retrieved by an old couple who came by foot to Ormond Yard, a pair who appeared to be unable to afford a ransom fee. Their dog was only a mutt of lovable but mixed breed who had been a particular favourite of Lewrie's men.

The mops, brooms, pails, and rakes were returned to the stables, and Deavers was despatched to Duke of York St. to flag down a coach to take them home, at last. Lewrie had re-dressed, with his overcoat slung over one arm, his weapons stashed on his person, and looking round to see that nothing was left behind.

"Hallo, who's this?" Yeovill said, kneeling down. "What are you doing here, puss? The smell of food draw you?"

The cat was a young one, recently weaned, a black-and-white tom who showed no distress at being picked up and cuddled to Yeovill's chest in one arm as Yeovill picked up a scrap or two of the stewed chicken left-overs that they'd been feeding to the dogs. Lewrie was drawn to it at once.

"Isn't he a fine one?" Lewrie cooed, stroking its head with one finger as it avidly chomped on the chicken scraps. "Long ago, I had a cat much like him. Bit of a disaster that I adopted at Toulon, so that was his name . . . one disaster *found* at a disaster. He was a fine cat, for all that."

Done with his scraps, the kitten regarded Lewrie with jade green eyes, blinked slowly as if contemplating, then wriggled and reached out a paw to take hold of Lewrie's coat lapel. Yeovill let him go and the kitten scrambled into Lewrie's grasp, sniffing him over. It had a white mask, a black nose, white paws, and white belly, with a streak of white down its back like a bolt of lightning. As Lewrie stroked it, it began to purr, once more raised its gaze to look him in the eye, and licked his fingers. It began to throb with its purr.

"Think you just got adopted yourself, sir," Yeovill sniggered. "A kitten on his own, round here, wouldn't last out the week. Maybe you should . . . to make up for losing Chalky."

"We'll need to buy a barrel of dry sand, build a box for it," Lewrie said. "But aye, I think I'll take him with us. Something good comes o' this, after all. Come on, puss. You're going t'have a home. Don't piss all over it, please? Claw up the upholstery? My wife'd not care for it. We'll figure out what t'call you. Hmm, how would you like . . . Buffer?"

CHAPTER TWENTY-FOUR

Oh, you're feeling better!" Lewrie exclaimed one morning a few days later as he sat at-table in the smaller morning room, having his breakfast, when Jessica came sweeping in, dressed in one of her older gowns.

"I could not, in good conscience, lounge in bed a minute longer," she said as he rose to pull out her chair for her. "You're spoiling him," Jessica told him, jutting her chin at the kitten, Buffer, which was chewing away at a slice of a wee sausage from his bowl, atop the table.

"Nonsense, pets are meant t'be spoiled," Lewrie japed, "most especially cats."

"Only you could go off to rescue two animals, and come back with three," Jessica said with an amused shake of her head.

"Your head doesn't hurt anymore?" Lewrie asked, watching her careful movements to pour tea for herself, cream and sugar it with her left hand, and stir it up.

"The ice reduced the knot, and all I feel now is the pull of the sutures," Jessica told him, "and Doctor Stansfield is coming today to remove them." She set her cup down, pulled back her hair and leaned forward so Lewrie could see. "It's not much of a red scar, and that will subside after a time, I dearly hope."

"I'm sure it will," Lewrie agreed, "though it *will* make you more mysterious."

Buffer had had enough breakfast, and pounced on Lewrie's right wrist, giving out a rather loud *Meow!* for such a small kitten, and flopped on his side to play, and when Lewrie rubbed his belly, Buffer rolled full on his back, wriggling happily, his belly fully exposed.

"My poor upholstery, and drapes," Jessica said with a sigh.

"We've half an hundredweight of sand in a barrel belowstairs," Lewrie explained, "and he's taken to the boxes right off. Had himself quite a prowl, from the kitchen to the garret, over three hours of it.

"By the way," Lewrie said with a smirk, "Hazelwood denied him access to the kitchens. He says cats make him break out in a rash and sneeze his head off."

"I don't know whether to feel sorry for him, or take joy of his suffering," Jessica said, trying to butter a thick slice of toast, but making a one-handed muck of it. "Lucy and the chambermaids tell me that he's quite the tyrant with our servants."

"Then Buffer may need a warm and comfy place to sleep this winter, close to the ovens and fireplaces, instead of our bedchamber," Lewrie suggested, almost cackling with glee. "Here, let me help. How's your wrist?"

"Oh, stiff and still a bit sore," Jessica had to admit, raising her right hand and flexing her fingers, and rotating her hand, wincing a little though she tried to put a bold face on it. "The ice, again, helps, though it's going fast. That and the willow bark tea. With any luck, I can get back to painting Hugh's portrait that I promised, say another week or so?"

"Poor darling," Lewrie commiserated, kissing her fingers, "You must be frustrated beyond all temperance. So many sketches you wish to turn into oils.

"What the Hell's that?" Lewrie asked of a sudden, cocking his head to catch some noisy commotion belowstairs. He rose from his seat and raised the sash window that overlooked the back garden, wondering if there was some civil riot erupting, stirred by some Captain Tom of the Mob. He stuck his head out and looked straight down, just in time to see Yeovill and Hazelwood emerge from the basement entrance, stamp up the stone stairs past the water pump, and go at each other, arms and fists flailing, and both cursing a blue streak!

"Hoy! Avast, damn yer eyes!" Lewrie shouted down.

Deavers and Desmond, and the lads, Dasher and Turnbow, emerged a moment later, followed by the scullery maid, all three dogs, and the chambermaids, hooting, shouting, and barking.

Peacekeepers, or spectators? Lewrie asked himself; *Layin' wagers on who cracks the other's head first?*

"You two stop that, at once, hear me?" he shouted louder, but the combatants paid him no heed. Lewrie snatched his napkin from his shirt collar and bounded for the stairs. "The damn fools are havin' at each other!" he shouted over his shoulder to Jessica, who also rose to look out the window to see which "damn fools" he meant.

By the time Lewrie tore through the kitchens and out to the back garden, he could see that Hazelwood had armed himself with a long soup ladle, and Yeovill had snatched up a thin lath that had been supporting a so-far-unsuccessful rose bush. Neither one of them had any combat experience, beyond the occasional foray ashore that Yeovill had made, which usually resulted in him doing more camp cooking than fighting, so it was an awkward pairing with mis-matched weapons.

To make matters worse for Hazelwood, his face was beet red and he kept sneezing. A wild swing of the lath knocked his silly tall white hat off, making Hazelwood howl as if his skull had been cracked!

"You bloody thief, I'll lambaste you!" Yeovill shouted.

"Liar!" Hazelwood shot back, panting. "At-atchoo!"

"You can't boil an *egg* 'thout instructions, *thief*!" Yeovill accused. His lath broke in two, and he began to pummel Hazelwood with both pieces, driving Hazelwood back into a flower bed.

"Here, don't trample the . . . *yellow* things!" Lewrie roared.

That roar made Hazelwood look back for a second to see what he was standing in, an opening that Yeovill took advantage of, using his clenched fist to pop him one on the mouth, sending Hazelwood sprawling atop the flower bed.

"Stand fast!" Lewrie yelled, taking Yeovill by his left arm as if to give him a shake, and Desmond and Deavers finally came forward to haul Hazelwood to his feet, taking the soup ladle away.

"He *hit* me, sir!" Hazelwood spat, astonished, his lip split and his nose and eyes running freely. "There was no reason to . . . !"

"Sneaking at my receipts, sir, stealing from me!" Yeovill shot back. He had dropped the broken lath pieces, shaking his right hand as if he'd broken his knuckles with his punch, and wincing. "He took my book!"

"What book?" Lewrie demanded, hands on his hips.

"My receipt book, sir," Yeovill explained, impatiently swiping his hair back. He'd picked up splinters from the lath and suddenly said "Ow! D'ye see, sir, everywhere we've sailed since I became your personal cook, the West Indies, Georgia and the Carolinas, the Bahamas, Gibraltar, Spain, Cape Town, Buenos Aires, Portugal or Sicily . . . I've gone ashore for provisions, and tasted new dishes and foods. I ask the street vendors, restaurant cooks, old women in the shops, how to cook them, what spices they use, what the sauces are. My *secrets*, sir! He had no right to copy them, barring me from the kitchens, then using my receipts as his own, sir! No right at all! As if the un-talented clown could follow them proper. He could turn a Cambridge Burnt Cream or a Spanish *flan* into blackened *soup*!"

"Me? Un-talented?" Hazelwood screeched, "Why . . . ah-ah-*atchoo*!" He tried to argue, but his reaction to cats cut him off in mid-screed, forcing him to raise the hem of his apron to wipe his reddened eyes and his streaming nose. "God *damn* that cat . . . ah . . . *atchoo*!"

"Use a handkerchief, for God's sake," Lewrie snapped, backing up a pace or two.

"I caught him writing one down, sir, on a scrap of paper. He's got it in his waist-coat pocket," Yeovill accused, jabbing a finger at the offending pocket, then returned to picking splinters from his palms. "You look, you'll see, sir."

"Hazelwood?" Lewrie demanded, holding out an open hand.

With bad grace, still snuffling, coughing, spitting, and sneezing, the usually feisty fellow dug a square snippet of foolscap out of one of his pockets and handed it over, trying not to look guilty.

Lewrie glanced it over.

Tomato—Marinara—Pasta Sauce
  Dice fine 2 cloves garlic, 1 large onion doz. pitted black olives. Fresh oregano, basil rosemary, thyme, & sage, pestled if nec. Brown in olive oil in large deep skillet or large pot.
  Add doz. to 2 doz. peeled roma tomatoes, add 1 cup red wine chianti or montepulciano best. Simmer 3 hours, stirring to thick puree, parmesan, provolone mozarella fine grated to thicken, ½ cup sugar if desired. No feta!

"It seems as if the proof is in the pudding, Hazelwood," Lewrie said, glowering at him.

"Remember the chicken parmesan I made, sir?" Yeovill said. "All the pasta dishes I cooked when we were anchored at Milazzo? That's my sauce to a tee, sir, and he had no right to take it, and claim it as his own."

"Yeovill might have shared his receipts with you, Hazelwood, if you would've allowed him equal access to the kitchens," Lewrie said.

"No, I wouldn't've, for he's a sneering tyrant," Yeovill snapped. "He's been looking down his nose at me since I set foot in the house!"

"That's right, he wouldn't share," Hazelwood carped, between his sneezes, "He's jealous of my skill, and my position! Too many cooks sp . . . spoil the . . . *atchoo!* . . . the sauce, Sir Alan. He may be good enough with salt meats and a porridge, but I am the better . . . *atchoo!*"

"Admirals, and foreign dignitaries, have tried to lure Yeovill away from my service, Mister Hazelwood," Lewrie countered, "so he's good enough for me. You run a very taut kitchen, or so the other house servants say to me and my wife. Dictatorial, and tyrannical were the words used. The two of you are supposed to be professionals. Can you not co-operate?"

"With him?" Hazelwood sneered. "Never, Sir Alan! If you prefer his slop to me, then you are welcome to him." He raised his chin and runny nose in a superior look, stamping his feet.

"Stop killing my flowers!" Jessica shouted down at that moment, which took Hazelwood down a peg. All shifted to the gravel walk.

"I cannot work in such conditions, Sir Alan," Hazelwood said, stripping his apron off over his head. "I fear I must give you my notice." He tried to make it sound formally stiff, but the phlegm that had built up in his throat made him break into a coughing jag.

"Very well, Mister Hazelwood, if that is your choice," Lewrie replied. "We will pay you your wages through the end of this week, and wish you the best of luck in your future endeavours. I'm sure there's a house that will have you."

'Til they get t'know you, Lewrie qualified to himself.

"I will pack my things and go, then, Sir Alan," Hazelwood said with a slight bow from the waist.

"Can you be out by dinnertime?" Lewrie could not help asking.

"Yes, sir, I can," Hazelwood said, bowing again, and marching off towards the basement door.

"Deavers," Lewrie said, summoning him with a crook of his finger, "you know what we bought for the kitchen. Keep an eye on him so that he don't make off with anything that isn't his."

"Aye, sir," Deavers said with a grin.

"Yeovill, it appears the house is in need of a new cook. Would you consider taking over?" Lewrie asked him.

"Thank you very kindly, sir," Yeovill answered with a relieved and happy grin, "and I'd be that glad to."

"Now, with that out of the way, I think I'll go finish my breakfast," Lewrie said, chuckling now that Hazelwood was out of sight. "Fun's over, all. Wasn't much of a bout, anyway. Back to your usual duties," he added, waving his servants into the house as well.

One more wee domestic problem's solved itself, Lewrie happily told himself; *But, when's the other shoe drop?*

After the incident with Hazelwood, life in the Lewrie household took a distinct turn for the better. The victuals improved, more to Lewrie's tastes, as did the economy with which Yeovill ran his kitchen, the scullery maid waif could actually be heard singing or humming at her duties, and there were more smiles on the faces of the other servants.

Jessica's feared scar on her temple turned out to be much less noticeable than she had dreaded, and her sprained wrist improved, as soreness disappeared and flexibility returned, to the point that Lewrie was drawn at a rush from his newspaper in the drawing room to her studio one morning when he heard what he took for a shriek.

"What is it?" he demanded, pulling his hanger sword from the ceramic umbrella stand in the entry hall.

"Look!" Jessica exclaimed, all but dancing round the room, waving her right hand in extravagent motions, bending and rotating her wrist. "It *works* again! I just *drew* this with no trouble at all!" She had a large sheet of paper in her left hand, a drawing of a kitten toying with a ball of yarn.

"Startled me out of year of growth, you did," Lewrie whooped as he sheathed the bared blade and embraced her with equal joy.

In point of fact, the only bothersome part of his life were his weekly visits to Admiralty to tout Hugh's and Charlie's prospects. And when Jessica was having her "monthlies" and he slept alone.

"Alan, dearest," Jessica said one evening over a tasty supper, with a serious look on her face.

Uh-oh, what've I done now? he thought.

"Yes, dear?" he replied, after dabbing his lips with his napkin.

"Pettus and Lucy's marriage," she said. "We must have workers in to make the rooms above the coach house and stables into a lodging for them. And, we must go shopping for furniture for them."

"They won't be needin' a kitchen of their own, will they?" he

"Oh, they'll still take all their meals belowstairs with the rest of the servants," Jessica replied more perkily, now that she had a project, "but the ability to make early morning tea, or heat water for bathing would be nice. Who could we call upon?"

"Ehm, there's that fellow who first rented me the house," Lewrie mused, "what's his name? Penneworth? He'd know some workers who put up houses."

"Good!" Jessica congratulated, grinning. "If you see to that, I can take Lucy to Clotworthy Chute's emporium. Or, we could take Lucy *and* Pettus, so the furnishings are *their* taste, not just anything we pick up on the cheap."

"Cheap is sometimes good," Lewrie pointed out, in jest.

"Alan," she responded with a mock glare, and he knew what he would be doing for the next fortnight; he was under strict orders.

Mr. Penneworth, it turned out, was a speculator who bought up rickety old properties and refurbished them, alongside his realty business, so he had a work crew of skilled carpenters, brick masons, and plasterers and painters ready on call. A quick walk-through, and they set to creating a proper parlour, two bedrooms, a wee dining room, and privy chamber, after a consultation with Pettus and his intended.

"Lord, sir, this is really quite kind of you and Dame Lewrie," Pettus thanked them again as they got down from a hired coach in front of Clotworthy Chute's establishment, which had grown from one store to a row of them.

"Think nothing of it, Pettus," Lewrie told him, "your and Lucy's future comfort, and happiness are reward enough."

And costly enough, Lewrie thought.

"Oh my," Lucy exclaimed as she looked round the interior, taking hold of Pettus's arm. "It is all so *grand*!"

And indeed it was, in some portions of the emporium, where there were framed paintings on display, along with Greek or Roman statuary and busts, tall vases from ancient times to Chinese, ornately carved tables, armoires, desks, and dining rooms.

All of it frauds, most-like, Lewrie thought, remembering how Clotworthy Chute could turn a new bronze statue into one just dug up in Italy, after a fortnight in salt water, or hire someone talented to "restore" common woodwork into William & Mary or Queen Anne pieces in even less time. In the centre of the vast combined shops, in the back, stood the average pieces that *didn't* cost a duke's fortune.

"May I show you anything in particular, sir?" a salesman dressed in the latest dark Beau Brummel fashion enquired.

"We're looking for Clotworthy Chute," Lewrie told him. "He's an old school friend of mine."

"Of course, sir," the salesman said with a nod and a slight bow. "You would prefer to deal with the owner himself. I will summon him, if you will excuse me for a moment?"

Once he departed, Lucy turned to Jessica, saying, "Everything is so expensive-looking, ma'am. Are you sure we're in the right place? Our needs are far more humble than any of this."

Jessica's assurancing reply was cut off by Clotworthy as he came rumbling from a back office, arms spread wide in welcome.

"Alan, me old!" Chute boomed, "You old tarpaulin man! Been cutting and thrusting with dog nappers, I heard? Give ye joy, my man, give ye joy!"

"Hallo, Clotworthy," Lewrie replied, simply having to smile, for the old rogue and "Captain Sharp" was the same as the day they'd been expelled from Harrow. "It's good t'see you, again," he added as they vigourously shook hands. Other shoppers in the emporium turned to peer at the noisy greeting, whispering to each other as they recognised Lewrie from the newspaper accounts.

"And Dame Lewrie, a delight to see you in my store, again, too," Clotworthy went on, only slightly less loud, kissing the back of her hand. "And what brings two of my favourite people to my store?"

"Clotworthy, this is Pettus, our butler, and Lucy, Dame Lewrie's maid," Lewrie said, doing the introductions, "they are to be married soon, and we wish to furnish a separate lodging for them."

"And you came to me, first, aha!" Clotworthy enthused. "Good! Topping! Capital! Table and chairs, settee and chairs, end tables and night tables, and most importantly, a bedstead. Come this way and let me show you what we have at the back of the store. I'm mortal-certain you'll find what you like. Even some carpets for the parlour and bedchamber, to keep your feet warm in winter, too, perhaps?"

"Well, that would be nice, but . . ." Lucy tried to object at the expense.

"Nonsense, Lucy, let's see what they have," Jessica insisted.

She would brook no false modesty, no objections of "it's too nice" or "it looks too expensive" from Lucy, and, slowly, furniture was gathered for the couple, with Jessica and Lucy beginning to compare tastes and laugh about the project. This left Lewrie little to do but dawdle round behind them for a time, then wander into the more expensive wings of Chute's emporium.

"Almost done," Clotworthy announced about an hour later, coming to join Lewrie with the bill. "I think we did them proud, Alan. All they need for a parlour, a bedchamber, and a place to dine, and it only comes to eighty-four pounds, eight shillings."

"I'll give you my note of hand on Coutts' Bank," Lewrie told him with a wince; Jessica's "project" was more expensive than he'd imagined.

"And the delivery?" Clotworthy enquired.

"Hmm, I'm told the painters will be done tomorrow," Lewrie said, cocking his head in speculation, "say a day t'let it dry, then deliver on Thursday? It's to go to the coach house out back, so your waggon can use the back gate to the garden and stables."

"I think I remember it well, from when we furnished the house," Clotworthy said with a knowing nod.

"Let me ask you, Clotworthy," Lewrie said with a sly grin, leaning his head close. "Just how much of all this stuff is the genuine article?"

"Alan," Chute pretended to be scandalised, "I am a respectable businessman these days!"

"Whatever *that* means," Lewrie scoffed. "No one even *heard* the word 'respectable' ten years ago."

"Quite right, my old," Chute responded with a laugh. "It is the new way of doing things, all prim, prudish, and pucker-arsed, haw haw. I expect Harrow, our dear old *alma mater,* has gone so far as to expel young sprogs for even *thinking* about topping a barmaid, much less putting a hand up their skirts. One must be sobre and righteous . . . or, do a good job of pretending.

"Confidentially?" Chute said, laying a hand on Lewrie's shoulder. "There *may* be some treasures brought back from some rich fool's Grand Tour of the Continent that may not be, ah, all *that* old, but for the *most* part, what I display for sale *is* real, these days. God, I adore the people who can't keep from gambling deep, and have to sell up to pay their debts. Done on the sly, so Society doesn't know how skint they've become."

"Good Christ, you really *have* been redeemed!" Lewrie laughed out loud.

"Well, not completely," Clotworthy qualified, almost crossing his fingers against complete Redemption. "Take these paintings, for instance. This 'un's *The Toilet of Venus* by François Boucher. Over there, *The Embarkation of The Queen of Sheba* by Claude Lorrain, done round Sixteen Fourty-eight."

"I rather like that one," Lewrie said.

"Of course you do," Chute sniggered, "it has ships in it."

"Well, I do," Lewrie insisted. "That old, is it? And it costs . . ." he peered at the dangling price tag. "Three thousand pounds?"

"On consignment for a French *émigré* who had the good sense to get his arse out of France before The Terror began," Clotworthy said, hands behind his back and rocking on his heels, "a fellow who brought off his most valuable treasures, hoping to live the same life he led before the Revolution . . . a Baron, Count, a Marquis or something other, who is now reduced to renting a dingy set of rooms. Threadbare suitings, frayed stockings . . . you've seen them, but still with the airs of an aristocrat."

"It isn't real, is it?" Lewrie asked with a wink.

"Of *course* it ain't," Chute happily confessed. "Somebody very good at doing them from memory, as far as I know. A real down-at-the-heels Frog brought it in for sale, and God only knows where *he* got it."

"What's consignment?" Lewrie asked.

"I don't pay him ha'pence 'til it's sold is what it is," Chute explained, "If some dunderhead buys it for three thousand pounds. I pay the fallen Frog twelve hundred and pocket the rest. He gets to eat and drink, buy new clothes . . . and frankly, so do I haw haw!"

"You keep sixty percent?" Lewrie marvelled.

"You can still do sums, I see, good for you Alan old son," the cagey conniver congratulated, "I have my expenses, my overhead to care for, and he don't, so . . . sixty percent commission is my usual. That goes for most of my stock, except for the few items that I have, ah . . . made," Chute grinned, laying a finger to his lips. "Somewhere in the world, in the Louvre in Paris most-like, the real painting is hanging. *I've* never seen it, so it may be big enough to cover an entire wall, or it's as small as a tea tray."

"Ehm, can't you get in trouble with them?" Lewrie wondered, waving a hand down the wall where the pictures were hung. "Forgery, or something?"

"Ah, but that's the grandest part of it, Alan," Clotworthy insisted, most gleefully, "I take things on *consignment*, I don't buy, so I'm taking the seller's word for authenticity, so who's to know? If the whole Royal Academy came charging in the door, I can just shrug my shoulders and say that I was diddled, hah hah!"

"Now, as to your note of hand," Chute mentioned, getting back to business, "I've pen and paper at that desk yonder. Because it's you, I threw in a pair of *slightly* used Turkey carpets, *gratis*. We can't let your people start wedded life on splintery, cold floors."

". . . at Saint Anselm's, of course," Jessica was happily scheming as she took off her bonnet, sat on a settee in the drawing room, and slipped off her street shoes. "Ah, that's better. Sunday will be the final reading of the banns, and then we can think of a place for the wedding breakfast. Or, should we have it here, and ask Yeovill to do the menu preparation? With enough warning, there's nothing that he can do. Do you not think so, Alan?"

"Hmm, how many will attend, though? A chop house'd be better," Lewrie replied, "somewhere where they ain't servants for a bit."

"I suppose you're right, dear," Jessica said, after a moment of thought. Then she got impish. "I saw you admiring some of the paintings at Chute's today. Did one strike your fancy?"

"A harbourscape called *The Embarkation of The Queen of Sheba*, with high ramparts like Valletta Harbour at Malta," Lewrie said with a sheepish grin as he threw himself down into an armchair, "with a pretty sunrise or sunset, and clouds all aglow. Admired it, aye, but three thousand pounds worth."

"Who did it?" Jessica asked.

"Some Frog artist, Claude Lorrain or something," Lewrie told her. "It's supposed t'be old, the sixteen-hundreds. Clotworthy said an *émigré* in need o' rent money brought it in, on consignment."

"Mister Chute should be careful, Alan," Jessica said, turning sobre, and leaning over an arm of the settee closer to him, "Do you remember the day we went to Ackermann's in the Strand, to look at all the paintings that didn't suit the Royal Academy's annual contest?"

"Aye, it was damned crowded," Lewrie sniggered, "and you got propositioned by a cad I had to threaten."

"Yes, Madame Pellatan got all excited when she saw what she took for a painting by one of her old friends in Paris, Jacques-Louis David, except it wasn't the real thing, but a smaller forgery. If someone buys that one you liked . . . Heavens, three thousand *pounds*? . . . then discovers it's a fraud, Mister Chute could end up in gaol, and his business ruined! Does he know much about art, or . . . ?"

"He took the seller's word for its authenticity," Lewrie said, "and on consignment, which means he isn't out a penny 'til it sells, so he didn't seem too concerned."

"Well, he *should* be," Jessica firmly stated, "or have someone on call who could advise him. Perhaps an older member of the Royal Academy? A painting that old will have tiny cracks in the surface, from drying out over the years. The expert could judge by the brushstrokes, the authenticity of the signature. By the very size of the work!"

"Like I said, he didn't seem too concerned," Lewrie repeated, "I'd imagine he sells things 'as-is,' or whatever, perhaps gets the seller t'come in and speak with the buyer, first."

"But, even so, Alan," Jessica insisted, "if it turns out to be a forgery, he'd have to return the buyer's money, *and* be out what he gave the owner who brought it in, who would most-like be long gone. He is in a *most* vulnerable position. I should warn him."

"Well, if you think that best," Lewrie said, wondering what his old school friend would make of that. And, would Clotworthy's weaseling explanation convince Jessica that he was *not* a sharp criminal?

"I should take Madame Pellatan with me," Jessica said, leaning back into the settee, "she's an educated eye."

Oh Christ, now I'll have to warn Chute that the sky's about to fall on him! Lewrie thought in dread of that duty; *And if she thinks my friends are shifty, what will she think of* me?

CHAPTER TWENTY-FIVE

*I*n lieu of making a second trip to Chute's emporium, Lewrie penned a quick warning letter and sent it off instanter, a day before Jessica collected Madame Berenice Pellatan from the manse at Saint Anselm's and set off on another of her "missions," with the same infectious drive that she put into learning how to groom her new horse, or the zeal she put into her artwork. Was she imagining that she set off to expose chicanery, Lewrie feared.

That woman can be ruthless, when she's got the bitts in her teeth! Lewrie thought. No shrinking violet, was Jessica, and no wonder her father, Reverend Chenery, despaired of her interests that were so *not* womanlike, ladylike, or silently, obediently "miss-ish."

Does she ever discover Good Works and Poor Relief, she'll turn into another Hannah More, ready t'mount the orator's corner in Hyde Park, he silently feared. All Lewrie could do was sit at home, play with the kitten and the dogs, read the newspapers, and await a final judgement from his wife and Madame Pellatan.

It came hours later. A bustle at the front door, hats, gloves, and parasols collected in the entry hall, then footsteps on the stairs. Lewrie pretended to be reading a paper as they entered the drawing room, looking up at their presence, smiling and giving out an enthusiastic "Aha!" and offering to ring for tea.

"And how was Clotworthy?" Lewrie asked, still smiling.

"His usual charming self, Alan," Jessica told him, smoothing her gown as she sat down on the settee beside him.

Is that good or bad? Lewrie wondered.

No judgement was rendered . . . yet.

"*Oui,* the gentleman is most *amusant,* Sir Alan," Madame Berenice Pellatan said as she sat down in an armchair and smoothed the skirts of her gown, then primped with her extravagantly styled hairdo. "I find his emporium a fascinating place, so filled with such intriguing items. The Greco-Roman things, the decorative urns, oh la! Unfortunately, he is not so knowledgeable when it comes to paintings."

"Oh?" Lewrie asked, trying for innocent surprise. "Chute sounded as if he knew what he was talking about."

"The man knows what others tell him," Madame Pellatan said with a raised brow, and a hint of superior amusement, "but a connoisseur of art? *Non.* Only a superior and glib tradesman."

"Well, he always was a quick study," Lewrie said, shrugging.

"He has, however," Madame Pellatan went on, "managed to collect some interesting paintings, and has priced them below what I would think a *real* gallery would. It is to say, some valuable paintings on the *bon marché,* hah hah."

"A florin to the pound, d'ye mean?" Lewrie interpreted.

Jessica had to translate for Madame Pellatan that a florin was a two-shilling coin, a tenth of a pound, which made the arch older French émigré simper with laughter.

"So, they're real?" Lewrie asked, much relieved.

"I cannot dispute their authenticity, Sir Alan," Mm. Pellatan said as the tea arrived, "for the good reason that, for the most instances, I have never seen them. My late husband and I, and all of our artistic friends, *haunted* the Louvre, attended almost every artist's showing, and regularly visited every sales gallery in Paris, but we never saw the ones your friend has on display."

"Madame Berenice told me that the ones Chute has for sale came from private collections, Alan," Jessica said as she poured for all.

"Where only family and guests could admire them, alas," Madame Pellatan said with an exaggerated sigh as she spooned in lots of sugar and cream to her tea. "As people of wealth, who could afford to own such fine art, they would have been the first victims of The Terror. It is possible that they fled France, and the guillotine, with them, as I and my husband did, trying to save a bit of their wealth as they went into exile."

"Paintings are a bit large t'smuggle out, aren't they?" Lewrie asked.

"We could not hope to take *all* of our favourites with us," the old girl said with a *moue*, "but, the ones we could not part with, we removed from the frames, pulled the little nails that held the canvas to the back frame, and rolled them up carefully, the smallest inside the bigger, and hid at the bottoms of chests and luggage.

"Unfortunately," Madame Pellatan explained with another deep sigh, "we had to sell them off, bit by bit, to support ourselves here in England, and when Jean-Claude got sick . . . alas . . . the physicians were so expensive, and so, I have but two small pieces left, hanging in my room at Saint Anselm's manse."

"They are exquisite, Madame," Jessica commiserated.

"So many of us, our old lives lost forever, drudging by at any work we could find," Madame Pellatan told them, looking as if she'd openly weep, "aristocrats with no skills but being elegant, wealthy landowners without land, and no money to buy land here in England . . . I can see why the people who own those paintings at *M'sieur* Chute's sell them at any price they can get to keep body and soul together.

"Is it Shute, or Chute?" she asked suddenly.

"It's Chute, as in 'Chew,'" Lewrie told her.

"Ah, *merci*, Sir Alan," Madame Pellatan said, nodding. "Mayhap, some waiter or wine steward, a chef to a great house, a store clerk has to part with his last remembrance of better times . . . so he can pay the rent on his meagre set of rooms, *non*? Clothing, shoes, and the school fees for his poor children?"

"I still can't afford *The Embarkation of The Queen of Sheba*," Lewrie japed, pulling a comic face, "even if it's the genuine article."

"Clotworthy *does* have some forgeries, though, Alan," Jessica stated.

"Ah, *mais oui*," Madame Pellatan brightened. "There are two that are more contemporary that I have seen in Paris before we left. Those *are* copies, and I told *M'sieur* Chute so. Marvellously well-forged by a talented man, but forgeries. He said he would return them to the fellow who brought them in."

He'll flog 'em on another dealer, more-like, Lewrie thought.

"And, on consignment, he isn't out a penny," Jessica happily said, "the same way Ackermann's and other galleries sell my paintings."

"Well, that's something," Lewrie commented over the rim of his tea cup. "I wonder . . . perhaps the man who did those two forgeries at Chute's is the same man who did that *Belisarius* by David that we saw at Ackermann's. Do you know any of your fellow artists who fled to London, Madame?"

"I know very few, Sir Alan," Madame Pellatan told him, looking a bit redder in the face, "the émigrés that gather once a week that I know are not artistic. Nostalgic, perhaps, but I cannot remember any of our group even mentioning paintings or statuary. Petit-fours and crème brûlées, Parisian café coffee, and our old lives is what we recall, hawn hawn."

"Oh, Yeovill made us some ginger snaps," Lewrie said, lifting a napkin from a plate on the tea table. "Have some, Madame? Quickly, for I'm a dear lover of them, and stand likely t'gobble 'em all up!"

"You are too kind, Sir Alan," the older lady said with a laugh, scooping four off the plate at once.

Good, Chute's in the clear, Lewrie told himself; *and I'm not associated with criminals, hah!*

Before Jessica could complete her plans for Pettus and Lucy to wed in at least a modicum of style, there was the pesky matter of a trial for the dog buffers to deal with. Lewrie escorted Jessica and Lucy to the Old Bailey early one morning where they would all testify, with Dasher and Turnbow fetched along in case their part in the affair would be necessary.

The lads were dressed in their Sunday best, fresh-blacked shoes with shiny pewter buckles, white cotton stockings and un-accustomed tan breeches, white shirts with black neck-stocks, at which they continually tugged, tan waist-coats, and dark blue coats. When Jessica commented that they looked like cherubs, it was almost too much for Dasher.

"A bath in th' middle o' th' week, I asks ya!" he carped to his mate, Turnbow, "Breeches cleavin' my 'nutmegs' like an axe, trussed up like a rib roast, an' stranglin' on this bloody neck-stock. I can't wait t'get home an' get back inta my slops! Don't see how *anybody* can stand bein' dressed this way all th' time, I don't!"

"But Tom," Turnbow sniggered, "if th' breeches squeeze yer crutch so bad, ya can *sing* like a cherub angel!"

"Ah, geroutofit!" Dasher shot back with a pout.

"Behave, you two," Lewrie ordered. "You might have to testify, so you want t'make a good impression."

"Lord, I hope they don't need us," Turnbow sulked.

"Then all this is for nothin'? Ceehrist!" Dasher spat.

As Lewrie and his party entered the court room, he spotted the gang of dog buffers being led in and shoved into the box together, the wee girl, the cart driver, the stringier fellow, and the side of beef who had struck Jessica. They all had been cleaned up and given new clothes by their attorney for the occasion. The bigger fellow glared at everybody, Lewrie most of all, and mouthed a silent curse. He no longer had a right arm, so his borrowed coat was a bad fit and threatened to slip off the stub of shoulder that the surgeon had left him, after Lewrie's pistol ball had shattered the joint. The rest of them looked scared.

The barrister who would prosecute was a silk-robed King's Bencher with a starched and pressed white stock at his throat, and a natty sprigged peruke atop his gingery hair. He spoke with Lewrie, Jessica, and Lucy and made some notes, but didn't seem too concerned, barely paying any attention to Dasher and Turnbow, or what they had to say of the attack, before the cry of "Oyez, Oyez, Oyez!" as the Justice came in and took his seat above everyone, gavelling the court to silence.

The charges, and the names of the accused were read out, and the felons declared their innocence by turns, the big fellow snarling that everyone present could go to the Devil, for he was *not* guilty!

The jury was already seated, so Jessica was called to the witness box and sworn on the Bible.

Were you and your maid in Green Park on such and such a date? Near the North verge and Piccadilly St.? Your were walking your dogs? And you both were accosted by two men who demanded that you give up your dogs? Aha. Do you recognise the men who did it? Were they armed? And Jessica pointed to the accused, pointing out the bigger man who struck her and dragged her by her wrist in the leash. Do you recognise the second man who showed you his knife? Yes, she did, and pointed him out, too. She had not seen the man who drove the cart, or the urchin girl.

Lucy was put through the same questions and pointed out the men she recognised. Then it was Lewrie's turn.

He related the events of that morning, the urgent summons by one of his servants, Turnbow, and his rush with his other servants to the park, recovering his wife, the visit by the Physician, and the chase that Dasher had made to follow the cart, without luck.

How did he find the criminal's lair?

Lewrie shared a look with the police chief constable who sat in the far side of the court, behind the prosecution table. How could he declare that he'd had government aid, in open court?

"I was informed that the dog buffers' manner of ransoming dogs was to send a child round with a verbal message, or a note, telling me to place an advertisement in a specific newspaper as if offering a reward for our dogs' return, sir. If paid, our dogs would be returned," Lewrie carefully laid out. "The next morning, a messenger *did* arrive at my house. Do I recognise her? It was a little girl, that'un in the box. I and my butler, Pettus, were in the entry hall when she handed over the note. I have it here, if you wish," he said, pulling the folded-over scrap of foolscap from a waistcoat pocket.

But, how did he discover their lair?

"There was an itinerant young fellow by name of Haddock," Lewrie slowly explained, "a knife grinder who does business in Dover Street and the neighbourhood. He struck me as a clever young lad, and he and I struck a bargain, that he would be at the servants' and delivery entrance the next day, sharpening knives 'til the messenger arrived, then he would follow her. Haddock suggested that I hire on two girls, as well, one who sells posies in the parks and streets, and one girl who could pretend to be a beggar.

"The three took turns trailing the messenger, followed her into Ormond Yard off Duke of York Street, heard the commotion of many barking dogs in an abandoned barrel works . . . and caught the smell of it, even stronger than the hackney stables nearby. They reported back to me, and I put a party together," Lewrie said evenly.

Who did he take? His son, his wife's younger brother, his Cox'n, cabin steward, and cook. Armed? Of course. And why do so? Could you have not alerted the police?

"I wanted our dogs back, sir," Lewrie told the prosecutor, "but my wife had been assaulted and injured, her maid slashed at with a knife, and I could not let that stand," Lewrie stated. "I wanted revenge."

And did the accused resist your entry?

"They did, sir," Lewrie told the court, "They would not give up their dogs. Including my two, there were fifteen in all held in there, representing at least one hundred and fifty pounds profit to them."

The audience, and the jury, found the image of Liam Desmond with a criquet bat for a weapon quite amusing, but then coughed into their fists and leaned forward, rapt, as Lewrie described the brief fight; pistols pulled and fired, Midshipmen's dirks and sailors' clasp knives whipped round, with butcher knives and fire pokers opposing them.

"The big ugly brute yonder, the one with only one arm," Lewrie said, jerking a hand at the box full of the accused, "he shot at me, and missed wide, then I shot him. He pulled a butcher knife off the table in his left hand, I sliced him cross the face with my old dirk, and dis-armed him."

In more ways than one, the prosecutor drolly commented, raising another laugh. The ugly brute snarled, doing his case no good.

Then the prosecutor led Lewrie through what transpired after, the guarding of the dogs overnight, feeding and watering them, taking them for a leashed walk so their pens could be washed out, and the next morning, when the newspaper advertisements drew their owners to the barrel works, all at Lewrie's cost.

He was dismissed from the witness box and rejoined Jessica and Lucy and the lads as the barrister for the defence, a young and in-experienced fellow in a "stuff" gown, who might have been "eating his terms" in one of the Inns of Court not six months before, tried to put up a convincing argument.

Just loving dogs and small animals, they took in strays and the run-aways they found on the streets. Oh, fed them capital, yer honour! Good, safe, and snug pens for each dog. Knives? Being in Green Park? Oh no, sir! Attacking fine ladies? Not in their nature! The wee girl we let sleep there, for she's no one and no home! She loves all dogs, too! *She* didn't have no knife in her hands, nossir, when those fellows burst in with guns and wee swords, and what were we *supposed* to do in a situation like that, just throw up our hands and surrender? Why, it was likely it was dog buffers come to steal them!

The jury was led out to make their decisions, and Lewrie and his party left the court room for a breath of fresher air in the halls.

"What's the verdict, father?" Hugh asked as he and Charlie, who had coached over separately, came up to them.

"Aye, are they to be imprisoned?" Charlie Chenery pressed.

"The jury just went out, lads," Lewrie told them, peering about the vast halls in search of a pick-pocket. Years before, at his own trial for stealing a dozen slaves on Jamaica to crew his fever-ravaged ship, or "liberating them" as he thought of it, right after he had been acquitted, a young, pre-sentable lady by name of "Three Handed Jenny" had lifted his pocket watch, and he only got it back through the good offices of Clotworthy

Chute, who seemed to know a slew of unsavoury people. "Guard your wallets, coin purses, and watches," he warned them. "There's a lot of crime in the Old Bailey . . . real crimes."

There was a stand just outside the doors to the courtyard, where piping hot tea could be purchased, and they thought to go out and take a cup, but a court officer stepped out of the courtroom and bellowed that the jury was back, and all involved should re-enter.

"My word, but that was quick," Jessica said as they went back to their pew seats neat the prosecutor's table.

London might have a new-fangled, French-style police department, and the old night wardens called the Parish Charlies, but England's justice was harsh and swift. Take anything valued more than fifteen shillings, and it was usually a hanging offence, or being transported for life to New South Wales, on the other side of the world.

Take fifteen dogs ransomed on average for ten pounds apiece, and throw violence into the bargain, and it usually meant a ride in a cart to Tyburn to be hanged.

The wee girl and the felon who had driven the cart were found guilty as abetting their crime; transportation for life.

The one who had shown a knife and slashed at Lucy, and the big brute with one arm were condemned to death.

"Ye moight'z *well* 'ang me, ye barst'd!" that man shouted at the judge, "f'r wot'd I do wif one bloody arm t'other side o' th' world but *starve* t'death! God rot an' damn th' lot o' ye!" he added as he was hauled out by the bailiffs. "I gie ye my curse o' death!"

"Well, that was dramatic, I must say," Hugh said with a nervous laugh. "Is anyone else hungry?"

"Excuse me, Captain Lewrie?" a weedy fellow in a worn suit and crushed farm hat implored, following them out, "Sir Alan, if you can spare me but a few moments. I'm with *The Times,* and I wonder if you could speak with me regarding this crime, and your reaction to the verdict just handed down."

"My reaction," Lewrie barked, frowning. "My *feelings,* d'ye mean?"

He had an innate suspicion of newspapers, for they usually got things all wrong. Oh, whenever he sent an official action report to Admiralty, it was printed in its entirety, in proper Naval-ese in the *Naval Chronicle* and sometimes in *The Gazette.* The other civilian papers, though, were just *too* damned inventive, with a taste for gore by the hogshead, heads blown off in detail, limbs shattered, people cut in half by roundshot, and oak splinters flying as thick as raindrops, or the cloud of arrows the Persians shot at the Spartans at the Battle of Thermopylae! And they weren't even there! No, some civilian clot grubbing at a corner desk amid piles of old papers, in the light of the single tallow candle that his miserly salary could afford, could spin a tale worthy of Don Quixote or Tobias Smollett, inflating a few broadsides into a storm of smoke, flame, and flying iron so loud and furious that coastal mountains shivered and slid into the sea! Fish leaped to their deaths in terror, to hear them tell it!

"Your thoughts on it, Sir Alan," the weedy fellow corrected himself, "Are you satisfied with the verdict?"

"Well, aye, I am," Lewrie allowed at last, "To my lights, Justice was done, though I do regret that that wee girl was convicted, for she's had no chance in life, and was drawn to crime so young."

"Pardon me, sir, and allow me to name myself," the reporter said, plucking off his hat, "I am John Wardell. I cover the courts. What you did to find and raid the miscreants is what our readers have come to expect of a naval hero such as yourself. I'm told that in the Navy you are known as the 'Ram-Cat,' Sir Alan?" For the way you go at our country's foes?"

"Oh, that," Lewrie said with a grin, "it's more for my choice of pet I keep in my cabins. When I was a new Lieutenant, I was aboard a hired-in brig, under an older fellow, Lieutenant Lilycrop, and he kept dozens of cats to keep the rats down, and he liked them a lot. I was continually going aboard any ship we spoke to offer litters of kittens or grown mousers. It does beat 'Black Alan' all hollow, though, I do admit."

"Liberating slaves as free men, liberating dogs now," Wardell said with a hint of hero worship, hastily scribbling a thought onto a small ledger book with a stub of pencil.

"Oh, let's not go all adoring," Lewrie warned. He had been the paragon for William Wilberforce and his Abolitionists during the trial, and still shivered with disgust for being labelled "Black Alan" Lewrie or "Lewrie the Liberator."

"Might you describe to me the raid on the thieves, Sir Alan," Wardell pressed as Lewrie made a half-turn to walk away.

"You were in court, sir?" Lewrie asked, turning stern. "You made notes? You can obtain a transcript? That's all I'll say about the matter. Now, if you will excuse us, Mister Wardell?"

"But of course, Sir Alan," Wardell said, bobbing like a robin on a worm and doffing his hat once more. "And thank you for your time."

I'm going to sound like Saint George slayin' the dragon tonight, he sorrowfully told himself; *Gad, it'll be* lurid! *Three criminals'll turn into a battalion of Bonaparte's Imperial Guard by the time* he's *through!*

"A cold collation, or a late breakfast?" Hugh tossed over his shoulder as he held the heavy doors so they could leave the Old Bailey to whistle up a hackney or two. "Who was that fellow, father?"

"A writer for *The Times*," Lewrie said with a groan. "Nothing good can come from that."

"He makes you sound like a hero, sir," Charlie piped up, "that's just proper. We all know what a scraper you are."

"Oh, for God's sake," Lewrie groaned again, and felt like cuffing Charlie on the head, "do 'piss down someone else's back!'"

"Alan!" Jessica snapped. "Such language!"

CHAPTER TWENTY-SIX

*L*ewrie was right; that writer for *The Times*, Wardell, had waxed rapturous as he wrote up the results of the trial, and what he *thought* Lewrie had said to him. It was "Black Alan" Lewrie and "Saint Alan The Liberator" all over again, a recounting of his victories over the foes of his country at sea, mention of the "Ram-Cat" sobriquet among the Navy, his knighthood and baronetcy awarded by the King himself in 1804, and a suggestion that the nickname "Bulldog" be added for the tenacious way Lewrie had gone after the dog buffers, then paid for the advertisments to re-unite stolen pets with their owners out of his own generosity, and his own purse!

"Oh, for God's sake, what a lot of flummery!" Lewrie had groaned over breakfast the day the article was printed, wadding it up and tossing the whole paper at the dogs. "It's embarrassing!"

"Well, *I* hold that it does you justice, Alan," Jessica sweetly praised. "It shows your nobility of character, and your courage."

"I never wish t'see that rot again, my entire life!" he declared.

No fear of that happening, though, for Jessica sent Margaret, one of their maids, out to buy up five copies of the morning's *Times*, and snipped the article out of each one to press into a large ledger that she termed her memory book.

Thankfully, not everyone in London read *The Times*, preferring the

other dailies, or their trade papers, but when Lewrie was sent out on er-
rands or shopping for the up-coming wedding, there were more than
enough of them in the shops and stores to gasp at the mention of his name,
clap hands to their mouths, and fawn over him, and even rudeness didn't
put them off their hero-worship. Evidently, the West End was simply stiff
with *Times* readers, or people who'd moved their humbler establishments
there and *thought* that some *ton* came with it, now that they had made it
into the fashionable set!

And the wedding was another of Jessica's projects. Oh, she'd consult
Lucy or Pettus as to their tastes, but the menu for the wedding breakfast . . .
the most important part . . . and its location would be more a reflection of
her, as if she'd been given a new dollhouse to furnish and fill with stuffed
creatures to play with.

Take the oysters, for one example.

Pettus expressed his liking for fresh oysters, revelling when he could
get them at a dozen at a sitting, and, during his talks in the kitchens with
Yeovill and the lads, and the maids, so did the rest of them. They were
cheap and plentiful in the Billingsgate Fish Market.

"Oh, Alan," Jessica said, though, frowning with one brow up in faint
distaste, "Oysters, I ask you? One might as well serve bread and cheese,
an apple and a pot of ale."

"I like oysters, common as they are, dear," Lewrie told her.

"Yeovill tells me that he could boil shrimps and serve them with a spicy
red sauce and lemon," she suggested, instead.

"Pettus and Lucy don't even know what shrimp are, Jessica," he countered, "it'd be like trottin' out a bowl of spaghetti, some beef kebabs from
the Middle East, or a Hindoo curry. They can't be expected t'experiment
with foreign kickshaws on their wedding day. Let 'em have oysters to begin with, and follow it up with good, English food."

"Besides," Lewrie added, "with boiled shrimp, you have t'pull the heads
off and peel the tail t'get at the meat, and that'd be very messy. I've had
'em at Wilmington, Charleston, and Savannah, and I know. Oysters can
be slurped off the half shells."

"But . . ." she tried to protest.

"Slurp slurp . . . yum yum," Lewrie japed. "It's *their* day."

"I know, Alan," she almost wailed, fretting, "but I want it to be perfect, and memorable, and . . ."

"Believe me, dearest love, it will be," Lewrie reassured her, reaching
cross the breakfast table to take her hand and squeeze.

Then, there was the matter of where the wedding breakfast would oc-
cur. Jessica thought that the banquetting hall where they had held theirs
would be grand. Too grand, perhaps, Lewrie thought. When they wed,
there had been an host of guests from Jessica's side of the family, and all
her girlhood friends and their husbands to accommodate, along with many
parishoners of St. Anselm's who had been sent invitations more for politi-
cal or social reasons than kinship or close relationships.

How many guests would there be? Pettus's family lived far down South
round Brighton, and they rarely exchanged letters since the day he'd been
swept up by the Impress Service and sent to sea years before. Lucy's parents, two brothers and a sister, lived in London. Outside of them, there
was only the house servants she worked with, Agnes and Martha and Margaret, Yeovill, Deavers, Desmond, and Dasher and Turnbow. Reverend
Chenery had to be there, of course, and they could count on Sir Hugo,
Hugh, and Charlie Chenery, plus the Lewries themselves, say, a total of
twenty?

Once again, it was Pettus and Lucy who suggested a hall in Old Bond
Street that they saw on strolls on their one day off each week, a much
smaller and older place, but more to their liking after attending the Lewries'
wedding at the grander place.

"I suppose you're right, Alan," Jessica gave in, slumping on the settee
as they had their afternoon tea in the drawing room. "You have looked
into it?"

"Pettus and I went there to 'smoak' it out," he assured her with a firm
nod, "It's clean, they do a lot of weddings, and they have the kitchen space,
and cooks on staff to prepare almost anything we wish. I checked out their
plates, glassware, and utensils, too, and it's all good quality. The room's
large enough to handle a long table for all, sitting on one side and at each
end, with lots of space left for musicians and dancing, if anyone feels like
it. They can even hire on the musicians, if we like."

"Hmm, Old Bond Street isn't all that far from Saint Anselm's," Jessica
allowed after a moment of thought. "We could almost walk."

"Nonsense!" Lewrie hooted in mirth. "We *have* t'hire hackneys, so
everyone can hang out the windows and shout the chivaree. Tie old shoes
to their coach . . . beat drums, tootle on tin horns . . ."

"Oh, Alan," Jessica despaired, putting a free hand to her brow, "it's beginning to sound as if the constables will turn up and read us the Riot
Act!"

Buffer the kitten took that moment to leap into her lap, almost spilling her cup of tea, and meowing right loudly in hopes of getting a bite of human food to eat. Buffer didn't quite know what scones and jam were, but if people were eating, shouldn't he?

"You named him wrongly, Alan," Jessica said, nipping a bit of scone off and offering it to him. "I would have called him Oh Be Q."

"Oh Be Q?" Lewrie puzzled.

"For Oh Be Quiet," Jessica laughed, no longer in a fret over the details, "I have never *heard* such a loud and insistent cat."

At last, all the final details of the wedding and the breakfast were woven together like the patterns of a silk shawl on a loom, and they set off for St. Anselm's in several hired coaches, everyone turned out in their Sunday best, Pettus in a new suiting *à la* Beau Brummel with trousers a sobre dark grey, white shirt and waist-coat and a black neck-stock, topped by a gentlemanly narrow-brimmed thimble of a hat. "Gawd, he's done up like th' butler of a *great* house, as fine as wot he'd get on Boxing Day!" Dasher exclaimed when he saw him.

Lucy had chosen fabric of primrose yellow for her wedding gown to be made up at a reputable milliner's, trimmed with white lace, and a perky new bonnet on her head, and looked lovely.

At Jessica's insistence, dress uniforms were the order of the day for Lewrie, right down to sash and star, and his medals on ribbons for Camperdown and Saint Vincent, with his presentation sword on his hip. Hugh and Charlie Chenery had gone along with her, too. It was only Sir Hugo who had balked for a while.

"Full mess-dress for a *butler's* wedding, hah?" he had barked when Lewrie had gone round to tell him of it, "What's the world coming to? I know it's the West End, and your wife wants to make a show of it, but, Christ! I haven't worn my uniforms since the last Saint George's Day to the annual Order of The Garter at Windsor Castle!"

"She's got me in full fig, too," Lewrie pressed. "Do go along."

"How exotic does Jessica wish, hey? Fourth Regiment of Foot, the King's Own, or mess-dress Hindoo kit from the Nineteenth Native Infantry at Calcutta?"

"Oh Lord," Lewrie recalled from his time in India, and how outlandishly foreign *that* uniform would look in London. Foreigners in their native attire, ambassadors to boot, could get dunged and mired by the hooting Mob.

"Keep it English, if ye please, father?" Lewrie had pleaded.

It did not help that Sir Hugo's lips had turned up into an evil leer, and he'd let out an equally sinister laugh. Fortunately for all, he'd shown up in his gleaming private coach in British Army uniform of a Lieutenant-General, and had quite generously offered his equipage to the bride and groom.

The wedding went off without a hitch, since the Church of England, after several hundred years of practice, had their part down pat. Reverend Chenery could probably have conjoined the bride and groom in his sleep by then, but for Jessica's sake, he took extra pains with his role, offering up a thoughtful performance. There was only one ring offered, to the bride, as usual. It had been Jessica's preference that Lewrie agree to a double-ring ceremony, a fact that some officers in the Navy he'd encountered since found extremely odd and laughable.

And yes, on Pettus's lapel there was the same sort of sprig of rosemary for Fidelity that Lewrie had worn, and there was rosemary in Lucy's bouquet as well.

Seated in the family pew box, Jessica had seized his hand and held it in her lap as the ceremony began, obviously excited, and when they stood for hymns or prayers, they continued to hold hands, Lewrie now and then leaning his head towards hers as if to touch foreheads, and secretly smile at each other.

Fidelity, well, Lewrie thought, reminiscing; *God, I've gone a year entire without touchin' strange quim. Maybe there's a hex on rosemary, or something. Did it before with Caroline . . . before a war sent me back t'sea, and temptation. I s'pose I'll survive it.*

The smaller banquetting hall was ready for them, the place cards were set out to indicate where guests would sit, mingling gentlemen and ladies with servants, which made the house help nervous at first.

Lewrie saw to champagne poured into the correct glasses and rose to propose a toast, wishing everyone a grand day, the happy couple a long and loving life, and everyone a delightful time. The champagne loosened tongues and stiff, nervous backs before the bottles were empty.

He sat at one far end of the long table as host, and Jessica at the other, with the bride and groom taking seats in the centre of the long row of guests, who were now talking to each other freely.

"Aha! Oysters!" Sir Hugo cried as a plate of a dozen was placed before him. "Good ho!" Much slurping followed.

A creamy pea soup showed up, paired with a white wine, followed by pork chops and what vegetable removes were still available this late in season, paired with claret. The main entree was an enormous roast goose with roast potatoes, gravy, and red currant jam. More claret came forth, and laughter was the main sound, by then.

The hired musicians, fiddlers, cello, bass viol, and flutists, played happy airs that made people sway from side to side, wave their wine glasses aloft in time, and some drunker to try to sing along.

For dessert, there were plum puddings doused with a sugary glaze and soaking with brandy sauce, along with a cake that Yeovill had baked and delivered before the wedding. And, of course, champagne went best with the diners' choice of sweets, lashings of it.

"Where's the punch?" Margaret, one of the older maids who Lewrie had hired, and not for her looks, shrieked. "Punch, punch, punch!" And the rest took up the cry, stamping feet and fists.

Lewrie had thought of that, too, and an enormous punch bowl was brought out of the kitchens to rest on a smaller table in front of the "happy couple."

Jessica gave him a stern look from her end of the table, but he just laughed and rose to ladle out two glass cups for Pettus and Lucy.

"I'll fathom the *bowl*, I'll fathom the *bowl*! Gi-ive *me* the punch ladle, I'll fath-om *the* bowl!" Lewrie sang, if a bit off-key, and the guests took it up.

And, after everyone had partaken, Lewrie called for music for Pettus and Lucy to dance to. "Ladies and gentlemen, I give you Mister and Mistress Pettus! Success to them, and let them have the first dance!"

The musicians struck up "Pleasant and Delightful," and Pettus and Lucy shyly came round the long table and awkwardly took hands to begin to wheel round each other, for neither had much experience with the studied rounds of a formal ball, but they got into the spirit and shifted to a loose embrace, beaming at each other.

When that tune ended, and everyone applauded, the musicians put their heads together for a moment and urged everyone to dance, starting a livelier tune. Charlie Chenery leaned over the long table and asked little

Agnes to dance, Desmond stood up and took Martha by the hand to lead her out to the dance floor, and they both, being Irish, broke into a sort of a jig. Deavers pulled Margaret to her feet and did his best, which looked very much like a hornpipe.

"Whoo-hee!" Hugh shouted and took Madame Pellatan out, though she looked a trifle appalled by such high cockalorum.

"There ye go, there ye go, that's the way!" Sir Hugo, who had put away more wine than most, rose and clapped his hands and stamped a booted foot in time.

"Gettin' out of hand?" Lewrie asked Jessica as he went down to her end of the table and offered a hand so she could rise. "Ya *said* ya wanted it t'be memorable."

She had to laugh, press a handkerchief to her face, and accept his offer. "Memorable it will be, I suppose. Yes, let's dance. Show me a jig or a horn-pipe, or whatever you sailors call it."

"Saw people waltz in Paris," Lewrie suggested. "We might give that a try."

"Do you know how?" she had to ask.

"Oh, Hell no, but let's do it, anyway!" he hooted.

"You're drunk!" Jessica gawped. "Drunk, or daft!"

"I confess to both," Lewrie laughed, throwing his head back to say, "but only a part of the time."

A hand on her waist, a hand in the air to place her left hand on his shoulder, taking her right in his left and swooping round in a circle. He'd *seen* how the French moved their feet at the *levée* at the Tuileries Palace, but he couldn't recall, said to the Devil with it, and settled on twirling to his right, slowly moving out onto the dance floor, nearer the musicians. It *had* been 1802, after all!

"Something faster!" someone shouted at them. "Country dances!"

"Yee-yeep!" Margaret cried.

The clatter of shoes or boots on the wooden floors rose louder than the music. Hugh and Charlie broke off from their partners to go into a contest at the hornpipe, making the women shriek and laugh out loud. Madame Pellatan snuck back to the punch bowl, dipping, ladling, drinking, and fanning herself as if it was a High Summer day in the stuffiness of a small church, her mouth making "Ooh la la" shapes, with a "*Morte de ma vie!*" and a "*Mon Dieu, merde alors!*" thrown in.

"Ladies and gentlemen, ladies and gentlemen, please," the owner of the banquetting hall tried to implore, "some decorum, I beg of you! The wedding party in the next room can hardly converse for the racket! Sir Alan, Sir Alan, can you not control your . . ."

Liam Desmond, inspired and tipsy, produced his *uillean* lap-pipes and flung himself sprawling in one of the musicians' spare chairs and squealed his way into a reel or jig tune.

Martha, the other maid, rasped out a song that had nothing to do with Desmond's tune, "Whack for the Derry-Oh, there's *whisky* in the jar, whee!"

"Sir, if you don't stop this drunken carousing, I will have to ask you all to leave, this instant!" the owner bellowed. "I will call the constables, and . . . !"

There was a ceramic crash somewhere as a plate was broken.

"Oh, damn," Lewrie groaned, and let his wife go. "Avast! Avast, I say! Pipe down, this instant!" and the ruckus faded, the lap-pipes squawked to a halt, the foot-stomping dancers fell silent, and even the hired musicians stopped playing.

"Thank you, Sir Alan," the owner said, blustering to his side. "I do think it the best thing would be for your party to depart, anyway. For respect for my other patrons. Besides, this room will be used by a poetry society for their dinner, at . . ." he pulled out his pocket watch, "at noon, in an hour's time, scarcely enough time for my waiters to clean and re-stage the tables."

"Hugh? Charlie?" Lewrie called. "It's time to go. Do hail us some hackneys. Pettus, Lucy, my apologies for your wedding breakfast gettin' out of hand. I hope we didn't spoil it for you."

"Oh, Captain Lewrie," Pettus replied with a slightly pie-eyed grin, embracing his bride closely, "it was a proper high ramble, and we wouldn't have missed it for the world. No apology needed."

"A very merry way to send us off into the world, Sir Alan," Lucy seconded his opinion, beaming to beat the breeze as she gave her new husband a reassuring hug.

"But, there's still some punch left," Margaret dared grumble under her breath.

"No no, I think everyone's had more than enough," Lewrie said, "Me included, what? Father, is your coach still outside, and available? Let's see the Pettuses into it. Any addition to the bill, sir?" he asked the owner.

"Well, there was a dinner plate broken, and a few wine glasses cracked, or lost their stems."

"Would an additional two pounds cover that?" Lewrie asked as he dug out his wallet for some bank notes.

"Most admirably, Sir Alan," the owner agreed, taking the notes and stuffing them into his waist-coat pocket. "Uhm, sir . . . you do not have any *other* weddings in your future, do you, Sir Alan?"

"Ah, no," Lewrie told him. "None I know of."

"Oh, good!" the owner enthused, "but if you do, sir, I suggest, most humbly mind, that you hire another hall?"

"Point taken, sir, point taken," Lewrie said with a grin.

Hats, coats, bonnets, parasols, and reticules were gathered up as the wedding party, now much mollified, herded out into Old Bond Street to see the Pettuses into Sir Hugo's coach. Cheers and well wishes arose again as the bride and groom leaned out the door windows to wave back. Hugh and Charlie Chenery had managed to flag down some hackneys, and Reverend Chenery, a bit under an alcoholic weather, his son Charlie, and Madame Pellatan took the first one so they could go to St. Anselm's manse together.

The maids went into the next one.

"Ah, sir," Deavers said as they clattered off, "when Pettus and Lucy get to the house, how are they going to get in? Mean t'say, he gave me the front door keys. 'Til *we* get home, everybody's going to stand round and wait . . . and they're all half-drunk."

"Ah," Lewrie replied. "Oops. Damn!"

"I hope we didn't scandalise your father," Lewrie said through the door to the dressing room off their bedchamber as he stripped off his dress uniform to stow away, and put on looser, more casual garb.

"He did look as if he was enjoying himself," Jessica replied, voice muffled as she changed into a simpler day gown. "Most of the time, I mean. Towards the end, though . . ." She tittered to herself. The door opened and she went over to her vanity, un-pinning her elegant up-do so she could brush her long, dark, almost-black hair down.

"A waltz, Alan? Really?" she laughed as she brushed.

"Never can tell, it might catch on in England someday," Lewrie told her as he slipped his feet into a pair of loose, old shoes.

Satisfied that her hair was neatly arranged, Jessica bound it with a blue ribbon, studied herself in the mirror, beamed satisfaction, and rose to go to the window of their bedchamber, which looked out on the back garden and the coach house, now the Pettuses' lodgings.

"What are you doing?" Lewrie asked.

"Just looking," Jessica told him. "Wondering what they're up to."

"Nosy," Lewrie chid her with a "Tsk. A peepin' Tom, are you?"

The upstairs set of rooms above the empty stable and coach house had no windows on the back side, a pair either side of the stairs that led up from the garden, and two that faced the main house. Lewrie had a quick look for himself, but there was no sign of movement from the lodgings, and the new curtains on the windows were drawn. There was a thin skein of smoke from a chimney, though.

"Probably brewin' themselves some tea," he surmised.

"Perhaps," Jessica said, then turned to him, "Or, after all the nervousness of the morning, the ceremony and all, then that breakfast folderol, they're quite exhausted. We were, remember?"

"Aye, we were," Lewrie agreed. After their wedding breakfast, they had coached to Sir Hugo's estate at Anglesgreen for a week of "honeymoon," and had, despite his wants, fallen into bed late at night and had just slept! "But, they didn't have that far to coach."

"Oh, Alan, I just hope that they're going to be as happy as we are," Jessica cooed, coming to embrace him.

"I'm sure they will be," he assured her, holding her close and breathing into her hair.

"I just wish they could go away for a few days," Jessica said, "to a country inn, or a posting house. One night together, and they come back to service tomorrow morning?"

"Pettus couldn't afford it, and wouldn't let me pay for it," Lewrie said, shrugging, "at least their lodgings'll be pleasant for their first night."

On the sly, vases had been set out, filled with fresh flowers, and their sideboard in the wee dining area now held two bottles of wine, white and red, a flask of brandy, and a used caddy now held tea leaves, coffee beans to grind, and a cone of sugar.

"Let's go down and ring for tea, or coffee," Lewrie suggested.

"Alan," Jessica chuckled, "do you *really* imagine that any of our servants are capable of doing anything 'til suppertime? Hah. You got them all *drunk*!"

"I've ground coffee before," Lewrie told her. "I think that I can even manage t'boil water. Stoke a fireplace, stoke a stove, hey?"

Once they got to the kitchens, though, it looked a far more difficult proposition. Un-attended for several hours, the fire in the oven had reduced itself to grey kindling and coals, and the top felt cold. Yeovill was seated at the dining table, slumped over flat on his face, and snoring. Bully, the terrier that turned the spit and chased the rats and mice, slept in a wicker basket full of towels and aprons. And, from the male servants' bedchambers towards the front of the basement, there were even more snores.

"I'll settle for a glass of water," Lewrie whispered, unwilling to disturb anyone, "and a nap of my own. Which one of the drawing room settees do you want?"

"A nap, yes," Jessica agreed, her head lowered towards her chest, and her eyes half-closed. "In our bedchamber?"

"Oh, yes," Lewrie heartily agreed.

Once back abovestairs, they slipped off their shoes and stretched out, Lewrie's left arm under the pile of pillows to cradle her. One brief moment to sigh, stretch tense, and relax, and their dream of a nap dissolved, for here came Bisquit, Rembrandt, and the kitten, to whine and frisk about on the carpet.

"Hush, dogs," Lewrie bade, "curl up and sleep. Oh, hallo puss. Fine, you're on the bed. Settle down, now," he said as the cat made his way up between them. Lewrie stroked Buffer, and he began to purr, loudly as was his wont.

"Is he licking your fingers?" Jessica marvelled.

Buffer was.

CHAPTER TWENTY-SEVEN

*A*utumn wore on, the days grew chillier, and the London skies were mostly grey and overcast. It was time to prepare for the coming Winter, time for the chimney swifts to come round with their long brushes and young lads, their clothes and hides dark-smudged and stained the colour of coal, to squeeze themselves up the flues, raining down the hardened soot from the last warming fires of the previous year and late Spring, and the housemaids had to spread old sailcloth in front of the hearths to protect the floors and carpets.

In the front of the basement, near the delivery entrance, sacks of fresh coal was piled deep, bought by the hundredweight, along with bundles and bundles of wood kindling.

The markets were scoured for the last supplies of potatoes, and stored in the larder, along with dried peas, dried beans, bunches of red, green, and yellow peppers, bushels of them. Yeovill, out on his many shopping trips, managed to obtain small bags of spices to be ground to a powder and stored away, as well. He found white rice from Louisiana and the Carolinas, for when the potatoes went bad or shriveled up, covered with eyes, and from Martini's establishment, came the exotic *cous cous* from Morocco or Southern Spain, *polenta* from Sicily, various kinds of *pasta,* and sundried tomatoes that *might* keep through the Winter.

And when not out shopping, Yeovill kept the house staff busy at pickling all manner of vegetables before they disappeared from the market; beets, turnips, radishes, cauliflower, Brussels sprouts, onions, cucumbers, and the last of the fresh tomatoes that the greengrocers had, of any variety. Apples were bought by the ten-pound sack.

Winter blankets were brought out from cedar-lined chests, eyed for moth holes, and aired in the back garden before being draped at the foot of all the beds. Carpets were vigourously swept with brooms after the swifts were done, wood floors mopped, furniture dusted, and fabrics whisked with stiff brushes.

Lewrie, for the most part, stayed well out of the way, for it was the housewife's main duty before the first frost, his wife's, and Jessica threw herself into the task with brisk efficiency, and there was no telling her to relax, that it would all get done. She had finished her portrait of Hugh standing by his horse's head and given it to Sir Hugo, but that was the last artwork she did most-likely 'til it was Guy Fawkes Day. She went about in a plain older gown, an apron and a mob-cap, only rarely dressing up when they entertained guests, a married couple or two of their acquaintance, her father and brother, Sir Hugo and Hugh.

Lewrie had thought that the best place for him would be in the drawing room or his study over the entry hall, reading a new novel or the newspapers, but every time he settled in for some peace and quiet, here came ugly old Martha or Margaret, their substantial bulk shaking the floors as they bustled in to do even more cleaning, stoke one of the fireplaces which were now lit round the clock, or dust something at his elbow with a "Please ya, Sir Alan, just a wee bit o' dustin' there" or "If ya'd rise, so please ya, th' floor's dirty. Be just a shake of a wee lamb's tail,"

As irksome as it was, and how pointless it seemed by then, he dressed in uniform and tottered off to Admiralty for the day, eating at a two-penny ordinary for dinner, and not returning home 'till it was time for supper!

He had been left alone, for the most part, one drizzly morning, following the war in Spain and Portugal even as the campaign season was winding down in those climes, too, when there came a loud and impatient knocking on the front door, not just the genteel rap of the pineapple brass door knocker, but a fist demanding entry, and he cocked an ear to see what the disturbance was, half-rising from his armchair.

"Oh, welcome, sir," he faintly heard Pettus say, before feet on the stairs thundered upwards.

Have t'lay carpetting on those stairs, he told himself; *damme, more t'be swept, I s'pose.*

"Father!" Hugh boomed. "Father! The best of news! I've got a ship! I'm made Lieutenant!" he chortled as he dashed into the drawing room.

"Well, halleluah, it's about time!" Lewrie hooted, spreading his arms to welcome his son in and congratulate him. "Give ya joy!"

"I just got the letter from Admiralty this morning," Hugh breathlessly gushed. "I'm appointed Third Officer to the *Greyhound* frigate, she's a thirty-two gunned Sixth Rate, now getting re-launched at Deptford! Ain't it the grandest thing?"

"Let me congratulate you, my boy," Lewrie said, taking his son into a snug embrace for a moment, patting his back with both hands. "Remember the last time I held you so," he said, stepping back and letting go, "the morning you went aboard your first ship in Eighteen Oh Three. I know it ain't English, but you deserve that 'un, too! How soon d'ya report?"

"I'll have to coach to Admiralty to receive my Commission documents, and my active-appointment," Hugh told him, still giddy with his promotion, "then, I suppose they'll tell me."

"Tomorrow morning, then, a shopping trip's in order," Lewrie decided. "New uniforms, a proper sword, and whatever you need for your sea chest, and personal stores, aha. You've told your grandfather?"

"First to know, aye," Hugh said, nodding. "He said something on that head, that he'd love to come along."

"Fine, then we'll make it a threesome, first thing in the morning," Lewrie directed.

"What's all the tumult?" Jessica asked as she swept into the drawing room in her mob-cap and apron, with a brush in her hand.

"Hugh's been promoted to Lieutenant, and orders to a new ship, my love," Lewrie proudly told her.

"Oh, how grand for you, at last, Hugh!" Jessica cried and came to give him a fierce hug. "Congratulations! I know how long you've been waiting on tenterhooks for it. Bored, feeling idle and useless."

"Amen to that, Jessica," Hugh heartily agreed. "I just wanted to dash in, let everyone know of it, then dash out, again."

"No time for a glass of something?" Lewrie asked.

"Well, not really," Hugh said with a grimace. "Maybe a brandy, once I get back from Admiralty."

"And has your new Captain gathered his alloted number of Mids yet?" Lewrie asked him. "If he hasn't, you might put in a good word for Charlie."

"Aye, he's had some sea time, and he's a good lad," Hugh agreed. "And a fighter, too, after serving under you, father."

"Aye, he is that!" Lewrie laughed.

"Oh, poor Charlie," Jessica said, much sobred. It appeared that the idea of her little brother going back to sea, and its dangers, did not sit well with her.

"Well, I'm off," Hugh said, exuberant. "Nine in the morning, is that a good time, father?"

"Nine it'll be," Lewrie agreed, reaching out to slap his son on the top of his arm, "Congratulations, Hugh. God, I'm so proud of you!"

"'By, father . . . Jessica," Hugh said, looking somewhat modest, as he made his way down the stairs to the entry hall, feet clomping as loud as they had on the way up.

"Think we should carpet those stairs?" Lewrie asked his wife.

"Oh no, I rather like the shiny hardwood," Jessica said, shaking her head, openly frowning now. "Alan . . . I *am* glad for Hugh, but is it really necessary for Charlie to join him?"

"He's the beginnings of a career in the Navy, love," Lewrie told her, "a gentlemanly career. It's what he wanted when I took him aboard *Sapphire*, Your own father couldn't drive him to taking Holy Orders, as the rest of your family has. Charlie knows the risks, has seen 'em up close, and is still eager to serve, and progress. It's *his* decision."

"I know, Alan, I know," Jessica fretted, sinking into the nearest armchair, "He's sixteen, and almost a man, but Charlie will forever be a pestiferous imp who laughed over every prank he played me, and . . ."

"*Greyhound*'s new Captain may already have all his Mids, six if I remember how many a Sixth Rate carries on Ship's Books," Lewrie said, trying to mollify her, "He's known he'd get her for weeks, so he may've taken on cousins, obliged family friends, or brought a couple from his last ship. It's all favour, interest, and patronage, ye know. Hah!"

"I recall hearin' about one Captain, a real dandy-prat, who ran up such a high bill with his tailor," Lewrie sniggered, "that to clear his debt, he took the tailor's son on as a Midshipman!"

"So, Charlie may have to wait longer?" Jessica hesitantly asked.

"Could be," Lewrie allowed, throwing himself onto a settee, "It ain't *quite* as dangerous these days, as it was before. Spain's turned into our ally,

Denmark's fleet is about gone, Sweden has no argument with England any more, and Russia under their new Tsar Alexander, who isn't insane like his predecessor, has more on their plate against the Ottoman Turks than us. The Dutch still build warships, but don't do anything with the ones they have, and the Italian navies . . . Venice, Naples, Genoa . . . in all the time I spent at Sicily, raidin' up and down the coasts, I never saw hide nor hair of an Italian warship, or a French one, either.

"The French, well," Lewrie went on, "Bonaparte's gutted them of men, every time he wins a battle, he loses ten or fifteen thousand casualties, and he'll draft young, beardless boys and sailors. Our Navy on blockade has 'em bottled up, and their fleet hasn't left port since Trafalgar. It's more a brace of frigates out to raid our convoys that you see. If Charlie does go to sea, again, he'll most-like be bored, idle, and feel useless as he does now. Except for the daily routine, that is."

"I still wish he'd have chosen clerking at a bank," Jessica said with a wry cock of her head, and a wee shrug. "If you say so, I will no longer worry for him *quite* so much."

"He may still be with us in time for Winter in the country," Lewrie proposed. "Christmas at *Dun Roman?*"

"Oh, I'd love that!" Jessica perked up. "And I could ride Bobs through the snow! How I miss that horse!"

"I'm sure my father'd relish it, too," Lewrie said, reaching out to pat her hand.

"I'll get back to cleaning, then," Jessica said, rising. "There isn't much left to do for our house to be ready for the season."

"Thank *God!*" Lewrie exclaimed. "Peace and quiet, at last!"

Pettus came up from the entry hall with a packet of letters for Lewrie to read that afternoon, and Lewrie sped through the stack with eagerness, noting that his old First Officer, Geoffrey Westcott had written him, as had Rear-Admiral Sir Thomas Charlton in the Med, Rear-Admiral Benjamin Rodgers from the Eastern Med, and Lt.-Col. Tarrant on Sicily, the commander of the 94th Foot which Lewrie had used for their coastal raiding force. And, wonder of wonders, there was one from his elder son, Sewallis, on the North American Station at Halifax!

News from old friends and shipmates was one thing, but it was Sewallis's letter that he tore open first. His frigate, the *Daedalus,* had just come back from a cruise as far South as the Florida Straits, with no port calls except for St. Augustine, where the Spanish authorities had given them a fine welcome, the ship's officers a supper and a dance, and a slew of fresh fruit rarely seen in England. Sewallis admitted that he had gorged himself on bananas, oranges, lemons and limes, and even peaches! Barrels of lemon and lime juice had been brought aboard, and now every hand demanded lime and sugar with their rum issues, the same as the petty officers did. *Daedalus* was a happy ship in most respects with few discipline problems, and the days at sea reeled by as calmly as a peacetime passage, "all cruising and claret." Sewallis had bought up as much fruit as he could afford, and had just turned a tidy profit off it among the fruit-starved men of the North American squadrons. He was also of a mind to buy up ice during the Winter for sale at St. Augustine or even Havana, which he would love to visit. The Captain and all the wardroom officers were doing it!

You a Commission Sea Officer, or a street vendor? Lewrie fumed to himself, reading on; *He's a damned* . . . merchant!"

When in port at Halifax, there were jolly boat races under sail, ship-against-ship, some fine criquet, and scenic horse rides along the rugged coasts and hills. Some local young ladies came along when they took baskets of food and wine for *al fresco* feasts, and the beauties of Saint Augustine were un-matched.

"Bah!" Lewrie spat after he read the last lines, and tossed it aside with faint disgust.

Commander Geoffrey Westcott at least still had a whiff of powder about him. He'd made prize of another Yankee grain ship off L'Orient, pressing two obvious Englishmen into his crew, and had encountered a French *corvette* similar to his brig-sloop, taking her after only three broadsides. Geoffrey admitted that he was not making as much in prize-money as he had under Lewrie, but his was now a larger share, thanking him for forcing him to strike out on his own, at last!

Good old Thom Charlton imparted worse news. After a provisioning call at Malta, he had come down with some sort of ague, possibly, or so the Surgeons told him, a form of malaria; sweats, fever, then chills so violent that he could barely stand still, or hold a glass or eating utensils. It came and it went un-predictably, with a few good days in a row, then another bout would lay him low in his bed-cot for two days running, and he had decided to write Admiralty for someone to replace him in charge of his far-flung squadron. He would strike his flag and sail home, where he hoped to restore his health.

Thankfully, my Captains are well experienced at the work by now, and shew a great deal of Zeal and Initiative, so that my hand is not Necessary for our Foes to be foiled. Except for one Instance. Your replacement, dear Lewrie, is a most cautious Slow-Coach. Commodore Grierson is still training his re-enforced transports and troops, and has yet to launch any coastal raids. His lack of Aggression is most Distressing to me.

Brig. Caruthers, by the way, is now in command of Grierson's land force, having taken the 94th, which did us great Service, into his Brigade and trading off one of his former regiments; another fellow who wishes all his Tees crossed and I's dotted before he will undertake any Action. Despite my Orders to both men to get on with it, they drag their feet, so I do not Envy the task my replacement Inherits.

By the by, your Protege, Cmdr. D'Arcy Gamble, recently distinguished himself by intercepting a small convoy of coasters running down from Bari to Crotone in the dark, and made prize of all five of them. His family will be proud to see his name in the Naval Chronicle and the Gazette, and I am sure, Gamble will be greatful for the prize-money, which is become harder to garnish.

If I am forced to retire, I am sanguine. Fourty one years in my naval career may be long enough, and I recall all of it fondly.
Best regards to you, you old scamp, and to your good lady,

I am, your Humble & Thankful Friend
Sir Thomas Charlton

"Grierson, Grierson *and* Caruthers?" Lewrie fretted aloud, then went to Colonel Tarrant's letter, thinking that a bad combination of arrogance and aspiration.

Tarrant wrote that what he and Lewrie had dreaded had come to pass. The senior General commanding British forces on Sicily, having been favourably impressed with the work they had done before, should be re-enforced to achieve even greater results on the mainland of Italy. Since Caruthers had won the only battle against the French since the Battle of Maida years before, and was a "comer," it was only to be expected that he should be appointed to employ his brigade of three regiments in even larger operations.

Caruthers had been training one of his regiments in how to climb down boarding nets, then re-embark up them, on the sly even before Commodore Grierson had turned up with more transports in which to accommodate them, laying the groundwork for taking everything over under his sole command. Now, he would have a trained three regiment brigade to hand, and Tarrant feared that he would use them to make bigger raids; not just raids, but invasions that might last overnight and into the next day, drawing the attention of French forces in Calabria, so he could have himself a proper battle like his first at Siderno and at Locri, winning for himself even more fame, possibly a knighthood, or a promotion.

Sir, he simply won't stop harping upon the use of artillery, and is scouring Messina's harbour for big barges that could carry a fieldpiece, team of at least two horses, caisson and limber, and he has put a flea in Commodore Grierson's ear that he simply must scrounge something up. It'll be big cooking cauldrons and tents, next, as if he thinks to make a semi-permanent lodgement.

Tarrant despaired that they would attempt any moves before the Winter weather set in, for both Grierson and Caruthers needed to satisfy themselves that everything was "all tiddly." The 94th went aboard their transports twice a week, boarded their barges and rowed ashore, then back to the ships to sleep overnight, before being rowed back ashore for a ten mile route march and overnight camp, supposedly to "toughen" them up. Inspections and dismissive complaints ensued over the conditions of their uniforms, boots, headgear, brass, their lack of pipeclay to whiten belts. All the 94th who'd picked up those desirable French leather packs had had to revert to British issue. Tarrant's big and shaggy dog, Dante, had developed the habit of growling at the many officers of Caruthers's staff who came round to fuss over his soldiers' neatness. Oddly, Caruthers wished to conserve the ammunition, 'til they actually *did* something, so time on the firing range had been reduced.

Imagine, Sir, a British Army, the only one in Europe that regularly practices live, aimed, fire, being kept from doing so? It beggars the mind! At least we are still allowed to skirmish in the groves, though Caruthers has promised that we will be training in brigade movements. Our superiors have a great mis-trust in our means of gathering information, so much so that the games we held in camp, Army vs. Navy, are curtailed, in fear that local Sicilians, who attended, might be in the pay of the French. Our Mr. Quill is close to pulling his hair out with both hands. I have given him your London address, so you may hear

*from him in future. If you wish to write Quill, do so at the regimental
address, and I will give them to him.*

"I *told* Caruthers, over and over, it's a *raidin'* force, not an *invasion* force!"
Lewrie growled. But this sounded like the very sort of impending disaster that he'd warned Caruthers against, that Colonel Tarrant had deemed
too ambitious. Did the over-ambitious bastard even *care*? And Commodore Grierson, he and Lewrie despised each other like the Devil hated Holy
Water. He'd come into command in triumph, getting one over on Lewrie, changing everything about whether it needed to be changed, just
because it had been *Lewrie's* way of operation. And, if Brigadier-General
Caruthers had expansive plans that might lead to new glories, Grierson
would willingly go along with it, whether he and his flagship and two frigates could support Caruthers's raids or not.

Just how few pieces of wit does Grierson possess? Lewrie asked himself; *Just
enough t'order supper? Make change? Un-button the flap of his breeches t'pee?*

Sooner or later, Lewrie realised, those two lack-wits would set sail for
somewhere in Calabria, some town or small city that he and his limited
force daren't risk, and they would surely come a cropper! He had to
warn . . . *who?* Who could order them to re-think their operations to avoid
disaster, and a humiliating defeat?

For a wry second or two, Lewrie stretched his lips in an evil smile, wondering how big their come-down and embarrassment would be if he said
nothing and they went ahead with a rash plan. Courts-martial for each,
cashiered from the Army, "Yellow-Squadroned" along with the insane and
incompetent from the Navy, denied any military or naval role or command
the rest of their lives, like the nit-wit who'd lost a whole British army at
Buenos Aires in 1806 to a hastily gathered pack of hot-blooded rebel amateurs and militia?

No, he had to see someone in Admiralty, in Horse Guards, at the Foreign Office's Secret Branch, perhaps with someone at the Secretary of State
for War, like . . . Peter Rushton's brother, Harold!

No, let's start with Secret Branch, Lewrie thought best.

"Is Mister Peel in?" Lewrie asked the secretive clark, after he had been
passed through several vettings in the Foreign Office annex.

"And who is calling, sir?" the clerk asked, all hush-hush, and aloof.

"Captain Sir Alan Lewrie," was the response.

"I do not believe so, Sir Alan," the clerk said with a sniff.

"Head cold, is it?" Lewrie wryly asked. "Of course, Peel's in. That's his favourite hat and his walking stick yonder. And he really should purchase a new overcoat. That'un's gone seedy."

The clerk let out a long, put-upon sigh and went to the massive carved oak door to the inner sanctum, peeking round it, ajar.

"Oh, why not?" Peel's voice could be heard, in exasperation, "shove him in."

"Hallo, Mister Peel," Lewrie sunnily said as he shed his own hat and walking stick.

"What is it this time, Lewrie?" Peel asked with a frown. "You're missing an elephant? Thieves stole your shoe buckles?"

"No, have you *found* an elephant, though?" Lewrie japed. "I know a circus that might be interested. Actually, I've come, well before time, to invite you to dinner, as a way of paying thanks for your aid in getting my dogs back, and finding those dog buffers."

"Aha!" James Peel exclaimed, slapping a palm on his desk-top. "I do believe I will allow you to do so, old son. And, in point of fact, there is a new and rather tasty dining establishment not two blocks from here, where many in government offices dine these days."

"I assume the many enemy spies in London know of this?" Lewrie quipped some more.

"Oh, of course they do," Peel said, closing a few files in large brown paper envelopes that he slipped into his large desk and locked the drawer with a key hung on his watch fob. "Shall we go?"

"You know they're listening?" Lewrie wondered aloud as he and Peel left the inner offices and Peel donned his overcoat, slapped on his hat, and took up his walking stick.

"Only gentlemen obtain posts in His Majesty's Government, Lewrie, and English gentlemen never discuss business, religion, politics, or gossip about women when dining," Peel told him with a wink.

Peel's choice of restaurant was several cuts above the two-penny ordinary that Lewrie had expected. Once in the entry hall of what had been a grand mansion in the old days, there was a porter to take their hats, overcoats, and walking sticks, and give them pasteboard cards with a number on them. A maître d' led them to a table for two halfway along the ground floor and seated them. There was a snowy white tablecloth, up-ended

wine and water glasses, and *à la carte* printed menus. There were enough candles lit, on tables and candelabras hung above, to make reading menus, and discerning if what you ordered was what you were eating easy to do.

"I haven't seen a place like this since Paris, or the restaurant in Savoy Street, near the Strand," Lewrie marvelled.

"All the rage, I'm told," Peel said, grinning, "rivalling what a gentleman's club like Boodle's, Almack's or White's offers, without the high dues, and the vetting. All one has to do is come well-dressed, clean and sobre, and pay for what you order."

"What *will* they think of next?" Lewrie commented, scanning his menu. "Hmm, dover sole, with creamed potatoes, carrots, onion and peas sounds good . . . lemon sauce, gravy . . . a *shilling*?"

"My choice, you said," Peel replied with a beamish grin.

"What, we're served by bare-naked Chinese virgins?" Lewrie had to scoff.

"And, like a proper English gentleman's club, not a woman to be seen," Peel pointed out. "A welcome break from the wife and kiddies."

"Well, you rendered me good service, and I suppose this is a way to thank you," Lewrie said, laying aside the menu as a wine steward come to the table and suggested a smuggled Alsatian riesling to start.

"Knacky, how you avoided linking Secret Branch to your criminal affair, too," Peel told him. "How did yo put it? Haddock, an itinerant knife-grinder, and a likely lad who knew his way about?"

"I didn't see you in court," Lewrie said. "Sit in the back?"

"No, I read the transcript," Peel admitted. "Just to make sure you didn't blab something embarrassing to Foreign Office."

"You're beginning t'sound like old Zachariah Twigg," Lewrie complained, "always unsure if I had two wits t'rub together."

"Bless me, Lewrie, you've managed more than well without them!" Peel twitted him. It was good that the wine came, and a waiter to take their orders. "I see you had to toss the police a bone. Poor bastards. So many criminals in London, so few of them, and armed only with their wood truncheons. In the beginning, I thought a police department would be a tyrant's tool, like a huge standing Army, as dictatorial as the Prussians, the Russian Cossacks, or the French. But, now I'm starting to appreciate the idea, if they ever get round to *solving* crimes that they didn't witness and catch the perpetrators in the act."

"Well, the French," Lewrie said, savouring his first sip of the spicy

riesling, "their mobs and thieves must be more plentiful, and a lot more active, than ours. And their police *are* oppressive! To have police here . . . it's just not English!"

"It might grow on us, if crime is reduced," Peel prophecied.

"Ehm, I got some bad news from Sicily, Peel," Lewrie said, opening his plaint, "Rear-Admiral Sir Thomas Charlton's caught a recurring fever, and he's going to strike his flag and come home."

"Oh, poor fellow!" Peel sympathised. "Didn't you tell me that it was he who set you to planning how to land and recover raiding forces?"

"It was," Lewrie gladly confessed, "I can't take all the credit. One thing he said, that he doesn't envy his replacement, since he just can't goad *my* replacement, Commodore Grierson, into *doing* anything with the ships he has, and Brigadier-General Caruthers, who now commands a three-regiment force, seems more interested in drilling and training than having a go at the French. Colonel Tarrant complained to me that the man's still trying to find a way to get artillery ashore, so he can make a proper lodgement that'll draw the French to him for a battle."

"I was wondering if you'd heard from your Mister Quill," Lewrie asked, "to get his view on it."

"Yes, I have," Peel said, leaning forward over the table. "But, as I said, that would be a matter best discussed back in my offices, hey."

"Oh," Lewrie said, "then how's your family?"

Back in Peel's inner sanctum, the fellow, mellowed by his dinner and half a bottle of riesling, was much more informative.

"It's the same old story, really, Lewrie," Peel gloomed as he laid out several past reports to remind him, "proper gentlemen don't dirty their hands with espionage, and, when the sources of what information comes to them are criminals, smugglers, and strong-arm thugs, both Grierson and Caruthers are even more loath to listen. They deem *Don* Lucca Massimo and his men as scum of the Earth, have no truck with him or his *capos* and *barely* listen to what they learn when provided by Mister Quill. It's as if their plans for future operations over on the mainland have nothing to do with the partisans, and what Quill and Mister Sylvester are doing."

"Which is what, exactly?" Lewrie asked.

"Oh, they've made great inroads!" Peel boasted, "Sylvester most especially. He can now deliver reports to Sicily like a penny post, and has recruited *hosts* of listeners, observers, and informants among almost

every French garrison town. They can't saddle up for a road-march or do close-order drill without us knowing of it. Children, tavern waitresses, whores . . . recall that a lot of the French in Italy are Italians from other regions, so no one has to learn French to listen to their drunken boastings and complaints and pass them on.

"Sylvester has also managed to smuggle in several shipments of arms and ammunition," Peel went on, "along with small kegs of gunpowder and slow match fuses. A lot of mountain roads have been blocked with fallen trees or rockslides, and when the French try to clear them, the partisans are lurking high above in the mountains and shoot at them or drop lit kegs on their heads, and the French troops aren't mountain goats, nor are their cavalry horses, hah hah!"

"So, it sounds like Grierson and Caruthers *are* hoping for a big battle, and the partisans' aid isn't necessary for that," Lewrie said, making a face. "They, and Quill, are working at cross-purposes."

"It sounds very like it, yes," Peel agreed.

"And if they do land all their regiments and then sit and wait to draw a French army to them," Lewrie surmised, "they're courting a disaster. If they go beyond the range of Grierson's guns. Peel, someone has to slap them down before they do. Horse Guards, Admiralty, your branch, Lord Castlereagh?"

"Hmm, I suppose a report sent round to the various offices that you mentioned *might* stir some interest," Peel said, scratching his chin. "You haven't written Admiralty yourself?"

"I go to beg for a new command," Lewrie gravelled, "but gettin' an interview to criticise Grierson and Caruthers'd look like I was chewin' sour grapes. I could prevail upon my father to visit one of his old friends at Horse Guards . . . and an old school friend has a brother who works for Castlereagh, but . . ." he ended with a helpless shrug.

"Ah, that's right," Peel commented, "you have few patrons of high enough influence to play politics for you. I'll do what I can with a cautionary report, but . . ." Peel, too, lifted his hands in a shrug of his own.

"Well, at least we had a good dinner," Lewrie said, sighing.

Lewrie took himself home in a puzzlement, striving to come up with the wording of a letter, or letters, he could send to all parties involved in the command of far-flung military operations against France. Yet, who was he but only one Post-Captain of More Than Three Years' Seniority on the Navy List, and one ashore on half-pay at that? Peel was right; he *had* no powerful patrons with influence and the ear of those who led the war. Those who had arranged for him to be stripped of his ship and his command on Sicily would always prevail. He could only sit back and wait for foreign events to unfold, for good or ill.

And commiserate. He would definitely write letters in answer to the ones he'd just received, to Quill, Colonel Tarrant, Lt. Fletcher who led the first batch of troop transports when he'd first anchored at Sicily. And Harold Rushton at Lord Castlereagh's offices?

He would give that one a try, too, so long as he avoided pleading, or angrily exhorting; he could not sound like a Cassandra, who always knew the future, but was never believed, then slain at last when her dire predictions grew too bothersome.

He'd write Sewallis, too, and ask if he was aboard a warship or a trading brig.

He rapped at his own pineapple door knocker, and scraped some mud from his boot soles on the implements by the steps. Pettus opened the door and took his hat, overcoat, and walking stick.

"Damned good news upstairs, sir," Pettus told him, grinning.

"What's up?" Lewrie asked.

"Mister Chenery's heard from Admiralty, sir," Pettus told him as he headed for the stairs. Lewrie could hear some youthful whoops of joy.

"Well, hallo, Charlie," he said in greeting when he entered the drawing room, "had good news, have you?"

"Oh, it's grand, sir!" Chenery shouted. "Hugh . . . Lieutenant Lewrie, that is . . . met his new Captain, a fellow by name of Hogue who . . . !"

"Hogue?" Lewrie said, dredging his memory, "Oh, of course! He was with me in the Far East, and was in the Gironde River when I had the *Savage* frigate!"

"Anyway, Captain Hogue was delighted to have the son of one of his old shipmates as his Third Officer," Charlie happily babbled on, "and when Hugh . . . Lieutenant Lewrie . . . asked if he had all of his Mids, he said he still had openings for two more, so when . . . your son dared suggest *my* name, he was more than willing to take me on. Hugh, hang it! Your son just wrote that Captain Hogue would be delighted to offer a berth to someone who spent several years in two ships under a Captain who's won such a sterling repute. I'm off tomorrow, the first diligence coach, to Deptford, before he can change his mind, hah hah!"

"Captain Nathaniel Hogue," Lewrie reminisced, "in Eighty-Four, he

was a Master's Mate, just turned eighteen, as smart as paint. Got his Lieutenantcy in Eighty-Six, I think, and he was a Commander when we ran
into each other in the mouth of the Gironde. The lucky bastard . . ."

"Alan!" Jessica snapped. "*Language*!"

"Your pardons, my dear," Lewrie had to apologise. "Hogue made off
with one, maybe two, big three-masted merchantmen, both stuffed to
the deckheads with all sorts of fine, export wines and spirits, and made
a pile o' 'tin' in prize-money. A hell . . . a fine sailor and navigator, and I
expect a fine Captain. You're fortunate, Charlie. Need a shoppin' trip before you go?"

"My sea chest and dunnage are like Jessica's hope chest, sir," Chenery
dared jape, "all prepared and stocked, in hopes of orders. I have already
told father, and he's suggested a last family supper."

"Hang that," Lewrie countered, "we'll host you and him here this evening, and trust Yeovill t'lay the same sort o' feast that he did for Hugh
when we saw him off, right, Jessica?"

"But of course, Alan," his wife said, though she had lifted the hem of
her apron to dab at her eyes which were shiny with moisture. "Though I
hate to see my little brother sail away again."

"Did Hugh say anything of where Hogue's orders take *Greyhound*?"
Lewrie asked, knowing that he and Jessica would have to have a long discussion before that "joyous" supper.

"No, sir," Charlie said, "but then, he wouldn't be privy before she's fully
manned, and might not know 'til we're far out to sea."

"Either way, you and your father be back here by Seven, and we will
stuff you both 'til pudding comes out of your ears," Lewrie promised. "Off
with you, young Mister Chenery, and finish your packing."

"On my way, sir!" Charlie said, going to give his sister one more hug,
and a manly handshake to Lewrie.

"And he only got to ride his new horse but two weeks," Jessica said with
a sniff. "Now, it'll be years before he can go to Anglesgreen or sleep in
his old childhood bed at the manse."

"I think he's outgrown that childhood bed," Lewrie told her.

"Yes, I fear so," she said with a long sigh. "At least he and Hugh will
be together in the same ship. They've become good friends."

Lewrie didn't tell her of the gulf between a sixteen year old Midshipman and a Commission Sea Officer, or the private travails that Charlie
would face belowdecks in the Mids' cockpit among strange new faces.
Lewrie was sure that he would cope; he had so far.

"If you'd tell Yeovill what's wanting," Lewrie said, looking at his pocket watch, "I have some letters to answer."

"Oh, speaking of mail," Jessica said, taking a letter from her apron pocket, "you got this from that association of animal lovers, the . . . National Society For the Elimination of Cruelty Towards Animals In All Forms, or whatever they call themselves."

"Oh, *that* lot," Lewrie scoffed, grimacing. He tore it open to discover that those worthies had a monthly meeting coming up at the Nerot's Hotel near St. James's Palace and were extending an invitation to him to be their guest of honour. "Hah! I'm to be feted! Wish to come along?"

Jessica shook her head negatively, looking amused, more than anything else; at least it shook her from her sad study. "I had nothing to do with your raid, Alan. The honour is all yours. Ehm, Yeovill says he has a beef roast ready for tonight. Will that be grand enough, or should I ask him to be more lavish?"

"Oh, lavish is the word, my love!" Lewrie hooted, striking a comic pose with an arm upthrust, "Lavish! I *like* that word!" We use it so seldom. Say it with me! L . . . avish!"

"You're daft," Jessica tittered, and headed belowstairs.

At least I cosseted her out of her pet, Lewrie told himself as he headed for his study; *Hugh at sea, again, Charlie at sea, again, and only me still "beached." Two down, one to go. And maybe Peel can put Grierson and Caruthers in their place before they do something stupid.*

CHAPTER TWENTY-EIGHT

$\mathcal{G}$ood evening, Pettus," Lewrie said on greeting as he returned home late. "A nippy damned night," he added as he handed over his damp hat and overcoat.

"Yes sir," Pettus agreed as he shut the front door against the chill wind and a misty, cold rain. "The new thermometer by the doors to the back garden says it's in the mid-fourties. You'll be wishing hot tea, and some rum or brandy, sir?"

"In front of a roaring fire, aye," Lewrie agreed, shivering for real as he rubbed his hands together.

"Dame Lewrie is still up, sir, in the drawing room," Pettus said, pointing upwards. "I'll have Deavers fetch you a fresh pot and a glass of something."

"Good, good," Lewrie said, pulling something from his overcoat pocket.

"And what is that, sir?" Pettus had to ask.

"A loving cup, Pettus," Lewrie said with a laugh. "See? It now appears I'm a champion to all animals."

The cup, a chalice really, was about eight inches high, with a wide, scrolled base, and ornate scrollwork round the lip, fitted with two handles. It was sterling silver, rather heavy, and bore an inscription—Capt. Sir Alan Lewrie, RN, Bt. Champion of All Animals.

"Perhaps if I drink from it, I'll be able to converse with the dogs, and the cat, what?" Lewrie japed as he trotted upstairs. "Hallo, Jessica my darling. I'm back!"

"So, how did your supper go?" Jessica asked, too comfortable and warm to rise from her armchair by the fireplace, with her feet up on a hassock, and a throw on her from the waist to her shod feet. She did lower the book she was reading, and seemed amused.

"Oh, what a horrendous bore," Lewrie said, leaning down to give her a kiss. "But, I got this. They *told* me it was sterling silver."

Jessica took it to look over, and read the inscriptions.

"The *National* Society To Eliminate Cruelty In All Forms Against Animals, well well, that's a mouthful," she commented with one brow up in wry wonder. "Tell me all about it."

"Well, there was about half an hour before we sat down to eat," Lewrie said, going to the fireplace to spread the lapels of his coat and warm his chilled hands. "All sorts of bowing and curtsying, and handshakes. Milord this, milady that. They have at least two Barons, a Viscount, and a Marquis as members, and their ladies along. All the names went right past my head, anyway, for I never heard the like. They're not so much about preventin' cruelty as they are doin' away with any sports that involve beasts. Oh, hallo, Bisquit, can you guess where I've been? Can you smell supper on me?"

He felt a tug on his trouser leg, looked down, wiggled fingers, and Buffer scrambled nimbly up to his chest, far enough to touch noses, and give Lewrie's a licking.

"What sort of sports?" Jessica asked, still studying the cup.

"They're not high on horse racin', for one," Lewrie told her, "they think steeplechasin' is too dangerous for man or beast, besides what it does to poor people's crops, fox huntin' is pretty much just as bad, and of course, dog fightin', bear baitin', cock fightin,' and all things like that should be banned.

"Anyway," he went on, turning to present his chill backside to the fire and stroke the cat, "it was all rather pleasant, at first. We sat down to a tasty supper, beef barley soup, salad greens, and only God knows where they got 'em this time o' year. Cod for fish, game hens for fowl . . . rather ironic if you think about it . . . then roast beef, and lots of vegetable removes, and again, who knows where they found 'em. Maybe have their own hot houses. There was even asparagus and Brussels sprouts!"

"*Fresh?*" Jessica exclaimed. "My word, I wish I *had* gone with you!"

"Aye, fresh, or fresh-ish," Lewrie assured her. "And Nerot's Hotel has a decent wine cellar, to boot. As the guest of honour, they treated me quite well, and everyone wanted t'chat me up.

"'Til we got to the business part of the meetin'," he went on, tossing off a quick scowl. "They simply *had* to read the minutes of the last meeting, which went on and on and on, then open the floor to present matters, and *everyone* wanted t'stick their oar in about what they discussed last month, how much they'd spent on printin' tracts and was it too much, would they hire an artist to draw a carter beatin' on his burro, or his pony. Someone rises to propose this, is there anyone who'd second it, and they're wranglin' like so many bears that've read *Robert's Rules of Order*. I began t'nod off 'til they got round to me and the cup, chalice, or whatever it is.

"I wasn't told I had to speechify, love," Lewrie said, sighing as he sat down in the opposite armchair, his backside warm at last.

"Were you sobre enough by then?" Jessica teased.

"Barely," Lewrie said with a scoffing laugh. "I told you the wine cellars at Nerot's are good. I told them I was that mad that anyone'd dare steal our dear dogs . . . yes Bisquit, I'm talkin' about you," he cooed as Bisquit laid his front paws on his leg, earning him some pets and head rubs. ". . . and physically harm you or Lucy, and that I'm not the kind t'wring my hands and trust to the police, or a ransom, to get them back. I told 'em how rewardin' it was t'clean up the other dogs, place advertisements so people could come and reclaim *their* dogs, and I was humbled and honoured t'be honoured for what I'd do to the Frogs if *they* were in the business of stealin' dogs, and thankee kindly," he concluded. "Then I got out o' there as quickly and courteously as I could, and hope never t'hear from that giddy lot the rest of my days."

"Oh, you poor dear," Jessica sniggered, a hand over her mouth as she laughed. "You bear a hero's burden *so* well!"

"And there's the proof of it," Lewrie japed, pointing at the cup in Jessica's lap.

Bisquit shifted closer, got his front end and his head onto Lewrie's lap for more "wubbies," which irked the cat, who jumped down and went to Jessica's chair, scrambled up the throw over her and padded up to stick his head into the bowl of the chalice, looking for a treat.

"Your master is champion of all animals in the world, Buffer," Jessica cooed to it as she rubbed his head and chest, "did you know it, little one?"

Buffer dropped to his belly and crawled up to lie on her chest, purring so loud that Lewrie could hear it from his chair.

"Are you sure he was a stray, Alan?" Jessica had to ask. "He's so very good at using his sand box, he hardly ever climbs the drapes, and he only sharpens his claws on that tree limb you set up in my parlour. I suspect he was someone's housepet, let out for the morning near the thieves' lair, and just wandered in hoping to catch himself a mouse amid all the barrels in that abandoned building."

"Hmm," Lewrie mused aloud, eyeing Buffer more closely. "He *was* remarkably clean for a stray, at that. Used to people, and came right up to us, and not just for some leftover scraps. He even gets along with the dogs, like he's used t'bein' round 'em. Hmm."

"Buffer," Jessica whispered to the cat, "your master just may be a cat buffer. Poor baby, you've been *kidnapped* and held against your will!"

Whatever Buffer thought of that made no difference; he just went a little higher up her chest and began to lick her nose, doing a very thorough job of it, and purring even louder.

It was days later when his father, Sir Hugo, coached round and asked if Lewrie would join him for a supper at the Madeira Club. It had been a long time since Lewrie had haunted the place on a temporary basis when up to London to call upon Admiralty. He'd taken his house in Dover St., then bought it when Jessica accepted his proposal, and with a wife and a home of his own he hadn't even thought of going there since.

"It's more of a quarterly meeting on club business," Sir Hugo told him as a porter took their hats, overcoats, gloves, and walking sticks.

"Oh, *now* you tell me?" Lewrie said with an exaggerated groan of protest, "What am I here for, then, to nudge you awake when you nod off? They get to numbers and debts, and my *own* eyes'll glaze over!"

"Sir Malcolm will be here," Sir Hugo said. "He'll be glad to see you, as I'm certain you are glad to see him. It's been a while. Ah! Mister Hoyle!" his father cried as he shook hands with the long-time club manager. "I must say the results of the expansion are delightful, and the re-doing of the decor masterful, as grand as any gentlemen's club in London."

"Thank you for saying so, Sir Hugo," Hoyle replied, "she is now properly grand, isn't she? And Sir Alan! Welcome back. It has been far too long since you've dined with us. Come along, sirs, and join us in the Common Room."

Part of the far wall had been knocked down to create a double door passage into the new annex, made into a library, expanding the older Common Room to twice its previous size. There were new carpets, brighter paint, more chandeliers overhead, and even more settees and leather chairs. They'd even added a second fireplace, and warm air wafted into the room, making even faraway seating comfortable.

"Sir Malcolm" Lewrie said, extending a hand to Sir Malcolm Shockley, one of the original group of founders. He had been of only middling wealth before coal was found on his estate, and now he was a most prosperous looking older fellow. Sir Malcolm, though, had the misfortune to have been besotted with the much younger Lucy Beauman, a girl Lewrie had lusted after in the West Indies in his teens. He and Lucy had married, and Sir Malcolm had worn a "cuckold's horns" ever since, whether he knew it or not; Lewrie suspected that he did not, for Sir Malcolm was just *too* decent a gentleman.

"Aha, Lewrie!" Shockley boomed, "Or should I say Sir Alan now. As fit as a fiddle, and the very image of the man I last saw in the Adriatic. Grand times in Venice, before you dealt with the Serbian pirates. You don't age at *all*, do you, sir, haw haw! I read of your marriage, though I was sorry I could not attend, but both Lucy and I pray that you and your lady wife are happy and content."

"Well, thank you, Sir Malcolm, aye, Jessica and I wished that you could have attended, but we are both very happy, and well settled."

"Dame Lewrie's an artist, sir," Sir Hugo boasted, "She does the most remarkably lifelike portraits, illustrations for novels, and amusing paintings suitable for children."

When did he *get proud of her?* Lewrie wondered.

"You and Lucy must dine with me some evening," Sir Hugo went on, "and see some of her work. I'd not force *my* aged likeness on a club wall, but you might consider being painted to hang in here as one of the founders."

"Why, I and my wife would be delighted, Sir Hugo," Shockley said with some joy, "if you invite Sir Alan and his talented lady. We must meet this prodigy."

"Well, if it ain't Sir Alan Lewrie," older Mr. Giles, who was big in leather goods, cackled as he came up to greet them. Behind him were Mr. Showalter, in town for deliberations in the Commons, Mr. Pilkinton, who was in corn, and a gloomy sort usually sure the markets would crash the next morning, even ex-Major Baird, along with an host of members, most new ones unknown to Lewrie or his father.

Lewrie left his father's side to greet the older members whom he knew, and allow himself to be introduced to the new ones.

"Sir Alan's a fighter, gentlemen," Baird boasted to the circle of younger members, "a proper hero of our Navy, and the victor of more sea battles than most of us have had hot suppers, hah hah! He's been particularly dashing when he's ashore, too. Can't keep an active man idle, what? I'm certain that most of you read about it in the papers?"

Whether they had or not, Baird, with occasional assisting comments from Mr. Showalter, told the story of the kidnapping of the family dogs, the injury to Lewrie's wife, the ferreting out and the raid on the dog buffers' lair, their arrest and trial, and the reclaiming of all the other pets.

"Now now, gentlemen," Lewrie said, trying to sound modest, "it was nothing."

"But sir, why then have you been crowned the champion of animals?" a younger fellow blurted out.

"What?" Lewrie asked. "Where did you hear about that?"

"You have not seen these tracts, Sir Alan?" the young man said, pulling them from a breast pocket of his coat.

"Good God, how . . . lurid!" Lewrie gawped. One tract, done by a dab-hand caricaturist, depicted children weeping, praying, lifting hands to Heaven over the corpses of their dead dogs and cats, with a large WILL YOU HELP END THIS?, the text decrying a long list of cruelties inflicted on domestic animals, urging people to donate and join the Society.

Another showed a carter, with an evil grimace on his face, whipping a starving horse that was already down on the cobblestones, sure to die in its traces, from abuse and lack of food.

The third was the worst.

END SUCH DEPRAVITY TOWARDS ANIMALS! it blared, JOIN US! FOLLOW OUR LATEST HERO! That caricaturist must have been at that supper at Nerot's Hotel, for he'd done a fair depiction of Lewrie, a large and flaming sword in one hand worthy of an avenging angel, and the other hand thrust upwards holding that damned chalice. Lewrie's hair was waving in the wind, and at his knees, he was dubbed CHAMPION OF ANIMALS!

"Oh, mine arse on a bloody *band-box*!" Lewrie spluttered as the circle round him began to laugh.

The major patrons of the Society were listed, with Lewrie's name at the bottom of the list, right above a long screed about the goals. They would ban horse racing, fox hunting, steeplechasing, cock fights, dog fights, bear baiting, greased pig races, duck pulling, the mis-use of whips, spurs, quirts, and horse whips on draught animals and riding horses, the drowning of un-wanted puppies and kittens, the fiendish torture of strays in the streets, starving and over-working, and lashing working beasts by ignorant un-Christian common folk.

"No no no, oh no!" Lewrie gawped, getting louder by each word. "I *never* agreed with those lunaticks! I never joined their damn-fool Society, I never gave 'em tuppence! Gentlemen, this is all a lie, I tell you! I'm not one of them, and never *will* be! They dined me out for gettin' those dogs back, I said thankee and left! They had no right to think I buy their . . . shite! God damn it, and God damn *them*."

But, each protestation only seemed to goad the guffaws louder.

"I'll bloody *sue*!" Lewrie roared.

"What's all this?" Sir Hugo asked, drawn by the laughing.

"This!" Lewrie barked, shoving the tracts at him. "Vouch for me, father. I've ridden to hounds, gentlemen, I've hared cross-country at steeplechasin' when I was younger, and foolish, I've been to cock fights . . . lost money on the birds I picked. It's what two cocks *do* when they meet! Bear baitin'? Not a lot o' that happenin' lately, 'cause where the Devil do you find a bear in England? They import 'em from Sweden, Russia, or Spain! I went to *one*, and that was for the lack of a *bear*! I swear to you, I am maligned!"

"Haw haw haw!" from his own father. "The champion of animals? Hee hee hee!"

Just like *you, you* always *let me down!* Lewrie fumed in his head.

"All this is a lot of codswallop, sirs," Sir Hugo exclaimed once he got over his laughter. "My son puts his money on the wrong horse, or the wrong cock, but he adores all the grand outdoor pursuits of an English gentleman . . . racing, fox hunting, village games and county fairs, cock fights. We would breed fighting cocks if we were down in Surrey more often. I don't know if suing this pack of fools would avail, but . . . hmm. That supper you unfortunately attended. How many were there, besides the nitwits on this list?"

"Oh, fourty, fifty at best?" Lewrie told him.

"Sirs, where did you find these tracts?" Sir Hugo asked the men gathered round. "Did they have a lot of them? Were passersby taking them?"

"Ehm, I saw an elderly couple, sir," the young fellow who had shown them first said, "they had a small stack, no more than fifty or so, and hardly anyone was taking them, and those who did balled them up and tossed them away. Why, some who read them went back to curse them for a pack of fools."

"Aha!" Sir Hugo barked. "This list of patrons . . . I happen to know that this Marquis is merely scraping by on pride, this Viscount actually sold half his acres to keep himself from debtors' prison, ruining what his eldest son would inherit, and these Barons have been made so as reward for their long careers at Cambridge. Haw! Not an hundred pounds 'twixt all of them, so suing them's right out. Better you write a letter to *The Times* to clear your escutcheon, my lad."

"It *is* amusing, though," Mr. Giles wheezed, still wiping tears from his eyes. "Isn't it?"

"For a moment," Sir Malcolm told them. "And the moment's passed."

"I need a stiff drink," Lewrie declared.

"My dear sir, let me stand you one!" Mr. Baird declared. "Here, waiter! A double measure of brandy for Sir Alan."

"My thanks, Mister Baird," Lewrie said.

"Ehm, now that we have a quorum present, gentlemen, let's take seats and open the quarterly business meeting," Sir Malcolm directed.

"You want these?" Sir Hugo muttered, shoulder-to-shoulder with his son, offering the scurrilous tracts.

"Only do I need to run to the 'jakes' after supper," Lewrie told him, grimacing in disgust. "Mine arse of a band-box, what have I gotten myself into *this* time?"

"A very minor embarrassment, gone and forgotten by the world by tomorrow morning," Sir Hugo told him, wadding them up and ready to toss them into the nearest fireplace. "But I must say, you have the knack for looking like a fool. You always have."

"Oh, thank you so *very* bloody much . . . pater," Lewrie growled as his brandy came. He took a goodly swig, winced and bared his teeth, then sulked his way to a leather armchair, sure to be bored to tears with the reading of the minutes, and the listing of assets and debits.

Gettin' talked into comin' along is another of my mistakes, he told himself as he squirmed to get comfortable; *I hope he's right, though, that it blows over.*

But then, he was reminded that his father had never been that helpful with parental advice, on much of anything!

When he told Jessica about it, she was appalled, but her sympathy vanished as soon as *she* found it amusing, so much so that she buried her face in a settee toss-pillow and cackled so loudly that she wheezed for breath. At breakfast the next morning, sedately enjoying scrambled eggs and sausages, the word "champion" came to mind and her voice, and this time it was a napkin she used to stifle herself.

Later, when he announced that he would stroll up New Bond St. to look for some new books to read, she saw him off in the entry hall.

"Do see if there is something I might enjoy," she bade him. "And do not bring home any stray dogs or cats, seeing as how you are their . . . hee hee hee!" she laughed, spun round and dashed upstairs.

"Sir?" Pettus asked, handing him his gloves and walking stick.

"Never mind, Pettus," Lewrie said, groaning. "It's an old joke."

It was a nippy morning with a bit of wind, and there was light snow that had fallen in the night, a dusting that swirled about on the cobblestones and the sidewalks. Even so, despite the chill and the wind, dozens of men and boys had their noses pressed to the bookstore bow window to look at the latest caricatures and social cartoons.

Lewrie ignored them and entered the shop, pausing to pull off his gloves before going to the shelves where new fiction was kept.

"Oho, now that is funny!" a customer brayed.

Lewrie looked over and froze in dread. "No!" he muttered.

Rowlandson, Gillray, Isaac Cruickshank, all the leading artists had something about the National Society To Eliminate Cruelty In All Forms Against Animals! He *wanted* to see how badly he was depicted, but feared that all of London would be laughing about him by noon! Lewrie finally got his feet to move and went to peer at them.

"Oh!" he said. "Cruickshank's not so bad,"

They were having a parade, with two feeble old men in wigs leading, carrying their banner. Behind, a fat fellow carried sheep under both arms, an over-dressed woman with a gigantic wig hung with birds had her legs round a horse's neck, trying to plant her lips on the beast as she hung upside down, while two younger fellows presented fighting cocks to each other. Someone was being savaged by at least fifty cats, an angel with a trumpet soared overhead, carrying a basket of bewildered dogs, and impish boys dashed about chasing squirrels.

Our newest saviours was the headline.

Gillray's caricature was much the same, making buffoons of the society. It was only Rowlandson who drew a fellow in a Navy uniform, on the run from an host of animals and a crowd of Society members drawn as rabble rousers with signs on sticks, shouting "But You Are Our Champion!" and the Navy officer's ribbon of speech crying "Get away from me! I love animals, but I don't love you!"

"I wonder who the Navy officer is?" a customer close by asked.

"A most reluctant fellow, it appears," Lewrie answered with a sigh of relief.

How did Rowlandson know about me? Lewrie had to wonder; *And if he did, how'd he know I don't hold with them? Someone at the club?*

"What sort of people are in this horrible society?" the customer went on. "This is the most un-English prattle I've ever heard!"

"Bugger 'em," Lewrie commented. "I think I'll take one of each. No more fox hunting? No more cock fights? They're *lunaticks!*"

"Amen to that, sir, amen to that," the customer heartily agreed.

I'll still write that letter to The Times, Lewrie told himself; *Just t'make it clear that I have nothing t'do with 'em!*

"You wish the newest, sir?" a store clerk asked.

"Aye, one each for myself, and one each for my father," Lewrie told him. "The hand-coloured versions."

CHAPTER TWENTY-NINE

*R*eally?" the Reverend Chenery beamed, making sounds of amusement in a genteel way, then dabbed his lips with his napkin. "Who could have expected such a society could hold such views. The Lord in the Garden of Eden ordered us to be stewards to the whole Earth, with mastery over the beasts of the fields, the birds in the air, and the fish in the sea. But, I doubt if he wished us to honour them more than our fellow men! Why, one might as well allow rats, mice, roaches, and spiders free rein. No no. I'm sure those people read the Old Testament all wrong.

"But, as the Bard tells us, 'all's well that end's well,'" Reverend Chenery went on, as was his wont. "And you were most fortunate, Sir Alan, to not be tarred with the same brush. Bless me, but *someone* was privy to your identity, yet forebore to name you publicly. It is a mystery, indeed."

"Aye, I was fortunate, sir," Lewrie told him, "and aye, it is a mystery, and most-like will remain so. I *suspect* it might have been a member of the Madeira Club who knew Mister Rowlandson somehow, and asked him to spare me. Someone who attended the supper at Nerot's? Either way, their tracts were bad enough."

"Ah, the club, Alan," Sir Hugo, who had also been invited over to supper, said. "Perhaps we should take Reverend Chenery along as a guest some night."

"The Madeira Club, Sir Hugo?" Chenery asked, then turned his head as a good-sized currant pudding was brought to the table, and lit.

"One I, and several other gentlemen, founded years ago, sir," Sir Hugo boasted, "one to fill the social needs for gentlemen of trade, and middling status who could not aspire to be selected as members in the older, set-tled, or aristocratic clubs. At the corner of Duke and Wigmore Streets. Lawyers, Members of the Commons, men in corn, coal, leather, wool, and such? Their cooks, and the victuals, are superb. Never had a mediocre meal there, have we, son?"

"Superb indeed, father," Lewrie had to agree.

"And their wine cellars rival any club, or new-fangled restaurant, in London," Sir Hugo added. "But for the Rainwater Madeira, which sim-ply can't be found these days, sorry to say."

"Frankly, I've never had a single sip of it," Lewrie admitted.

"It sounds delightful, Sir Alan," Rev. Chenery said, "and I am now most curious to partake of it, and would be immensely grateful to you both for the kind invitation!"

"Capital!" Sir Hugo cried, slapping the table top. "We must set a day."

"Ehm . . . might I extend an invitation in return, Sir Hugo, Sir Alan?" Chenery said, getting an excited look on his phyz. "You know of my long interest in antiquities, and my brother Robert's post as the Chair of Antiq-uities at Oxford. Well, he and I, and several other prominent scholars, are proposing an expedition, or a series of expeditions, to America to track down some intriguing mysteries of our own."

Oh no, here we go again! Lewrie thought, though keeping his face pleasant.

"For instance, on one of the earliest maps of the coastlines on Massa-chusetts, done by Amerigo Vespucci," the Reverend enthused, "an eight-legged stone structure similar to a grist mill is depicted as a landmark for mariners, long before any White settlements, pre-dating the Puritans. How did it come to be there? Vikings? Templars fleeing their persecution? We wish to go see it. Study it, delve its secret."

"Ah, hmm," Sir Hugo pretended interest. "Intriguing indeed."

The Reverend began listing all the anomalies, the Roman coins pur-portedly washing up on a beach near Beverly, Massachusetts, a *stele* stone up the coast with Phoenician inscriptions, thousands of copper pit mines in the Ohio and Michigan Territories that supposedly produced far more ore than the Indians could have ever used, even for money or their own crude metallurgy.

"We engaged a clever and plucky fellow earlier this year to make the arrangements, list what we would need to take with us, and scout the areas we wish to explore, Sir Hugo," Reverend Chenery told them. "A Major Robert Beresford, late of the Thirty Third . . ."

"Oh, I do believe Alan mentioned his name to me, long ago," Sir Hugo perked up. Especially perked up as a portion of pudding was set before him by Dasher. "Mean t'say, he's gone and reconnoitered for you already?"

"Yes, Sir Hugo," Chenery happily said. "And a most thorough job he did of it, too! We are to have a meeting of our donors and participants here in London next week, with many coming down from Oxford for the planning of our first expedition in the Spring. I do believe that both of you, whether you would wish to contribute or not, would find it enlightening and eye-opening. Imagine, if we could prove that the Americas were discovered, even settled for a time, by Europeans, and not 'found' by Columbus! The world would stand on its ear!"

"Uncle Robert is coming down from Oxford?" Jessica asked, happy to see her far-off kin again. "Alan, you should meet him. He's a most interesting man, and so well educated and knowledgeable. When I was a girl, I stood in awe of his intellect, and what he knew!"

"Well, *I'd* go to your meeting," Lewrie had to say, under the eye of his wife. "Might be intriguing, at that. Father?"

"Just so long as no one expects me to hack my way through woods and hike ten miles a day," Sir Hugo allowed, harumphing. "I've *done* my expeditions in India with the *jangli admi*, tigers, cobras, and such. It *does* sound . . . enlightening, sir. Yes, I'll listen to your man."

"Mmm, mmm, this pudding is *swimming* with red currants," Reverend Chenery enthused between bites, "and veins and swirls of red currant jam in it as well. Sir Alan, your man, Yeovill, is a treasure, a true, national treasure."

"He's full of surprises," Lewrie heartily agreed, "but never a disappointment. Oh, this *is* good!"

Conversation fell off, leaving only the sounds of forks on the plates, and an occasional "yummy" sound. That was when all became aware of an irregular plop-plop-plop coming from the front of the house.

Lewrie looked out the dining room door to the hall, to see their butler, Pettus, making his way to the entry hall, and he rose to join him.

"Hail, Pettus?" Lewrie speculated. "It wasn't storming. It felt more like it may snow, but . . ."

"Doesn't sound like hail, no sir," Pettus said, un-locking the front door and swinging it open. "Oh, my word!" he exclaimed.

Lewrie stepped out to join him, his shoes crackling on the stone stoop, and on an host of shattered egg shells. He looked up and some yolk that had been oozing down from the Doric arch over the door fell on his hair and the side of his head.

"Don't see anyone in the street, sir," Pettus said, looking up and down Dover St. There wasn't enough fine snow to reveal footprints. They both went out into the street to survey the damage; luckily, the eggs had not been hard enough to break window panes.

"Who do you think did it, sir?" Pettus asked, bewildered.

"Some people who didn't read my letter in *The Times*, or can't read at all," Lewrie gravelled, "or people from that damned Society, who think me a traitor to their cause. God-*dammit*! It'll be cold as charity tomorrow, and our house staff'll have to clean all this up, sweep the walk . . ." He would have snarled more, but he stepped on a smear of yolk and almost slipped.

He led Pettus back inside, taking off the offending shoe and went to join the others in the dining room. "We have another mystery on our hands, it seems," he announced. "It appears we spoke too soon of people not knowing my identity. The house has just been very thoroughly *egged*! It ain't over, not by a long chalk. There's *someone*, one side or the other, who thinks me the Devil, with hooves, horns, and barbed tail."

"Well, I thought that letter to *The Times* would only add fuel to the fire," Sir Hugo said with a sniff, while licking crumbs from his fork.

"You never!" Lewrie accused. "I had t'clear myself!"

"Have it your own way," Sir Hugo breezily replied. "I think I'll have a bit more of this grand pudding, if nobody minds."

What a supportive father you are, you old fart! Lewrie thought.

"Uncle" Robert Chenery, the Professor of Antiquities at Oxford, made it down to London in a hired coach, and caused a great change in the daily routine. First of all, to save money on lodgings, he moved into St. Anselm's manse with his brother, Rev. Chenery, which turned the usually meek minister into a cringing, fawning addle-pate, eager to accommodate his elder brother's every whim. Prof. Chenery brought along two of his colleagues, a fussy fellow with a shock of unruly hair named Fogge, and a portly trencherman who could eat for three and still feel hungry, one Professor Dolittle. They took over Charles Chenery's vacant bedchamber and a guest room, and pretty-much made the manse their own, and they had not fetched along their manservants to help round the house, either.

Jessica was delighted to see her Uncle Robert, all but gawping at his side, kneeling by his chair, to hear his witticisms and his learned comments. Lewrie had to feed the lot of them at least three times over their extended stay, and a dry and dull time it was, to his lights.

In point of fact, Professor Chenery turned out to be a pluperfect ass, with the punch lines of his witty comments delivered in Latin or Greek, followed by a hearty *haw haw haw* brayed from himself over how clever he'd been, and simpered at or hurrayed by Fogge or Dolittle as they toadied up. At the various public schools that Lewrie had been sent to in hopes that *some* knowledge would stick to him, he had done passably well at Latin, but without practice necessary to the career of a rakehell, or a Navy officer, Latin was, indeed, a dead and ancient language to him. As for Greek, well . . . he didn't even know how to spell it, much less decypher Prof. Chenery's droplets of wisdom or wit.

Just as well I didn't go to Oxford, he told himself; *if all the Dons are tyrants and bullies like him. I even feel sorry for Reverend Chenery, who's turned into a shrinking violet. And when do they* leave, *please Jesus?*

At last, the day or the conference, or whatever it was, about the pending expedition, was to be held. Jessica's father had offered his church for the meeting, but his elder brother had rebuffed that; there *had* to be a dinner, and wine and spirits. A banquetting hall had to be engaged.

"A promise is a promise," Sir Hugo grumbled as they alit from his coach, in front of the banquetting hall where they had held the wedding break-fast for Pettus and Lucy. "Damme, d'ye think the owner will recognise us and boot us out?"

"Faint hopes, that," Lewrie said with a shake of his head. "In *mufti*, he might not notice we're here."

"Wish I wasn't," his father carped. "One supper with that lot and I'm ready to beg off and go grouse hunting in Scotland. My word, what a pack of pompous buggers! Aha, there you are, Professor!" Sir Hugo more loudly cried in greeting to Prof. Chenery. "Today's the day, what?"

"*Carpe diem,* Sir Hugo," Chenery boomed. "A day to be seized! And Sir Alan, good day to you as well, sir! Be sure to get good seats up front, for the discussions will be thrilling and informative."

Once free of hats, gloves, overcoats, and walking sticks, Lewrie and his father got glasses of claret and circled the room being introduced to the other attendees. One of whom was a surprise; Sir Malcolm Shockley!

"I say, sir," Sir Hugo said in greeting, "I had no idea you were interested in this. Donated, have you?"

"I must own to curiosity, old friend," Sir Malcolm said, "all this speculation about Phoenicians, Romans, Vikings, and Templars fair makes my imagination soar. Though, I do confess it would please me greatly to find that America was really discovered by Englishmen."

"Englishmen, Sir Malcolm?" Lewrie asked.

"The Templars, Sir Alan," Shockley said with a grin, "they had a sizeable trading fleet, and warships to protect them. In England and in Scotland, there were Knight Commanderies, Templar churches that still stand. Once the King of France and the Catholic Church rounded them up to confiscate their wealth, slew them as heretics, and freed the King of his heavy debts to them by the by, the survivors, and the Templars in Britain, had to go *somewhere* safe cross the seas where no-one knew to follow. My money's on England. Or some Scots, if it has to be. Shall we take a table together?"

There were many square tables set out for four, with one long table at the head of the hall where Prof. Chenery, Fogge, Dolittle, and a few other of the more learned sat, with one military-looking fellow in his late thirties or early fourties, whom Lewrie took for that Major Beresford that Rev. Chenery had mentioned.

Out came bottles or carafes of wine from the kitchens, followed by soup and bread rolls, then a fish course, a fowl course, then the roast beef, with vegetable removes, and merry, anticipatory conversation

Finally, after pudding, port, and coffee, Prof. Chenery heaved his bulk to his feet and opened the meeting formally, requesting his brother to offer a prayer for their enlightenment and success, and he then began a long, dry lecture.

He covered all the possibilities, from Phoenicians to Carthaginians, early Greeks who might have sailed beyond Italy and Sicily and out the Pillars of Hercules; teen Emperor Valentinus the Second, who would be murdered by his mother and a Goth general, and might have despatched his navies in search of a place of safety, citing possible evidence for each.

"Would it be impolite to pull out my watch to see how much time this windbag is wasting?" Sir Hugo whispered. "He ain't even up to the Vikings yet?"

Lewrie looked round the hall, eyes half-lidded, to note the few who had almost succumbed to the heavy dinner, and the attendees who sat rapt, nodding sagely. Rev. Chenery, at a table nearer the long table, seemed ready to squirm with eagerness.

At *very* long last, Prof. Chenery introduced Major Beresford who had been to America recently to scout the first goals of the expedition set for Spring, to warm applause.

"Gentlemen," Major Robert Beresford began, standing four-square in a military pose, and speaking in a voice that carried to the far corners of the hall, "I have lived a life of adventure and exploration so far, in travels with my regiment, and to the far corners of our world. India, Egypt, the Holy Land, and the forests and lakes of British North America, and many wonders have I and my travelling companions seen. On my most recent trip to the United States, mostly in Massachusetts and New England, I have found hints and clues, enigmatic so far, of what your society wishes to discover, and I am happy to report to you that the first expedition, first of many, could prove fruitful."

Loud cheers and huzzahs greeted those statements.

"Not only have I seen the grist-mill structure, I have asked the locals about its origins," Beresford went on, "and they have no clue about its age, or who built it, but some learned fellows who attended their local college, Harvard, have taken note that what look to be arrow slits high up above where a wood floor once stood, might be an arrangement to determine the timing of the solstices, and might be a religious artifact for some so far unknown tribe or community, but it is definitely *not* the sort of thing erected by the native Indians."

More cheers arose.

He had visited the sandy beaches by Beverly, Massachusetts, but saw no Roman coins, and most locals thought it a myth. He had ridden North into Connecticut and beyond and had found a massive barrow made of local rock, much like an ancient Irish barrow that also showed the signs of being able to determine the solstices that they would surely desire to explore.

He laid out all that would be necessary for the members of the expedition; pavillions, ground cloths, cooking ware, suitable clothes, blankets, pack mules and riding horses, which could be obtained locally, and laborers, cooks, hunters, and "mule skinners" to tend to the beasts. Survey equipment, map makers, an artist to sketch their finds,

"Would we need weapons, or hired guards?" someone asked from the audience.

"This year, sir," Beresford answered with a wee smile, "we will be in Boston, Beverly, Chatham, and coastal towns North of there, so an armed British party might go over badly. Boston *was* the birthplace of it all."

"Will we run the risk of meeting polar bears?" another asked.

Lewrie, Sir Hugo, and Sir Malcolm looked at each other, laid all aback, ready to laugh out loud.

"Ah, polar bears says it all, sir," Beresford carefully replied. "They are only found above British North America, in the Hudson's Bay Territories, and in the polar Arctic, of course."

"Should we bring along bed-cots and pallets?" someone asked.

"For the most part, sir, in Boston and its environs, there are sufficient inns and taverns who let rooms," Beresford told him. "It's only if we trek off to look for that stone barrow that we will sleep in pavillions, and bed-cots and mattresses will require too many waggons. I and my fellow adventurers have found that a pile of springy pine boughs, with a ground cloth, one blanket under one, and another over one, makes a very comfortable bed, sir."

"Are there any protections to be taken against rattlesnakes in such conditions, Major?" a callow younger fellow asked.

"Rattlesnakes, my God!" Prof. Chenery scoffed.

"I've seen them, pickled in alcohol," the callow young man shot back. "Are they rife? I'm told they crawl into bedding seeking human warmth. Cold blooded, you know. Are they in those woods, sir?"

"They usually den up in groups 'til Spring, sir," Beresford patiently tried to explain, "and, yes, they are in the woods throughout the region, but not in Boston or the coastal towns. One must be cautious in the *woods*, look where one steps, look before stepping over any fallen log, and carry a long staff to pound the ground to drive them to a quick retreat. Snakes fear people. And if they are in one's path, they will coil up to defend themselves and rattle their tales, so one can be warned to stop, look round, and back away."

"But they *do* crawl into bedding?" the fellow persisted.

"I saw a display," another man chimed in from the far side of the hall, "their scales blended with leaves, twigs, and dirt so well that it was nigh invisible!"

"*Bears* come out of their dens in the Spring, too, don't they?" the polar bear fellow spoke up. "What sort of bears? Will they attack us?"

Major Beresford lowered his head for a second and pinched the bridge of his nose before speaking up.

"There *are* brown bears and black bears, gentlemen, and they *do* emerge from their dens in Spring," he told them all, "mostly in search of nuts, berries, some fish in the streams, to replace the weight they lost during their hibernation. That is what the hunters are for, sirs, do we trek into the backwoods. Believe me, attacks by hungry bears are rarities, does one go well armed, and pay attention to one's surroundings."

"Should we take along salt meats?" a portly man asked.

"God, I hope not!" Lewrie sniggered.

"I have found that the back country in New England is well-populated, sir, and piglets, chickens, turkeys, and eggs are available for sale if one asks nicely. The hunters we hire are mostly crack shots with rifled muskets, and the woods are full of squirrel, rabbit, wild pigeons, raccoons and opossums, all of which are tasty camp meats, and deer abound. Venison may well be a staple of our diet."

"Does bear taste good?" someone asked, sounding tongue-in-cheek rather than ignorantly curious. "Like chicken, or beef?"

Sir Hugo by then was chuckling aloud, pressing a napkin to his lips so he wouldn't guffaw.

"*Rattlesnake* tastes like chicken, sir," Major Beresford hissed, finding that holding his disgust was getting harder and harder. "Bear is even gamier than venison. Some swear that basting in beer or ale reduces the gameyness. Beef, unfortunately, will be rarely available, except in inns and taverns."

"Milk or cream?" another man wondered aloud.

"From the local farmers, sir, though it will not keep," Major Beresford said. "Now, as to the tools we will need for any excavation or prying rocks aside, I recommend that we take all we need with us, since metal tools are mostly imported to our former Colonies, and the smiths in America mostly *repair* things."

"Ehm, what sort of clothing do you find suitable?" one gentleman sensibly asked. "Are moccasins and buckskins better in the woods?" he added, inanely.

Lewrie's table all grinned widely as they saw Major Beresford visibly wince.

"Only if one wishes to gather souvenirs of our journey sir," Beresford said, casting his gaze all about as if looking for escape. "Stout top-boots, wool *and* sailcloth trousers, warm waist-coats that one may wear if the weather turns cold or rainy, a coat, an overcoat, and a painted or oiled cloth foul weather coat that one may obtain at any ship chandlery."

"Are you considering *going,* sir?" Sir Hugo asked Sir Malcolm.

"Oh, Gracious God, *no* Willoughby," Shockley said with a hearty laugh. "And, after the idiotic questions, and the looks on many faces, I doubt if many others would, either, hah hah. They'll donate to be one of the patrons, should results be found, and be dined out on their small fame, but to go and rough it among the crude Americans? Hah!"

"Most sensible, sir," Lewrie told him. "D'ye think we could slink off without notice? This is gettin' dry, again."

"What, and miss some more ignorant questions?" Sir Hugo scoffed. "This is as good as a comedic play. Besides, I wish to speak with the gallant Major Beresford, if only to offer my commiserations."

So they sat through it to the end, and another long parting speech from Professor Chenery, before being allowed to dismiss, come sign up to volunteer, or make a sizeable donation.

Major Beresford was swamped by a crowd of hangers-on wishing to ask just one more question or two, so it took some time before their party, and Reverend Chenery, could approach him.

"Major, allow me to name to you Major-General Sir Hugo Willoughby, Captain Sir Alan Lewrie, Royal Navy, and Baronet, and Sir Malcolm Shockley," Chenery intoned.

"Gentlemen, happy to make your acquaintance," Beresford replied, though he looked to be a man more than ready to mop his brow and get out of the hall, soonest.

"Good Lord, I do not envy you, sir," Sir Hugo said, "your role here today, or your task of herding this pack of fools this Spring."

"Oh, I don't know, sir," Beresford said with an easy grin. "Back in the day, I've put together explorations up the Nile, to the ancient temples and relics of Egypt, to Jerusalem, with all sorts of in-experienced academics and enthusiasts. I'm used to amateurs."

"Polar bears, though, my God," Lewrie said, chuckling, "one might as well ask you about unicorns."

"As for that fellow," Beresford agreed, "I wasn't sure whether he feared that polar bears abound in Massachusetts, or he really wished to see one."

"And have you travelled far enough North to see one, sir?" Sir Malcolm Shockley asked.

"Only once, and no, I did not," Beresford told him, "but I did meet an old hand with the Hudson's Bay Company who told an amusing tale about polar bears. He was breaking in a newcome sent out from London, and he advised the young man to always carry several muskets with him should he have to dog sled into the ice fields. Then, if he met with a polar bear, he must take careful aim if it approached him, loaded with buck and ball, and at sixty yards, a decent range, shoot the bear in the chest.

"What if I miss, the newcome asked," Beresford went on, "and the old hunter told him to snatch a fresh musket off his sled, take aim, and about fourty yards, shoot the bear. What if I miss again, the fellow asks? Snatch up another musket, and at twenty yards, shoot him."

"What if I miss again, the newcome asks, and the old hunter says when the bear gets within swatting distance, you fling a handful of shit in the bear's eyes and run for your life," Beresford said, starting to laugh. "And where does the shit come from, the young man asked? And the old hunter sagely tells him, if the bear is close enough to rip your face off with his claws . . . believe me, it *will* be there, haw haw!"

They said their goodbyes on that amusing note and left the hall to find their waiting coach. Rev. Chenery, who had done the most to organise the meeting, had been overlooked by the attendees who gathered round his elder brother and the other noted professors, sidled up as if begging a ride back to his manse at St. Anselm's, and Lewrie and his father took pity on him and offered him a seat.

"He wishes another planning conference, and Robert will have to hire out the Crown and Cushion in Oxford," Chenery complained, "let *him* make the arrangements."

"Professor Chenery and his compatriots depart tomorrow, sir?" Sir Hugo asked.

"Only if God is indeed just, Sir Hugo," Chenery said with a sigh. "My brother is brilliant, possessed of a keen intellect . . . but he can wear out the kindness of the Good Samaritan. After he is gone, I will summon Madame Pellatan and my servants to the drawing room and urge all to sit in the dark and be very, very quiet!"

"I wish you at least one peaceful hour before they leave that hall, then, Reverend," Lewrie offered.

They dropped Chenery off, then coached to Dover St. to drop off Lewrie.

"Oh, my Christ!" Lewrie roared as the coach clattered to a stop in front of his house. "Mine arse on a bloody *band-box*! They've done it again!" he shouted as he alit on the sidewalk and gawped. People of his house staff were gathered in front, bundled up against the cold, mopping, swabbing, and sweeping up the mess, trying to reach high with one hand at the end of a mop or broom to get at the splatters on the second floor level.

"In broad daylight?" Lewrie fumed, "Who *are* these bastards? Did anyone see 'em at it?"

Dasher held a dust pan, now oozing with egg yolk and shattered shells, making a face of disgust. "Can't be animal lovers, sir. See? They threw eggs with *chicks* growin' in 'em."

He picked up a dead, unborn chick by a tiny leg.

"Wasn't that a delicacy at Canton?" Sir Hugo commented, leaning out the door window. "Or was it Macau, or the Philippines?"

"God damn whoever they are," Lewrie growled. "I'll set watch, I'll thrash 'em within an inch o' their miserable lives!"

"I'll leave you to it, me lad," Sir Hugo cheeerfully said as he thumped his walking stick on the roof of the coach to set his coach-man to lash up and drive on. "Good luck with all that. You *might* send a new letter to *The Times* to complain, hee hee!"

If Lewrie had had an unbroken egg, he would have hurled it at his father's smirking face!

CHAPTER THIRTY

*I*s it safe to leave your house for a few hours, Alan," Peter Rushton, Viscount Draywick, and an old school chum from Harrow, teased as Lewrie got into his coach a few days later. "Mean t'say, do your tormentors only strike when you're away? And is my coach safe if I'm seen with you?"

"They haven't been back since," Lewrie was happy, warily happy, to tell him. "We've spoken to all our neighbours, and they've promised to keep a lookout, as my house servants will. I spoke with the police, as well, and they said a constable would stroll up my street now and then. One hopes they'll be daunted."

"Champion of All Animals, was it?" Peter tittered. "I saw the caricatures. Bought the complete set."

"Lady Draywick amused?" Lewrie asked as the coach lurched into motion.

"My wife has not been amused by *anything* since the Act of Union," Peter said with a dry laugh, throwing back his head. "Possibly she has found nothing funny since William Pitt the Younger first became Prime Minister. *Everything* is a great dis-appointment to *her*. Thank God for Tess."

Long before, Lewrie had found Tess in a Panton St. brothel, a sweet, impoverished girl fresh come from Ireland. He'd rescued her from a daft

Russian nobleman who'd been so besotted that he'd tried to kidnap her, and kill anyone who'd had her favours. Sadly, when Lewrie couldn't make her his mistress, he'd introduced her to Peter, and they had been a mutually pleasing item ever since.

"And how is Tess?" Lewrie asked.

"Simply delightful, as always," Rushton said with a longing sigh. "I *think* the wife knows of her . . . but then she suspects every pretty girl or young woman we know, and half the housemaids. So, where is this new restaurant?"

"A few blocks from the Foreign Office," Lewrie told him. "James Peel, a fellow I know there, introduced me to it. You'll like it, I think."

"Then I'm sure that Clotworthy will, too," Rushton said. "We'll end up paying his share, you know. 'Why, I've come away without my coin purse, or my wallet!' he'll claim. Always does. Just like at Harrow when we ate off campus."

"And yet he's making such a pile of the 'blunt' these days," Lewrie agreed, nodding. "He's branched out into fine art, ye know."

"Clotworthy? What does *he* know about art?" Peter Rushton exclaimed. "At school, the best he could draw was stick figures!"

"You'll see," Lewrie promised.

They alit in front of Chute's emporium, which, by the numbers of shoppers stopping to gawk in the bow-windows, or stroll inside, was indeed doing a thriving business. They made their own way in, skirting round couples admiring the furniture, the statuary, both the real and the "reproduced," or outright fakes.

"My word, it is a big place, ain't it?" Peter Rushton marvelled at the expanse, and how much there was by way of merchandise.

"Ah, there he is," Lewrie said, as Clotworthy Chute came from a back room. "We'd best pat him down t'see if he has money on him."

"Well, hallo, Peter, Alan," Chute cried, spreading his arms in welcome. "Welcome to my humble establishment. Care to look round for a bit? You never know what you may find that strikes your fancy."

"Alan tells me you've began selling fine art," Peter said.

"Indeed I have, but only in a small way," Chute pooh-poohed. "On consignment only. You know my way."

"Oh, indeed we do," Lewrie heartily agreed.

"Yayss, I see," Rushton drawled, slowly strolling down the row of paintings hung on an open, stud-framed wall, or leaned against the odd chair or hassock. "Hmm, quite nice," he commented over one, made a face over a second, then stopped dead in his tracks. "I *say*, where did you get this'un, then?"

"*The Embarkation of The Queen of Sheba*, by Claude Lorrain, done in Sixteen Fourty Eight or so," Clotworthy boastfully told him, rocking on the balls of his feet. "Quite nice, isn't it. Alan here loves it, 'cause it has ships in it, hah hah."

"No," Rushton said, "Where, and when, did you get it?"

"About a fortnight ago, as I recall," Chute said, "I'd have to look at the paperwork. Some *très élégant*, but seedy, Frog émigré was in need of selling off his last heirloom . . . starving babes, house falling down, a bad night at the card tables, one of the usual problems. Why? I'm only asking three thousand pounds."

"Remember Bagby Blakeley?" Rushton asked them.

"'Rajah' Blakeley?" Lewrie asked, grinning. "That pompous ass? Thank God none of us ever fagged for him. Whatever happened to him? Something evil, I hope."

"He's with the East India Company," Rushton told them. "Just as he predicted when we were at Harrow, since his father's a member of the board, of long standing. He boasted that he's pulling down twenty-four hundred pounds a year, and actually goes in to work at least four days a week."

"Well, what of him?" Lewrie said.

"The wife and I attended a supper party at his house five nights ago," Peter Rushton said, "so he could show off his art collection . . . and his latest acquisition . . . *that*! *The Embarkation of The Queen of Sheba*! For a minute, I thought Blakeley'd brought it in here to sell for some reason. Maybe his wife or father said he'd paid too much for it . . . five thousand pounds, he boasted. The purse-proud pig."

"Five thousand pounds?" Chute gasped, then fingered the paste-board price tag of the painting in question. "I should mark this up."

"Clotworthy!" Lewrie exclaimed, "What if it's a forgery?"

"Ssh! Not so loud, old son," Chute cautioned, with a finger laid to his lips. "It *can't* be a forgery. Your wife's friend, that Madame Whos-it, with the yard-high wig and the *oo la la* royal airs. Isn't she supposed to be a noted Frog painter, and when she and your wife were here in the store, *she* thought it was real. From a private collection, smuggled out by some aristocrat running from the guillotine."

"Madame Pellatan, aye," Lewrie pointed out. "She said it *could* be real, but she'd never seen it hangin' in a Paris museum, so it *may* have come from a private collection, or it could be a fraud, and she really couldn't say, one way or another. Nothin' *sure*."

"Well, if there's two of them, as alike as two peas in a pod . . . which they are . . . one of them's *sure* to be a fake," Rushton declared.

"Where did 'Rajah' Blakeley get his?" Lewrie asked Peter.

"Ehm . . . I *think* he said he found it at Boydell's Shakespeare Gallery, in Pall Mall," Rushton told him, squinting to recall. "A very reliable place, or so I've been told."

"Well, why don't we go there and ask where *they* got it?" Lewrie suggested.

"Alan, we can't just barge in and accuse Boydell's of foisting fake art on people!" Clotworthy objected.

"We can be more subtle than that, old man," Rushton rejoined with a tap of a finger alongside his nose. "Can't we? Mean t'say, we coach over, in my coach with my coat of arms on the doors, *stroll* in as if my wallet is about to burst if I don't find something that, ah . . ."

"Matches your carpets, or your settees," Lewrie snidely stuck in.

"Yes, thank you, Alan," Rushton said, nodding. "We have always been able to count on your quick wit."

"We're not going to eat, are we?" Chute despaired. "And here, I made sure to fill my wallet with five pound notes this morning."

"Say this, then," Lewrie suggested, "You were at 'Rajah's' supper party, and were quite taken with his *Sheba*, and wished to have a look round. The owner, or one of his sales clerks'll tour you about. When he thinks you would buy something, ask him who brought it into the gallery. Private sale, private collection, the last of the family treasures? Might that person have more squirrelled away, and be so in need to maintain life in London that you might be able to buy one for a song, like 'Rajah' did? Only five thousand pounds for an old master? Really?"

"Hmm, that might work," Rushton said, trying to gnaw the lining of his mouth in thought. "Yes, let's go."

"And we'll eat after?" Clotworthy said with a sigh.

Boydell's Shakespeare Gallery, 52 Pall Mall, quite put Chute's emporium to shame. For one, it was hushed; boots and shoes didn't clop on hardwood floors, they faintly swished on half an acre of Axminster or Turkey car-

"Any weapons at your shop, Clotworthy?" Rushton asked.

"Well, I've a brace of 'barkers' should anyone rush in and rob us of the day's take, but . . ." Chute explained, or tried to.

"Topping!" Lewrie cheered. "Once we've eat, Peter and I can arm ourselves, just in case. And you can use your walking stick."

"On *what*?" Clotworthy gawped. "Alan, does all this derring-do, neck-or-nothing stuff *ever* wear thin with you?"

"Not since we burned down the school governor's coach house!" Lewrie happily told him. "I'm just a simple sailor, me."

"And a lunatic!" Chute grumped, slumping on his seat.

The address of the purported owner of the Claude Lorrain painting, Didier Chalmont, was in Old Compton St., a far better neighbourhood than they would have expected. In Lewrie's mind, a shady Frog forger would hole up in the East End, or cross the Thames in Southwark, where anonymity, and cheap rents, abounded.

The house looked rather average, built to rent out sets of rooms, with a well-painted door, good white Portland stonework, and un-broken windows at the front, all showing drapes or curtains.

"He's in Number Four," Peter Rushton said in an exaggerated whisper. "That must place his rooms on the upper storey."

"Why are you whispering?" Chute asked.

"Aye, what's that about?" Lewrie added.

"I don't know," Rushton shot back. "I thought it proper for this sort of work. And Clotworthy, where *did* you buy these pistols? From a scrap ironmonger? There's something rattling in mine," he complained, rotating his wrist to turn the pistol from side to side.

"Probably the rammer's loose," Lewrie told him.

"So sorry, Peter, that they're not a matched set of dueling pistols from Manton's," Chute grumbled. "It's a single-barrel, so it only has to go off once. And when's the last time you shot anything?"

"I *was* a Captain in the Seventeenth Dragoons, you will recall," Rushton said archly. "I know my way about firelocks."

In point of fact, the Honourable Peter Rushton's military career had been rather short; only a few years after expulsion from Harrow, before his elder brother had died of food poisoning by a foreign kickshaw, a "made dish" that his fiancée had prepared on her own, using too much sauce May-

pets, and with the more expensive versions hung vertically on some of the walls so they wouldn't get even a speck of soil before they sold. In several areas there were ancient Greco-Roman columns, or segments of them, the upper plinths with their ornate carvings, along with newer, shorter columns upon which ancient busts and torsos sat. If one wished to create a decorative villa garden from scratch, then Boydell's was the place to go. If fountains were your pleasure, then look no further, for half-dressed maids stood ready to endlessly pour water from their jugs, ewers, claret, and *amphorae* whilst angels and chubby cherubs waited to pee for you, once the plumbing was installed.

And there were paintings galore, small ones, middling ones, and large portraits done by famous artists. One could have a Round-Head general or cavalier, a dandy *à la* Charles II or King James in armour to hang on one's wall and hint that he was a distant relation, if the ceiling was high enough. There were landscapes, portraits, religious themed artwork, Greco-Roman classical scenes that *could* have arrived at the end of some rich and titled man's Grand Tour of the Continent, then brought here to be sold when he went smash over some investment.

Did one prefer Dutch painters, German, Spanish, or Italians, or did one specialise in French or British? There they hung, grouped by national origin. Paintings covered almost every inch of wall space.

"My word, your shop's miserly, compared t'this," Lewrie muttered.

"Don't remind me," Chute said with another sigh. "I wonder what consignment fees he charges."

"May I help you gentlemen?" a tall clerk asked, gliding up with a grim and haughty look on his phyz, garbed head to toe in the best of Beau Brummel fashion.

"Peter, Viscount Draywick," Rushton said, introducing himself with a grin and a tilt of his head. "Sir Alan Lewrie, Baronet, and an old school chum, Clotworthy Chute, sir. I was at a supper party some nights ago where another Harrow man showed us his art collection, and a new acquisition, and wished to look round to see what you have."

Oh, play the titled fool, Peter! Lewrie thought, hiding a smirk; *He can work his walking stick like a royal rod and scepter!*

"Any particular country, or era, milord?" the clerk suggested, extending one arm to sweep them towards the row-upon-row of artworks.

"He had just discovered a Lorrain, *The Embarkation of The Queen of Sheba*, and it opened my eyes. The composition, the vividness, and the ah . . . overall, uhm, you know?"

"Of course, milord," the clerk said with a sage nod, as if this new customer was particularly ripe and ready.

Lewrie's eyes were caught by a large painting filled with nude women, titled *The Bath of Diana*; he'd always favoured the titillating, and still rued that the harem scene he'd bought in 1784 had been sent away when his first wife, Caroline, had laid eyes on it.

"Too bad Blakeley beat me to it," Peter tossed out to see what the sales clerk might say. "He said it came from a private collection?"

"I remember it well, milord," the clerk replied as they slowly strolled down one row. "From a private collection, indeed. The owner has brought us several pieces over the last year or so. The high cost of London life, sadly. To go to such lengths to save her family valuables from the savage, ignorant mobs when the French Revolution turned so bloody and beastly, then have to sell them at the last, is quite sad. But," the clerk perked up and donned a wolfish smile, "hopefully, she gained a sustaining windfall, and someone else gained the pleasure of possessing such a magnificent piece."

"On consignment, I'd suppose," Clotworthy idly commented.

"That is the usual practice, sir, yes," the clerk agreed.

"Brought several in, did she?" Lewrie asked. "I wonder what else this lady might have for a hard turn in future?"

"I could not say, Sir Alan," the clerk smarmed.

"Aha!" Peter exclaimed as he got to the English section and took a closer look at a painting of a group of horses. "I like this'un!"

"*Mares And Foals In A Landscape*, milord, by George Stubbs," the clerk announced, "done in Seventeen Sixty-Two."

"How much is it?" Peter enthused.

"Ehm, it is five thousand pounds, milord," the clerk said.

"Egad, too rich for my blood," Peter said with a fake shiver.

"I do believe that piece is also available as a reproduction, engraved from the original, milord," the sales clerk imparted, with a faint hint of distaste.

"No no, an original, or nothing," Peter said, sighing. "We *are* late to dinner arrangements. I'll just have to keep looking round the galleries 'til I see what takes my breath away. Sir Alan, Mister Chute? Shall we go?"

"Yes, I'm famished," Chute declared.

"So, what have we learned?" Rushton asked once they were back in his carriage and on their way to the restaurant by the Foreign Office.

"'Twas a woman, brought it in," Lewrie said. "And, I begin to suspect it's a woman we both know, hey, Clotworthy?"

"That Frog mare, Madame . . . oh, what's her name?" Chute struggled to recall.

"Madame Berenice Pellatan," Lewrie supplied.

"Why her?" Chute carped.

"She sold one at Boydell's for five thousand, claiming it was from her family collection," Lewrie told him, "and then one of her compatriots put an identical painting at your place. She never came out and said it was real, only that it *could be*, so you priced it at three thousand pounds. What's Boydell's consignment fee, do you imagine?"

"Probably not much above thirty percent," Clotworthy grumbled. "That would've netted her thirty five hundred pounds or so. And if I sold the other, she'd get twelve hundred."

"And God knows how many other fake paintings are on the London market, this instant," Rushton added. "Chute, who's the bugger that brought your version in? How's your elegant Frog to know to come and collect once you've sold it?"

"Well, I've his address, of course," Clotworthy said. "When the time comes, I write him, tell him no one'd pay the asking price, then say it went for two thousand pounds, not three, so he gets only eight hundred, and I pocket the rest.

"What?" Chute barked as they stared at him "No need to gawp at me. Fine art's a fickle market, and one takes one's chances!"

"I think we need to go to that Frenchman's address to see if he has any other paintings in the works," Lewrie told them.

"We'd have to go back to my emporium to get the address, first," Chute complained, "else, I wouldn't know him from Adam, or where he lives. And, d'ye think there might be a pieman on the way? I really need a meat pasty about now. I'm not at my best when hungry. A pasty and a beer, perhaps?"

"Oh, alright then," Peter said, flinging himself back into his upholstered bench seat with a sigh. "We'll go eat, *then* back to your shop. There's no real urgency. It's only a painting."

"When we do, though," Lewrie speculated, "what if the forger has others with him? If we catch him red-handed, he may put up a fight. Maybe we should be armed."

"Is this going to turn out like your raid on the dog buffers' lair all over again?" Chute seemed to quail. "I'm a businessman, not a soldier. I don't do heroics."

onnaise, and left out far too long at a sunlit garden party dinner, making Peter a Baron and the eldest, no longer to be put at risk.

"Let's just go and get it done," Lewrie all but ordered.

"And do what?" Chute insisted on knowing. "Do we just put our shoulders to his door and bash it open, then rush in with guns drawn?"

"Hmm . . . this Chalmont's expecting t'hear from your shop that the forgery's been sold," Lewrie extemporised, frowning. "Just knock on the door and announce yourself."

"Well, alright then," Chute glumly agreed, "but if there's more than him in there, you two will do the barging."

They left the carriage and crossed the street, pistols and hands in their overcoat pockets.

"*Saunter,* for Christ's sake," Lewrie hissed at them. "We look as if we're a team o' housebreakers sneakin' in the dead of night!"

As was Lewrie's wont, he took the lead, went up the steps of the stoop, tried the shiny painted door and found it open for all tenants to use, looked at a signboard above a side table in the entry hall, and found that Mr. D. Chalmont was on the first storey abovestairs.

Rushton gave Chute a wee shove when they got to the door, urging him to knock and announce himself.

"Mister Chalmont? Are you in? Chute here, from the emporium?" Clotworthy called out, rapping a second time.

"Ah, *oui?*" came a voice from within. "*M'sieur* Chute? *Une moment.*"

There were other voices behind that door, and Lewrie and Peter stiffened and griped their pistols more tightly.

"Sounds like an argument," Peter said, whispering again.

"I hear a woman," Lewrie said, pressing an ear to the door.

It was a long moment before a key clacked in the door lock, and a bolt was withdrawn. The door opened a mere crack, revealing an eye and a bushy Gallic moustachio.

"*Oui, M'sieur?* You come yourself?" a man they assumed to be Chalmont asked.

"With your money, Mister Chalmont," Chute lied, smiling sweetly.

"Ah, *oui,* come in, come in? *Alors,* who are they?"

Lewrie and Rushton pushed past Chute, shouldering the door wide open and sending Chalmont skittering to the far side of a four-place table, where he picked up a rickety-looking chair for a weapon raised over his shoulder.

"We're here about your *forgery,* sir!" Lewrie barked in his best quarterdeck voice. "*The Embarkation of The Queen of Sheba?* You've been *exposed*! The police are coming!"

Someone in a bedchamber beyond wailed "*Mon Dieu!*" another cried "*Emmerdement!*," forcing Lewrie to pull his pistol, point it at the quivering Chalmont, who dropped the chair and dashed to a corner of the parlour. Lewrie then kicked open the flimsy door to the next room to see who was wailing, and if *they* were armed.

"Well, just God damn my eyes!" he roared.

It wasn't a bedchamber, it was a dining room, one with no more furniture than some tall stools and some easels, and a book case along the outer wall just piled with brushes, paints, and cleaning rags.

There was a tall, lean fellow wearing a smock, interrupted in mid work on a painting just taking shape.

"God Almighty, a third one?" Rushton cried as he looked into the room, for there on an easel was another *Embarkation of The Queen of Sheba*. On other easels there was a finished landscape scene that reminded Lewrie of Italy, and its twin, at that stage mostly charcoal or pencil sketches.

"Oh, that is *most* un-appetising, I say!" Rushton exclaimed, making a face.

There were two other people in that room, one a man hastily hauling his trousers up, and a woman clad in only a chemise.

"Madame Pellatan?" Lewrie cried.

She *was* most un-appetising at that moment, for her usual tall, decorated white wig was on the floor, leaving her head covered with a short, mannish mop of frizzy auburn hair, and in only a chemise, her breasts sagged almost to her waist, much like old crones Lewrie had seen in Calcutta, and there was no gown to hide wide hips, rounded belly, and stuffed sausage-like legs.

"Stay in that corner, or I'll cudgel you senseless!" Chute was warning Chalmont in the parlour behind them. "*Parlez-vous* cudgel?" The door was locked once more, and the bolt securely thrown to prevent any escape. "Cheat an honest fellow like me, will you, hey?"

"Oh, cover yourself, Madame," Lewrie ordered.

"Oh yes, please!" Rushton agreed.

"*M'sieur chevalier*, it is not what you think you see . . ." Madame Pellatan began to explain, returning to her arch and artful self.

"It's plain enough what I see, Madame," Lewrie shot back, "and I think you're a little long in the tooth t'be playin' the innocent *coquette*. You and your *amis* here have been paintin' fakes and sellin' 'em to the galleries for thousands. And *still* livin' on the good will of Saint Anselm's church. The good Reverend, *and* Jessica, are going to be so angry and hurt when you're exposed as a common criminal."

"Zere eez nozzing *common* in what ve do, *M'sieur*!" the man in the smock most arrogantly said, raising a paint brush on high as if it was the sword of truth. "Ve are *artistes*! Ze creativity moos be given its reward."

"Yes, ten years in prison, or transportation for life!" Rushton hooted. "You reside in England, you obey our laws, or we just might send you back to Bonaparte."

"I would *adore* returning to Paris, and serving the Emperor!" the half-dressed one cried, puffing out a rather thin chest.

"Oh, put a shirt on, and a sock in it," Rushton growled, waving his pistol about. "And buss my blind cheeks, you snail-eatin' Frog."

Madame Pellatan and the half-dressed fellow opened the door to a bed-chamber and Lewrie got a sight of a bed not only messy, but strewn with overturned wine glasses, plates still containing food, and several used cundums.

"Well now, what shall we do with them?" Rushton boldly demanded.

"Send for the police," Lewrie suggested.

"What do *they* know about art, and forgeries?" Clotworthy sneered, having need to thrust the brass tip of his walking stick at his prisoner still cowering in the corner.

"They know about forged currency," Lewrie said with a shrug, "so the people who deal with money fraud *must* be able to do something about paintings that go for thousands of pounds."

"You could go, Chute," Rushton suggested.

"Me, a fellow with a fraud in his own shop, looking to make three thousand pounds off it?" Clotworthy objected. "No thank you! You're a Viscount, though. They'd listen to you, Peter. Practically get down on their knees and grovel, most-like. *You* go hunt them up."

"Oh, very well," Rushton said with a groan, loath to miss any of the action. "Here, Chute. Take this pistol of yours. Does anyone have a clue where one might find a constable?"

"Eh . . . ah," Chute said as he took the pistol, then fumbled for the key to unlock the door.

"Back in a tick, I hope," Rushton said as he left.

"I'm getting tired of looking at these Frogs, Alan," Chute said, unsure of what to do with his own pistol. "Why don't we just lock the door and stand guard in the hall 'til Peter comes back."

"Fine with me," Lewrie agreed. "Hoy, you . . . Chalmont. Get back in your studio or whatever it is, with the others," he ordered, waving his pistol to direct him. "*Vite, vite!*" he added, using what little French he knew.

The large iron key worked from both sides of the lock, clanking securely. Lewrie took hold of the door knob, tried turning it, and gave the door a hard shove, satisfying himself that the ones they had apprehended were truly locked in with no way out short of using an axe to tear the door apart.

"Oh, put it in your pocket, Clotworthy," Lewrie told him, "your pistol ain't even at half-cock. It's safe as houses . . . unless you got a pair of *real* bad'uns. Why'd you buy 'em if you don't know the very first thing in how to use 'em?"

"The bores look big if one's on the receiving end, Alan, and the clack of the whatyecallit when one cocks it sounds menacing," Clotworthy said, taking off his hat and using a handkerchief to mop his brow. "I never even loaded them 'til you insisted. Damn. I've some *cigarros,* but not a candle in sight that's lit. I should've lit one inside, before we looked them in."

"Never loaded 'em before . . . ?" Lewrie gawped. "Good God, what's the world comin' to?"

It took Peter Rushton nigh an hour before he clumped back up the stairs, joined by two constables with their truncheons already drawn, *and* a chief constable who was much better dressed.

"Right, then, gentlemen," that fellow said with authority, "You are the other two who discovered the hiding place of the art forgers?"

"We are, sir," Lewrie replied, introducing himself and Chute.

"Well, let's be at them, sirs," the chief constable ordered, and Clotworthy produced the large key and turned the lock mechanism, then shoved the door wide open.

"Well, where are they, then?" he demanded, fists on his hips as he scanned the room. The parlour was empty, and so was the dining room beyond. The easels and fake paintings were still there, but nobody was home.

"Perhaps they've hidden in one of the bedchambers," Lewrie said.

"Root them out, lads," the chief constable ordered his men, and they went to both bedchamber doors, kicking them open.

"Ain't nobody 'ere, sir," one of the policemen reported.

"There were four of them," Chute spat, "three men and a woman, we locked them in!"

"'Nother door 'ere, sir," one of the police said from the left-hand bedchamber. "H'open, h'it is. There's back stairs, for servants, goin' down. Dusty, like they ain't been used in a long time. Shoe-prints in th' dust."

"Back garden's not fenced, or walled, neither, sir," the other policeman said, looking out a rear window in the other bedchamber. "A sea o' mud. More prints goin' out South t'Tisbury Court. Shaftesbury Road is just over. Looks like they scampered."

"Aha! And *did* they, now?" the chief constable barked, most-displeased, and casting black glares at Lewrie, Rushton, and Chute. "It appears we've come on a goose-chase."

"Look there, sir," Rushton pointed out, thrusting a finger at the unfinished *The Embarkation of The Queen of Sheba*, and the identical landscapes. "This is the third copy of this painting we've seen, and these two are twins. And here's a detailed sketch of yet another, ready to be painted. Evidence of their crimes, sir!"

"The third?" the chief constable asked.

"One was bought from Boydell's for five thousand pounds, one to Clotworthy Chute, here, at his emporium in New Bond Street, and this!" Rushton told him.

At the mention of his name, and his connection to one of the fake paintings, Clotworthy began to look nervous, and in need of his handkerchief, again. "I was *assured* it was real by the seller, and one of the miscreants, a Madame Pellatan, a noted French portraitist, vouched for it. She was here with the others when we first entered the rooms."

"It's at your shop now?" the chief constable demanded.

"Yes, it is," Chute admitted. "I haven't sold it, yet. It's on consignment only, so no one's been cheated."

He gave the name of the seller, who lived at this address, and a brief description. Rushton supplied Bagby Blakeley's name and home address. "He keeps offices at East India House," he added.

"We shall have to talk with him, and confiscate his copy of this painting," the chief constable said, making pencilled notes in a wee notebook.

"I suppose we should've scouted this place before we knocked and were let in," Lewrie confessed. "Didn't know what we would find."

"Yes, you *should* have, sir," the chief constable gravelled. "We shall take all this for evidence, and keep an eye on the place should any of them come back. Thank you for bringing the matter to the proper authorities. You can go, gentlemen."

Out in the street, re-boarding Peter's coach, they all three had the look of men who had fumbled, somehow, and let the side down.

"At least your copy of the painting'll be off your hands, Chute," Lewrie told him as he handed him the second pistol. "You've come off as innocent as a baa-lamb."

"I *was* looking forward to the money I'd've got for it, though," Chute confessed.

"You know, if you had someone paint over the faked artist's name, and put in, oh . . . *Etude,* 1802, like an art student's copy done in one of the museums in Paris, you could have gotten at least one hundred pounds," Peter suggested.

"You're breaking my heart, please stop!" Chute all but wailed.

"Or, taken it home and hung it at your house," Lewrie quipped.

"Alan, old son," Clotworthy said, getting arch. "I may pass off goods like that on *other* people, but never on myself!"

"I suppose you'll miss the fun of tellin' 'Rajah' Blakeley he's out his painting *and* his five thousand pounds," Lewrie told Rushton.

"Well, I *was* day-dreaming on how to go about that very thing, but now I think about it, it's best coming from the police," Peter said with a fetching smile. "I never liked him, anyway. Drop you off in Dover Street?"

"No, I think I'll flag a hackney," Lewrie decided. "I need to tell Jessica and her father, the Reverend. By the time I get there, and clue them in, Madame Berenice Pellatan should be showing up at the manse . . . her last place of refuge."

"Have fun, then, Alan," Rushton said in parting. "Ta ta!"

CHAPTER THIRTY-ONE

*D*ear Lord in Heaven," the Reverend Chenery said mournfully, and sank even further into an armchair in St. Anselm's manse's drawing room as Lewrie laid out the damning evidence. "How could she? All these . . . all these years, I never saw a sign. No one did! And all these years, from the moment that she and her husband washed up on our shores as refugees . . . do you imagine that *both* of them shammed poverty, lived on the church's charity, that all along they were forging paintings, and earning a small *fortune* with their criminal enterprise?"

"Well, I don't know about that, sir," Lewrie had to admit. "It's only a few paintings that we know are fakes, the Claude Lorrain, and a landscape that looks like Italy in their set of rooms. There could be more, but they may already be sold."

"This is so disturbing," Jessica said with an audible sniff. "I cannot believe it. I practically grew up under Madame Berenice's care and guidance. All these years she's been so helpful, so encouraging of my art, from my childish drawings to my first oil painting. Why, I cannot even *imagine* her guilty of such a thing. It seems so out of character!"

"Yet, we are warned that those who would beguile us and lead us astray practice the art of the sweet smile," Rev. Chenery reminded her, "the honeyed speech, and the gentlest, kindest, and most innocent facade. Ah, me."

There'll be a sermon on that Sunday, Lewrie cynically thought.

"Perhaps she can explain herself," Jessica hoped aloud. "Alan, you said there were others, *émigré* artists, who might have led her to join them. I know for a fact that Madame Berenice hasn't had all that many commissions for portraits, the last two years, or longer, really. Growing old, being out of fashion, living on the church's good will, and what little the parish can pay her to teach drawing at our grammar school . . . some money for her aged years must have looked so tempting."

"Aye, I s'pose so," Lewrie allowed, "but those dog buffers wanted money, too, and so do pickpockets, house breakers, and everyone who goes criminal. Need is no excuse, in the eyes of the law."

"If she's taken up and put on trial," Rev. Chenery said with a groan. "The shame of it, directed at our parish. On all of us!"

"I could almost wish that she found a way to escape all of that," Jessica declared, pressing a handkerchief to her nose. "What would the punishment be?"

"People who forge Bank of England notes, or counterfeit coins, are usually hung at Tyburn," Lewrie blurted without thinking.

"Oh merciful God!" Rev. Chenery almost wailed.

The heavy-set older housekeeper of the manse bustled into the drawing room, looking excited for the first time in months. "Beg your pardon, Reverend, but there's something odd going on in the garden. It sounds like a horse is tryin' t'push through the hedges."

Chenery and Lewrie leaped to their feet and rapidly went to the back of the house, with Jessica following along more sedately, even to the point of getting her warm cloak from the entry hall.

It must here be noted that St. Anselm's Church had been on its lot for over two hundred years, its lawns and the churchyard cemetery had been sodded for the same length of time, and could now rival the lawns of Windsor Castle, and its encircling yew hedges had grown to a dense, thick, and entertwined barrier, proof against battering rams.

Something, though, was trying to plough through it. As Chenery and Lewrie emerged into the back garden in all its winter bleakness, they saw a section of the hedge thrashing, bending, and creaking as if the hedge was struck by a powerful, limb-snapping gale, whipping back and forth in a dark green froth, and a figurative snowfall of leaves.

"What in the *world*?" Jessica gaped as she joined them.

"Should we arm outselves?" the Reverend fretted aloud.

That's the second *time someone's asked that today,* Lewrie thought, grinning despite what threat was to emerge from the hedge.

"It might be someone *desperately* in need of salvation, ye know," he japed, instead. "They might need a confessor."

Some colours began to appear as whatever it was finally forced its way through, almost into the back garden. There was a burgundy splotch, which turned out to be a cloak; then a blot of white Lewrie recognised— Madame Berenice Pellatan's high-piled and decorated wig. The sleeves of her gown appeared, shoving the last branches to part. Her wig snagged on the hedges as she wriggled her way free of it at last, as did her reticule. She stood before them, her clothing snagged and torn, overly done makeup smeared, and panting like a terrorised heifer. She turned and tried to tug her wig free.

"Couldn't you just come knock on the front door?" Lewrie asked.

He was thankful he did not know much French, for what little he could make out sounded remarkably similar to *"cochon," "salaud,"* and *"va te faire foutre."* It appeared that her coolly aristocratic mien had always been a sham, and Madame Pellatan could curse like a Billingsgate fishwife.

"Madame! Really!" Jessica scolded, frowning deeply.

"Pardons," Madame Pellatan said, snatching her snagged gown and cloak free of the last impediments, wrapping them into place, and then flouncing cross the back garden with her chin held high, even if her wig was now jammed on her head with a starboard list and turned halfway sideways.

"Madame Pellatan," Rev. Chenery began, glaring in righteous indignity. "We have heard some distressing news of you and some of your fellow *émigrés*. That you were caught red-handed at some lodgings in Old Compton Street, where you and they have been forging paintings, then selling them for thousands of pounds, defrauding gullible subjects of the Crown. As bad a crime as making counterfeit money, which Sir Alan tells me is a capital offence. What have you to say for yourself?"

"That I am in need of hot tea, *M'sieur Abbé*," Madame Pellatan said, one brow up, striving for her old superior airs.

"What? Tea?" Rev. Chenery spluttered. "What gall!"

"Gauls have a lot of gall, sir," Lewrie quipped.

"Oh, Madame, how *could* you?" Jessica all but wailed.

"If I have your permission, Reverend," Madame Pellatan said with an incline of her head, which set the wig to shifting more to the right, "I will go to my room and pack my things? You will not have to abide my presence any longer."

"But, *why* did you do it, Madame?" Jessica demanded to know.

"I must pack, Jessica, *chérie*," Pellatan firmly stated, "Then I will explain." And she swept past them into the manse with the air of a *Vicomtesse*, leaving them all gap-jawed and speechless.

There was naught to do but return to the drawing room and ring for tea.

It took quite a while for the tea set to arrive, with cream and sugar pared off a cone; there was no more lemon to be had in winter.

"I never *heard* the like," Rev. Chenery spluttered. "A bit more of the sugar, as you are playing 'Mother,' dear, thankee."

"How much was Mister Chute going to ask for that painting we saw at his shop, Alan?" Jessica asked as she spooned a bit more sugar into her father's cup.

"Three thousand pounds," Lewrie told her. "And the one she sold through Boydell's Shakespeare Gallery went for five thousand. Shared 'twixt all four, that's still a nice pile of 'the blunt.'"

"And none of it donated to Saint Anselm's, to repay our generosity," Chenery carped between sips.

"Of course, Boydell's probably kept thirty percent," Lewrie told them, "and Clotworthy's consignment fee is more like sixty percent. Even so, that's . . . fourty four hundred pounds, right there, and only God knows how much they made off other paintings we don't know about."

"You called the police?" Rev. Chenery asked him. "Do they have people who deal in such crimes?"

"We did," Lewrie said, which made the good Reverend flinch with potential embarrassment. "We gave them two names, and their descriptions, but who the other two were is a mystery, and all they have to do is to choose new names, move away from their old lodgings, and get clean away with it. There could be fake paintings turning up for years."

There was a bustle on the stairs as one of the housemaids came down with a pair of carpet bags that she sat down in the entry hall, followed by the stout housekeeper holding up one end of a wood chest, and Madame Pellatan bearing the other handle strap.

The men were English gentlemen; even the arrival of a criminal drew them to their feet in deference to a lady.

"Gentlemen, Jessica *chérie*," Madame Pellatan said as she swept into the drawing room, smoothed the skirts of a drabber woolen gown more suited to the weather, and for travelling, and attempted to give them all a reassuring smile. "Ah, *bien*. The tea. May I prevail upon you, Jessica? *Merci*."

"You said you could explain," Jessica impatiently snapped. "Do proceed to do so, Madame."

I'll wager this'll *be one Hell of a tale!* Lewrie thought, sitting back on the settee and making himself more comfortable.

"Yes, just how long *have* you been a forger?" Rev. Chenery said, looking down his nose at her.

"Only for a short time, actually," Madame Pellatan matter-of-fact-ly told them, after a warming sip of creamed and sugared tea. "Do you recall, Jessica, the time we went to Ackermann's in the Strand, before you and Sir Alan wed? And the marvellous supper we had at that restaurant in Savoy Street? There was a painting there, done by my old, old and dear friend, Jacques-Louis David . . . a painting of the Roman general Belisarius and his daughter, begging. I rushed to see it, wondering how such a masterpiece could make its way to England.

"But it wasn't a David," she went on, making a *moue* and sighing. "It was the wrong size, and while it was a remarkably good copy, it was not David's work, nor his brush work. It was his composition, but not his choice of colours."

"So, that made you think of faking . . . ?" Lewrie began to ask.

Madame Pellatan raised a hand to shush him.

"I spoke of that art show, and the grand quality of that meal when next I met with my French friends," the old fraud went on, "and I must confess that I lied to you, Sir Alan, and M'sieur Chute, when I was in his shop. I said none of my friends were artists, but that isn't true. Almost all of us are, and oh la, what a crowd we were in the old days in Paris, of the café set, wild Bohèmes, going to the museums, the galleries where our *amis* had pieces hung. We were popular, our art sold well, but, alas, people who lived creatively, with style, were too close to the 'aristos' who bought our art, and that condemned us all to the sham trials of The Terror that executed milliners and hairdressers who were close to the wealthy and titled."

"Old news, we've heard it before," Lewrie brusquely snapped.

"Here, in England, in London, once safe, we all had hopes that our art would provide a modicum of income," Madame Pellatan mourned, "but, alas again, we were *French*, the enemy once war was declared, so no one was interested in our paintings. My late husband, God rest his soul, found little market for his works, and my portraits were not of the desired style. We were all poor, working as house servants, waiters, *house painters*, tutors in French to children."

"And then you had an idea," Rev. Chenery accused.

"*Oui*, Reverend, we did," Madame Pellatan confessed, "And a most profitable one. Instead of getting together once the week to commiserate with each other and mourn our pasts, we began to draw from memory, collaborating on form and composition, mixing colours, then painting art we admired. And when the first one was sold, and we had thousands of pounds to share, we had a celebration worthy of our old days, and the die was cast."

"Just how many paintings did you forge?" Lewrie asked sternly.

"About a dozen, all told, *M'sieur Chevalier*," she boldly replied. "It takes a lot of work for the four of us to replicate any painting."

"Madame, Saint Anselm's, the Church of England, simply cannot let you reside under this roof for a single minute longer," the Reverend declared. "Your criminal activities have brought shame and embarrassment to our repute. You must finish your tea and go! For shame!"

"Oh, I intend to, *M'sieur*," Madame Pellatan replied with a hint of twinkling amusement. "We cannot remain in London, under a cloud. I assume your police may be looking for us, and have seized the works we were producing."

"Damned right they are," Lewrie told her, "and damned right they have."

"But, where could you go?" Jessica asked, still concerned for her old mentor, despite the woman's crimes.

"Vienna would be lovely," Madame Pellatan said with a gay smile, "if there is a way to get there, and I have heard that Dublin is becoming a lively artist community."

"Oporto or Lisbon, where most of our criminals flee," Lewrie said with a snort of derision.

"Perhaps America might be best," Madame Pellatan countered, still amused. "New York, Philadelphia, or Charleston? French people are honoured and considered fashionable there, and an *honest* living can be had with portraits of American ladies and the children, *n'est-ce pas?*"

"Your betrayal of our charity dis-appoints me greatly, Madame," the Reverend grieved, with a sad shake of his head.

"Your charity, *M'sieur*, and your school wages drove me to it," Madame Pellatan replied with a deep Gallic shrug, and a touch of anger. "*You* try being an object of charity, and see how *you* like it. Ah, my tea is done. I must depart. If one of you gentlemen will hail me a hackney?"

She wrapped herself in her cloak, pinned a bonnet atop her now-straightened wig, slung her reticule on her left arm, and pulled on a pair of kidskin gloves.

"*Adieu,* Jessica *chérie,*" she said from the stoop, "I wish you all the success you desire with your work. *Adieu,* Reverend, for I really did enjoy our long conversations, and *Adieu,* Sir Alan. I hope that you and Jessica shall be profoundly happy in life."

A hackney rattled to a stop, and Lewrie and the Reverend, along with the coachee, loaded her traps in the leather-covered boot, then stood to watch her coach away.

"And good riddance to bad rubbish," the Reverend sighed. "What will I tell the vestry board? The parishioners? Or the children she taught at our grammar school?"

"Hmm . . . that she suddenly came into a tidy sum and wished to go away somewhere warmer?" Lewrie japed.

"Oh, the . . . what?" Chenery spluttered.

"Into a tidy sum . . . that's a good one," Jessica said, and began to titter, to her father's utter confusion.

CHAPTER THIRTY-TWO

*H*e was just on the verge of waking, though he didn't want to, oh no. He was snug under a coverlet, two blankets, and a home-made quilt, and nigh-swaddled in a flannel nightshirt and wool stockings up to the knees. There was too much stirring about by the housemaids, the tick of the mantel clock, though, to fall back asleep.

He slid one arm under the pillows to his left to snuggle closer to Jessica and her heavenly warmth . . . but she wasn't there. She had already arisen and the heat of where she'd slept was dissipating.

To Lewrie's lights, there was nothing finer on a cold winter's night than a sleeping woman, for they all seemed to radiate warmth by God's design, warmth and their particular aromas. A woman in a nightgown was good; a woman sleeping nude was even better.

He smacked his lips, wishing for water to sluice the dryness, and the aftertaste, away. At last, he opened one eye, with a thought for the glass and carafe on the nightstand, but . . .

All he could see was the black-and-white face of the cat, which was touching noses with him. Sensing that he was waking, Buffer began to lick his nose.

"Thankee, Buffer," Lewrie mumbled, "Is it dirty? You're doin' a grand job." But, when Buffer started kneading his paws on the front of Lewrie's nightshirt, clever wee claws gripping and lifting, he groaned, stretched, and pushed himself up to a sitting position at the headboard. From that higher vantage, he could look down to see Bisquit and his wife's dog, Rembrandt, sitting at the edge of the bed.

"Nothin' for it, then," he muttered, "I'll have t'get up. Good morning, puppies. Good morning, Buffer."

Jessica came through the door to the hall, saw him awake, and smiled. "Awake at last, sleepyhead? I'll light another candle."

Lewrie rolled to the edge of the bed, groped with his toes for his pair of moccasin-like slippers, stood, and went for his dressing gown. "What's the weather like today?" he asked her.

"Cold, and grey," Jessica answered as she knelt by the blazing fireplace to ignite a rush that she used to start a second candle for more light. "When I looked out at the back garden, I saw snow, just a dusting. Enough to make out the Pettuses' prints on their way to the kitchens. Martha said she thinks she smells rain later in the day."

"A nice day t'stay inside, *brr*," Lewrie said, pouring himself a glass of water. "Shopping to do, though."

Christmas was coming, and with it presents for family, then more for Boxing Day. Jessica, ever the organised one, had already made out her lists for both, with a third, shorter one, for items to decorate the house for the season.

There was a knock on the door.

"Good morning, sir," Deavers said from without, "Do you need anything today?"

"Hot water for a shave and a sponge off, Deavers, and I'll take care of dressin' myself," Lewrie told him.

"Right, sir," Deavers replied, "and I've sent Dasher out for the morning papers. Be back in a bit."

Washed, shaved, clothed, and fed a hot breakfast, Lewrie took a glance outside at last, and the day did indeed look grey and depressing. Yes, there was a skiff of snow, soon to turn pale slate grey as the coal smoke rose, and if one of their maids, Martha, was correct, the rain she sensed would wash all that away. He leaned on the deep window seat in the front parlour on the ground floor, watching all the morning goings-on in Dover St., in every London street.

Milk sellers were out, trundling their push carts along, knife grinders cried their services, and children carried preparations for the holiday. Holly branches and sprigs, heavy with berries, lengths of ivy, and handmade

wreaths for windows and door fronts. Apprentices from the many baker-
ies carried trays slung from their necks, shouting that they had hot cross
buns, muffins, mincemeat pies, and pies made with dried fruits, trailed and
stalked by urchins and imps who would snatch free ones if the apprentices
weren't careful.

He looked up and down Dover St. and saw that several of their neighbours had already hung wreaths on their doors, draped holly and ivy on
the wrought iron railings that stood in front of the delivery entrances, and
in some windows, candles already stood aglow.

Lewrie looked down and grinned, for Jessica had already found a safe
way to illuminate their windows in all eight windows that faced the street
from all three levels. Instead of bare candles that could tip over, or set
drapes alight, she had discovered polished brass lanthorns with clear glass
panes, about ten inches high with wide bottoms that even curious dogs or
a cat could not knock over.

He thought of lighting the two in the front parlour that was also Jessica's art studio, but a knock at the door stopped him. He went to the entry
hall, instead, just as Pettus went to respond, as well.

"Mail, sir," a post boy said, handing over a substantial stack of letters
with one hand, and the other open for the postage fees.

"Oh, good," Lewrie said, sorting through them quickly, "lots of readin'
t'do, Pettus . . . indoors where it's warm."

"Yes, sir," Pettus said with a grin.

He trotted upstairs to the drawing room, shouting to Jessica to alert her
to letters for her. She was on one of the settees, leaning on one end, with
Rembrandt's head and paws in her lap.

Which to open first? There were letters from Colonel Tarrant and
Lieutenant Fletcher on Sicily, one from Hugh aboard his new frigate at
Gibraltar, one from Peter Rushton's younger brother, Harold, at the War
Office, one from James Peel of Secret Branch. Nothing from Admiralty,
unfortunately, but there was one from Rear-Admiral Sir Thomas Charl-
ton, from somewhere in the country, so he was still alive and healing up
with his family, and . . . a letter from Governour Chiswick at Anglesgreen?
Lewrie tore that one open.

Alan,
I take pen in hand to convey to you news of your daughter, Charlotte,
and her recent doings. Over the season of the harvest balls and celebra-
tory suppers for the cottagers and tenants . . .

No "Dear Alan," hey? Lewrie thought; *All the years we were in-laws, and he still can't bring himself to be civil!*

Diana, my own girl, was invited by her affianced, Capt. Wilmoth, to attend a grand regimental ball at Aldershot. She insisted that Charlotte must go with her. After considering the distance, the company, and risks most carefully, I assure you, I gave them both a cautious consent. I would have gone as chaperone but for my duties as Magistrate, the time of the Assizes being upon us, so, I sent Millicent and the boys to Aldershot too, to keep a sharp eye on the girls' safety and reputations. Imagine my utter chagrin when, this very week, your Charlotte announced that she is with child, and must be wed at once to the man who seduced her, one Capt. Alexander Courtney. I do believe that you have met him the last time you were down to the country.

"*What* the bloody *Hell?*" Lewrie howled, shooting to his feet and startling all the beasts.

"Alan, dear," Jessica asked, lowering her own letter to her lap and losing the sweet smile that she had worn. "Whatever is the matter?"

"Charlotte's the matter, love," Lewrie raved, pacing about the drawing room. "The silly chit's gone and gotten *pregnant*! Seduced by that smirky bastard, that Captain Courtney! She told Governour that they have to marry, instanter, or else. Hmm, he goes on . . ."

"Oh, Lord," Jessica said, surprising Lewrie that she did not leap to comfort him or assure him, smiling secretly, instead.

"She and Courtney *thought* of getting a church license, without a reading of the banns, so they could wed anywhere, damn her," Lewrie went on, reading from the letter. "Good Christ, they thought of coachin' off to *Scotland* to elope, but the roads are too uncertain this time o' year, and . . . God Almighty, they *planned* it this way, he writes! Climb into bed, get pregnant, and they *have* to marry! Because she *loves* him with all her *heart*, can't *live* without him . . . he might get sent to Spain in the next draught of the regiment . . . oh, mine arse on a *band-box*!" Lewrie roared, the mockery of Charlotte's emotions fair dripping bile.

"They're certain she's pregnant?" Jessica calmly asked.

"Aye, Governour had the local doctor come round, and it's true," Lewrie groaned, flopping down onto the other settee suddenly, as if he had exhausted himself. He waved the damned letter idly in the air.

"What do we know of this fellow, his family, his fortune?" his wife matter-of-factly went on. "It seems Charlotte intended all along to make him your son-in-law, so . . . is he a worthy man, do you think?"

"You're takin' this *far* too coolly," Lewrie told her, stunned by her attitude as if he'd never known her at all.

"Captain Courtney, was it?" Jessica said. "I thought him a bit too smooth. Handsome enough, I suppose, and certainly dashing enough. Good manners. But, Alan . . . which of them enchanted the other, with an eye to marry? That's more Charlotte's thinking than his, I'd wager. Captain Courtney does not strike me as the sort to fall head-over-heels in love so quickly or completely that he would contemplate dashing off to Gretna Green if all else failed, or taking such a risky way to the altar. They *must* marry, though."

"Aye, they do," Lewrie agreed, getting to his feet, again. "I'll go round and warn my father. We'll have to coach down to Anglesgreen at once, and *see* them wed at Saint George's, or at Aldershot. At sword point, or with a pistol to Courtney's head if he balks.

"*Damn* that girl, she's been a spiteful, hateful, *willful* pain in my side since she turned *twelve*!" Lewrie went on. "She's made her bed, now, and she'll have t'lie in it the rest of her miserable life! And just hear what Governour thinks of it! 'I blame Millicent and my boys for being so remiss in their watchfulness. How could Charlotte and Courtney find the time, or the privacy, to conjoin in secret? Diana is most distressed that her cousin will be married before she and her fiancé can go to their altar the properly chaste way, and believes that *your* daughter' . . . he underlined that, damn him . . . 'did it just to spite Diana, and steal all the attention from her.' Governour says he can't believe that, but I surely can."

"You and your father will be going tomorrow, or the next day?" Jessica asked him.

"Something like that," Lewrie told her, going to lean an arm and his forehead on the fireplace mantel. "Day after tomorrow, most-like. Clothes to pack for it, his Major-General rig, my Navy uniform, and the Order of The Bath. Speak with Charlotte, first, as distasteful as that'll be, then coach to Aldershot and beard this Courtney in his barracks. If he sounds like he might not marry the chit, we'll have to have a word with his commanding officer. He can *order* him t'do the right thing, or be court-martialled for conduct unbecoming. He might even have to sell up his commission to make restitution to Charlotte, though the shame of bein' an un-wed mother with a bastard is something money can't un-do. If all else fails, then aye, it's sword points and pistols."

"I'd admire to go with you, darling," Jessica said, coming to him at the mantel.

"Might get hot and angry," Lewrie warned her.

"I can stand it," Jessica assured him with a grin as she leaned on him, placing her head on his shoulder. "Christmas in the country is ever so much nicer than in the city. And, it may be the last time that I can see Bobs, and go riding, and endure the coach trip there and back."

"What? The last time?" Lewrie started. "Darling, are you ill? Have you come down with something that might . . . take you from . . . ?"

"My dearest husband," Jessica purred, "I may not be able to travel in the Spring."

"What? Why?" Lewrie demanded, putting both arms round her.

"Let me just say that Charlotte is not the *only* woman in your life who is with child," Jessica told him, getting on her tiptoes to give him a kiss, her arms round his neck.

"We're going t'have a *child*?" Lewrie gawped, completely, utterly stupefied. "We're going to have . . . ? Mine arse on . . . !" He censored himself, wondering how excited he *really* was, recalling at least three years of spit-up, foul nappies, wails at all hours of the night that nannies could not quiet, skinned knees and more wails.

"Oh . . . my . . . God, that's simply *marvellous*!" he decided that it would be politic to say. "Oh, Jessica, you're wonderful, this is goin' t'be so . . . grand!" I adore you, adore you, *adore you*!"

Good Christ on a crutch, he thought as Jessica bounced in glee, and squealed with joy; *Can't the Navy pluck me away, please, before I deal with all that, all over again? Still,* she's *happy, so I must be, too. Or do a hellish-good impersonation of it!*

AFTERWORD

Shall I crack any of the old jokes, master,
at which the audience never fails to laugh?

ARISTOPHANES, *THE FROGS*

As readers of the mis-adventures of Alan Lewrie have noticed, it has been quite a while since I allowed myself the luxury of an Afterword, most often because I usually fall behind on my publisher's deadlines (*Which* month? How *much* longer?) and figured that the brief Epilogue would satisfy everybody. Besides, I've had to join a Twelve Step Program for Prattlers who won't shut up—it's called On-And-On-And-On.

Another reason is that once I do finish a novel, I am usually mentally whipped and just want to go to Kinko's and UPS, get the book off, hit the liquor store for some champagne, and sleep the sleep of the just in, as Kinky Friedman called it, "my monastic little bed."

Over the last few novels, a lot of problems had arisen ashore for Lewrie, about which he could do nothing as long as he was at sea. I thought that they had to be faced, at last, and the only way that Lewrie could do so would be to get stranded ashore on half-pay. And as I've always told readers, Lewrie *always* gets in trouble on dry land, with time on his idle little hands.

First off, how will he find powerful support with Admiralty to get himself back to sea? And then comes his younger son, Hugh, who is also in need of a new ship, not to mention Midshipman Charlie Chenery, his teen brother-in-law in the same, pardon the pun, boat. And then there is Charlotte, who is *still* husband-hunting; too picky, or too arch and imperious, scaring off suitable beaus? Not to mention his former brother-in-law, Governour Chiswick and his brood of ne'er-do-wells. And just who *is* this Captain Alexander Courtney, and what are his motives? As we say in the South, "who are his people and what are they like?" If there's to be a sword-point wedding, will it turn out well?

Dog buffers were real, unfortunately. In Georgian and Regency London there were the Canting Crews, a loose association of criminals of various specialties, the kings of which were the dashing and bold highwaymen, and they went down in prestige from there in a hierarchy, the dog buffers being so far down they were sneered at by almost everyone else. It was rare they used violence to seize pets, but it wasn't unheard of. After all, what they did with the pelts and meat of the dogs they couldn't ransom, and the snatch-and-run crimes they committed doesn't take the sharpest knives in the drawer in the first place, and dog buffers would make bumbling criminals of today look like geniuses in comparison. I'm not saying they dragged their knuckles, but . . .

As for their trial at the Old Bailey . . . it would be enlightening to find and read a copy of *Albion's Fatal Tree*, Pantheon Books, 1975, which showed how quickly English Society was to hang lawbreakers after swift trials that might not last two hours, and for an ever-expanding list of capital crimes added to each year when the threat of the death penalty didn't seem to lessen the number of crimes. It did not help that when the condemned were carted to Tyburn to do their last jig in the air, massive crowds turned out to enjoy the spectacle, and those doomed to swing could have their fifteen minutes of fame, and shout not their innocence, but their bravado, whooping and cheering the mob on to delight and admiration.

That urchin girl, and the cart driver who showed no violence, didn't get off all that easily, either, when they were transported for life to New South Wales. Have you read the cautions about Australian wildlife? Everything on that continent may be out to kill you! And, if you had no job skills other than picking pockets, snatching silk handkerchiefs, or stealing dogs, what sort of work could you expect to find Down Under? But, do remember, before we won the American Revolution, we used to get those sorts of people dumped on *our* shores here in America. Talk about an immigration problem!

As for Claude Lorrain's *The Embarkation of The Queen of Sheba* that was the main ingredient in the forgery ring's doings, let me tell you where that came from.

In 1969, when I was a senior at Montana State University in Bozeman (Go Bobcats!) from Spring Break on the campus was inundated with salesmen trying to sign soon-to-be-graduates up for gasoline cards, some early versions of credit cards (okay, I confess, I stole a rubber door mat for a credit card company from the entry of the 4 B's Café and I still have it) and The Great Books from Harvard University Press. Like a halfway-educated fool, I went for The Great Books, which ran to over thirty volumes of the world's best thought, poetry, speeches, etc. and with it, a ten-volume set of art of the world. Madame Pellatan is, you may have noticed, French, and in the volume on French art I found *The Embarkation of The Queen of Sheba,* which I very much liked for how the artist rendered harbour waters, and a brilliant, glowing sky. And, as Lewrie did, I liked it because it had ships in it, no matter if they're not exactly Biblical.

Madame Pellatan, hmmm. When I first introduced her in *A Fine Retribution,* I had a feeling about her character. As we'd say up in Campbell County, "That woman just ain't right." I have no idea at this moment if she'll ever turn up, again, or if she gets clean away.

London's Police, the "Bow Street Runners," well. I can't think that they would have been as efficient back then as Scotland Yard is today. They had truncheons, and whistles were far off in the future, and might not even have had official uniforms yet. They patrolled the streets and *might* have gone into the criminal stews at some point, but that might have been a dangerous proposition. Look at their predecessors, the night watchmen and the "Parish Charlies" paid by the individual church parishes. They had guard posts, wooden booths in which they sheltered from the weather when not walking the bounds with a lanthorn, but were older fellows on the Poor List with their churches, and were usually found napping in their booths, making them vulnerable to being tipped over with the door face down, from which the poor old souls had no escape 'til dawn. If you can't tip cows in London, "Charlie" booths will do. Could the new-fangled police find a way to hunt a criminal down and arrest him or her in the first place? And would they have had people on staff with the expertise to prosecute art forgeries? Your guess is as good as mine.

So . . . here's Alan Lewrie, still ashore on half-pay, soon to be a father all over again, soon to give his daughter away in holy matrimony before she begins to show, and *still* can't even catch cold with the powers that be at Admiralty. Has his son Sewallis turned into a merchant or a Commission Sea Officer? Will the developing relationship 'twixt Liam Desmond and Abigail at the Old Ploughman take another stalwart from Lewrie's long-time retinue? Can Lewrie, Colonel Tarrant, Lt. Fletcher, and Peter Rushton's brother, Harold, scotch the vainglorious plans of Commodore Grierson and Brigadier-General Caruthers on Sicily before disaster strikes?

What will life be like when King George is declared insane, and the Prince of Wales, who wanted everyone to call him "Florizel" takes the throne as Regent, annul his secret marriage to Mrs. Fitz-Herbert, a Catholic of all things, and be re-united with his Princess Caroline?

And what's all this "Free Trade and Sailors' Rights" folderol over in the United States? Aren't they too poor and weak to complain about anything that Great Britain does? And how long would the American Navy last if they did? Might Captain Sir Alan Lewrie, Bt., have even a wee part in that?

And will dirty nappies, spit-ups, toddling babes, and general mayhem round the house drive him to distraction before he sails again, at last? I'm going to go to Kinko's, then to UPS, get some champagne, catch up on my laundry, and play with the cat. (Harry says hello, by the way—or he would if he would leave off licking my toes.)

ABOUT THE AUTHOR

DEWEY LAMBDIN is the author of twenty-four previous Alan Lewrie novels. A member of the U.S. Naval Institute and a Friend of the National Maritime Museum in Greenwich, England, he spends his free time working and sailing. He makes his home in Nashville, Tennessee, but would much prefer Margaritaville or Murrells Inlet.